CLASH

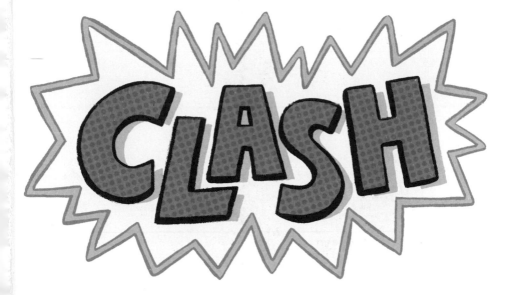

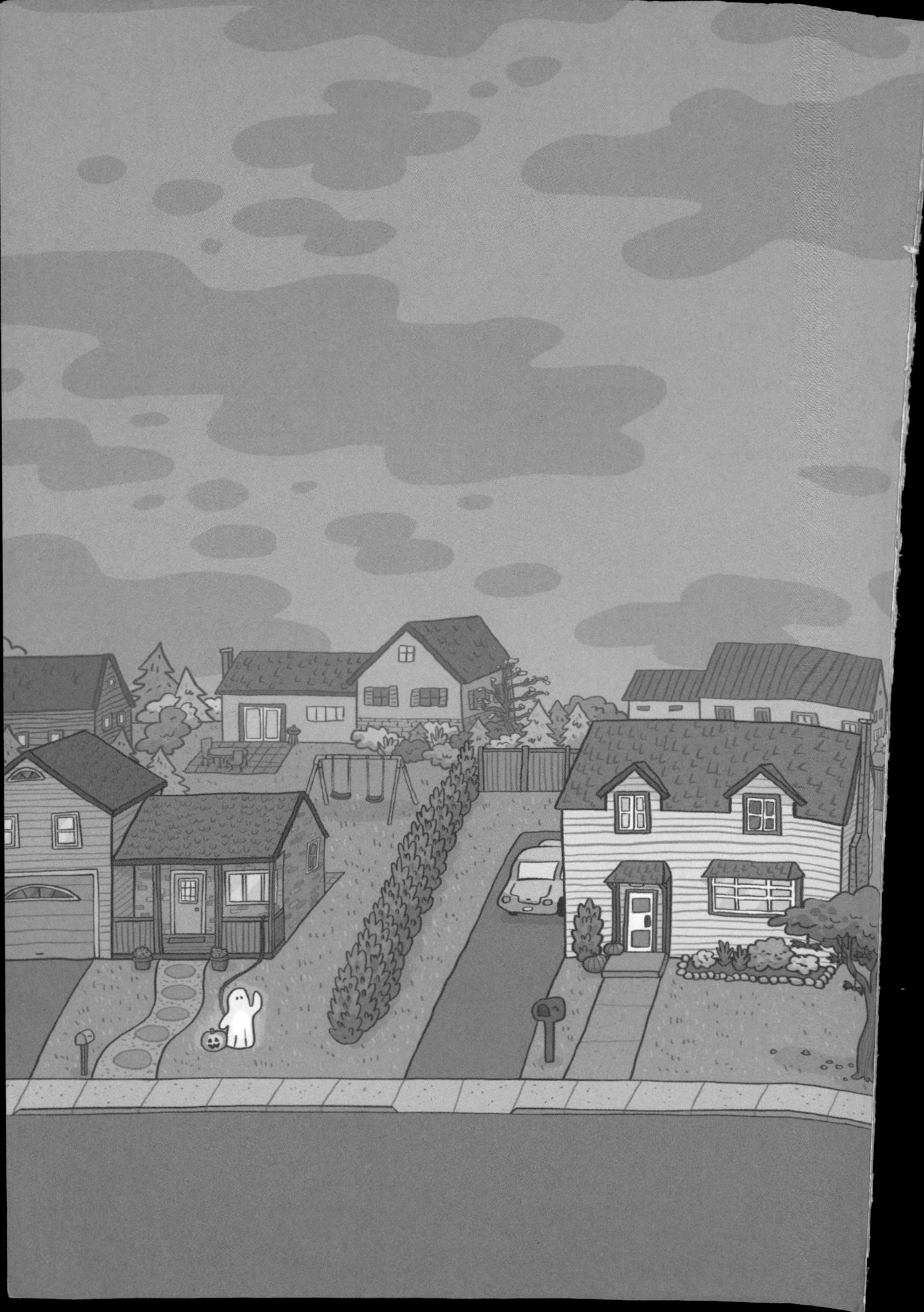

CLASH

BY KAYLA MILLER

ETCH
HOUGHTON MIFFLIN HARCOURT
BOSTON   NEW YORK

COLOR BY JESS LOME
LETTERING BY MICAH MYERS

Etch is an imprint of Houghton Mifflin Harcourt Publishing Company.

hmhbooks.com

The illustrations in this book were done using inks and digital color.

Design by Andrea Miller

ISBN: 978-0-358-24220-8 hardcover
ISBN: 978-0-358-24219-2 paperback

Manufactured in China
SCP 10 9 8 7 6 5 4 3 2 1
4500820332

FOR ANYONE WHO NEEDS
A LITTLE UNDERSTANDING -KM

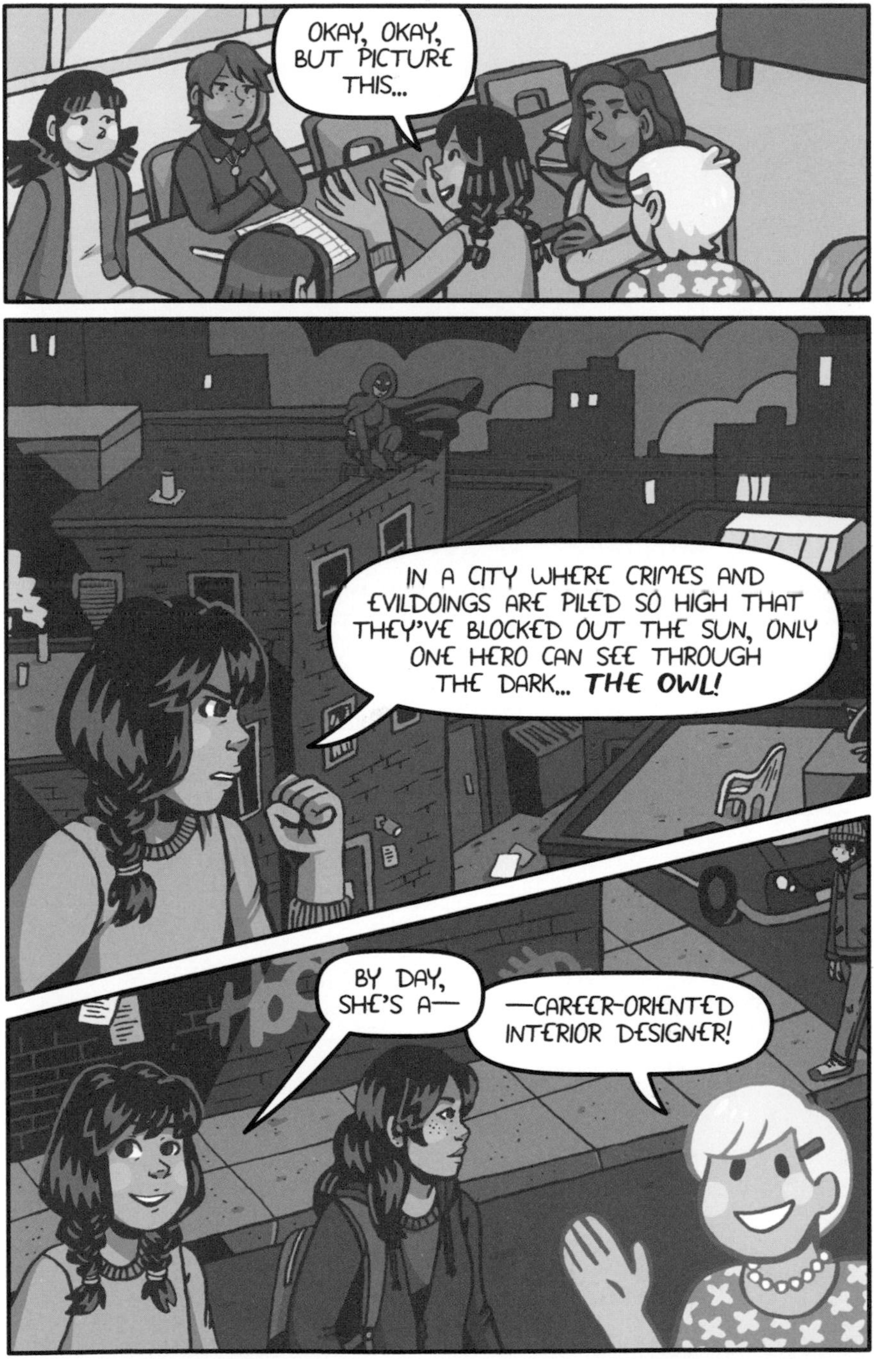
OKAY, OKAY, BUT PICTURE THIS...
IN A CITY WHERE CRIMES AND EVILDOINGS ARE PILED SO HIGH THAT THEY'VE BLOCKED OUT THE SUN, ONLY ONE HERO CAN SEE THROUGH THE DARK... **THE OWL!**
BY DAY, SHE'S A—
—CAREER-ORIENTED INTERIOR DESIGNER!

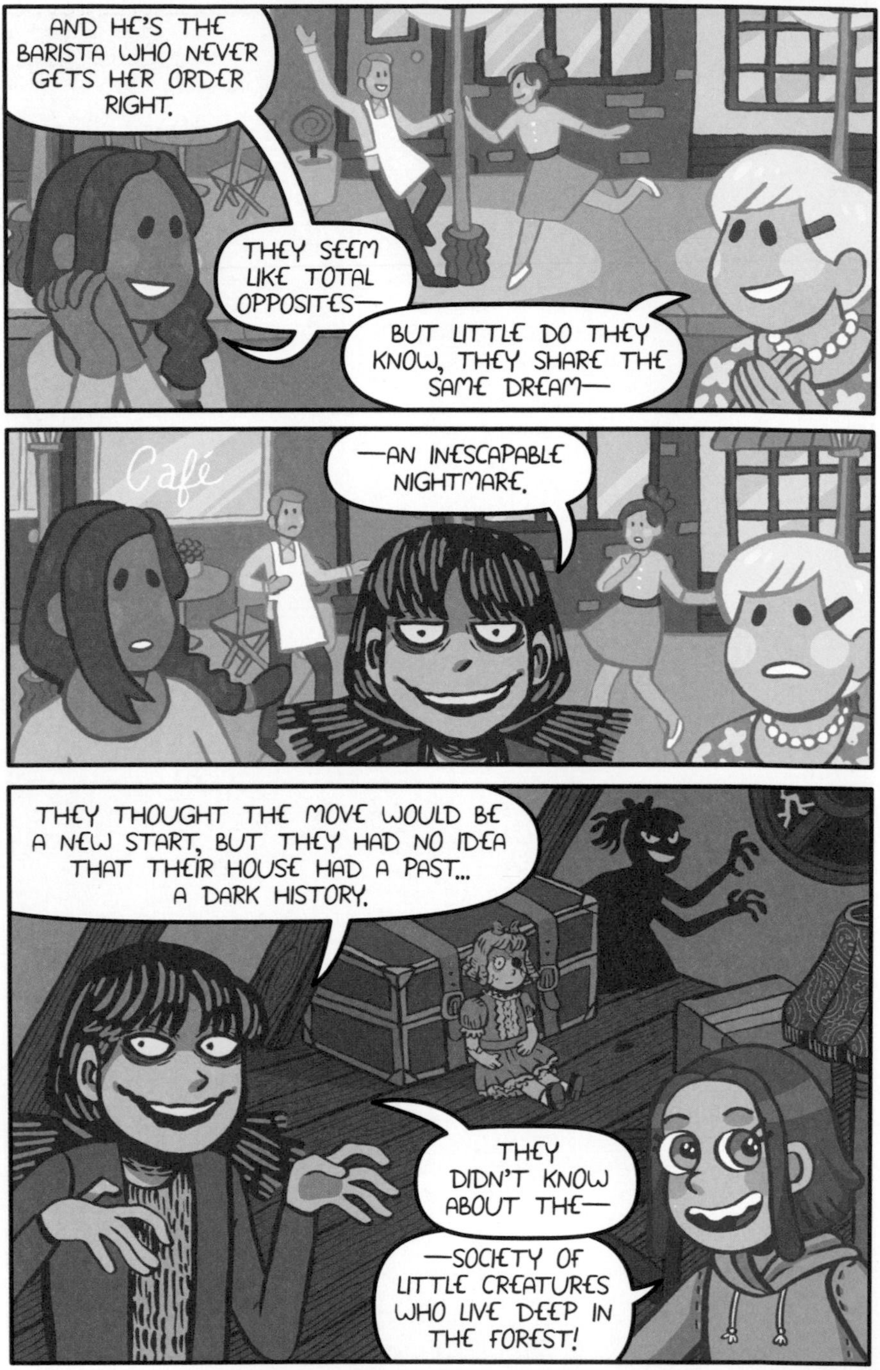
AND HE'S THE BARISTA WHO NEVER GETS HER ORDER RIGHT.
THEY SEEM LIKE TOTAL OPPOSITES—
BUT LITTLE DO THEY KNOW, THEY SHARE THE SAME DREAM—
Café
—AN INESCAPABLE NIGHTMARE.
THEY THOUGHT THE MOVE WOULD BE A NEW START, BUT THEY HAD NO IDEA THAT THEIR HOUSE HAD A PAST... A DARK HISTORY.
THEY DIDN'T KNOW ABOUT THE—
—SOCIETY OF LITTLE CREATURES WHO LIVE DEEP IN THE FOREST!

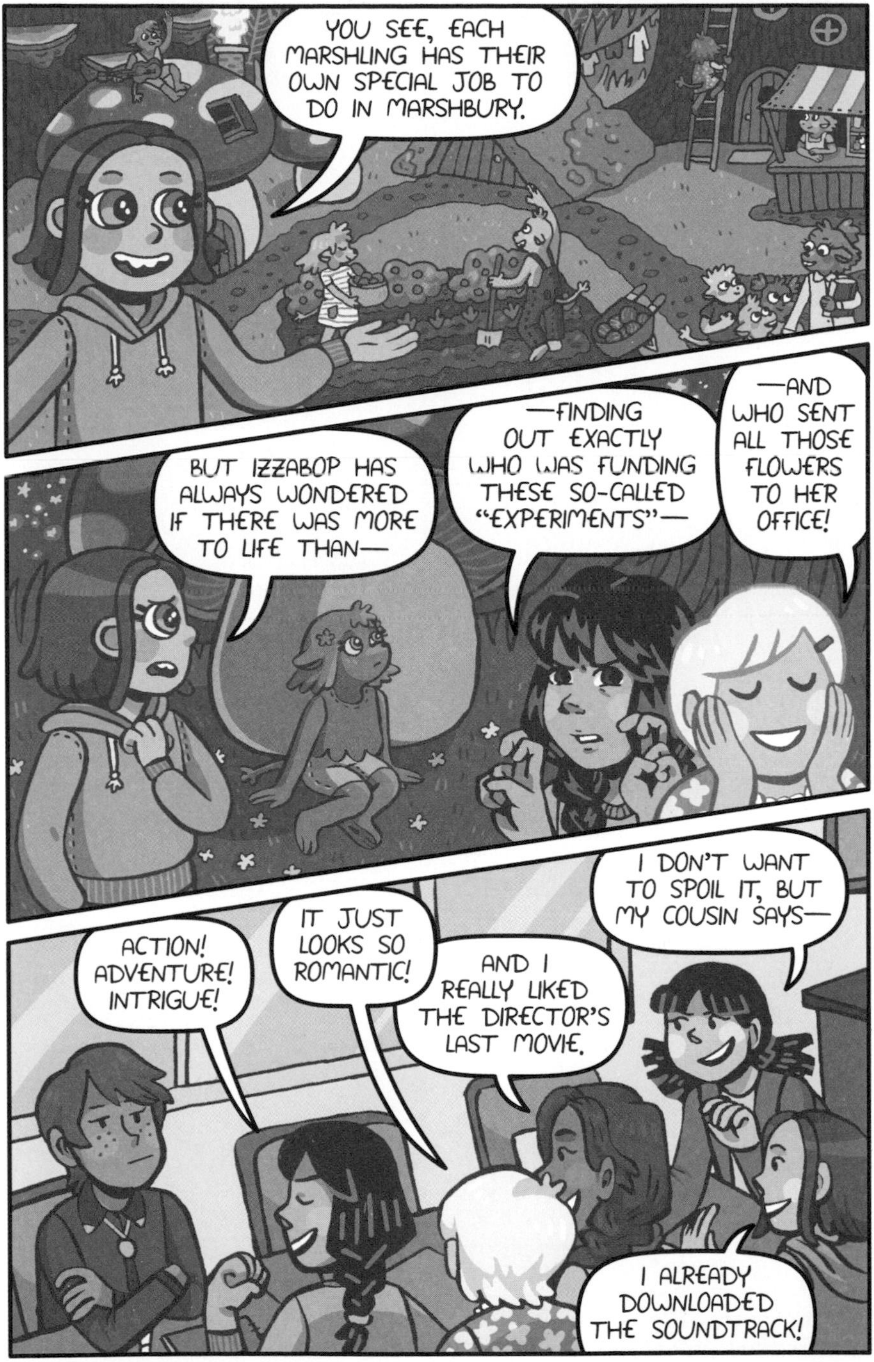
YOU SEE, EACH MARSHLING HAS THEIR OWN SPECIAL JOB TO DO IN MARSHBURY.
BUT IZZABOP HAS ALWAYS WONDERED IF THERE WAS MORE TO LIFE THAN—
—FINDING OUT EXACTLY WHO WAS FUNDING THESE SO-CALLED "EXPERIMENTS"—
—AND WHO SENT ALL THOSE FLOWERS TO HER OFFICE!
ACTION! ADVENTURE! INTRIGUE!
IT JUST LOOKS SO ROMANTIC!
AND I REALLY LIKED THE DIRECTOR'S LAST MOVIE.
I DON'T WANT TO SPOIL IT, BUT MY COUSIN SAYS—
I ALREADY DOWNLOADED THE SOUNDTRACK!

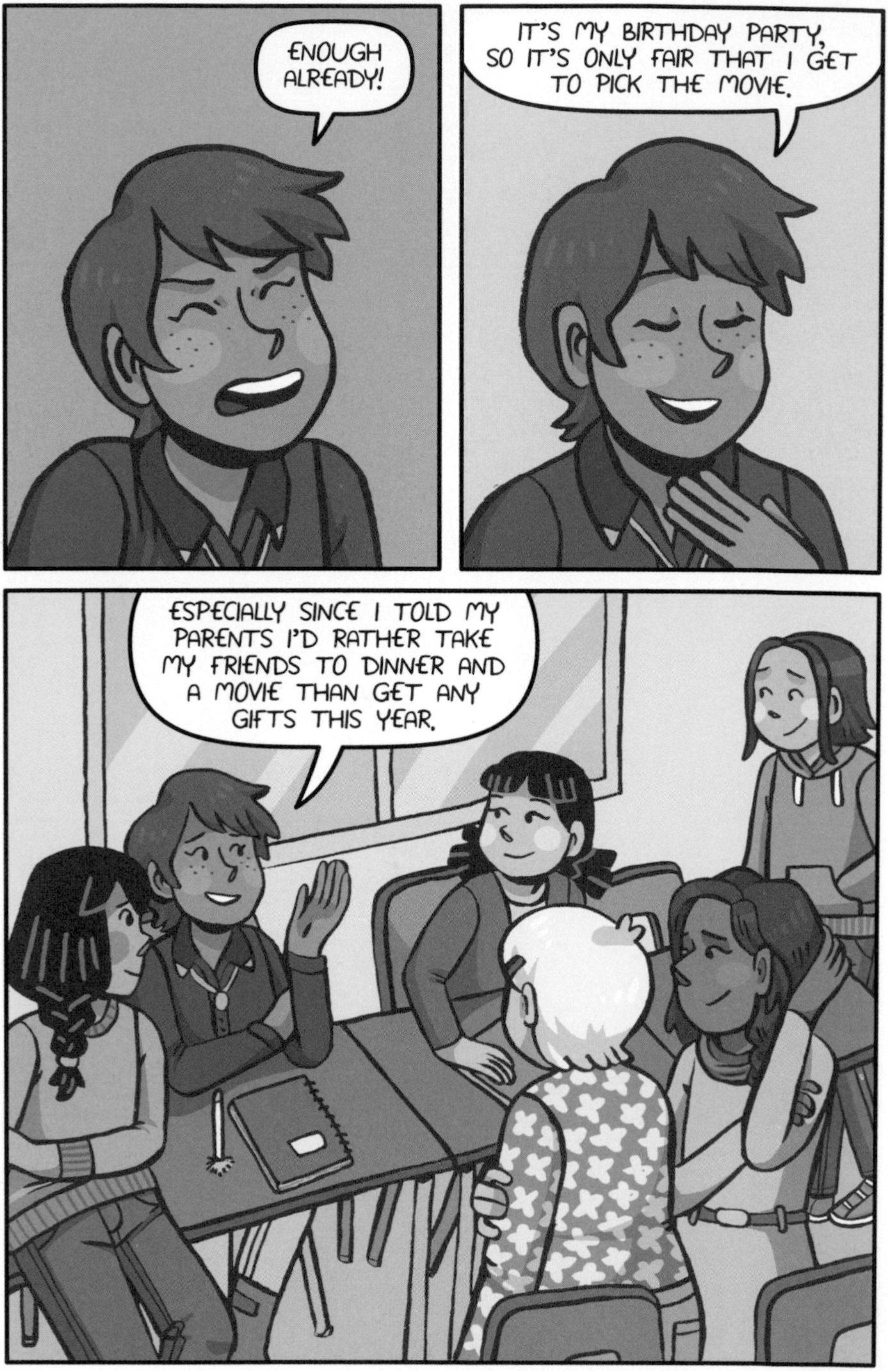
ENOUGH ALREADY!
IT'S MY BIRTHDAY PARTY, SO IT'S ONLY FAIR THAT I GET TO PICK THE MOVIE.
ESPECIALLY SINCE I TOLD MY PARENTS I'D RATHER TAKE MY FRIENDS TO DINNER AND A MOVIE THAN GET ANY GIFTS THIS YEAR.

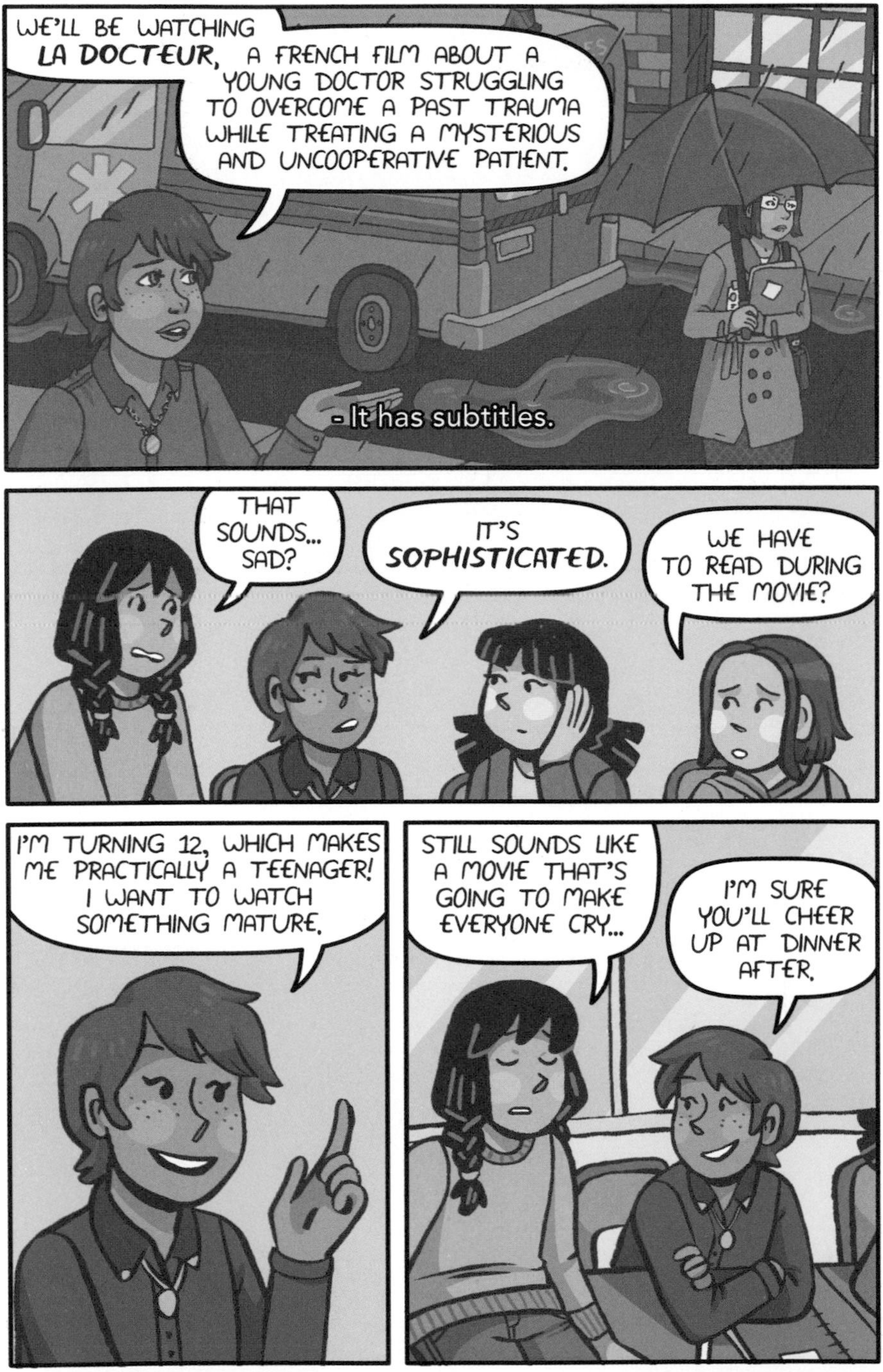
WE'LL BE WATCHING LA DOCTEUR, A FRENCH FILM ABOUT A YOUNG DOCTOR STRUGGLING TO OVERCOME A PAST TRAUMA WHILE TREATING A MYSTERIOUS AND UNCOOPERATIVE PATIENT.
- It has subtitles.
THAT SOUNDS... SAD?
IT'S SOPHISTICATED.
WE HAVE TO READ DURING THE MOVIE?
I'M TURNING 12, WHICH MAKES ME PRACTICALLY A TEENAGER! I WANT TO WATCH SOMETHING MATURE.
STILL SOUNDS LIKE A MOVIE THAT'S GOING TO MAKE EVERYONE CRY...
I'M SURE YOU'LL CHEER UP AT DINNER AFTER.

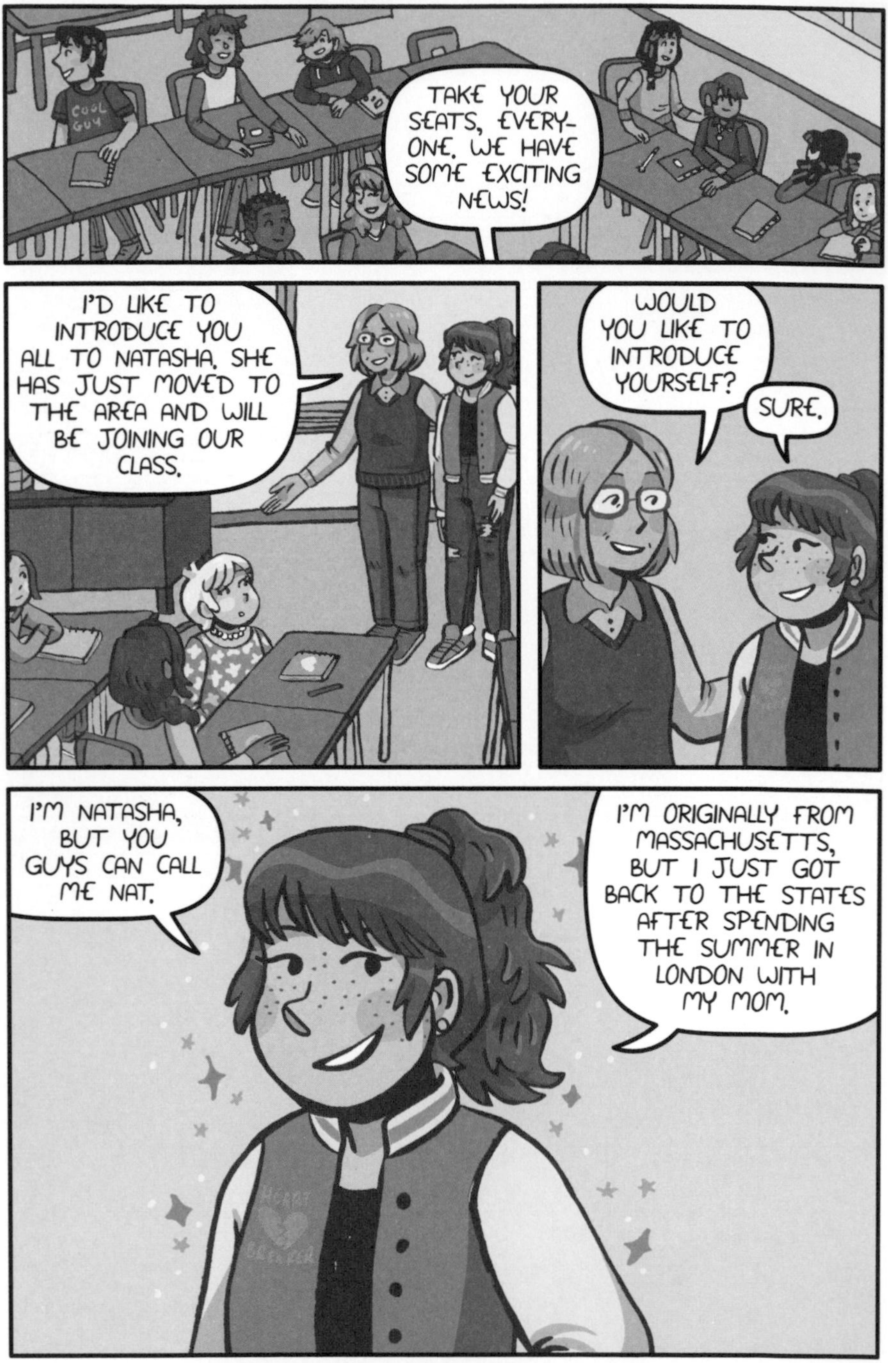
TAKE YOUR SEATS, EVERY-ONE. WE HAVE SOME EXCITING NEWS!
COOL GUY
I'D LIKE TO INTRODUCE YOU ALL TO NATASHA. SHE HAS JUST MOVED TO THE AREA AND WILL BE JOINING OUR CLASS.
WOULD YOU LIKE TO INTRODUCE YOURSELF?
SURE.
I'M NATASHA, BUT YOU GUYS CAN CALL ME NAT.
I'M ORIGINALLY FROM MASSACHUSETTS, BUT I JUST GOT BACK TO THE STATES AFTER SPENDING THE SUMMER IN LONDON WITH MY MOM.

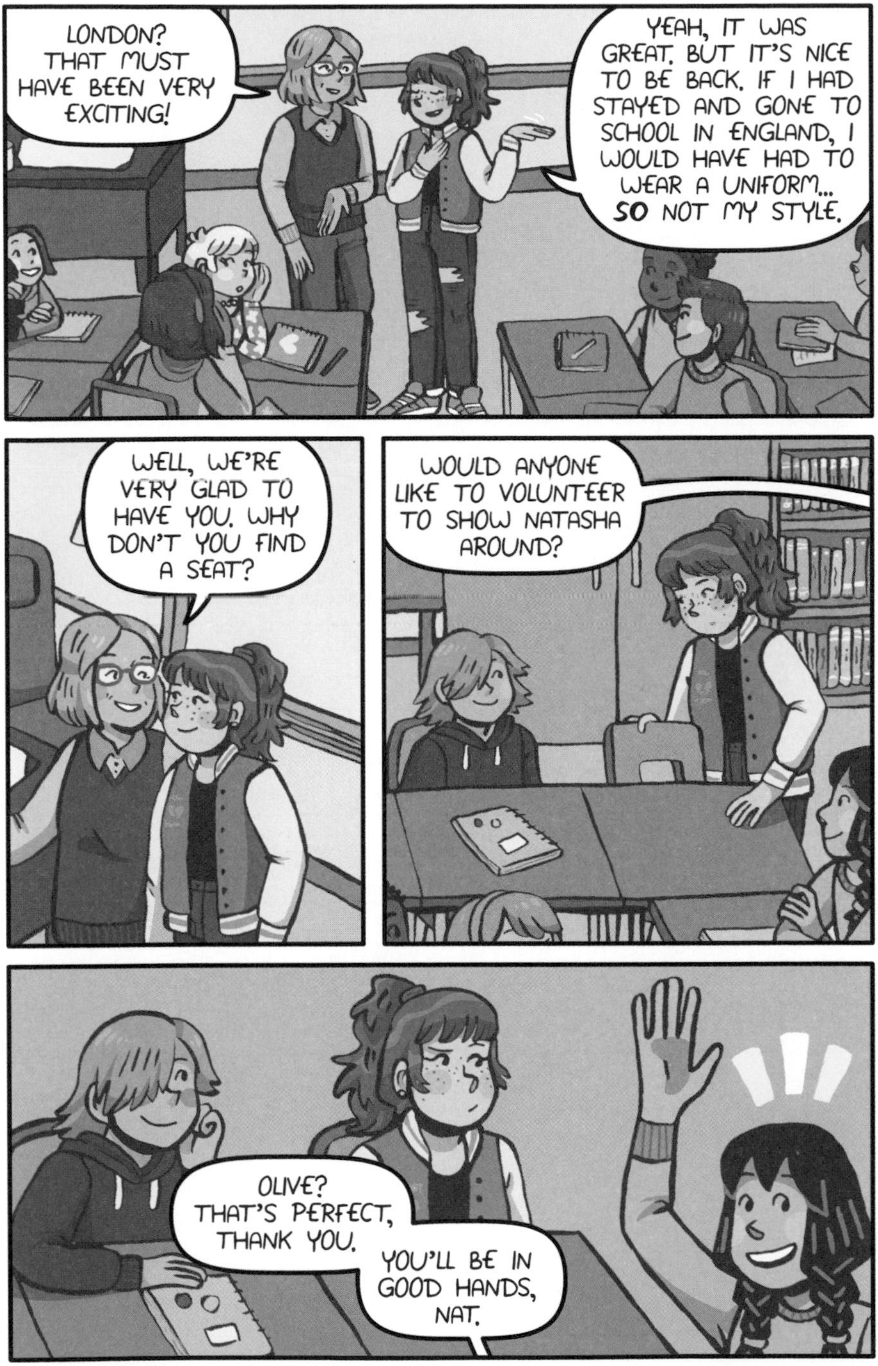
LONDON? THAT MUST HAVE BEEN VERY EXCITING!
YEAH, IT WAS GREAT. BUT IT'S NICE TO BE BACK. IF I HAD STAYED AND GONE TO SCHOOL IN ENGLAND, I WOULD HAVE HAD TO WEAR A UNIFORM... **SO** NOT MY STYLE.
WELL, WE'RE VERY GLAD TO HAVE YOU. WHY DON'T YOU FIND A SEAT?
WOULD ANYONE LIKE TO VOLUNTEER TO SHOW NATASHA AROUND?
OLIVE? THAT'S PERFECT, THANK YOU.
YOU'LL BE IN GOOD HANDS, NAT.

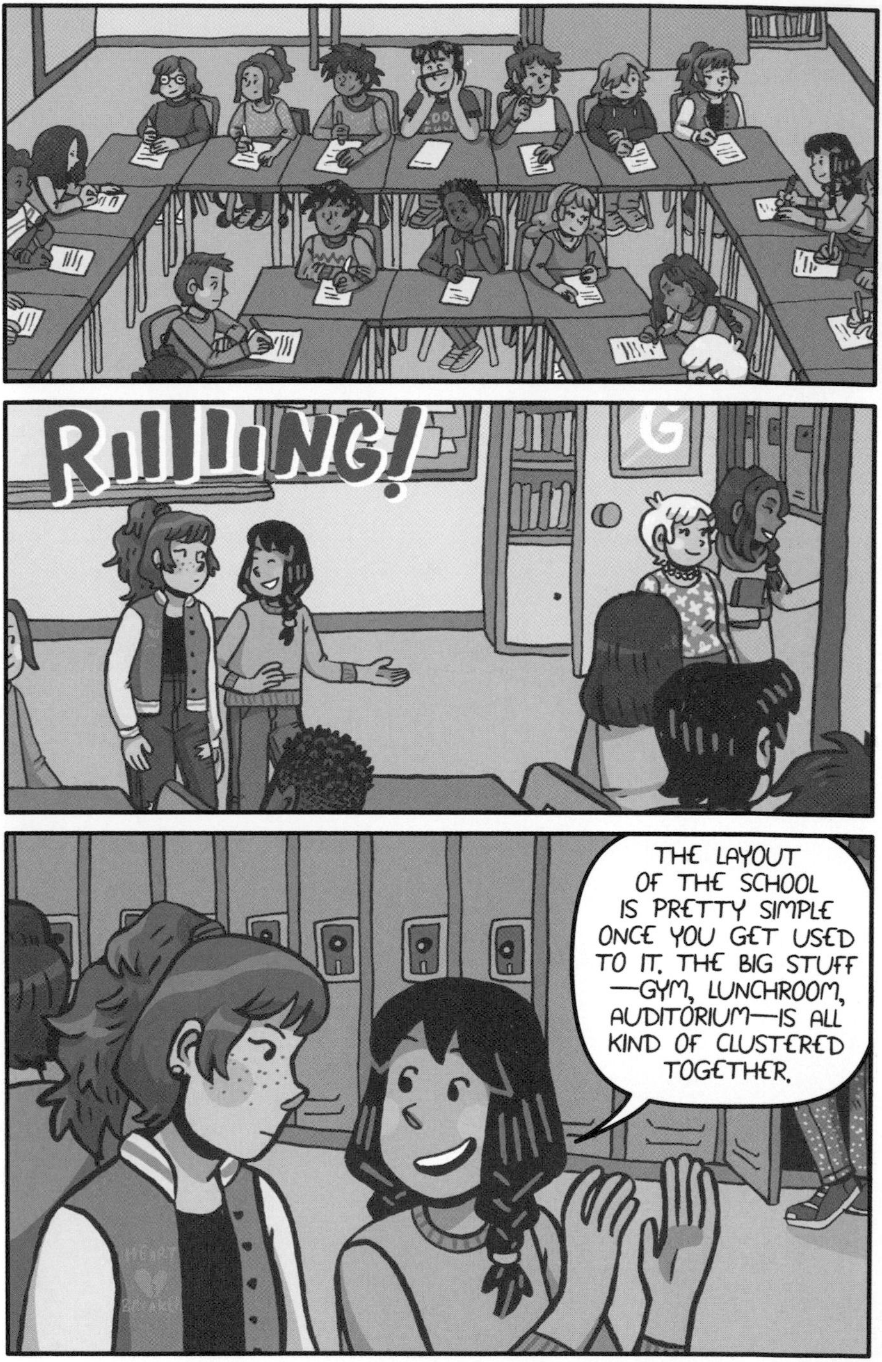
RIIIIING!
THE LAYOUT OF THE SCHOOL IS PRETTY SIMPLE ONCE YOU GET USED TO IT. THE BIG STUFF—GYM, LUNCHROOM, AUDITORIUM—IS ALL KIND OF CLUSTERED TOGETHER.

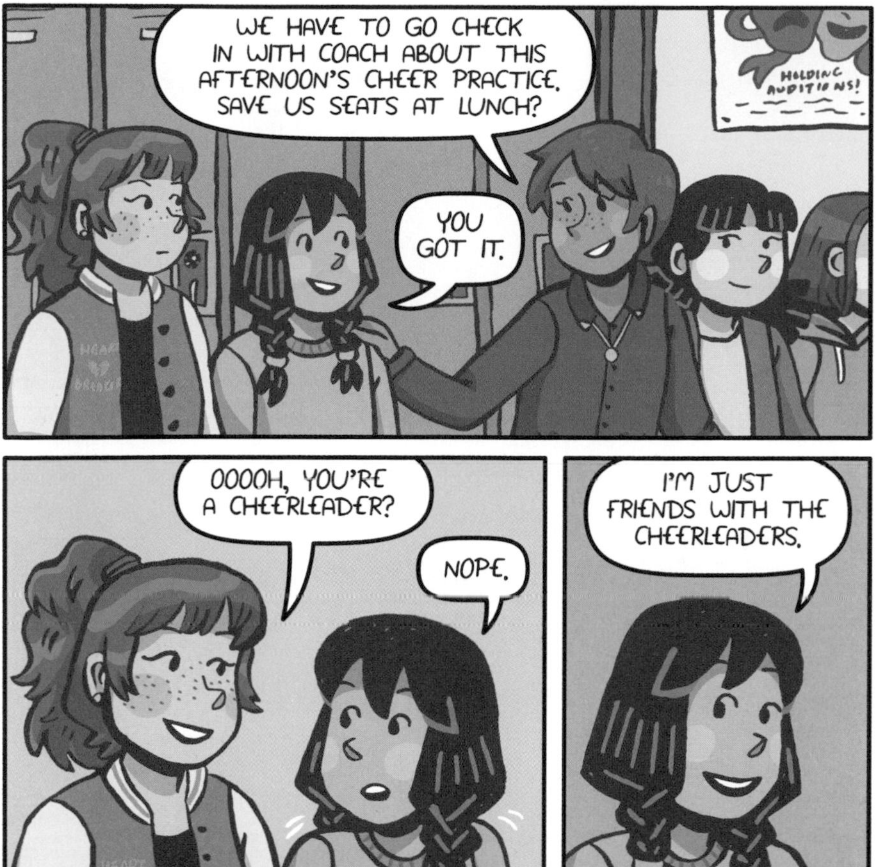
WE HAVE TO GO CHECK IN WITH COACH ABOUT THIS AFTERNOON'S CHEER PRACTICE. SAVE US SEATS AT LUNCH?
HOLDING AUDITIONS!
YOU GOT IT.
OOOOH, YOU'RE A CHEERLEADER?
NOPE.
I'M JUST FRIENDS WITH THE CHEERLEADERS.
ALL THE LOCKERS FOR SIXTH-GRADERS ARE ON THE FIRST FLOOR, SO YOUR LOCKER WILL PROBABLY BE AROUND HERE SOMEWHERE.

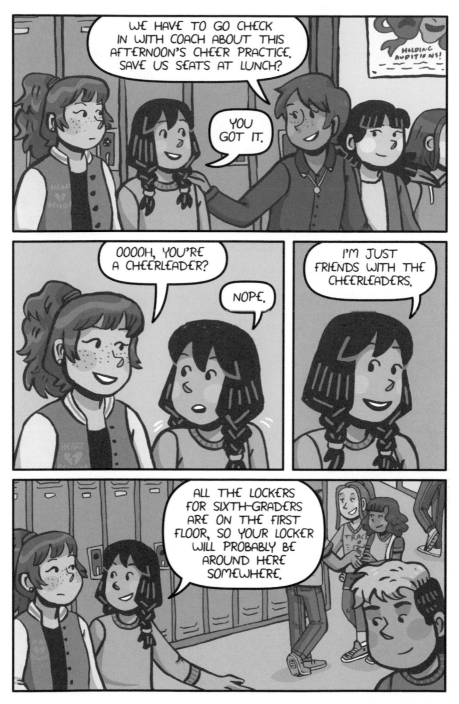

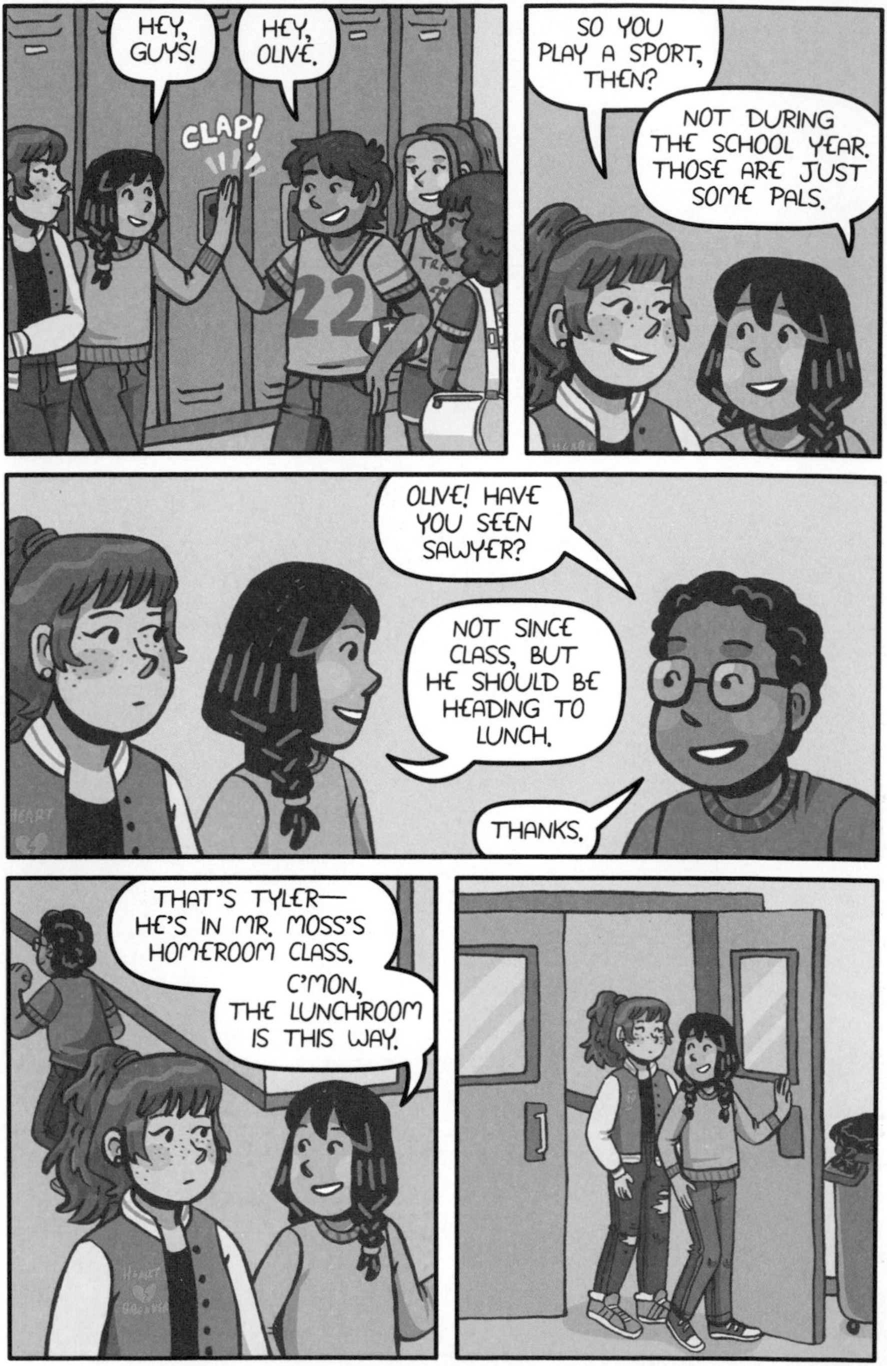
HEY, GUYS!
HEY, OLIVE.
CLAP!
SO YOU PLAY A SPORT, THEN?
NOT DURING THE SCHOOL YEAR. THOSE ARE JUST SOME PALS.
OLIVE! HAVE YOU SEEN SAWYER?
NOT SINCE CLASS, BUT HE SHOULD BE HEADING TO LUNCH.
THANKS.
THAT'S TYLER— HE'S IN MR. MOSS'S HOMEROOM CLASS.
C'MON, THE LUNCHROOM IS THIS WAY.

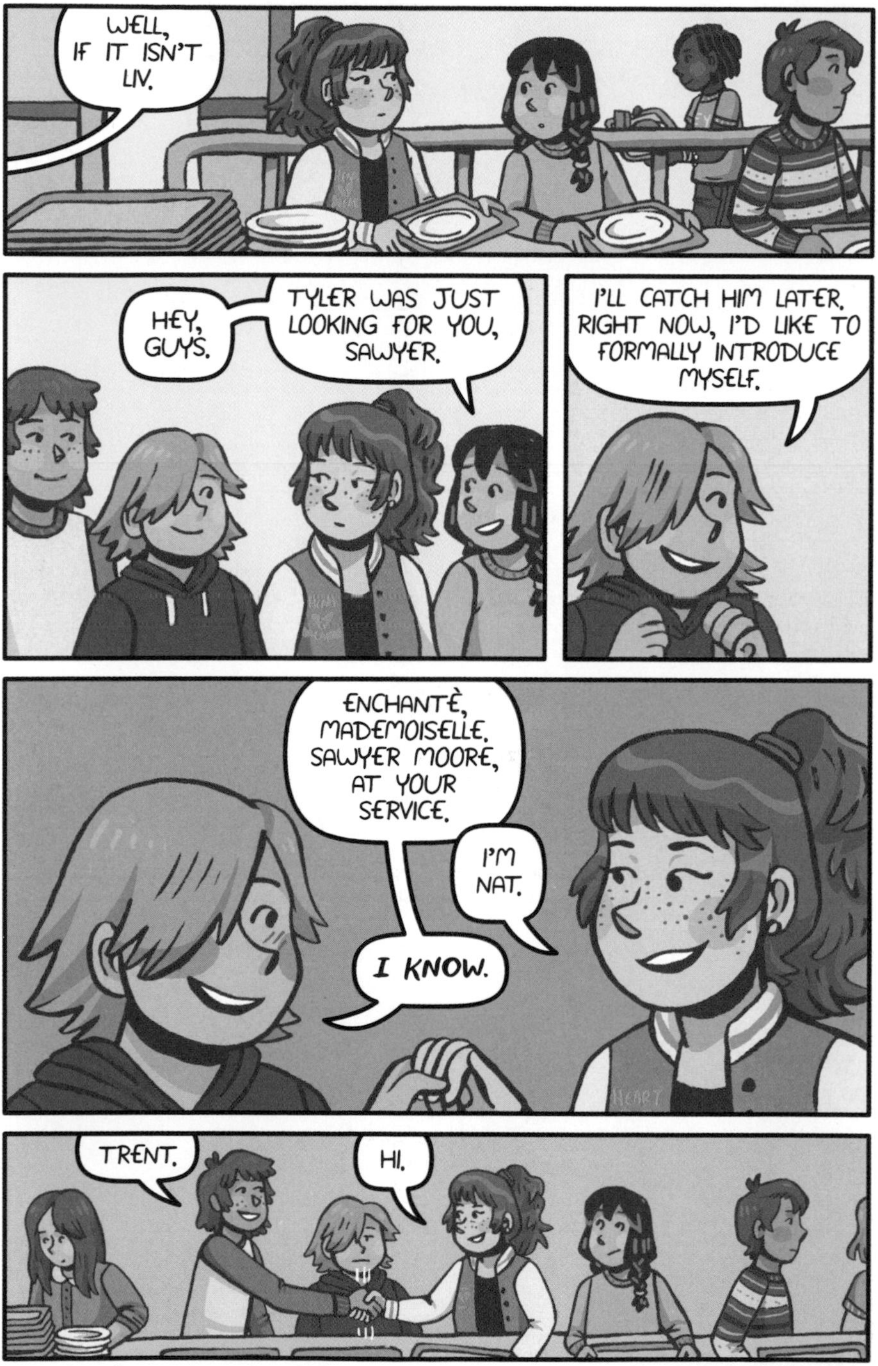
WELL, IF IT ISN'T LIV.
HEY, GUYS.
TYLER WAS JUST LOOKING FOR YOU, SAWYER.
I'LL CATCH HIM LATER. RIGHT NOW, I'D LIKE TO FORMALLY INTRODUCE MYSELF.
ENCHANTÈ, MADEMOISELLE. SAWYER MOORE, AT YOUR SERVICE.
I'M NAT.
I KNOW.
TRENT.
HI.

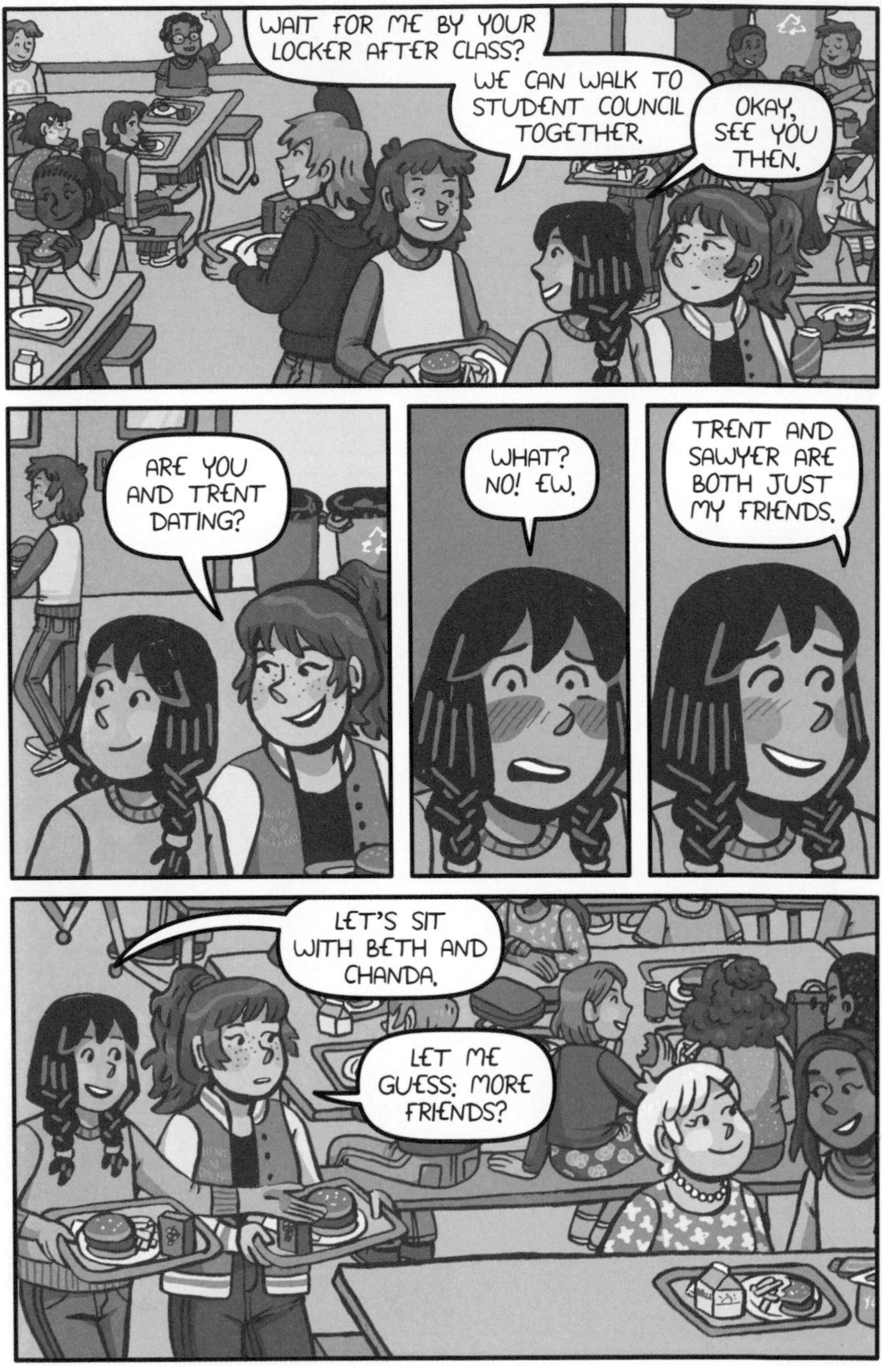

WAIT FOR ME BY YOUR LOCKER AFTER CLASS?
WE CAN WALK TO STUDENT COUNCIL TOGETHER.
OKAY, SEE YOU THEN.
ARE YOU AND TRENT DATING?
WHAT? NO! EW.
TRENT AND SAWYER ARE BOTH JUST MY FRIENDS.
LET'S SIT WITH BETH AND CHANDA.
LET ME GUESS: MORE FRIENDS?

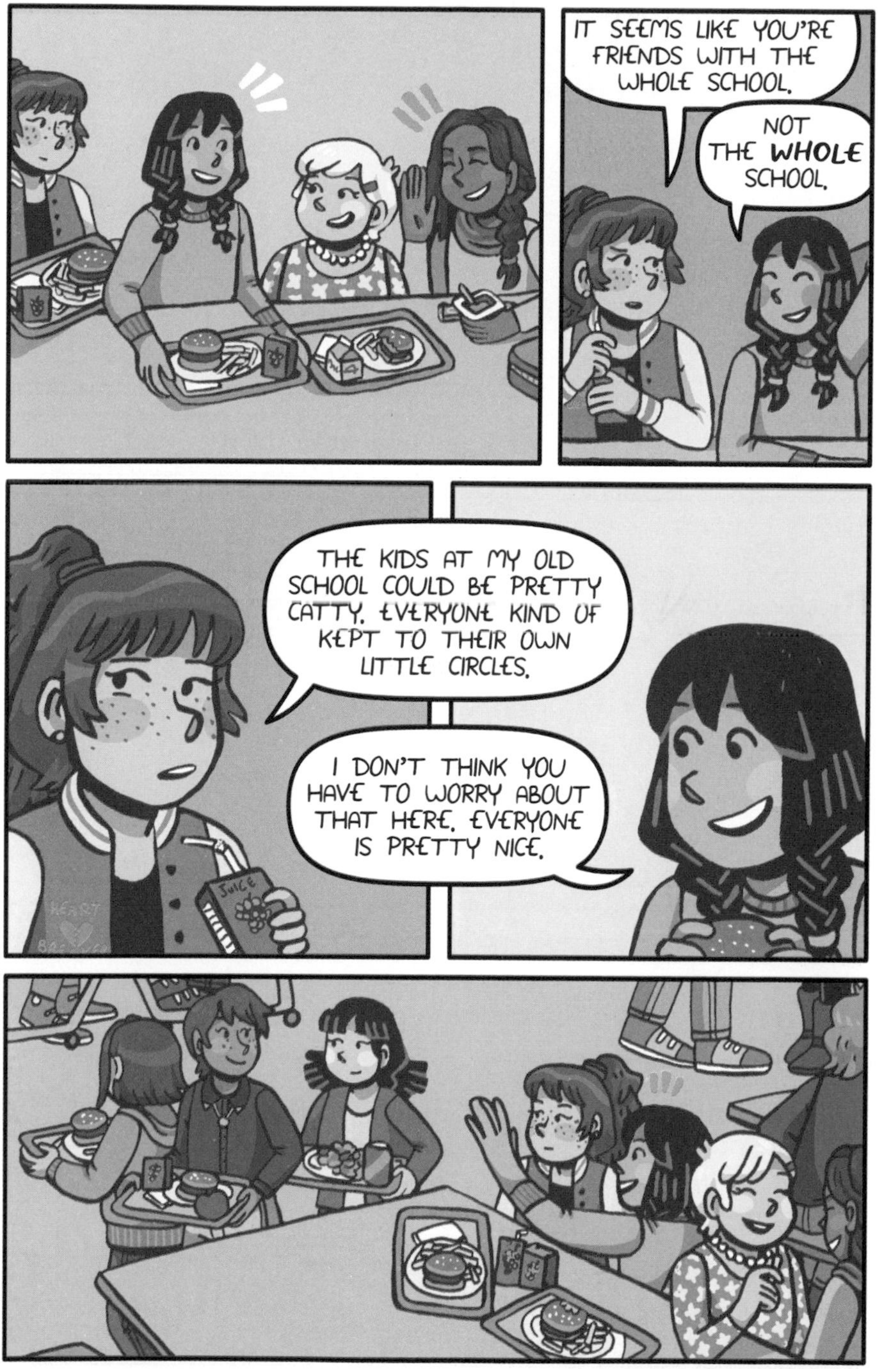
IT SEEMS LIKE YOU'RE FRIENDS WITH THE WHOLE SCHOOL.
NOT THE **WHOLE** SCHOOL.
THE KIDS AT MY OLD SCHOOL COULD BE PRETTY CATTY. EVERYONE KIND OF KEPT TO THEIR OWN LITTLE CIRCLES.
JUICE
I DON'T THINK YOU HAVE TO WORRY ABOUT THAT HERE. EVERYONE IS PRETTY NICE.

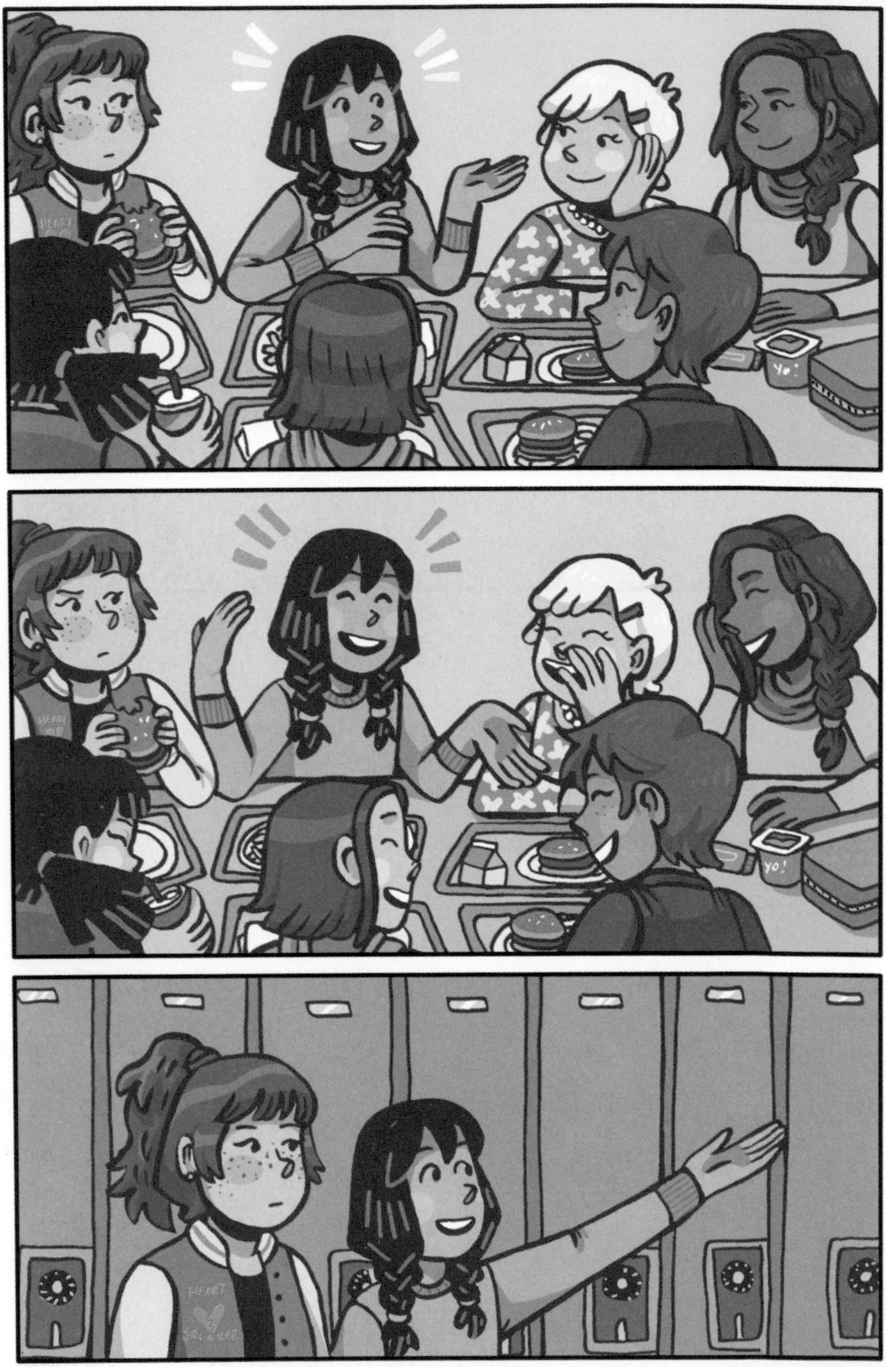
YO!
YO!
HEART BREAKER

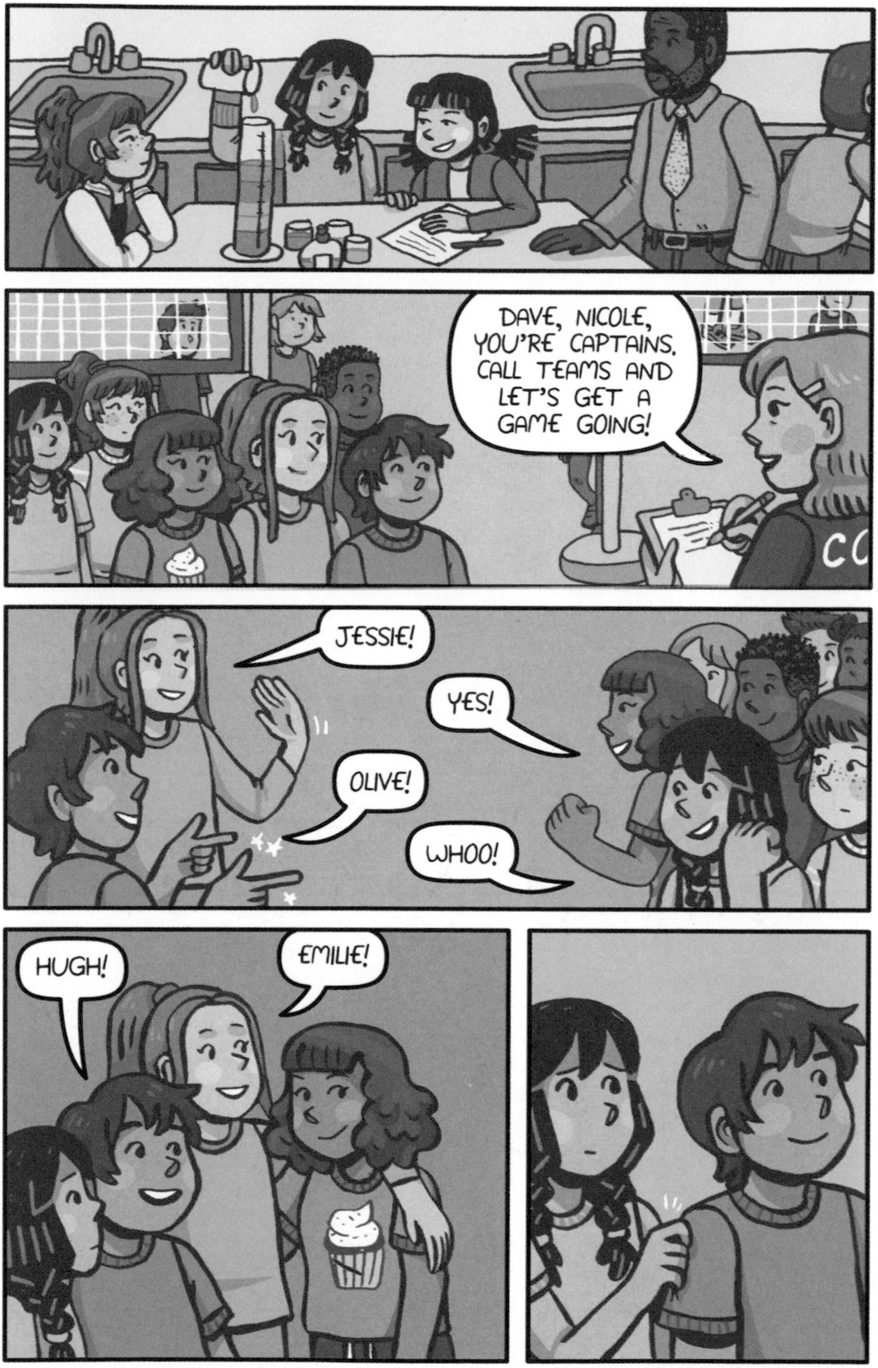
DAVE, NICOLE, YOU'RE CAPTAINS. CALL TEAMS AND LET'S GET A GAME GOING!
JESSIE!
YES!
OLIVE!
WHOO!
HUGH!
EMILIE!

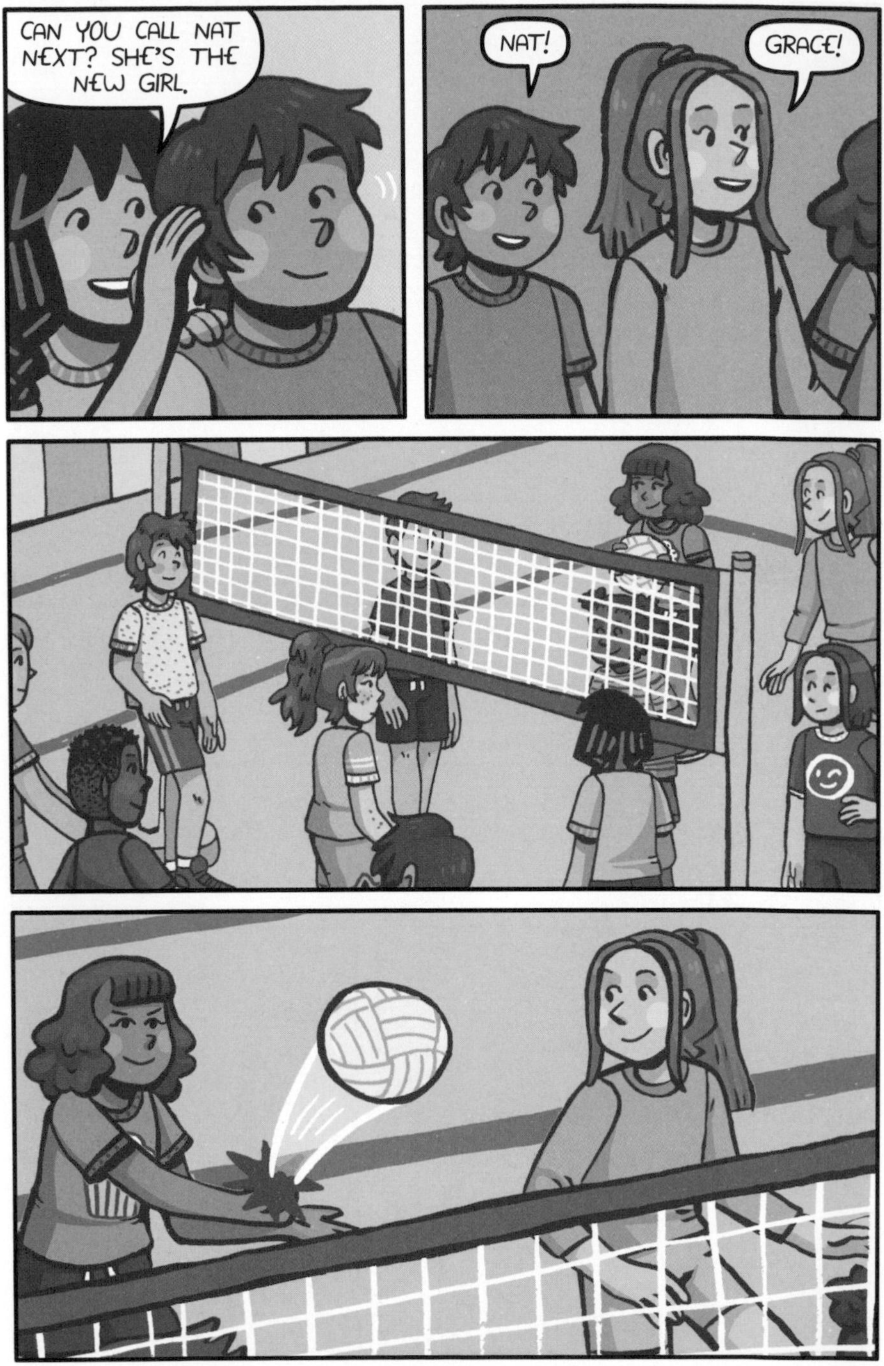
CAN YOU CALL NAT NEXT? SHE'S THE NEW GIRL.
NAT!
GRACE!

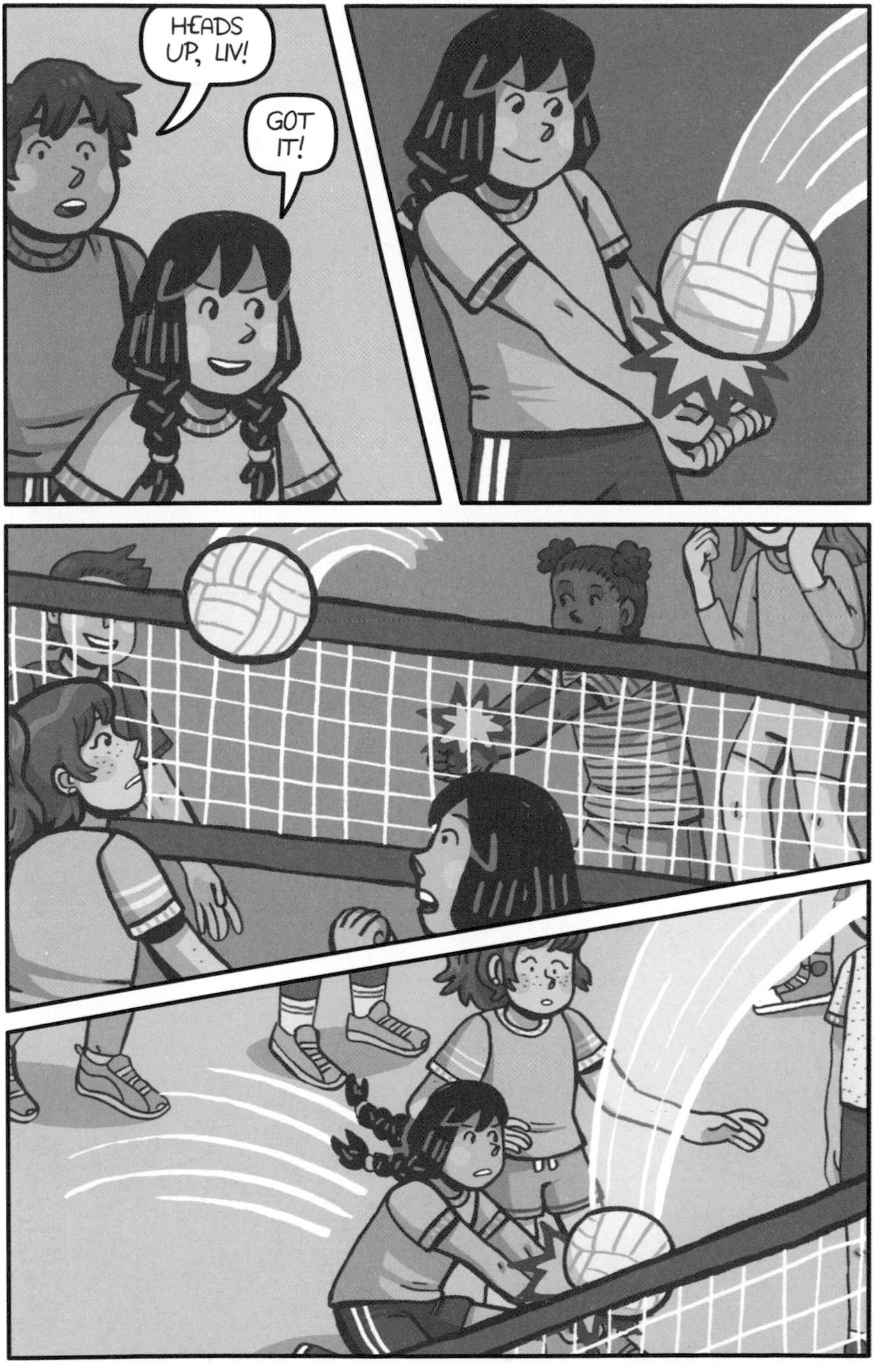
HEADS UP, LIV!
GOT IT!

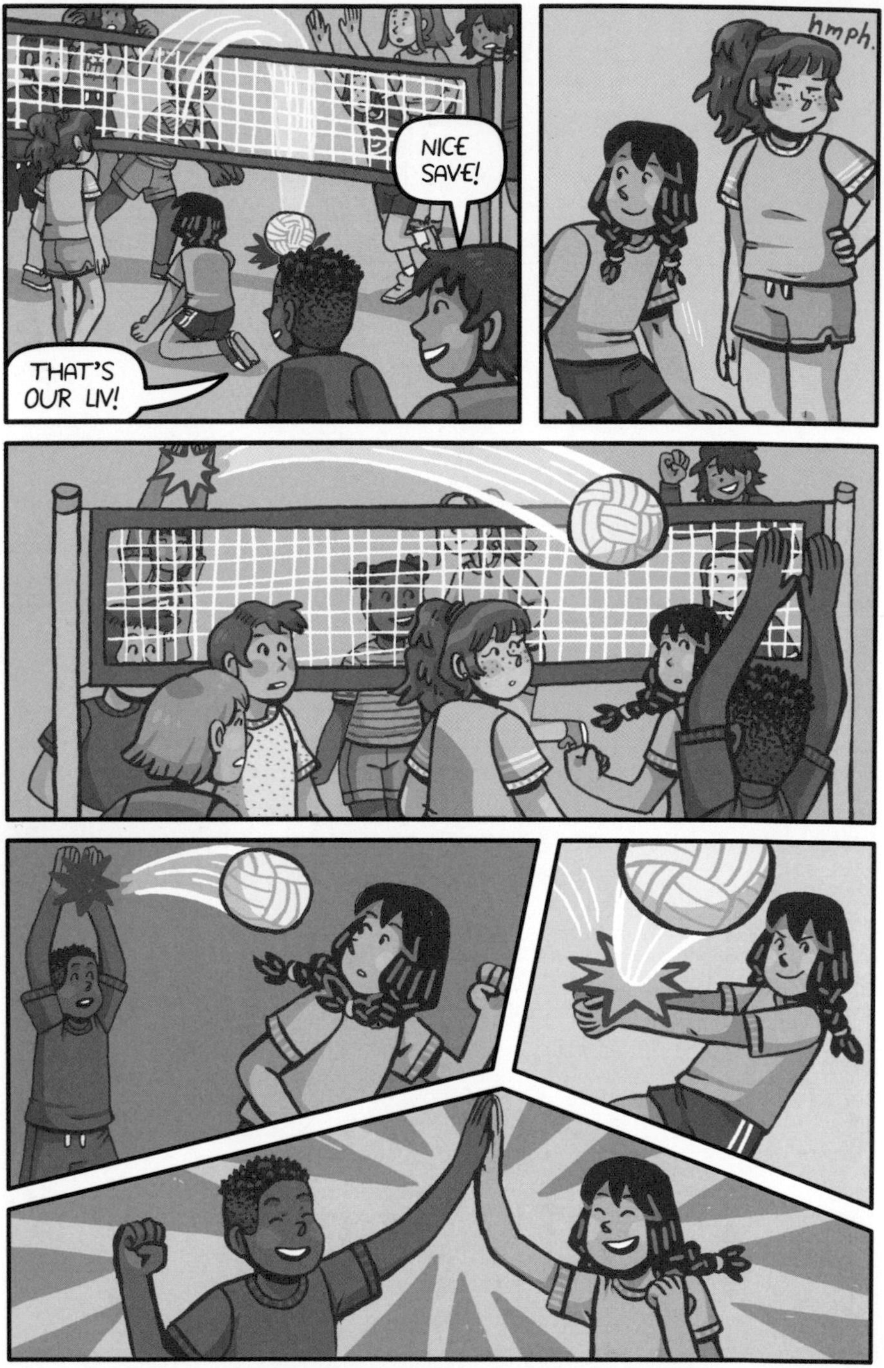
NICE SAVE!
THAT'S OUR LIV!
hmph.

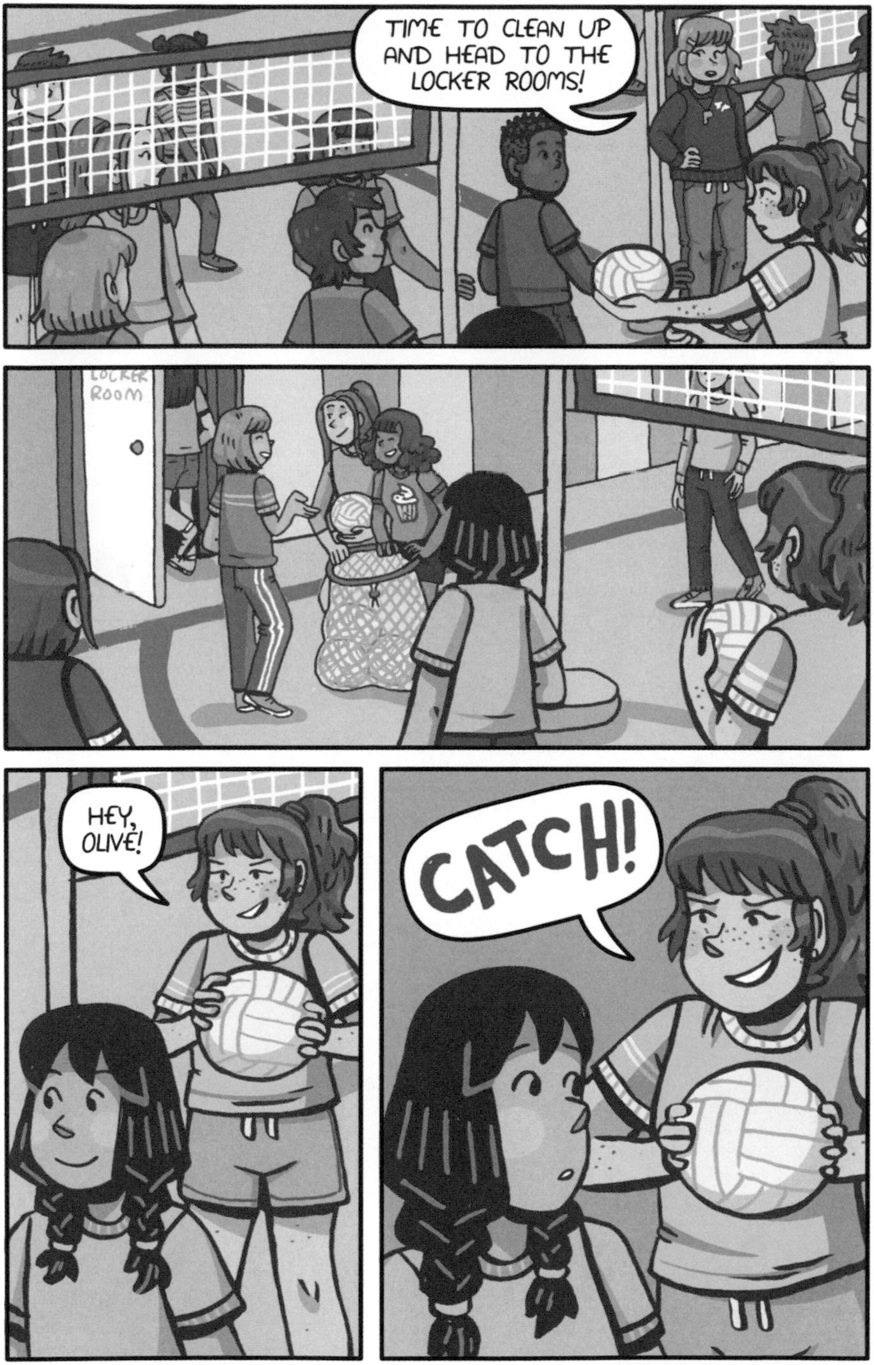
TIME TO CLEAN UP AND HEAD TO THE LOCKER ROOMS!
LOCKER ROOM
HEY, OLIVE!
CATCH!

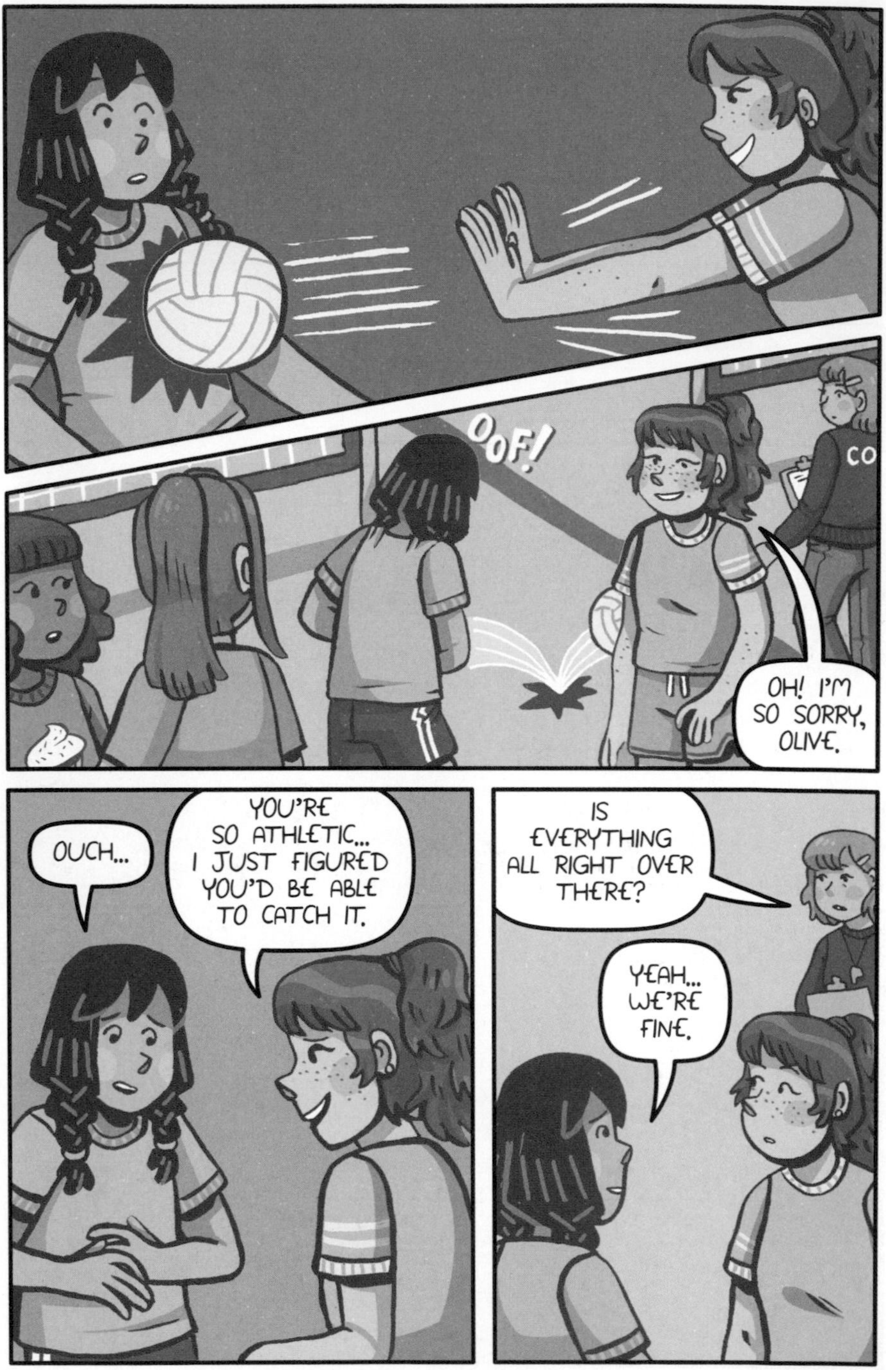
OOF!
OH! I'M SO SORRY, OLIVE.
OUCH...
YOU'RE SO ATHLETIC... I JUST FIGURED YOU'D BE ABLE TO CATCH IT.
IS EVERYTHING ALL RIGHT OVER THERE?
YEAH... WE'RE FINE.

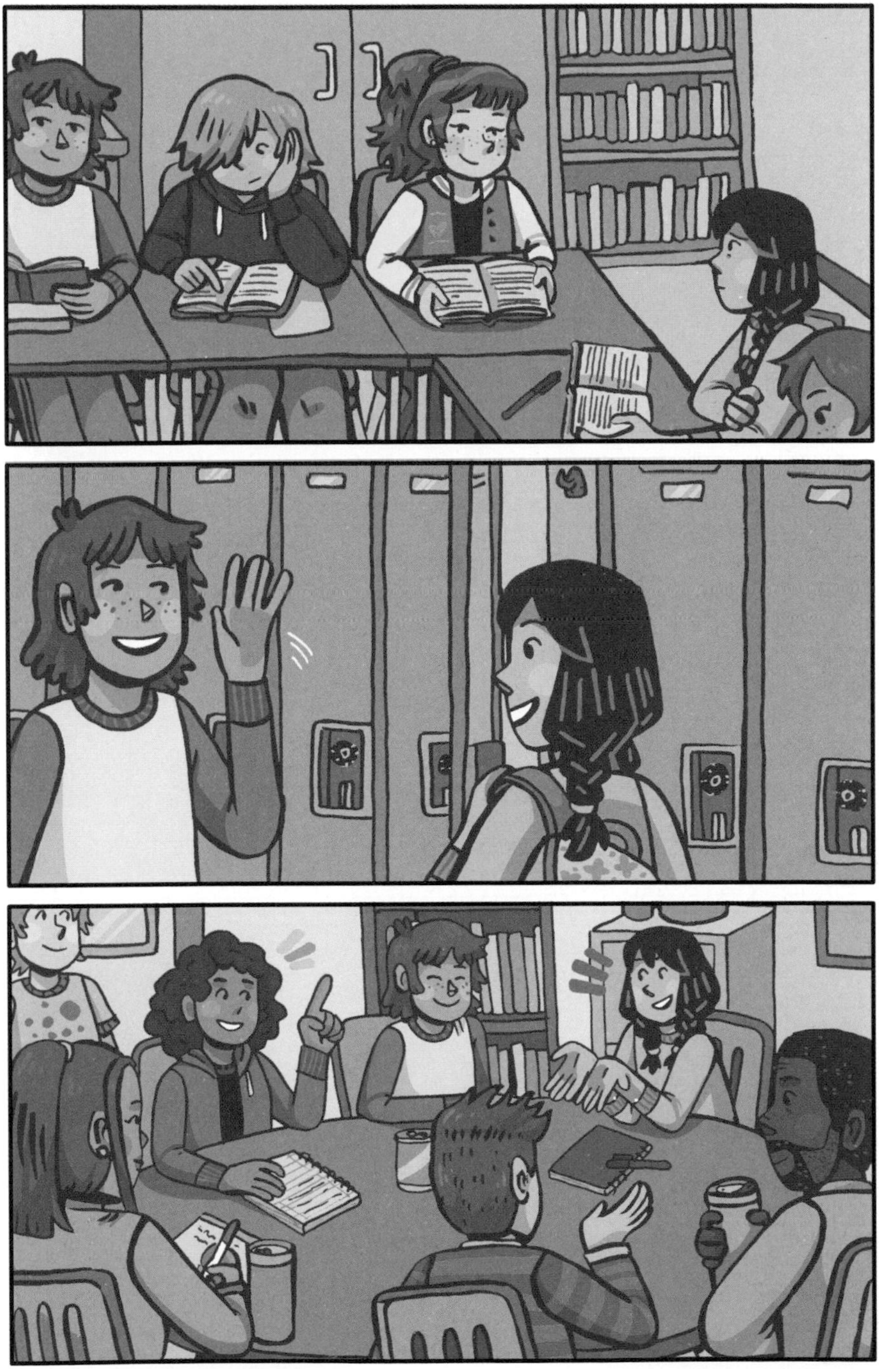

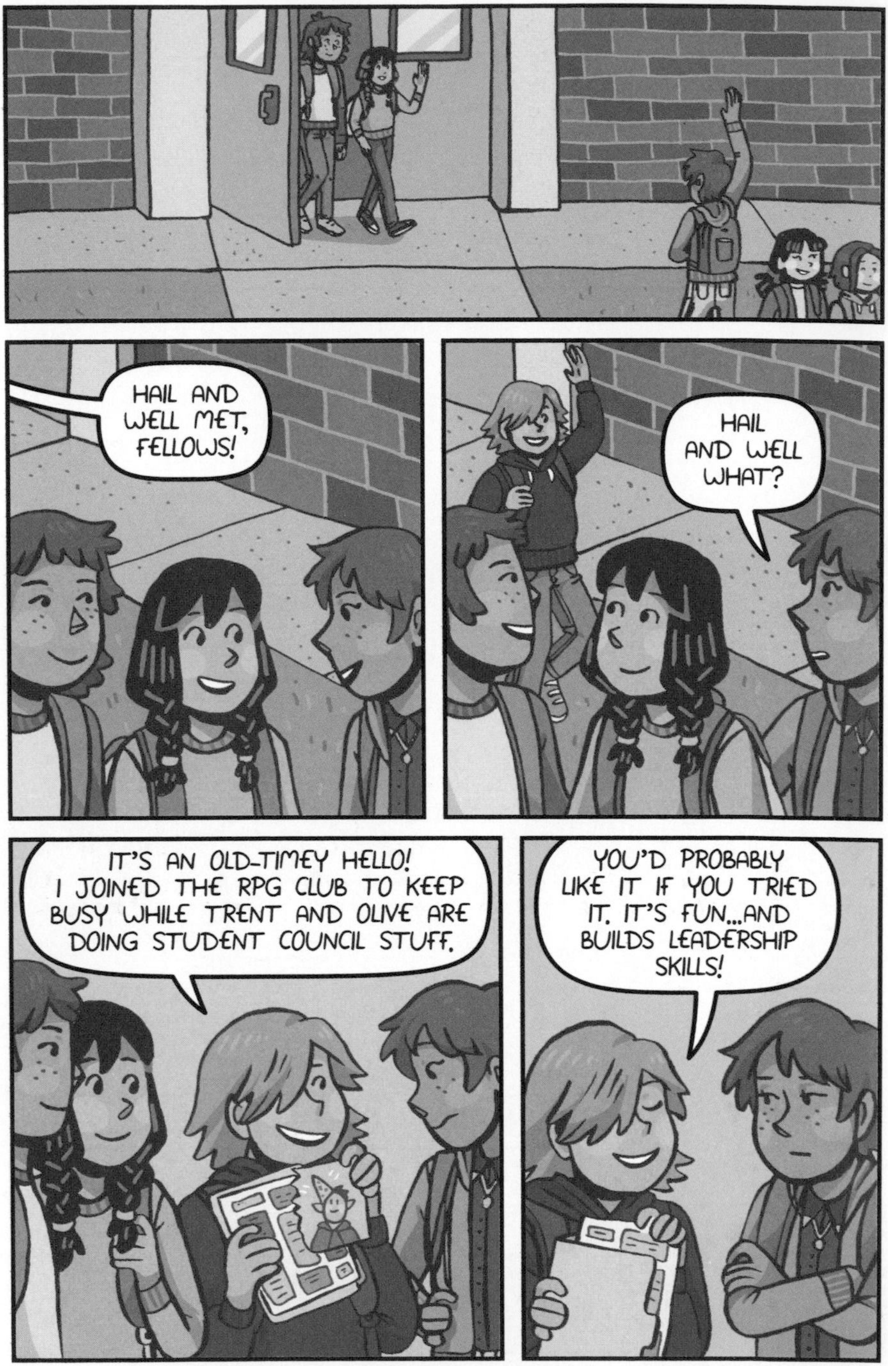
HAIL AND WELL MET, FELLOWS!
HAIL AND WELL WHAT?
IT'S AN OLD-TIMEY HELLO! I JOINED THE RPG CLUB TO KEEP BUSY WHILE TRENT AND OLIVE ARE DOING STUDENT COUNCIL STUFF.
YOU'D PROBABLY LIKE IT IF YOU TRIED IT. IT'S FUN...AND BUILDS LEADERSHIP SKILLS!

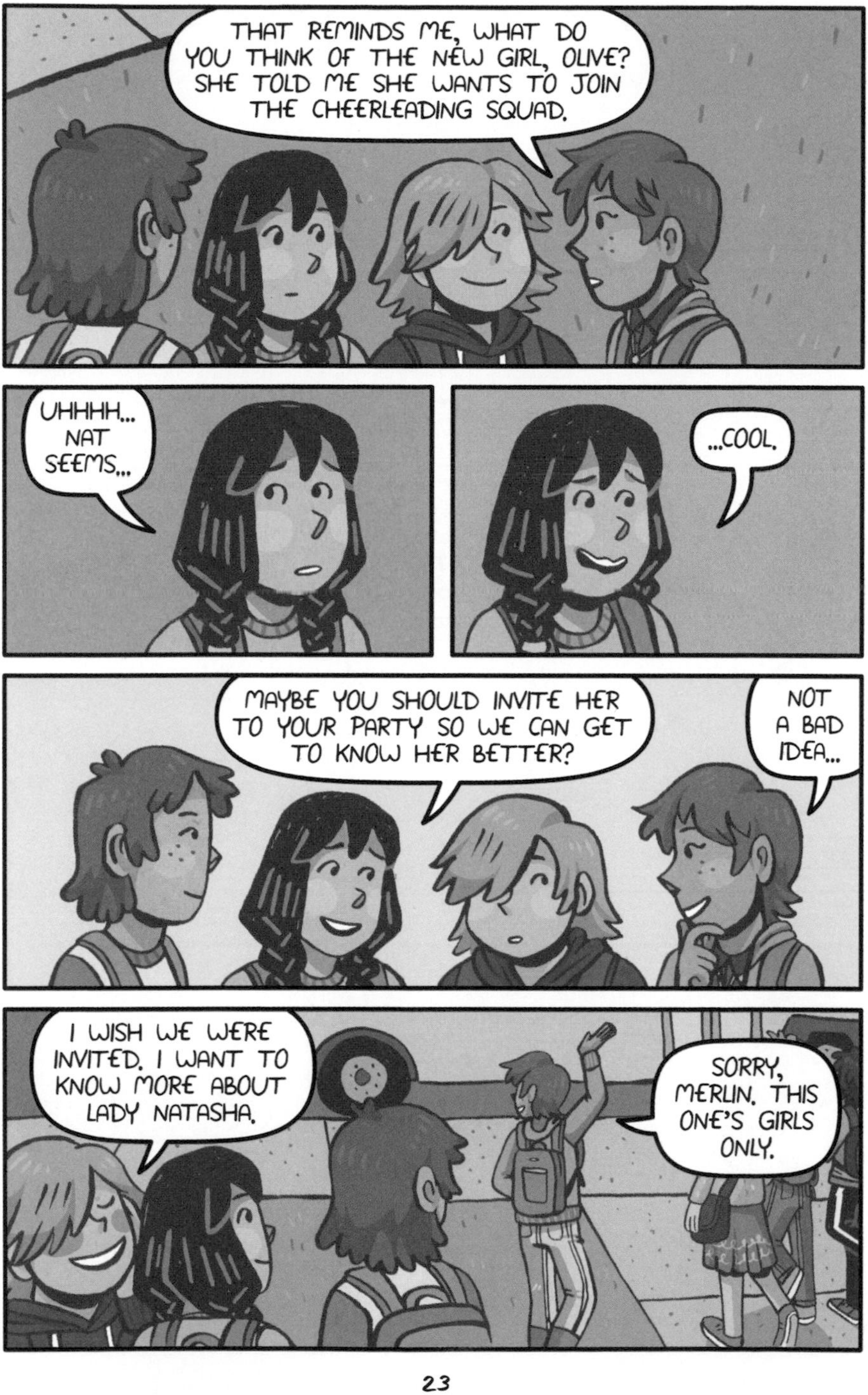
THAT REMINDS ME, WHAT DO YOU THINK OF THE NEW GIRL, OLIVE? SHE TOLD ME SHE WANTS TO JOIN THE CHEERLEADING SQUAD.
UHHHH... NAT SEEMS...
...COOL.
MAYBE YOU SHOULD INVITE HER TO YOUR PARTY SO WE CAN GET TO KNOW HER BETTER?
NOT A BAD IDEA...
I WISH WE WERE INVITED. I WANT TO KNOW MORE ABOUT LADY NATASHA.
SORRY, MERLIN. THIS ONE'S GIRLS ONLY.

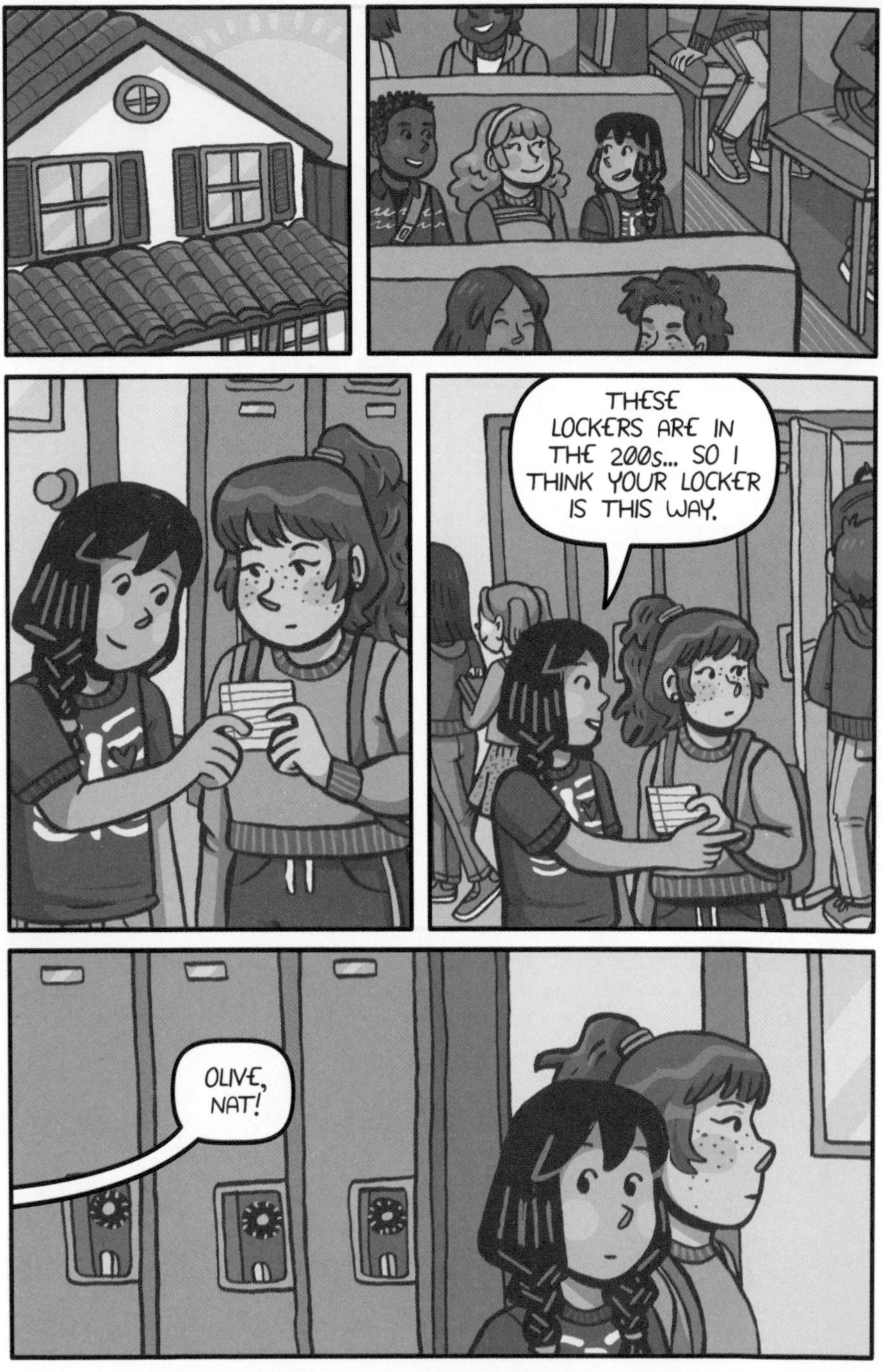
THESE LOCKERS ARE IN THE 200s... SO I THINK YOUR LOCKER IS THIS WAY.
OLIVE, NAT!

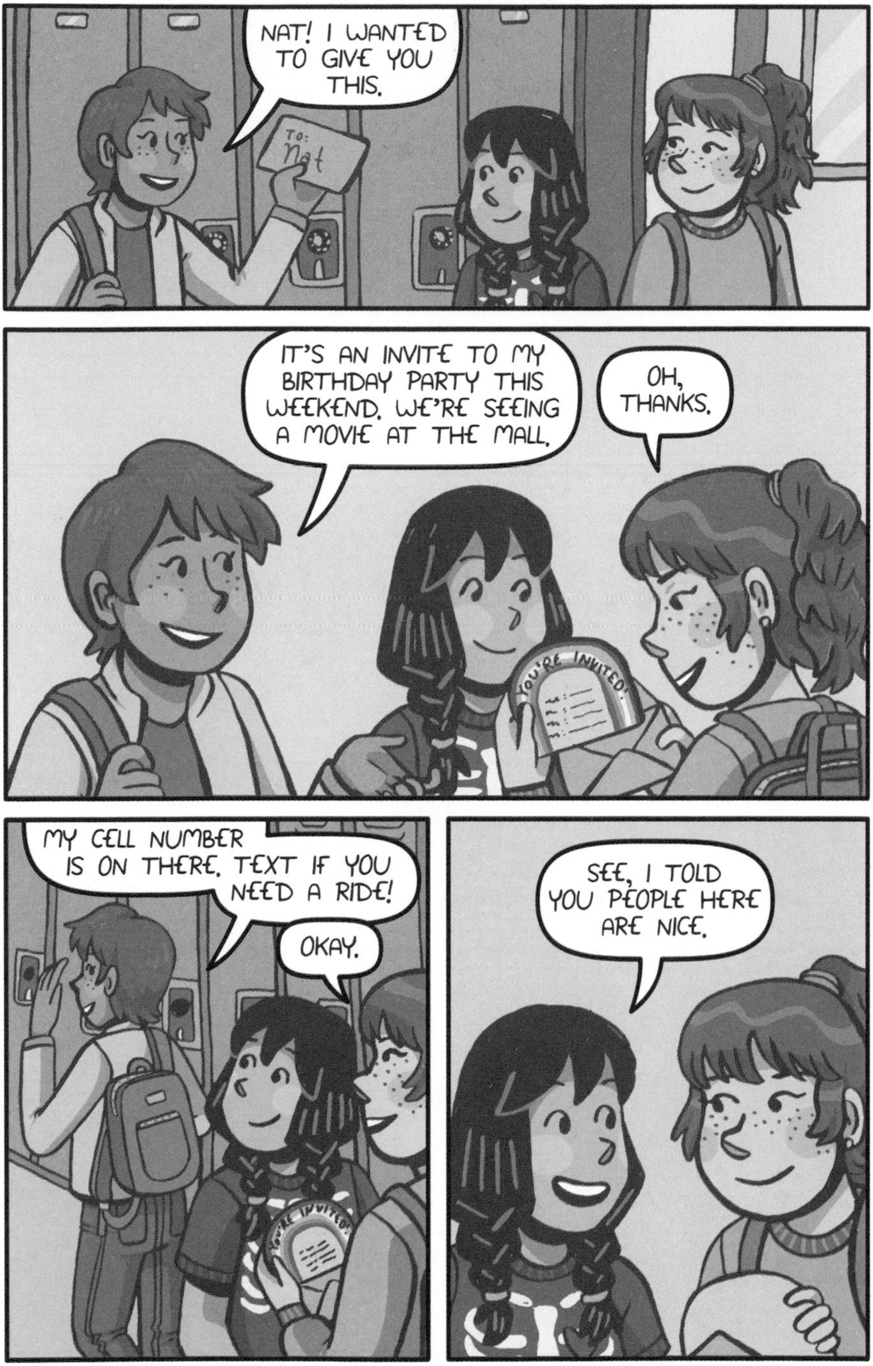
NAT! I WANTED TO GIVE YOU THIS.
TO: Nat
IT'S AN INVITE TO MY BIRTHDAY PARTY THIS WEEKEND. WE'RE SEEING A MOVIE AT THE MALL.
OH, THANKS.
YOU'RE INVITED!
MY CELL NUMBER IS ON THERE. TEXT IF YOU NEED A RIDE!
OKAY.
SEE, I TOLD YOU PEOPLE HERE ARE NICE.

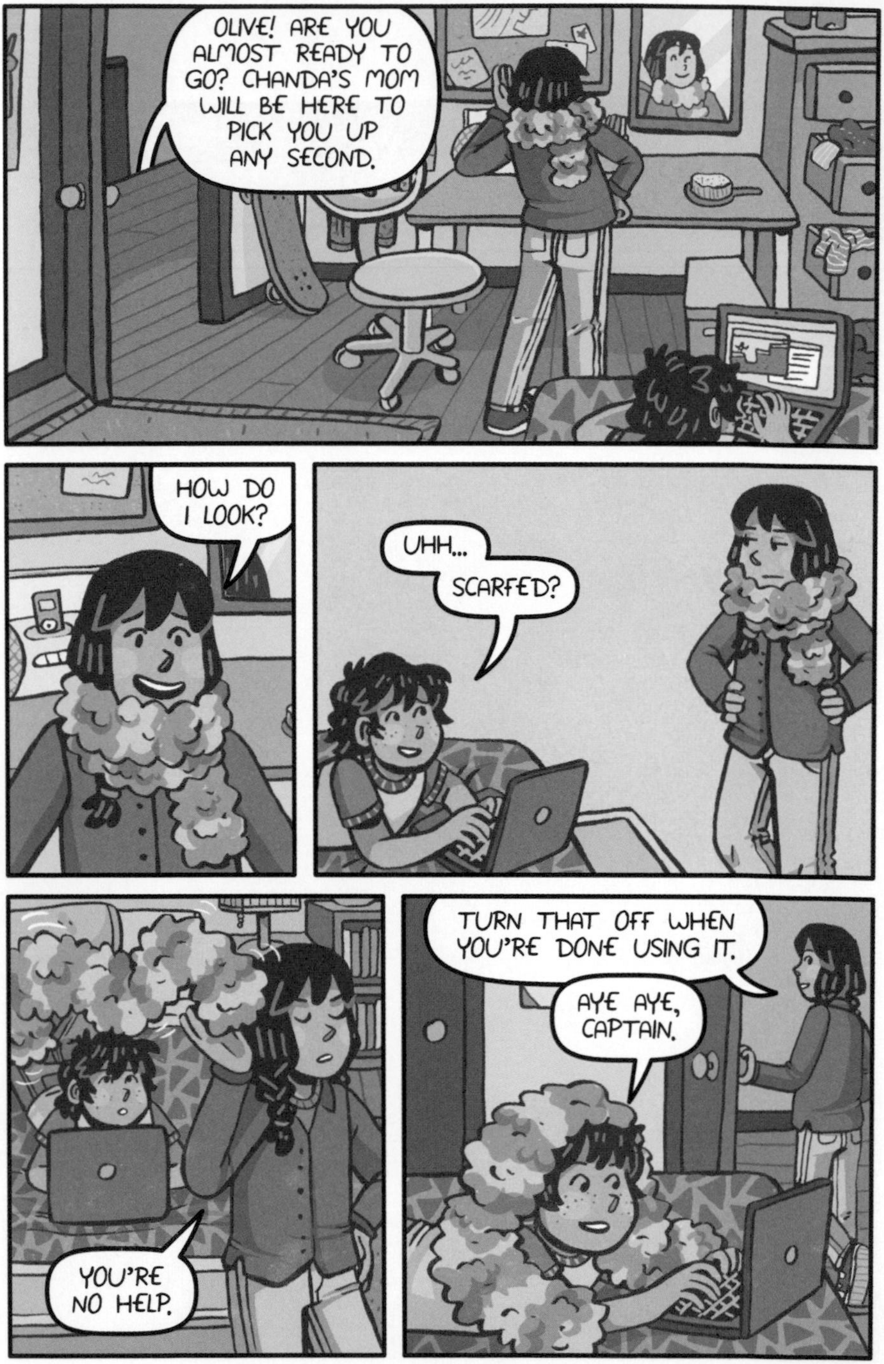
OLIVE! ARE YOU ALMOST READY TO GO? CHANDA'S MOM WILL BE HERE TO PICK YOU UP ANY SECOND.
HOW DO I LOOK?
UHH...
SCARFED?
YOU'RE NO HELP.
TURN THAT OFF WHEN YOU'RE DONE USING IT.
AYE AYE, CAPTAIN.

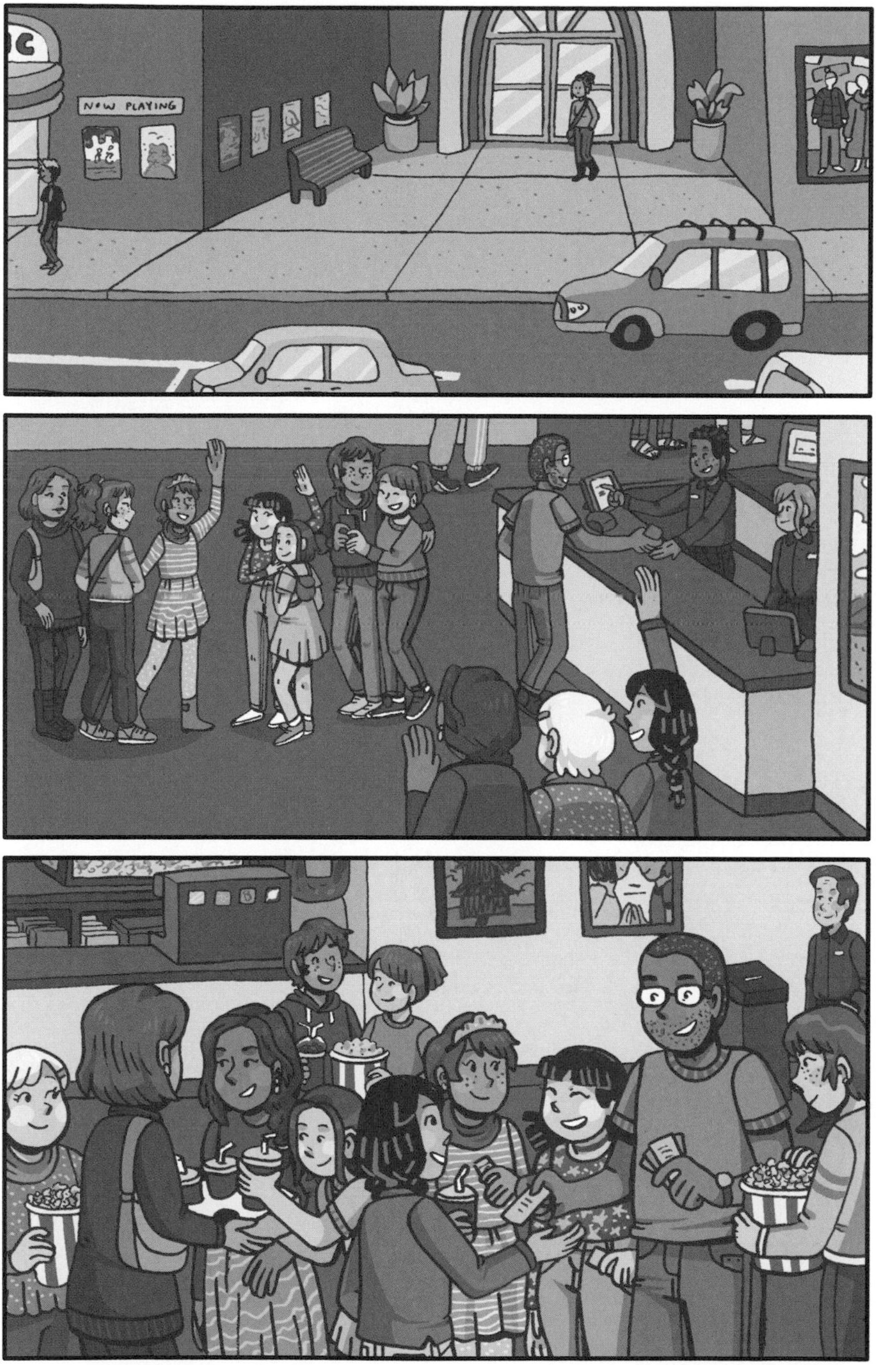
NOW PLAYING

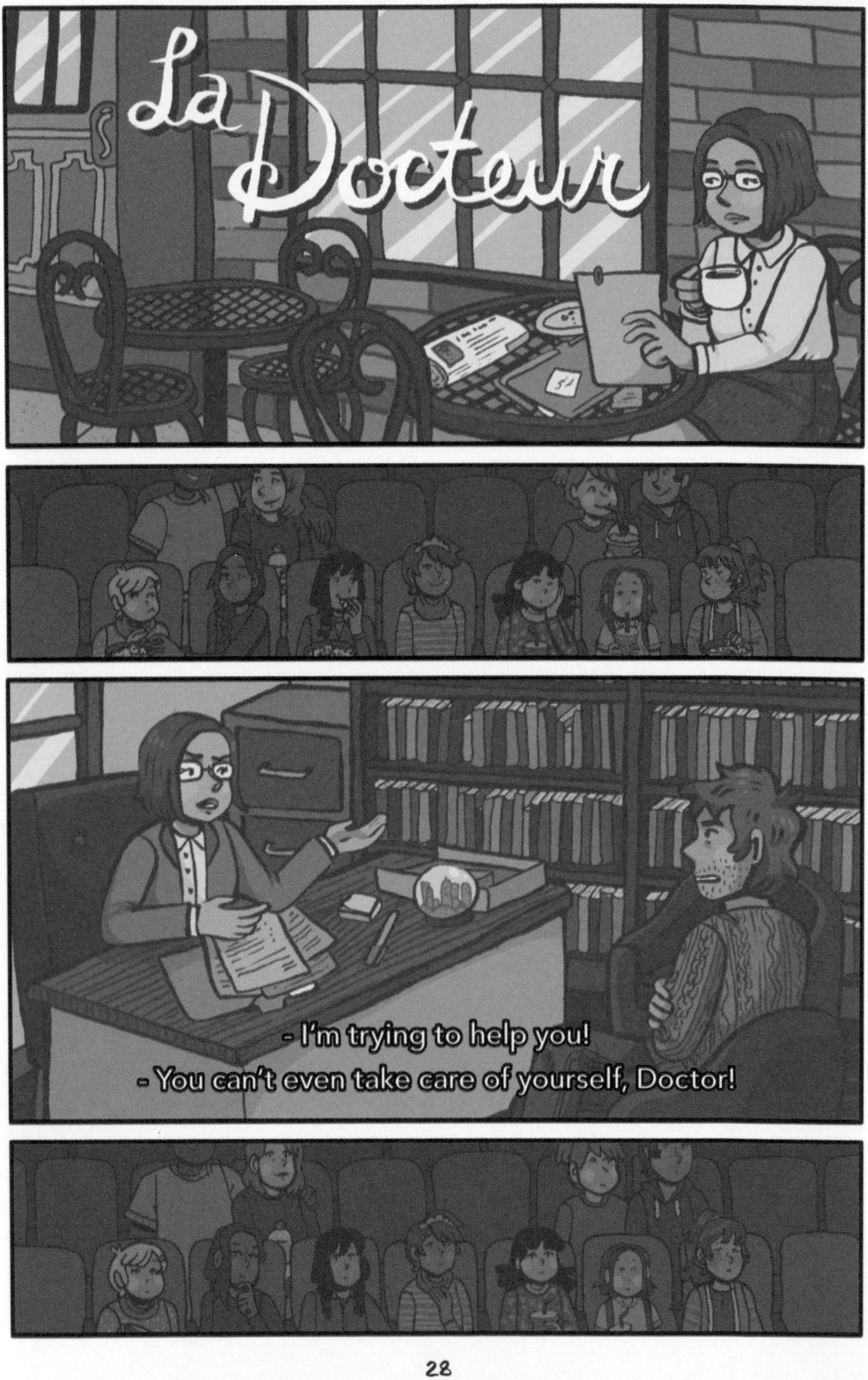
La Docteur
- I'm trying to help you!
- You can't even take care of yourself, Doctor!

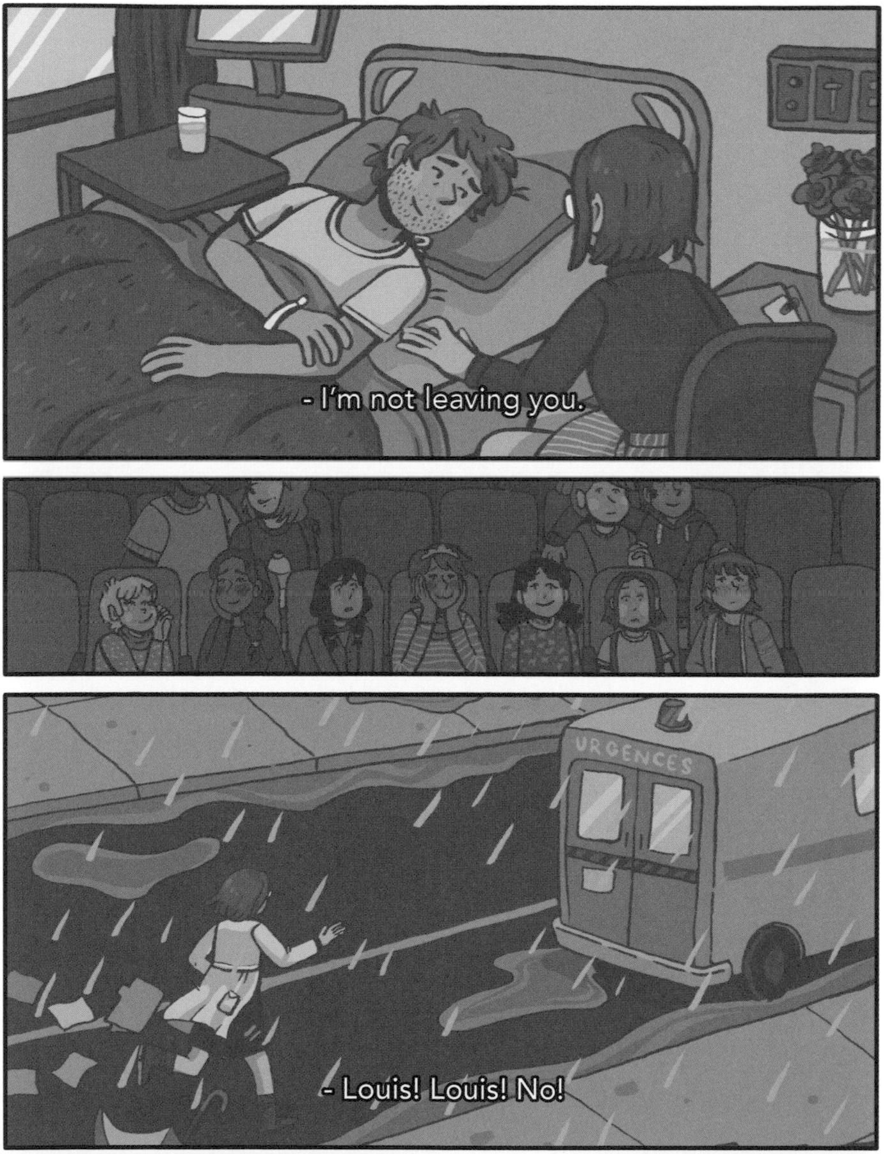
- I’m not leaving you.
URGENCES
- Louis! Louis! No!

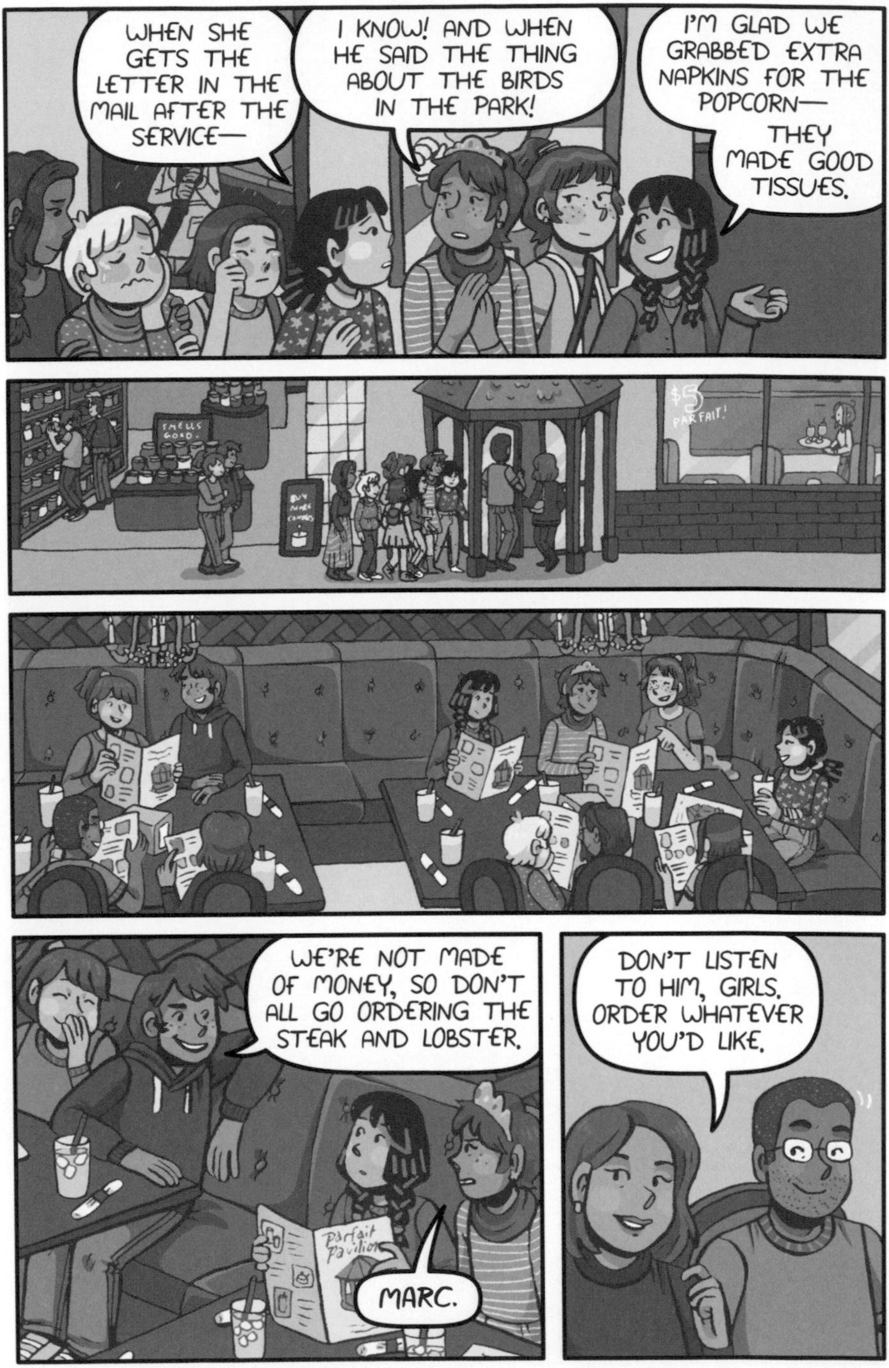
WHEN SHE GETS THE LETTER IN THE MAIL AFTER THE SERVICE—
I KNOW! AND WHEN HE SAID THE THING ABOUT THE BIRDS IN THE PARK!
I'M GLAD WE GRABBED EXTRA NAPKINS FOR THE POPCORN—
THEY MADE GOOD TISSUES.
SMELLS GOOD.
$5 PARFAIT!
WE'RE NOT MADE OF MONEY, SO DON'T ALL GO ORDERING THE STEAK AND LOBSTER.
Parfait Pavilion
MARC.
DON'T LISTEN TO HIM, GIRLS. ORDER WHATEVER YOU'D LIKE.

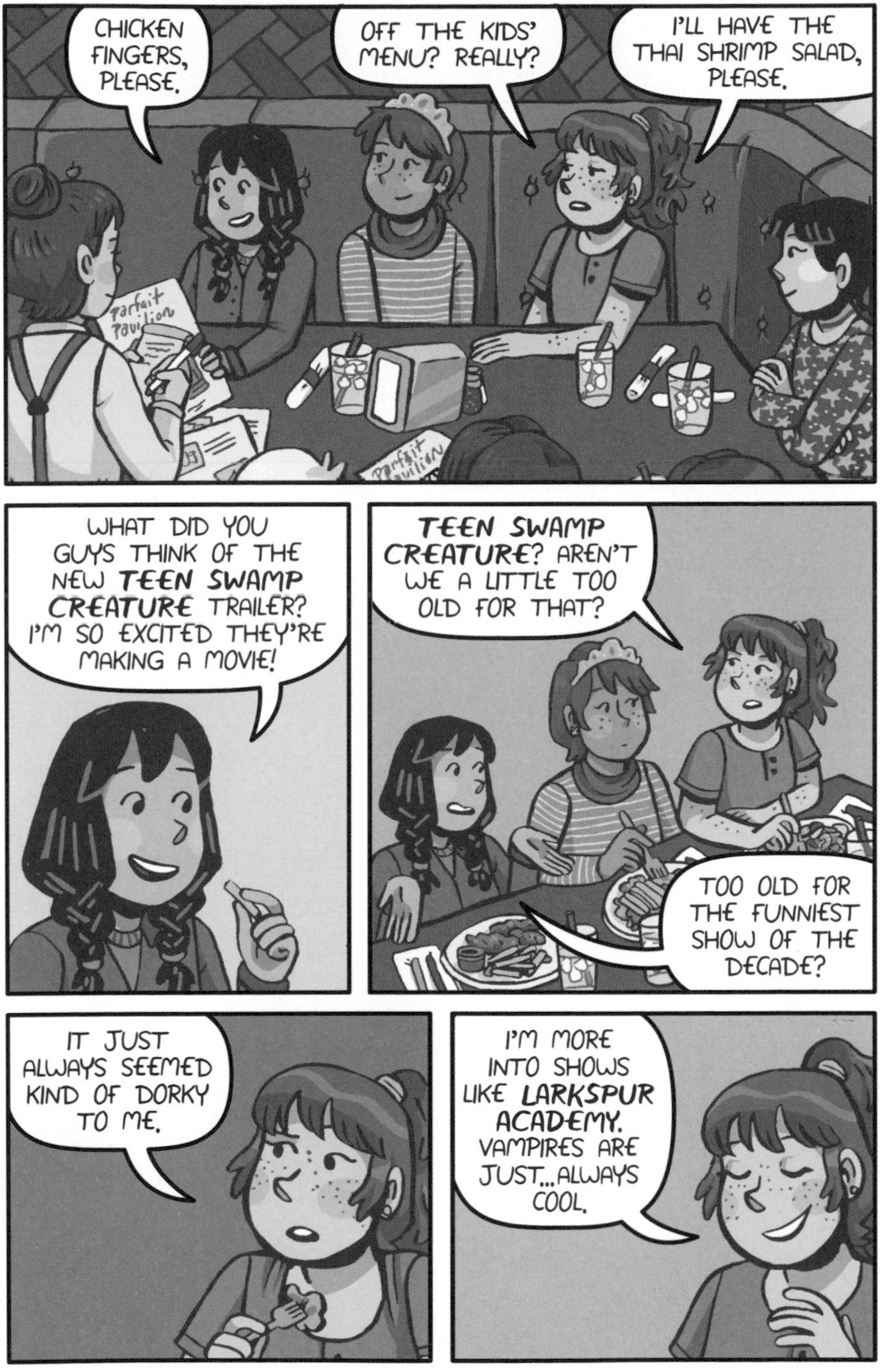
CHICKEN FINGERS, PLEASE.
OFF THE KIDS' MENU? REALLY?
I'LL HAVE THE THAI SHRIMP SALAD, PLEASE.
Parfait Pavilion
WHAT DID YOU GUYS THINK OF THE NEW **TEEN SWAMP CREATURE** TRAILER? I'M SO EXCITED THEY'RE MAKING A MOVIE!
TEEN SWAMP CREATURE? AREN'T WE A LITTLE TOO OLD FOR THAT?
TOO OLD FOR THE FUNNIEST SHOW OF THE DECADE?
IT JUST ALWAYS SEEMED KIND OF DORKY TO ME.
I'M MORE INTO SHOWS LIKE **LARKSPUR ACADEMY.** VAMPIRES ARE JUST...ALWAYS COOL.

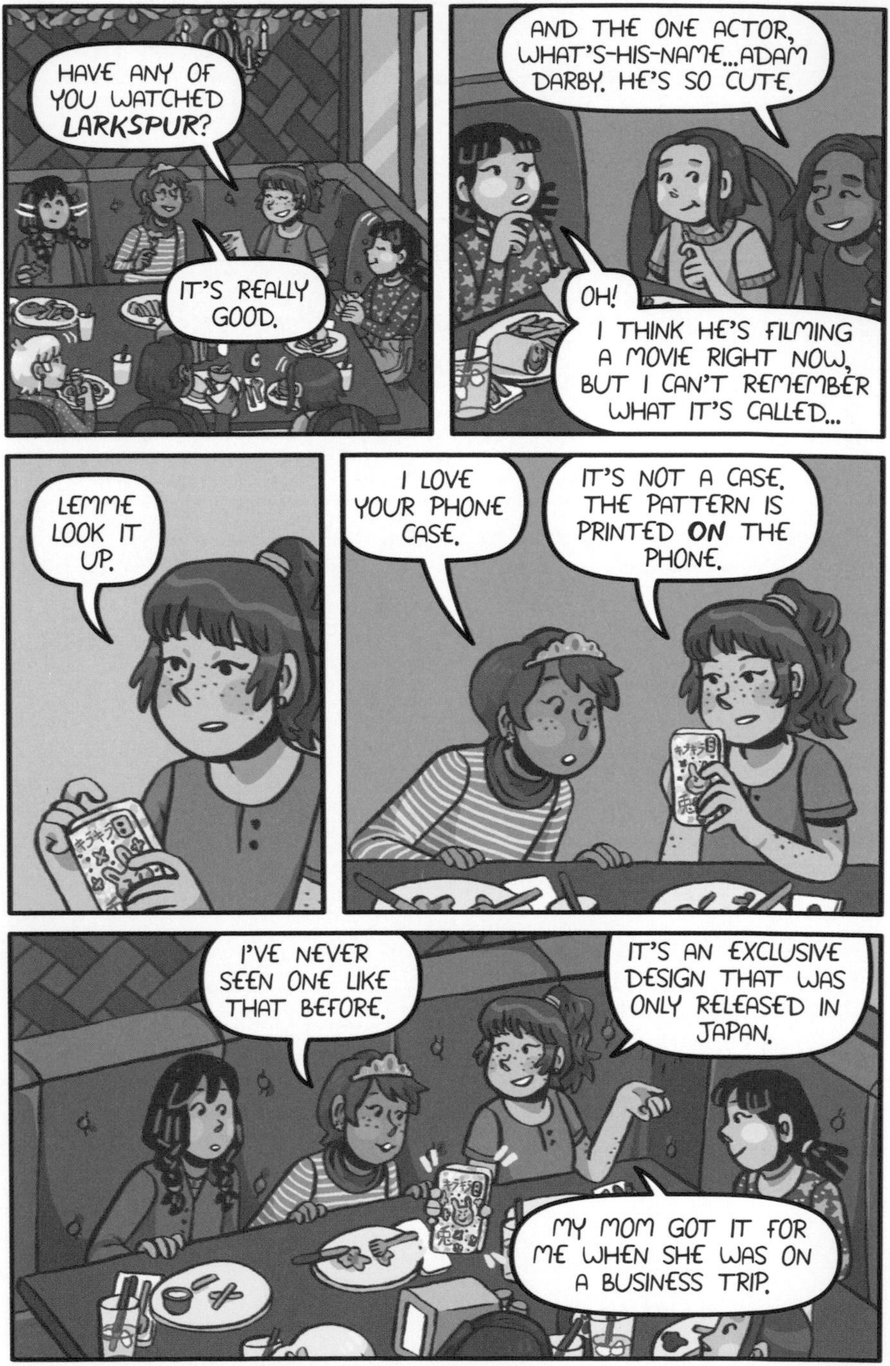
HAVE ANY OF YOU WATCHED LARKSPUR?
IT'S REALLY GOOD.
AND THE ONE ACTOR, WHAT'S-HIS-NAME...ADAM DARBY. HE'S SO CUTE.
OH!
I THINK HE'S FILMING A MOVIE RIGHT NOW, BUT I CAN'T REMEMBER WHAT IT'S CALLED...
LEMME LOOK IT UP.
I LOVE YOUR PHONE CASE.
IT'S NOT A CASE. THE PATTERN IS PRINTED **ON** THE PHONE.
I'VE NEVER SEEN ONE LIKE THAT BEFORE.
IT'S AN EXCLUSIVE DESIGN THAT WAS ONLY RELEASED IN JAPAN.
MY MOM GOT IT FOR ME WHEN SHE WAS ON A BUSINESS TRIP.

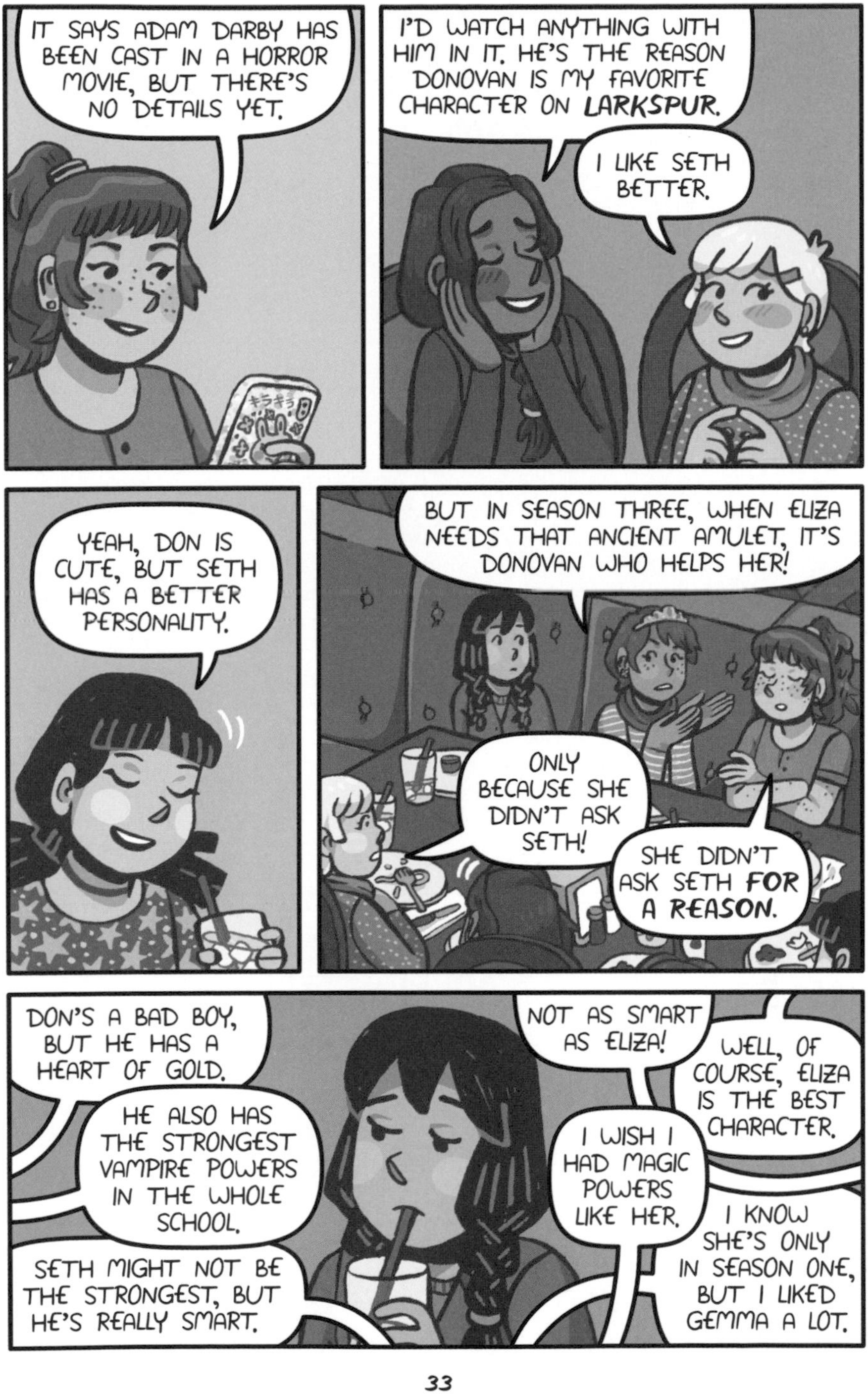

IT SAYS ADAM DARBY HAS BEEN CAST IN A HORROR MOVIE, BUT THERE'S NO DETAILS YET.
I'D WATCH ANYTHING WITH HIM IN IT. HE'S THE REASON DONOVAN IS MY FAVORITE CHARACTER ON **LARKSPUR**.
I LIKE SETH BETTER.
YEAH, DON IS CUTE, BUT SETH HAS A BETTER PERSONALITY.
BUT IN SEASON THREE, WHEN ELIZA NEEDS THAT ANCIENT AMULET, IT'S DONOVAN WHO HELPS HER!
ONLY BECAUSE SHE DIDN'T ASK SETH!
SHE DIDN'T ASK SETH **FOR A REASON**.
DON'S A BAD BOY, BUT HE HAS A HEART OF GOLD.
HE ALSO HAS THE STRONGEST VAMPIRE POWERS IN THE WHOLE SCHOOL.
SETH MIGHT NOT BE THE STRONGEST, BUT HE'S REALLY SMART.
NOT AS SMART AS ELIZA!
WELL, OF COURSE, ELIZA IS THE BEST CHARACTER.
I WISH I HAD MAGIC POWERS LIKE HER.
I KNOW SHE'S ONLY IN SEASON ONE, BUT I LIKED GEMMA A LOT.

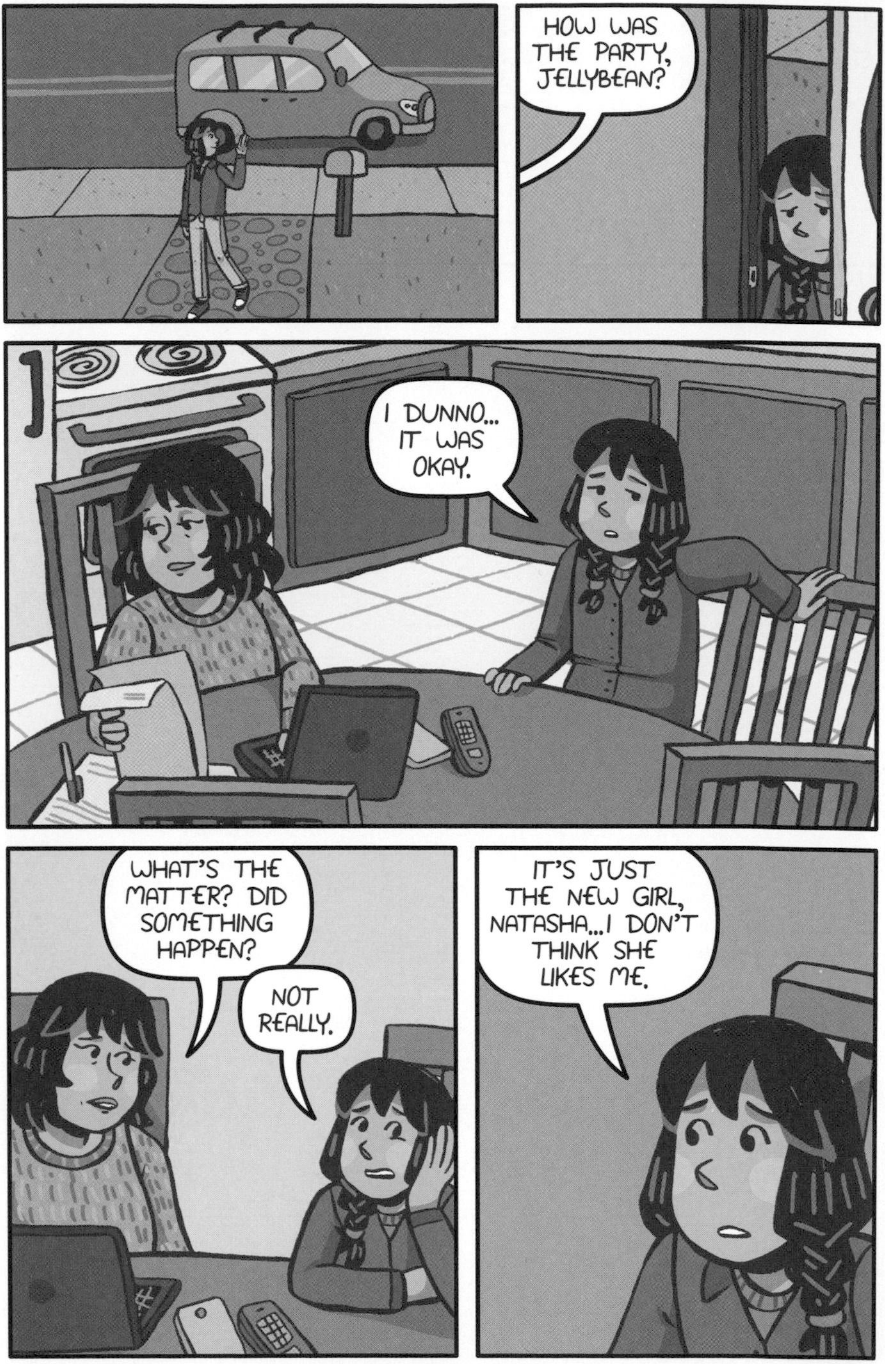
HOW WAS THE PARTY, JELLYBEAN?
I DUNNO... IT WAS OKAY.
WHAT'S THE MATTER? DID SOMETHING HAPPEN?
NOT REALLY.
IT'S JUST THE NEW GIRL, NATASHA...I DON'T THINK SHE LIKES ME.

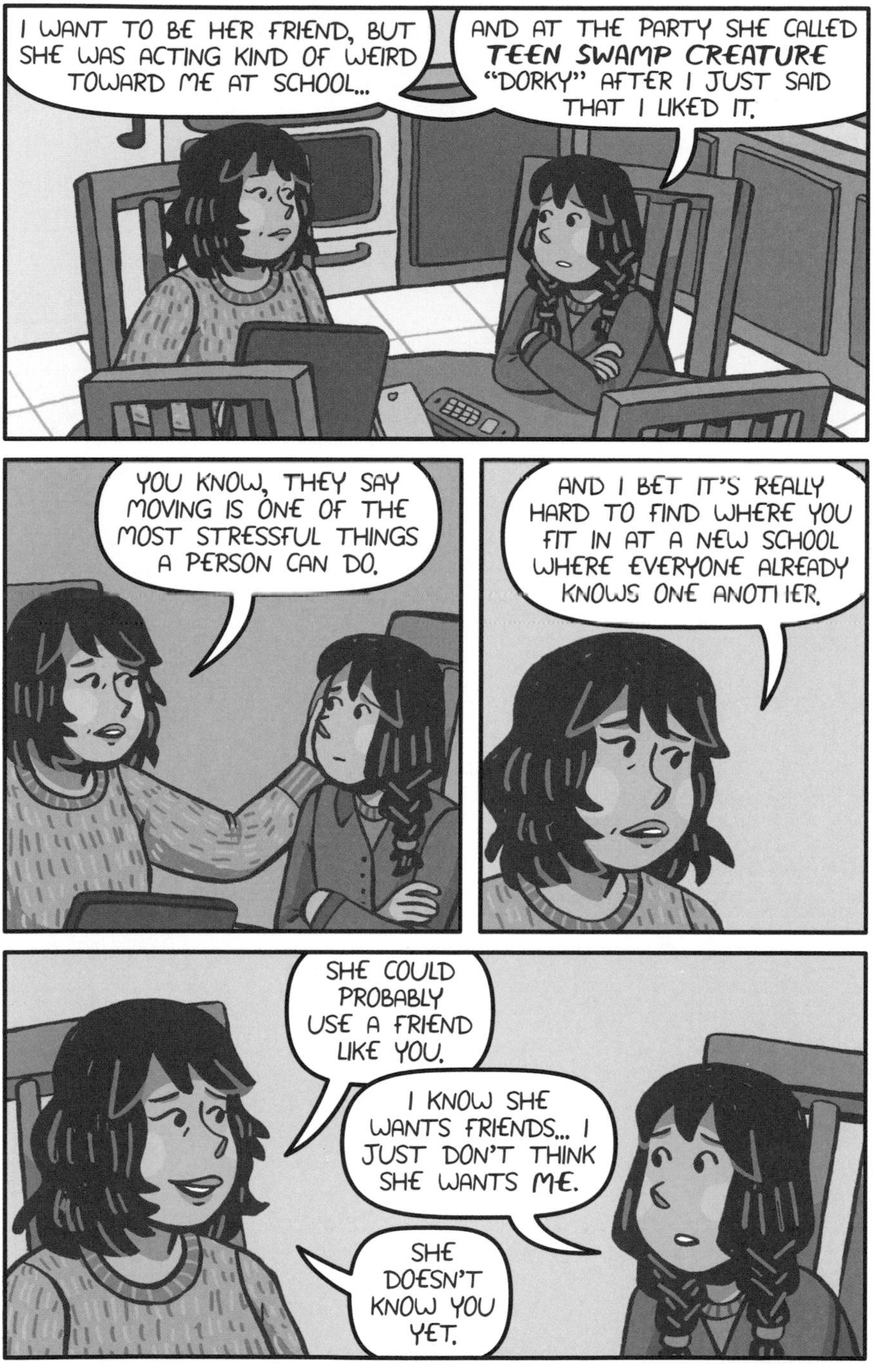
I WANT TO BE HER FRIEND, BUT SHE WAS ACTING KIND OF WEIRD TOWARD ME AT SCHOOL...
AND AT THE PARTY SHE CALLED **TEEN SWAMP CREATURE** "DORKY" AFTER I JUST SAID THAT I LIKED IT.
YOU KNOW, THEY SAY MOVING IS ONE OF THE MOST STRESSFUL THINGS A PERSON CAN DO.
AND I BET IT'S REALLY HARD TO FIND WHERE YOU FIT IN AT A NEW SCHOOL WHERE EVERYONE ALREADY KNOWS ONE ANOTHER.
SHE COULD PROBABLY USE A FRIEND LIKE YOU.
I KNOW SHE WANTS FRIENDS... I JUST DON'T THINK SHE WANTS ME.
SHE DOESN'T KNOW YOU YET.

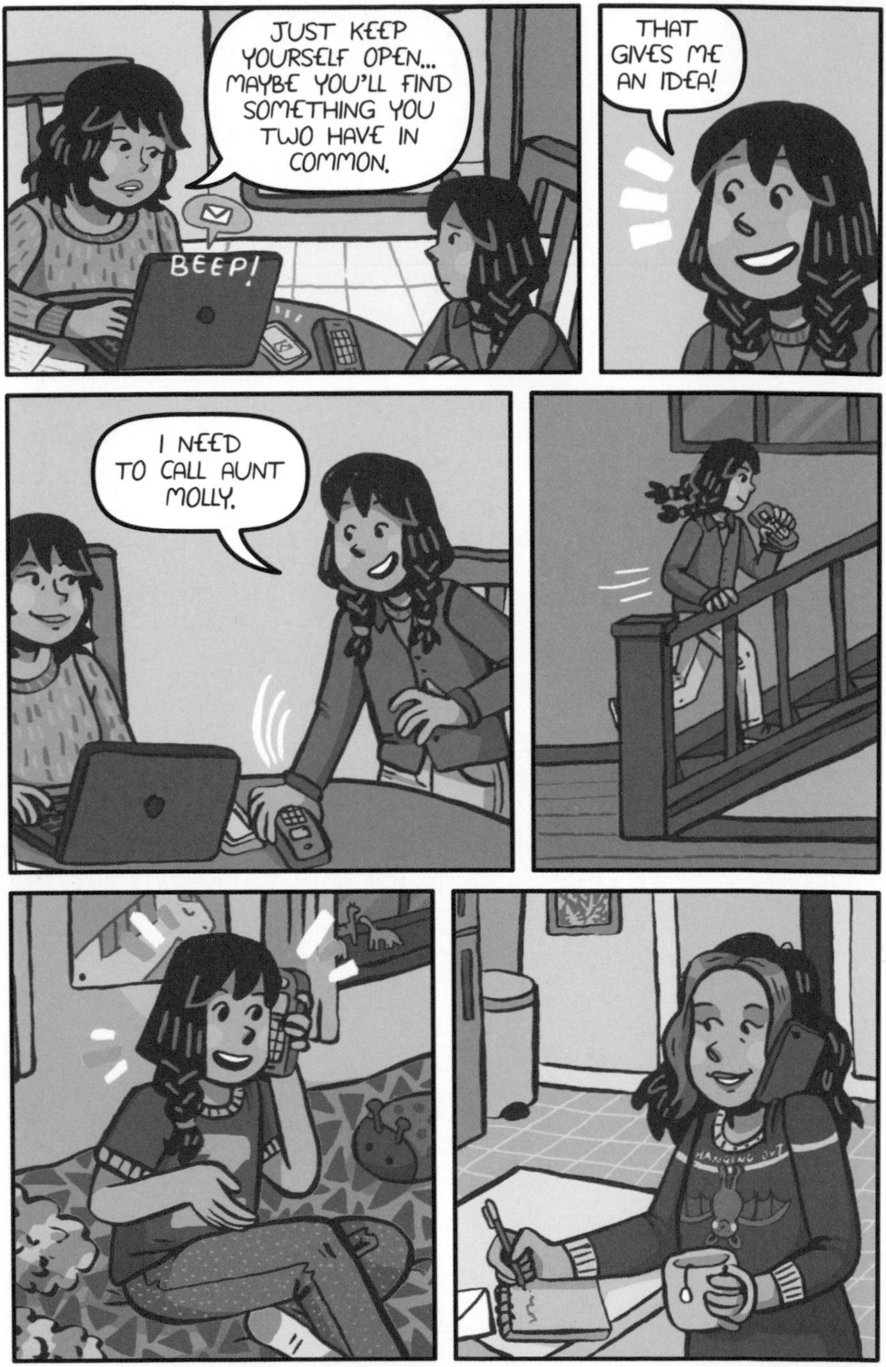
JUST KEEP YOURSELF OPEN... MAYBE YOU'LL FIND SOMETHING YOU TWO HAVE IN COMMON.
BEEP!
THAT GIVES ME AN IDEA!
I NEED TO CALL AUNT MOLLY.
HANGING OUT

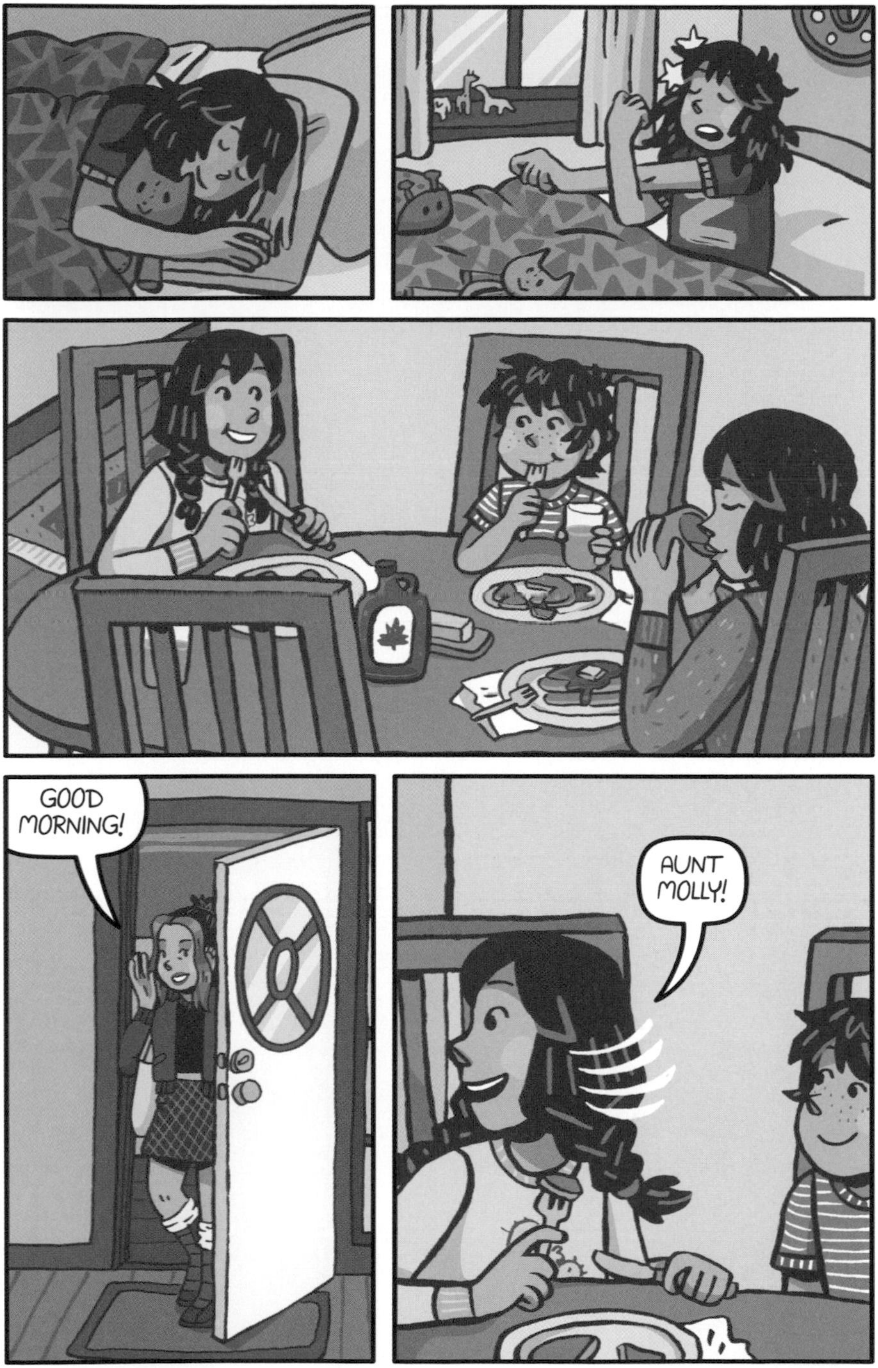
GOOD MORNING!
AUNT MOLLY!

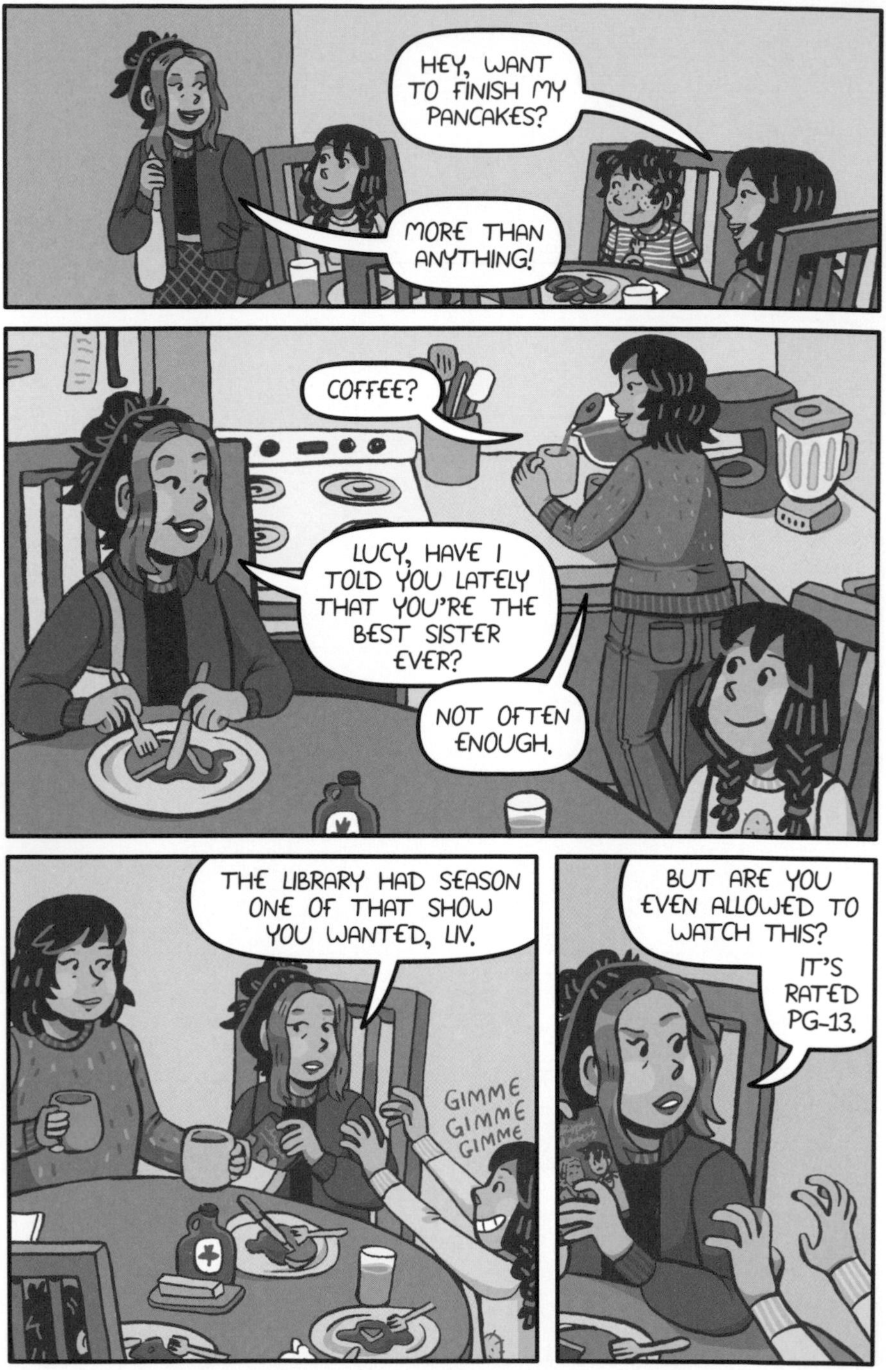
HEY, WANT TO FINISH MY PANCAKES?
MORE THAN ANYTHING!
COFFEE?
LUCY, HAVE I TOLD YOU LATELY THAT YOU'RE THE BEST SISTER EVER?
NOT OFTEN ENOUGH.
THE LIBRARY HAD SEASON ONE OF THAT SHOW YOU WANTED, LIV.
GIMME GIMME GIMME
BUT ARE YOU EVEN ALLOWED TO WATCH THIS?
IT'S RATED PG-13.

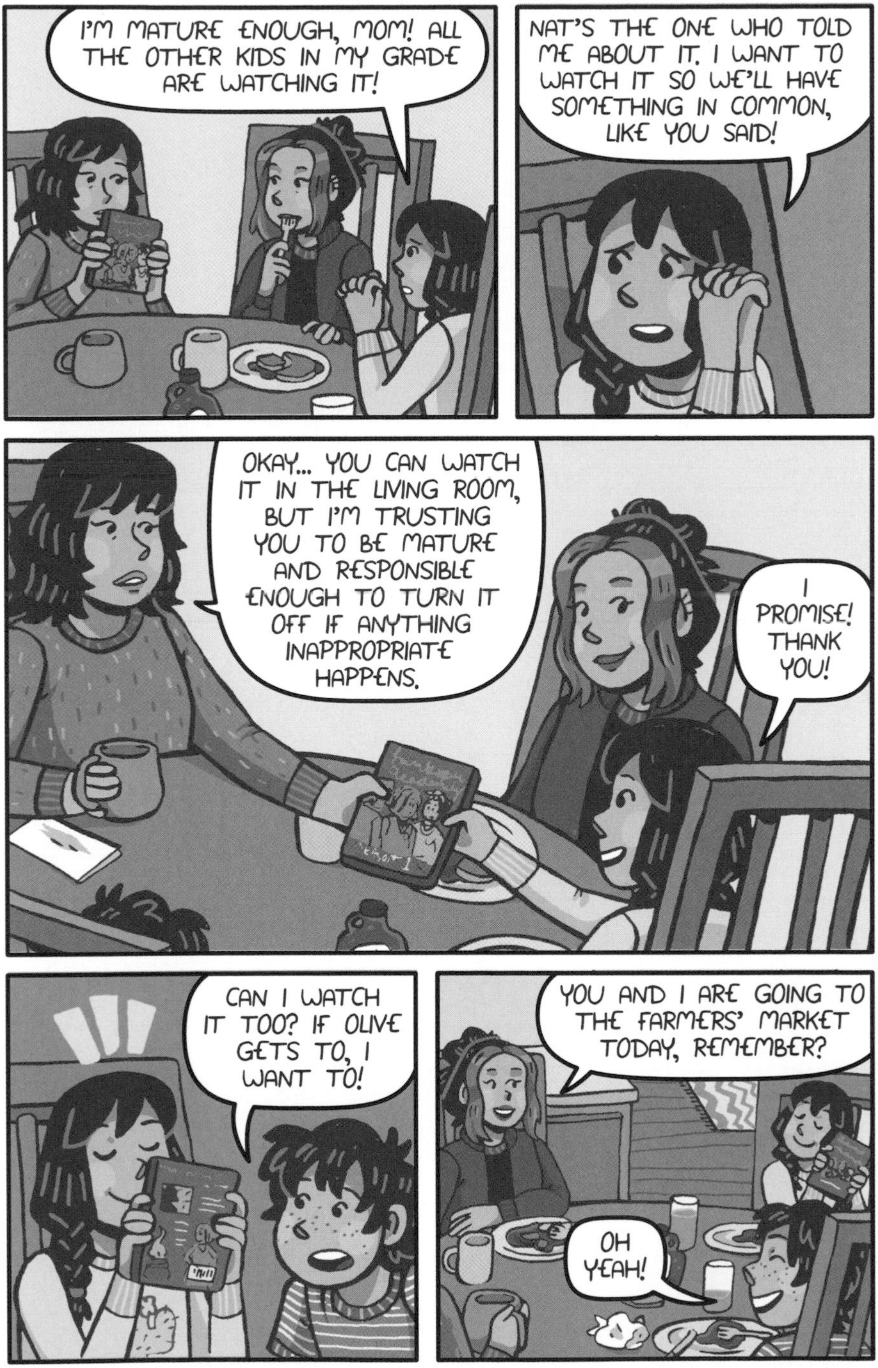
I'M MATURE ENOUGH, MOM! ALL THE OTHER KIDS IN MY GRADE ARE WATCHING IT!
NAT'S THE ONE WHO TOLD ME ABOUT IT. I WANT TO WATCH IT SO WE'LL HAVE SOMETHING IN COMMON, LIKE YOU SAID!
OKAY... YOU CAN WATCH IT IN THE LIVING ROOM, BUT I'M TRUSTING YOU TO BE MATURE AND RESPONSIBLE ENOUGH TO TURN IT OFF IF ANYTHING INAPPROPRIATE HAPPENS.
I PROMISE! THANK YOU!
CAN I WATCH IT TOO? IF OLIVE GETS TO, I WANT TO!
YOU AND I ARE GOING TO THE FARMERS' MARKET TODAY, REMEMBER?
OH YEAH!

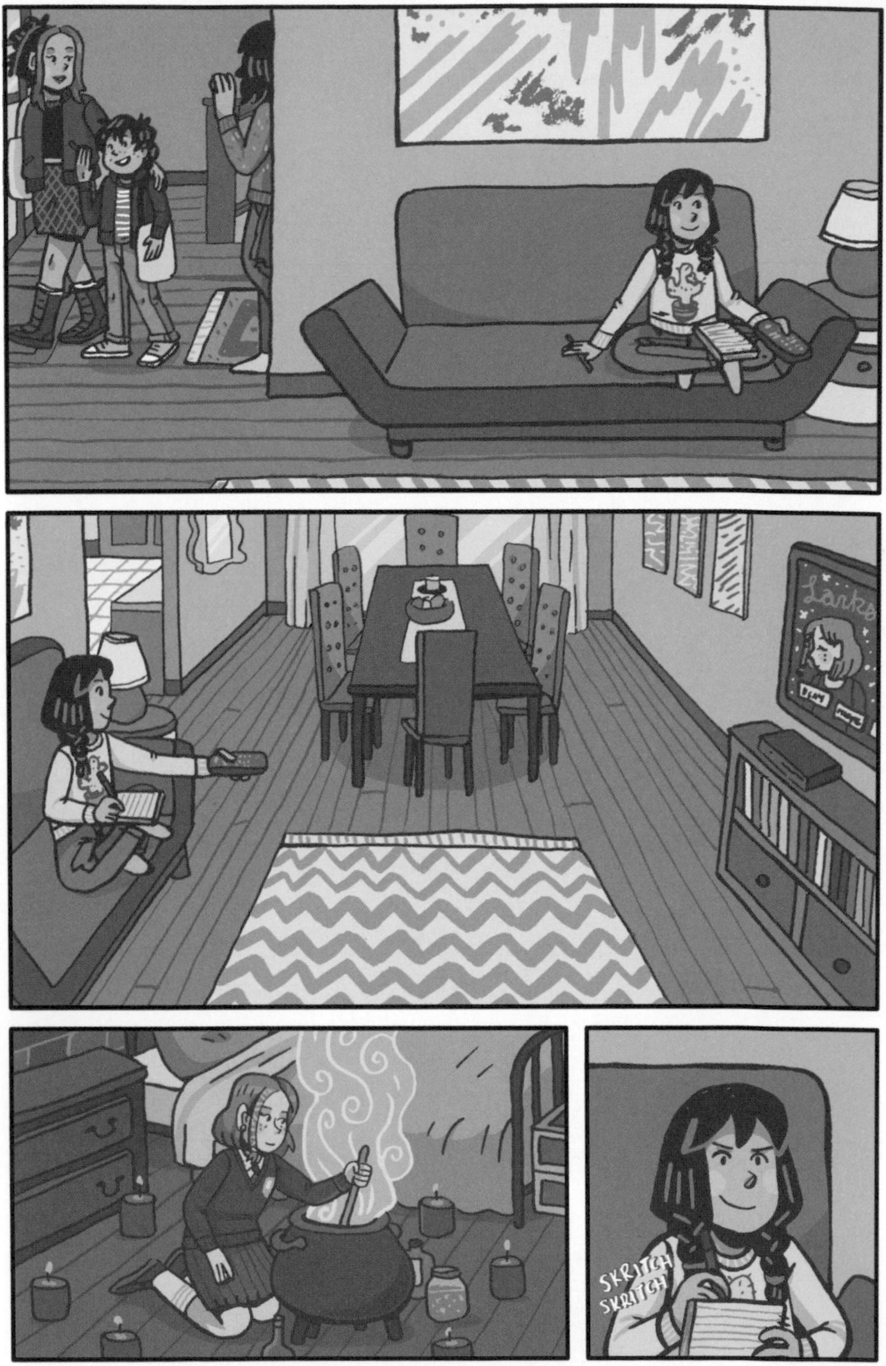
SKRITCH
SKRITCH

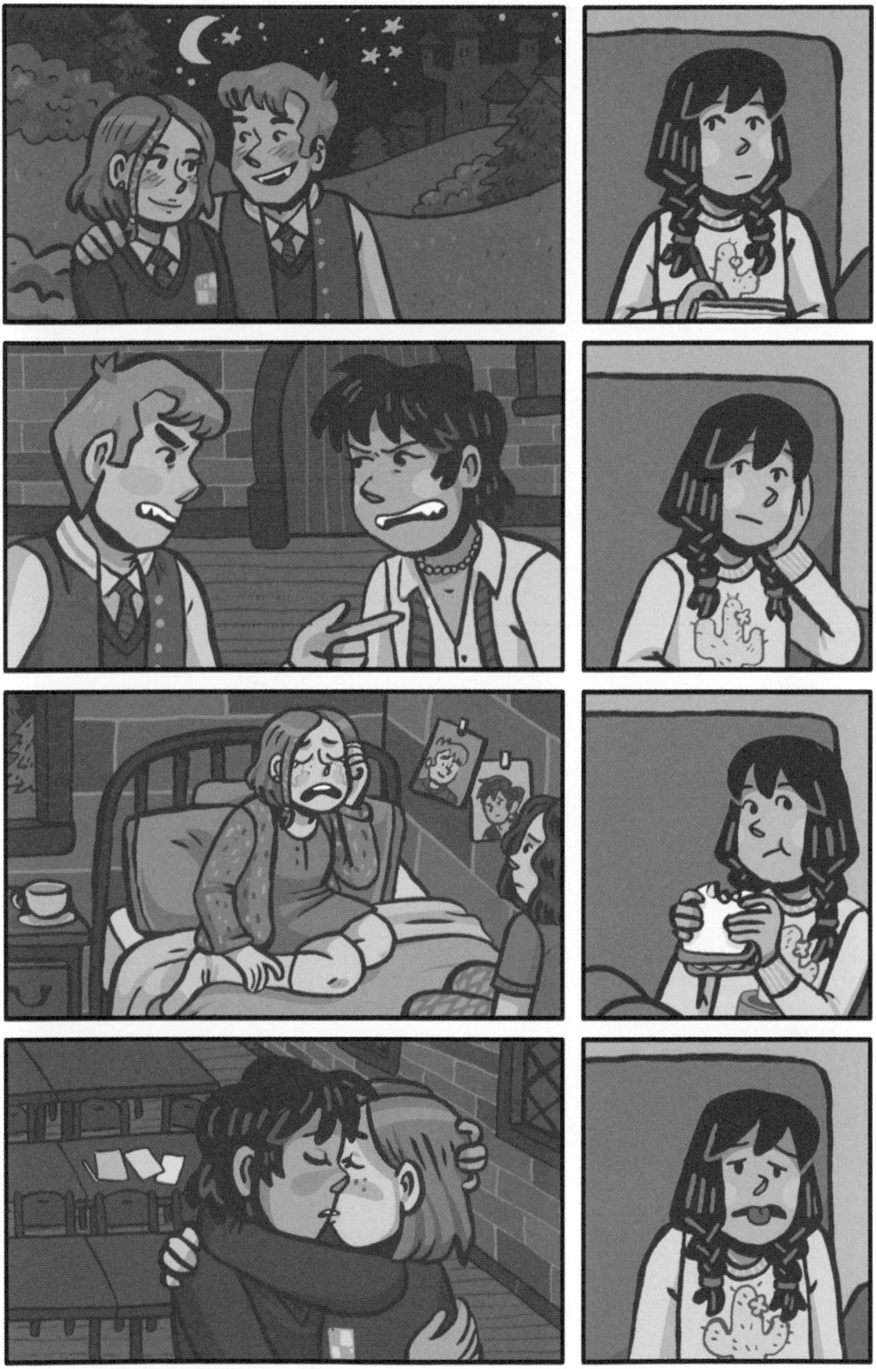

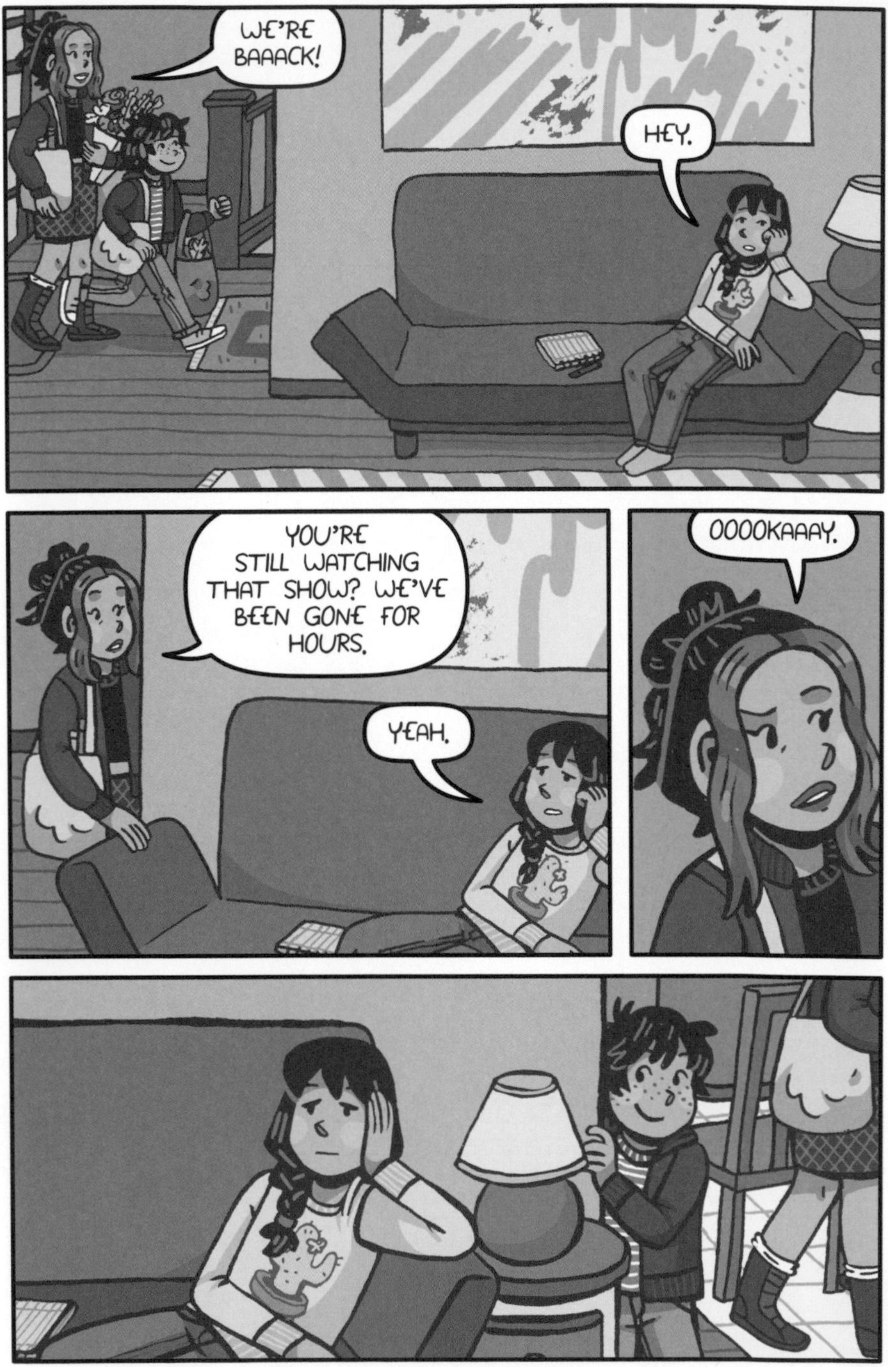
WE'RE BAAACK!
HEY.
YOU'RE STILL WATCHING THAT SHOW? WE'VE BEEN GONE FOR HOURS.
YEAH.
OOOOKAAAY.

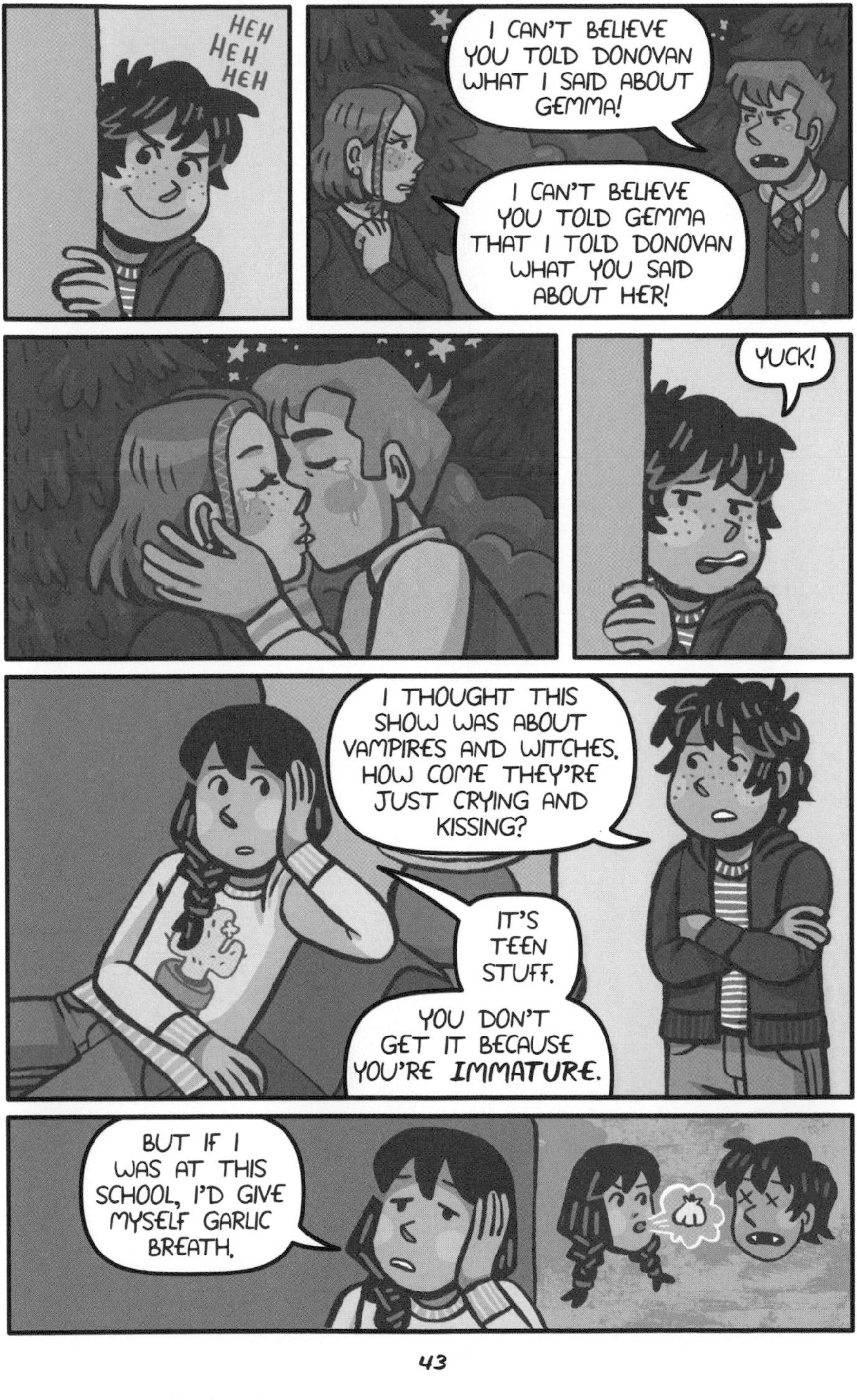
HEH HEH HEH
I CAN'T BELIEVE YOU TOLD DONOVAN WHAT I SAID ABOUT GEMMA!
I CAN'T BELIEVE YOU TOLD GEMMA THAT I TOLD DONOVAN WHAT YOU SAID ABOUT HER!
YUCK!
I THOUGHT THIS SHOW WAS ABOUT VAMPIRES AND WITCHES. HOW COME THEY'RE JUST CRYING AND KISSING?
IT'S TEEN STUFF.
YOU DON'T GET IT BECAUSE YOU'RE **IMMATURE**.
BUT IF I WAS AT THIS SCHOOL, I'D GIVE MYSELF GARLIC BREATH.

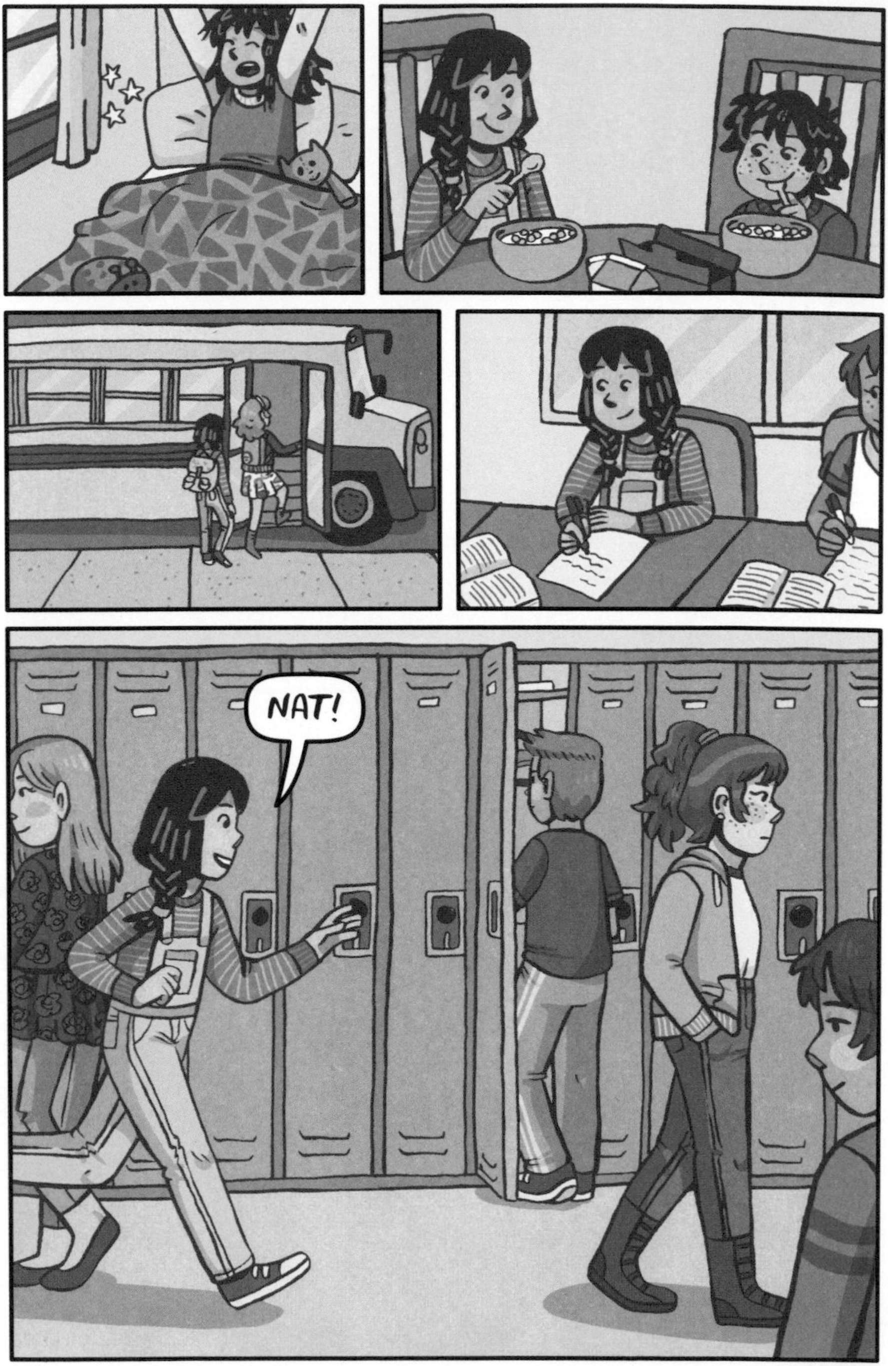
NAT!

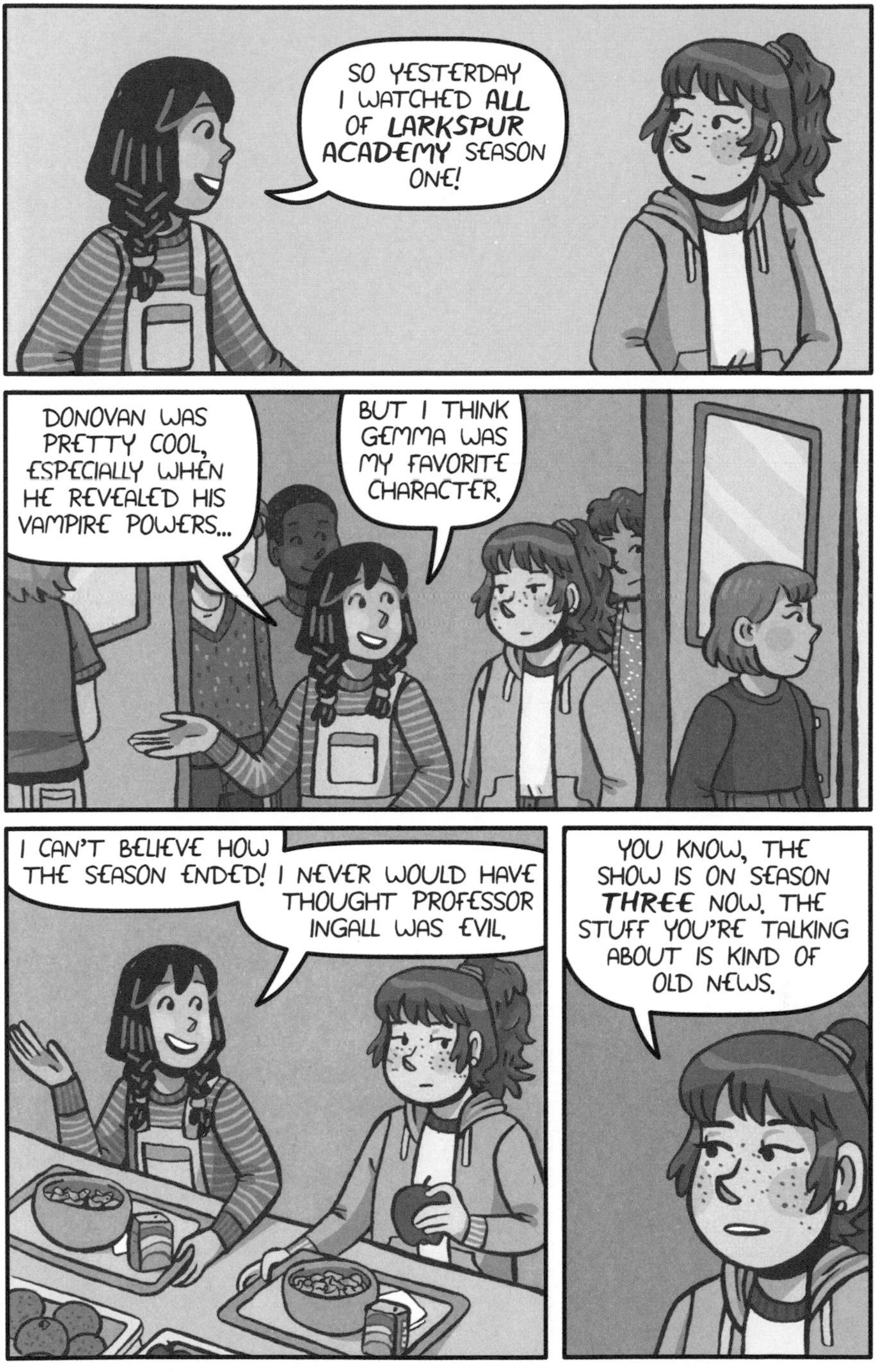
SO YESTERDAY I WATCHED ALL OF LARKSPUR ACADEMY SEASON ONE!
DONOVAN WAS PRETTY COOL, ESPECIALLY WHEN HE REVEALED HIS VAMPIRE POWERS...
BUT I THINK GEMMA WAS MY FAVORITE CHARACTER.
I CAN'T BELIEVE HOW THE SEASON ENDED! I NEVER WOULD HAVE THOUGHT PROFESSOR INGALL WAS EVIL.
YOU KNOW, THE SHOW IS ON SEASON THREE NOW. THE STUFF YOU'RE TALKING ABOUT IS KIND OF OLD NEWS.

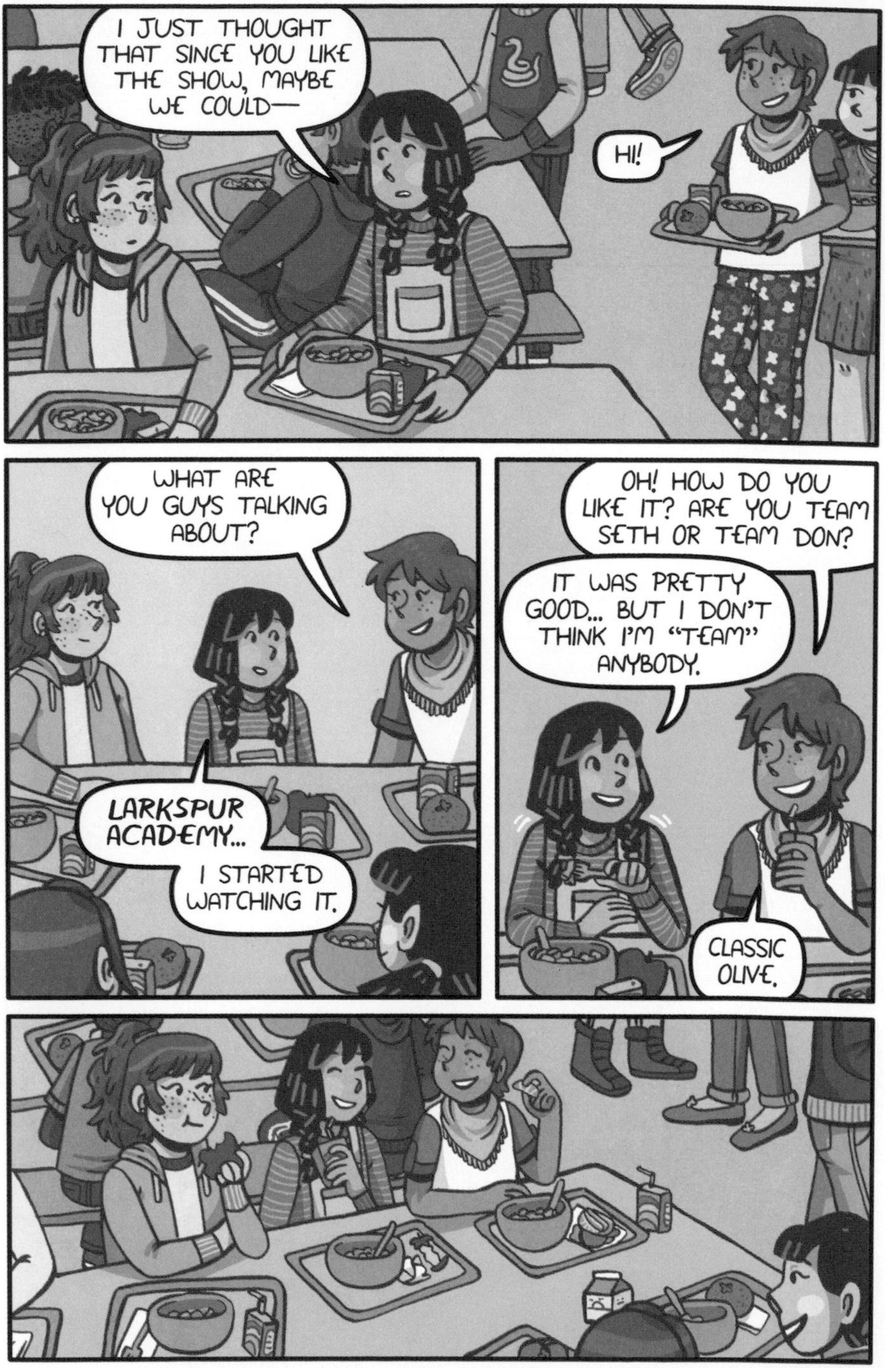
I JUST THOUGHT THAT SINCE YOU LIKE THE SHOW, MAYBE WE COULD—
HI!
WHAT ARE YOU GUYS TALKING ABOUT?
LARKSPUR ACADEMY...
I STARTED WATCHING IT.
OH! HOW DO YOU LIKE IT? ARE YOU TEAM SETH OR TEAM DON?
IT WAS PRETTY GOOD... BUT I DON'T THINK I'M "TEAM" ANYBODY.
CLASSIC OLIVE.

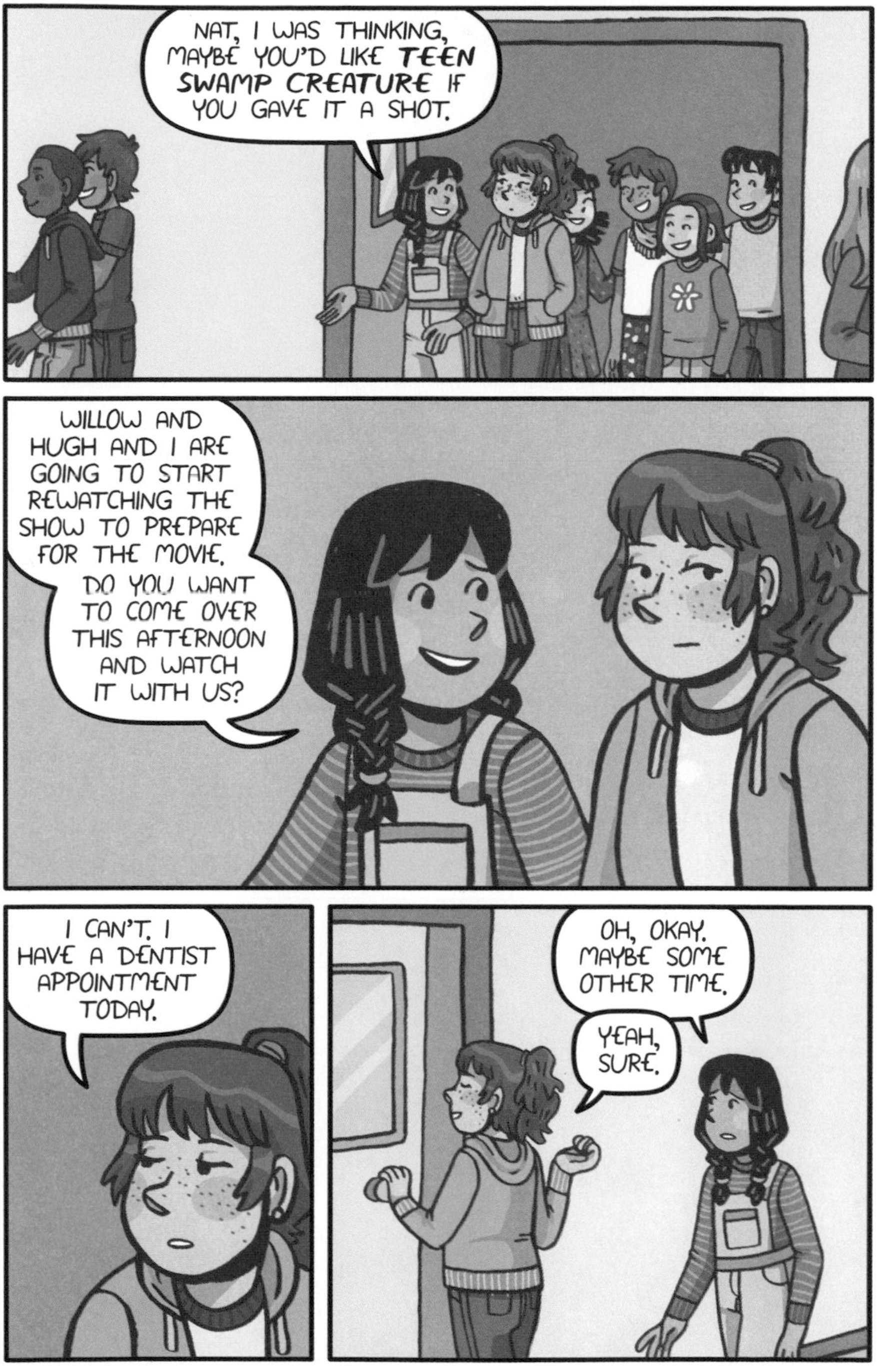
NAT, I WAS THINKING, MAYBE YOU'D LIKE **TEEN SWAMP CREATURE** IF YOU GAVE IT A SHOT.
WILLOW AND HUGH AND I ARE GOING TO START REWATCHING THE SHOW TO PREPARE FOR THE MOVIE.
DO YOU WANT TO COME OVER THIS AFTERNOON AND WATCH IT WITH US?
I CAN'T. I HAVE A DENTIST APPOINTMENT TODAY.
OH, OKAY. MAYBE SOME OTHER TIME.
YEAH, SURE.

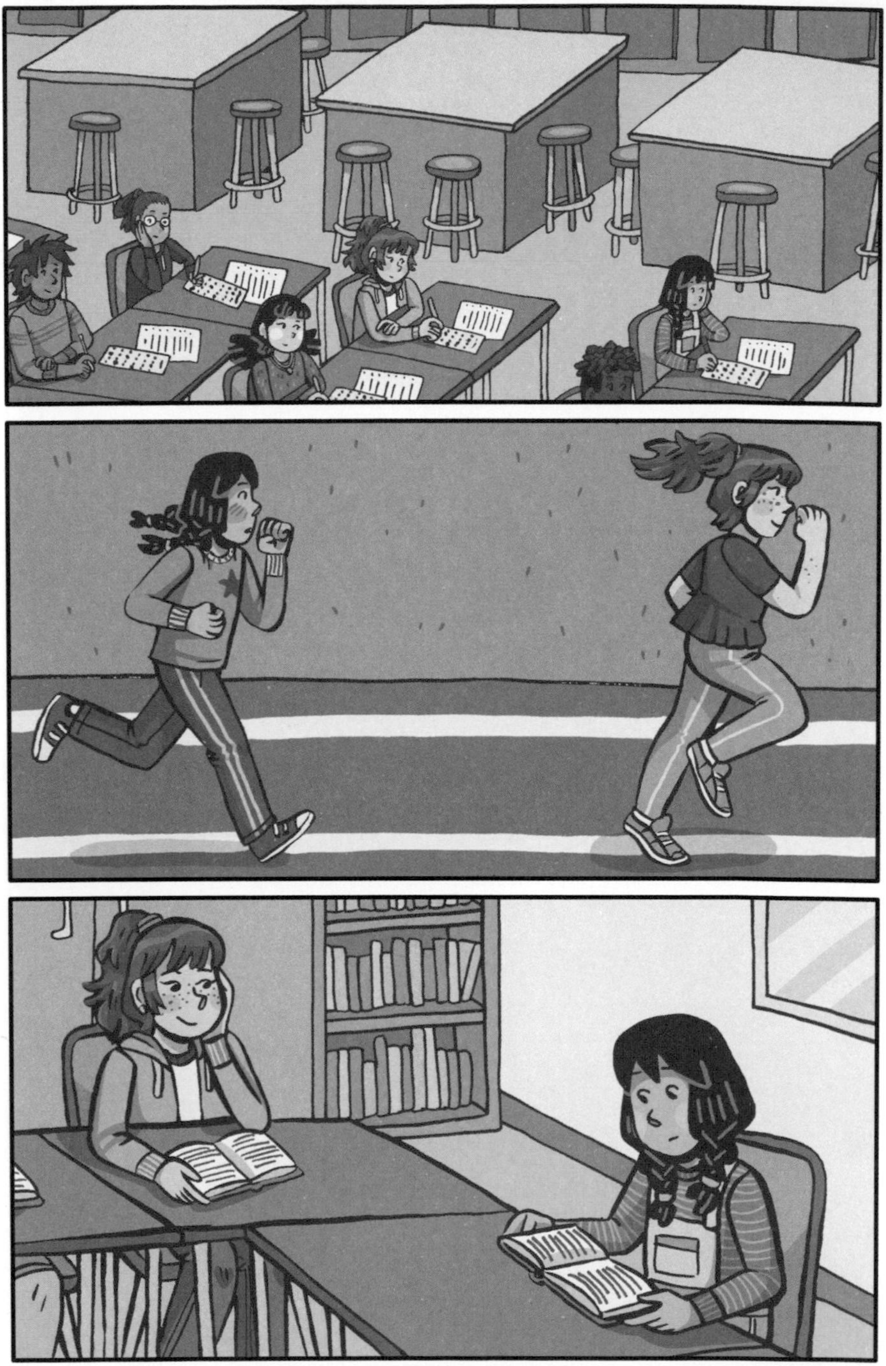

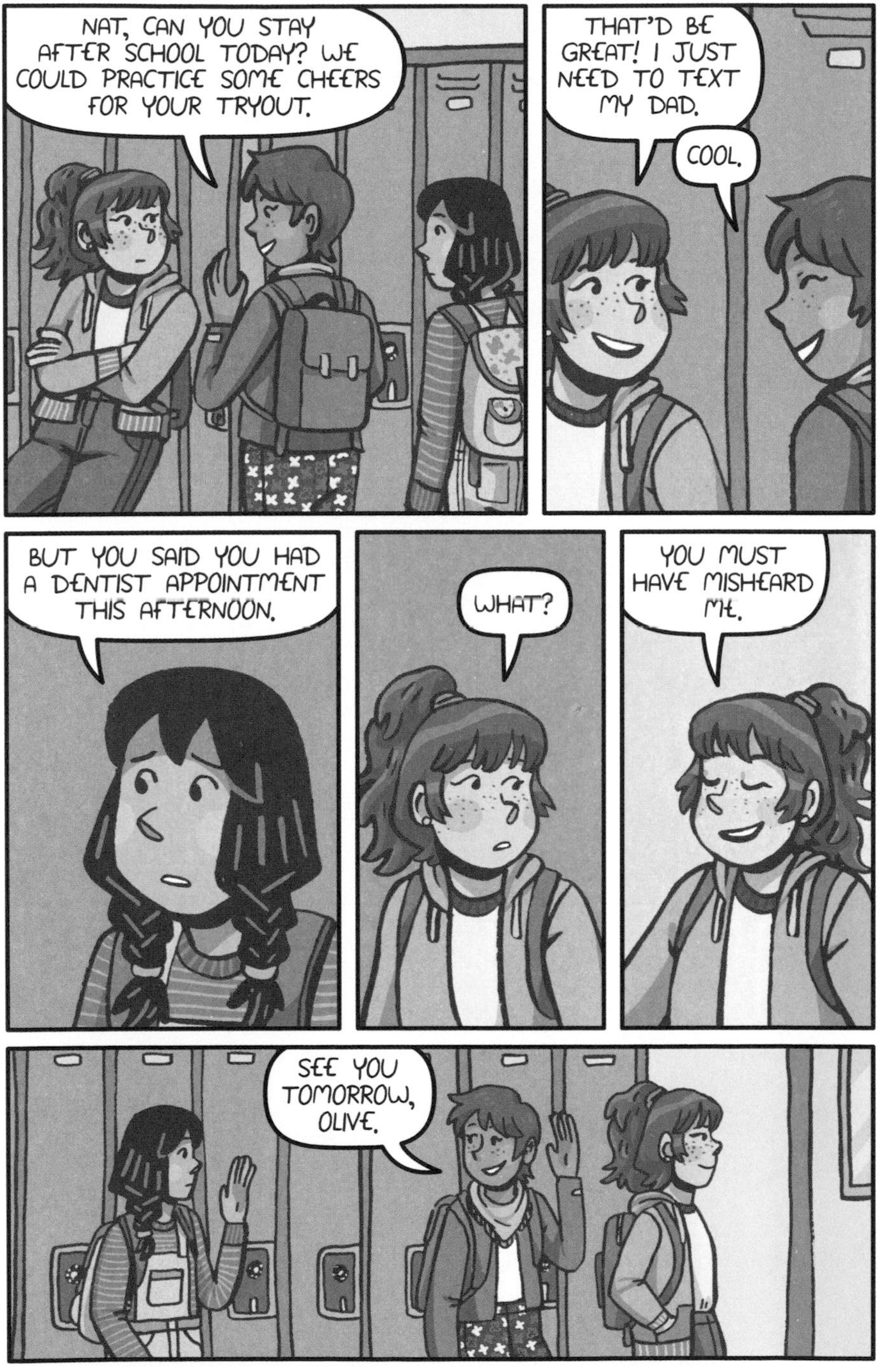
NAT, CAN YOU STAY AFTER SCHOOL TODAY? WE COULD PRACTICE SOME CHEERS FOR YOUR TRYOUT.
THAT'D BE GREAT! I JUST NEED TO TEXT MY DAD.
COOL.
BUT YOU SAID YOU HAD A DENTIST APPOINTMENT THIS AFTERNOON.
WHAT?
YOU MUST HAVE MISHEARD ME.
SEE YOU TOMORROW, OLIVE.

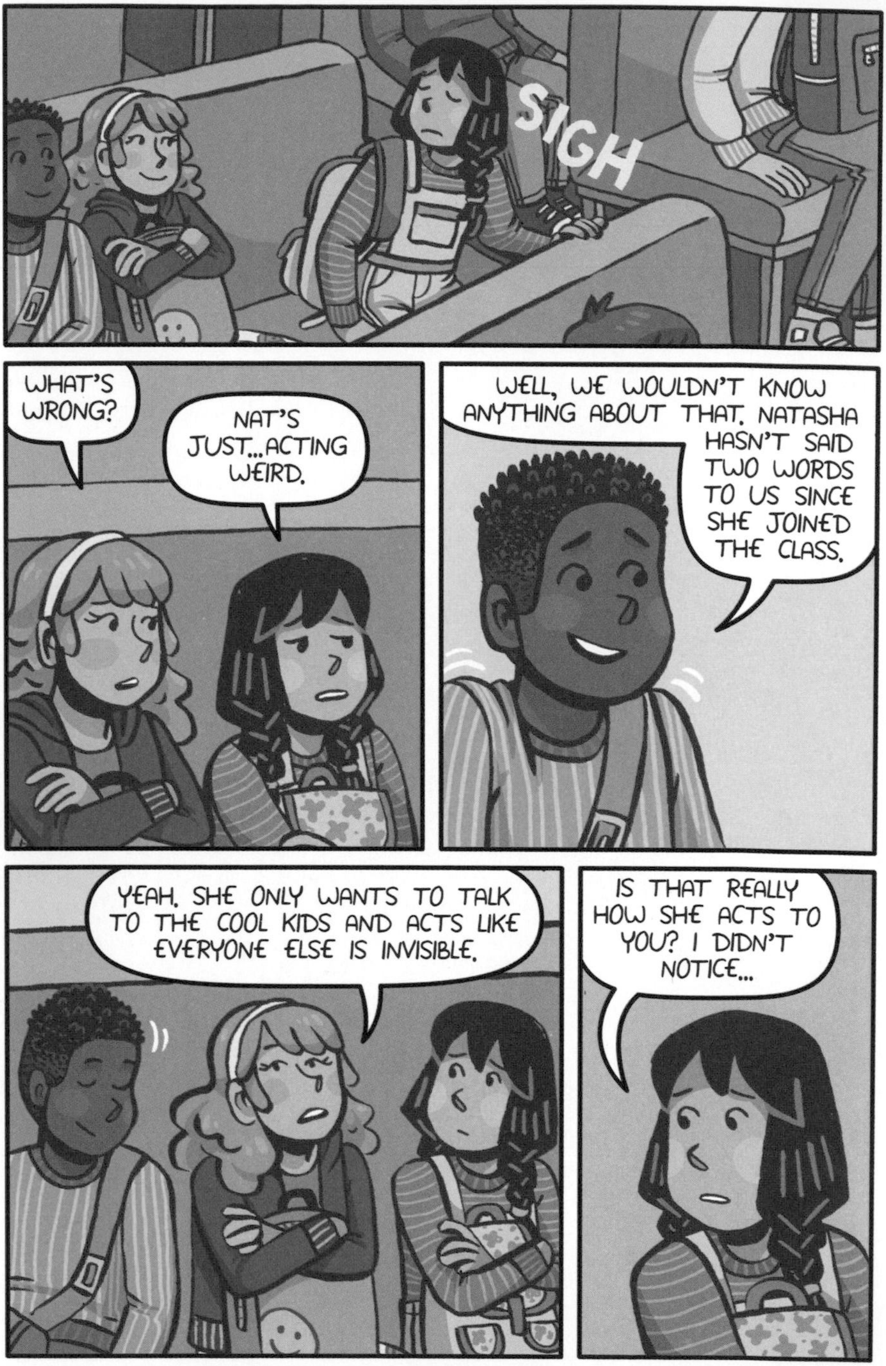
SIGH
WHAT'S WRONG?
NAT'S JUST...ACTING WEIRD.
WELL, WE WOULDN'T KNOW ANYTHING ABOUT THAT. NATASHA HASN'T SAID TWO WORDS TO US SINCE SHE JOINED THE CLASS.
YEAH. SHE ONLY WANTS TO TALK TO THE COOL KIDS AND ACTS LIKE EVERYONE ELSE IS INVISIBLE.
IS THAT REALLY HOW SHE ACTS TO YOU? I DIDN'T NOTICE...

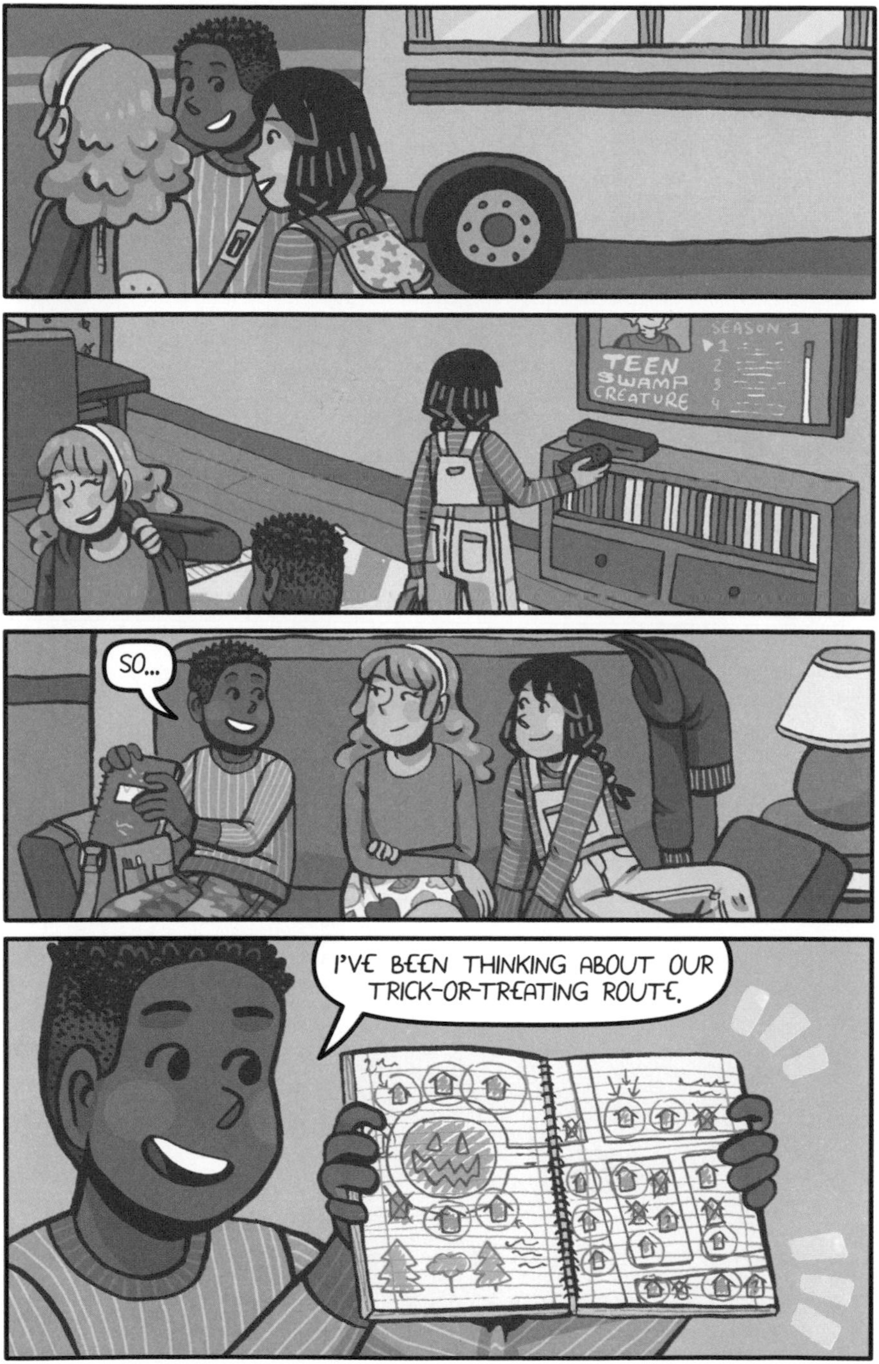
SEASON 1
TEEN
SWAMP
CREATURE
SO...
I'VE BEEN THINKING ABOUT OUR TRICK-OR-TREATING ROUTE.

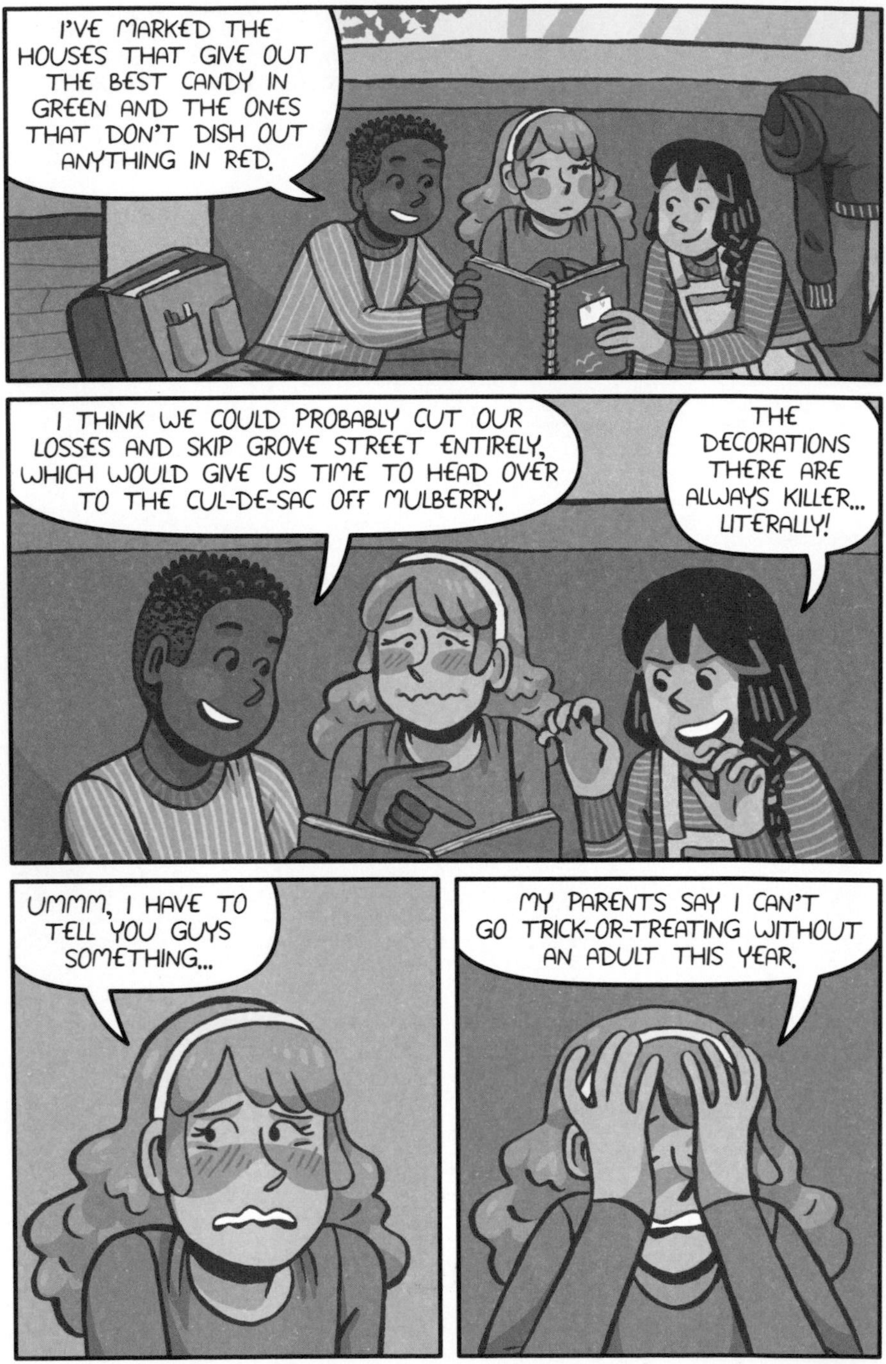
I'VE MARKED THE HOUSES THAT GIVE OUT THE BEST CANDY IN GREEN AND THE ONES THAT DON'T DISH OUT ANYTHING IN RED.
I THINK WE COULD PROBABLY CUT OUR LOSSES AND SKIP GROVE STREET ENTIRELY, WHICH WOULD GIVE US TIME TO HEAD OVER TO THE CUL-DE-SAC OFF MULBERRY.
THE DECORATIONS THERE ARE ALWAYS KILLER... LITERALLY!
UMMM, I HAVE TO TELL YOU GUYS SOMETHING...
MY PARENTS SAY I CAN'T GO TRICK-OR-TREATING WITHOUT AN ADULT THIS YEAR.

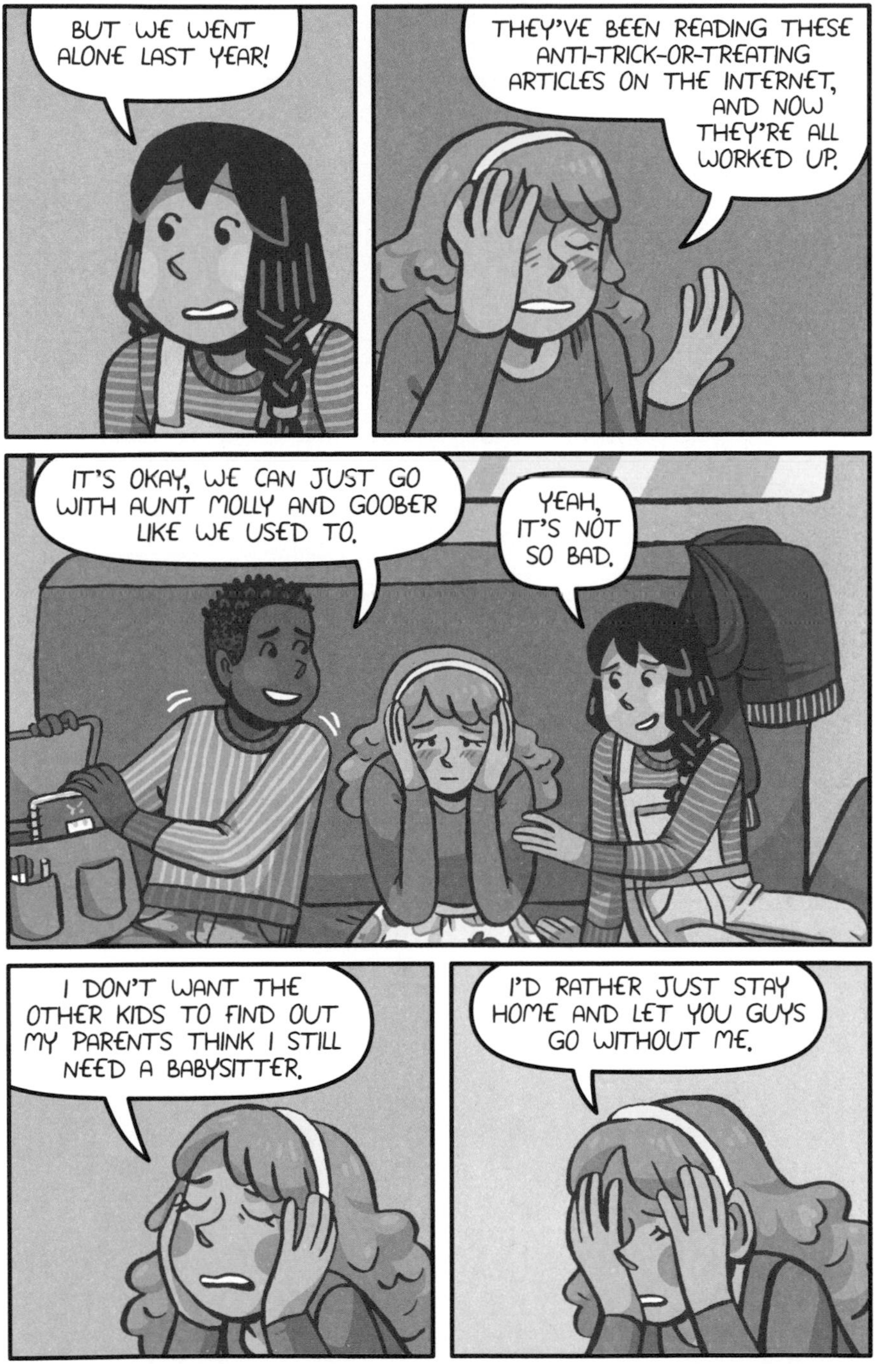
BUT WE WENT ALONE LAST YEAR!
THEY'VE BEEN READING THESE ANTI-TRICK-OR-TREATING ARTICLES ON THE INTERNET, AND NOW THEY'RE ALL WORKED UP.
IT'S OKAY, WE CAN JUST GO WITH AUNT MOLLY AND GOOBER LIKE WE USED TO.
YEAH, IT'S NOT SO BAD.
I DON'T WANT THE OTHER KIDS TO FIND OUT MY PARENTS THINK I STILL NEED A BABYSITTER.
I'D RATHER JUST STAY HOME AND LET YOU GUYS GO WITHOUT ME.

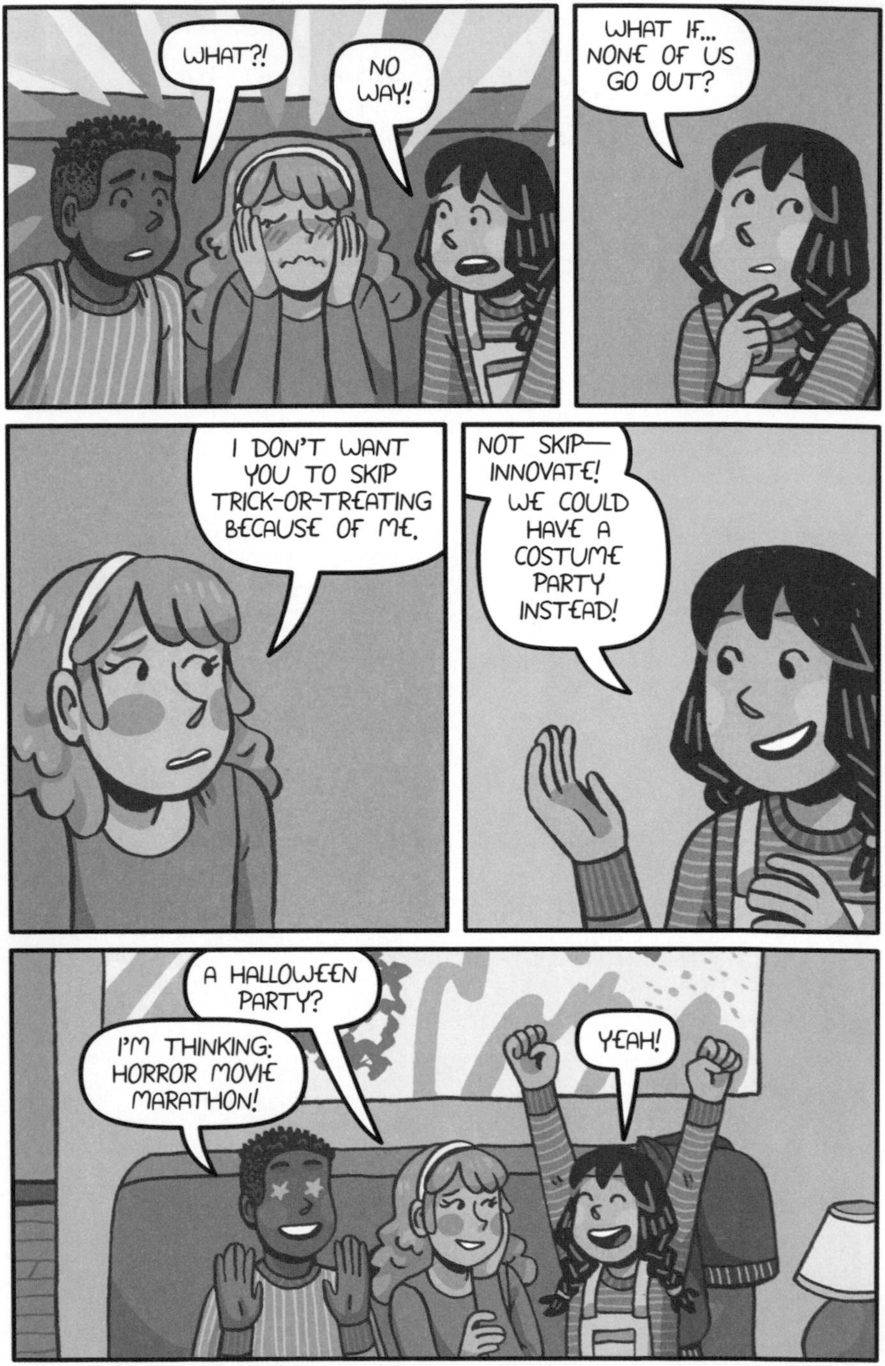
WHAT?!
NO WAY!
WHAT IF... NONE OF US GO OUT?
I DON'T WANT YOU TO SKIP TRICK-OR-TREATING BECAUSE OF ME.
NOT SKIP— INNOVATE!
WE COULD HAVE A COSTUME PARTY INSTEAD!
A HALLOWEEN PARTY?
I'M THINKING: HORROR MOVIE MARATHON!
YEAH!

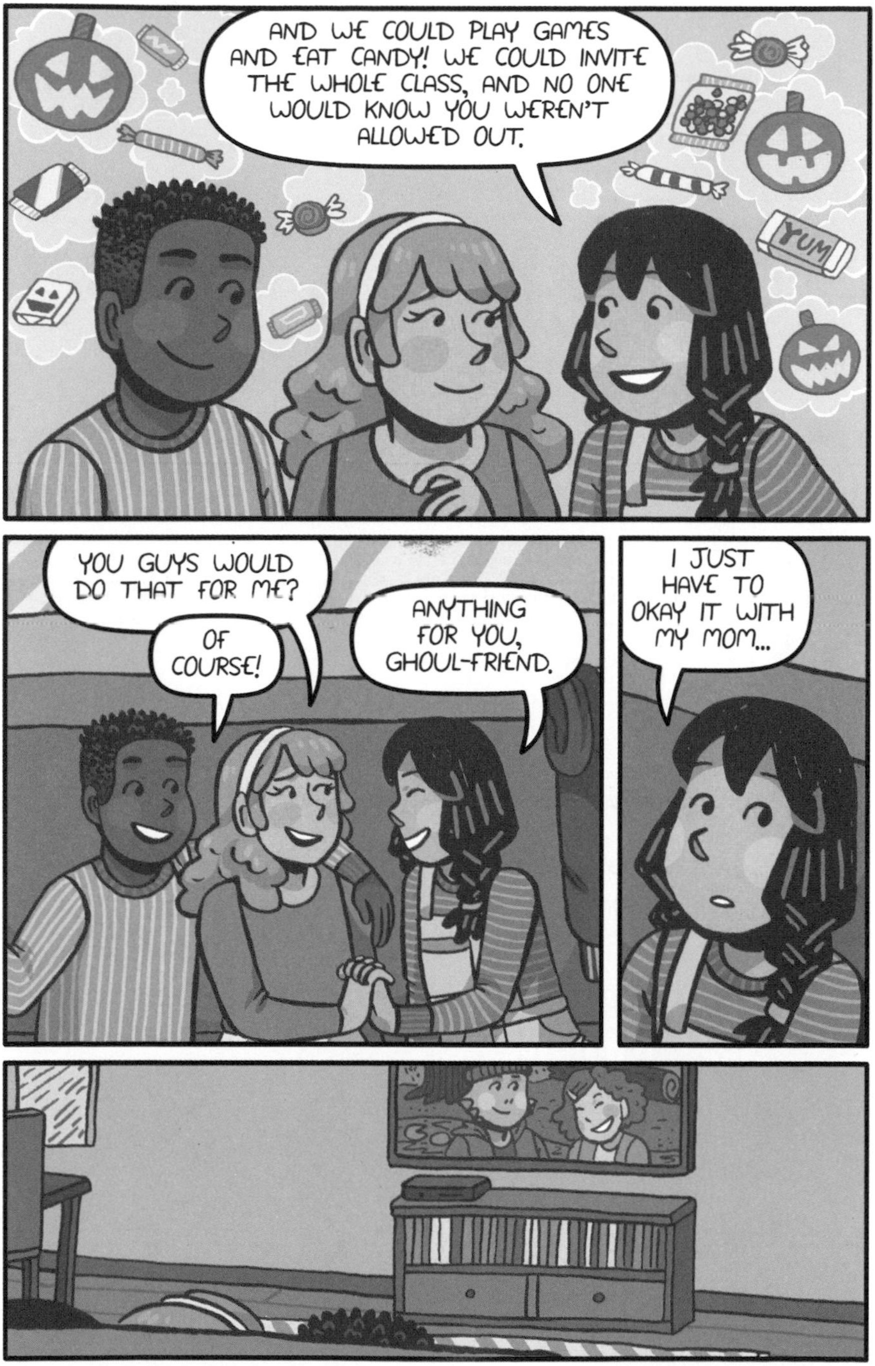
AND WE COULD PLAY GAMES AND EAT CANDY! WE COULD INVITE THE WHOLE CLASS, AND NO ONE WOULD KNOW YOU WEREN'T ALLOWED OUT.
YUM
YOU GUYS WOULD DO THAT FOR ME?
OF COURSE!
ANYTHING FOR YOU, GHOUL-FRIEND.
I JUST HAVE TO OKAY IT WITH MY MOM...

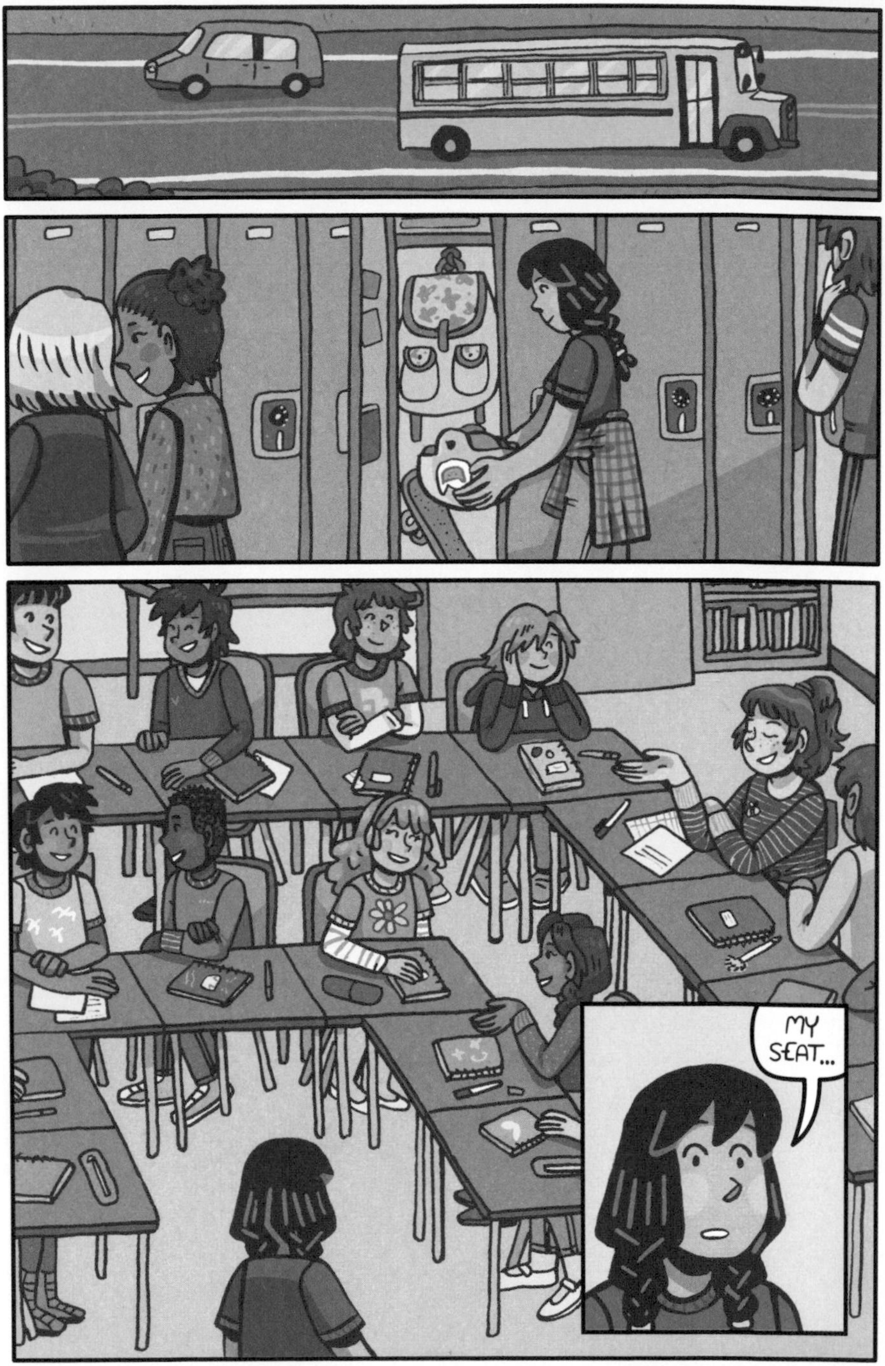
MY SEAT...

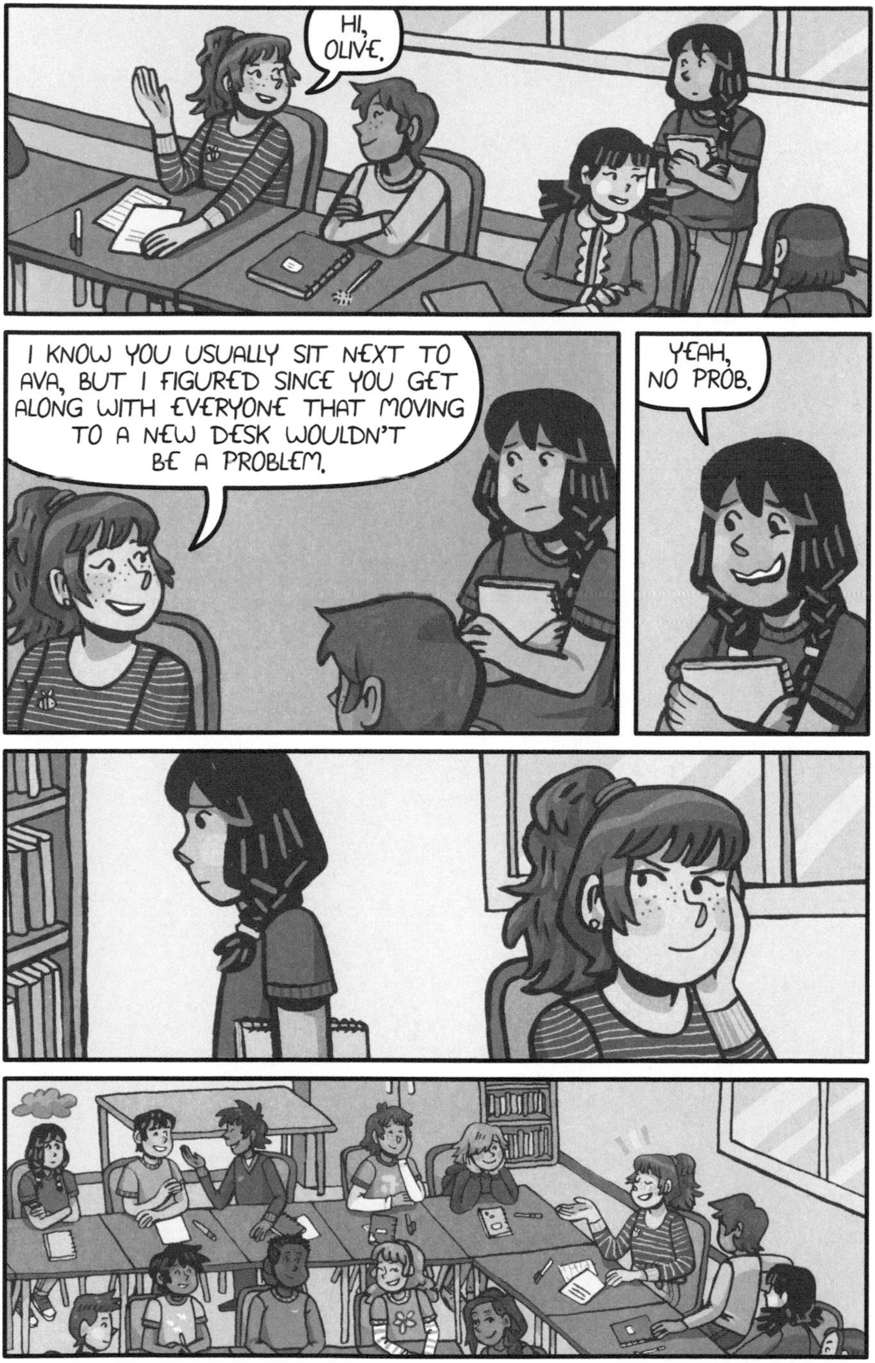
HI, OLIVE.
I KNOW YOU USUALLY SIT NEXT TO AVA, BUT I FIGURED SINCE YOU GET ALONG WITH EVERYONE THAT MOVING TO A NEW DESK WOULDN'T BE A PROBLEM.
YEAH, NO PROB.

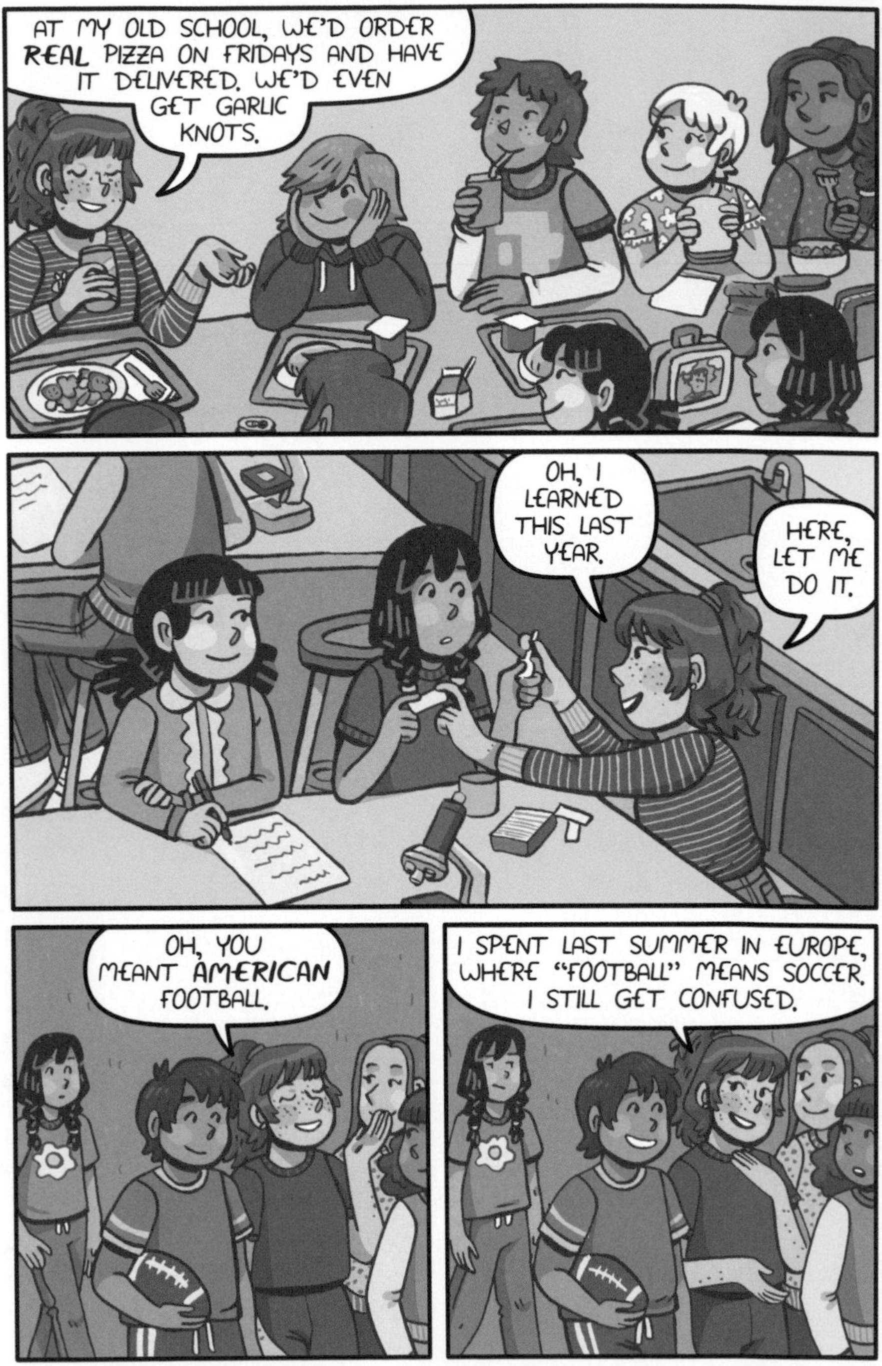

AT MY OLD SCHOOL, WE'D ORDER **REAL** PIZZA ON FRIDAYS AND HAVE IT DELIVERED. WE'D EVEN GET GARLIC KNOTS.
OH, I LEARNED THIS LAST YEAR.
HERE, LET ME DO IT.
OH, YOU MEANT **AMERICAN** FOOTBALL.
I SPENT LAST SUMMER IN EUROPE, WHERE "FOOTBALL" MEANS SOCCER. I STILL GET CONFUSED.

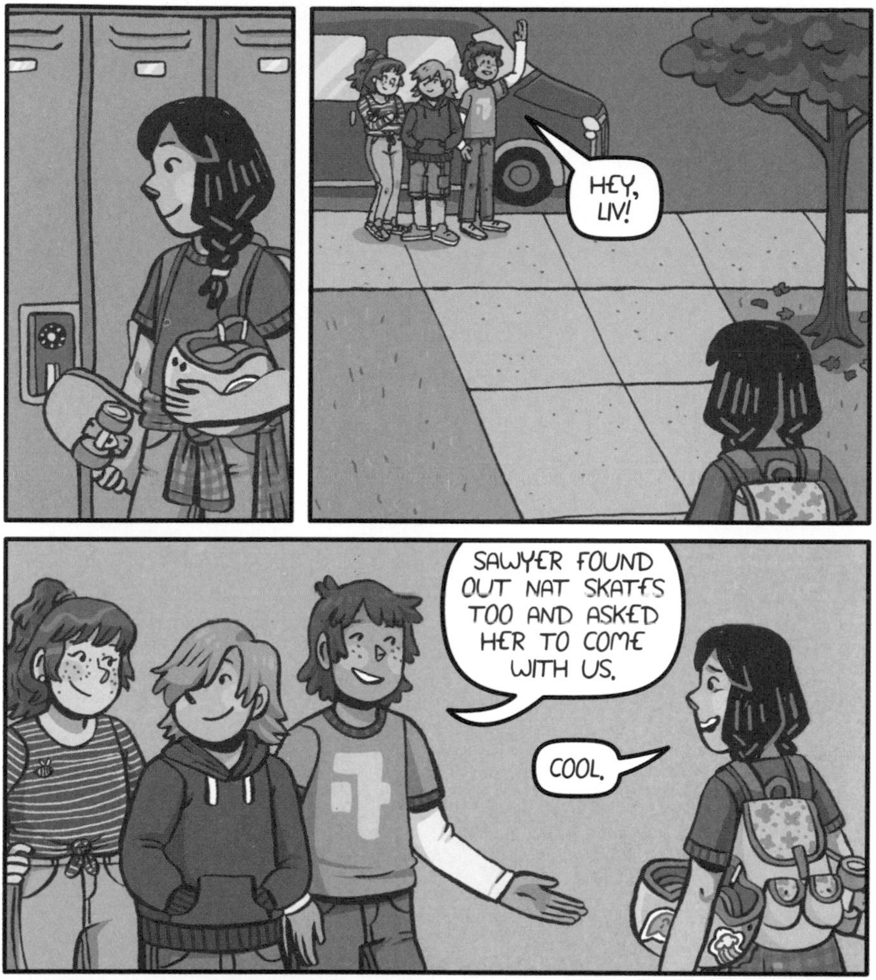
HEY, LIV!
SAWYER FOUND OUT NAT SKATES TOO AND ASKED HER TO COME WITH US.
COOL.

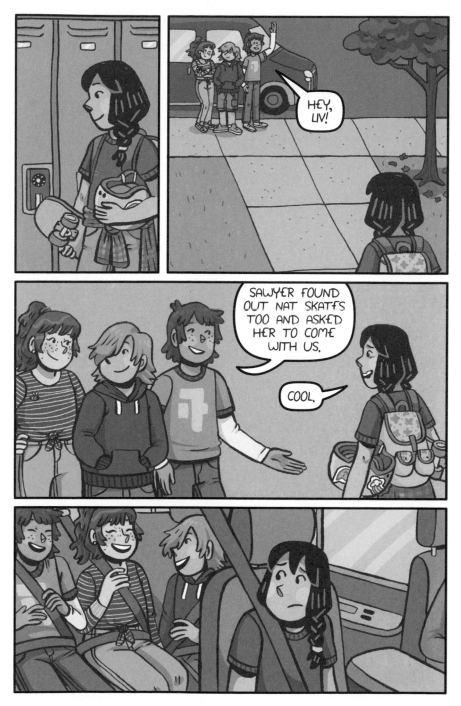

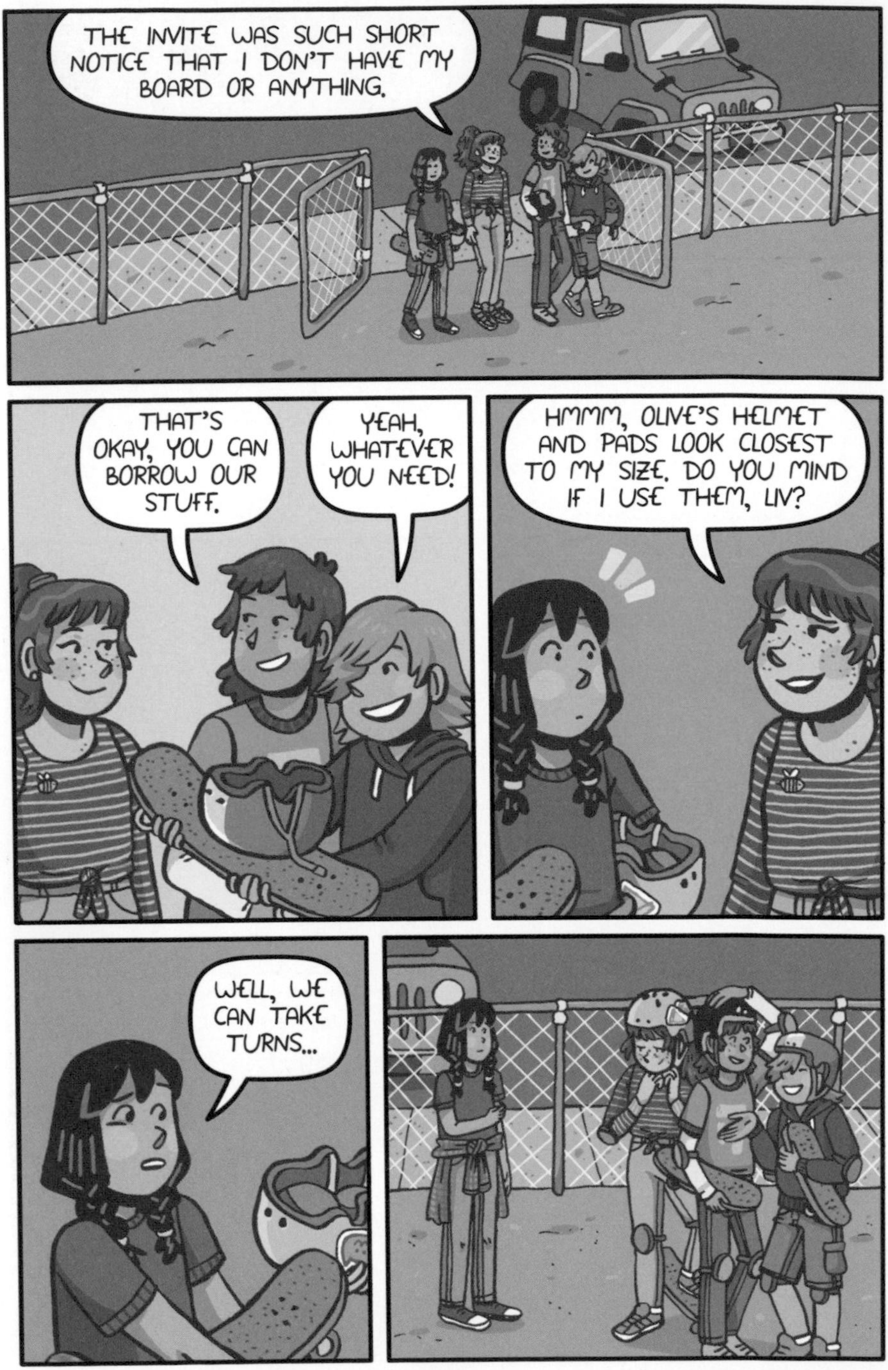
THE INVITE WAS SUCH SHORT NOTICE THAT I DON'T HAVE MY BOARD OR ANYTHING.
THAT'S OKAY, YOU CAN BORROW OUR STUFF.
YEAH, WHATEVER YOU NEED!
HMMM, OLIVE'S HELMET AND PADS LOOK CLOSEST TO MY SIZE. DO YOU MIND IF I USE THEM, LIV?
WELL, WE CAN TAKE TURNS...

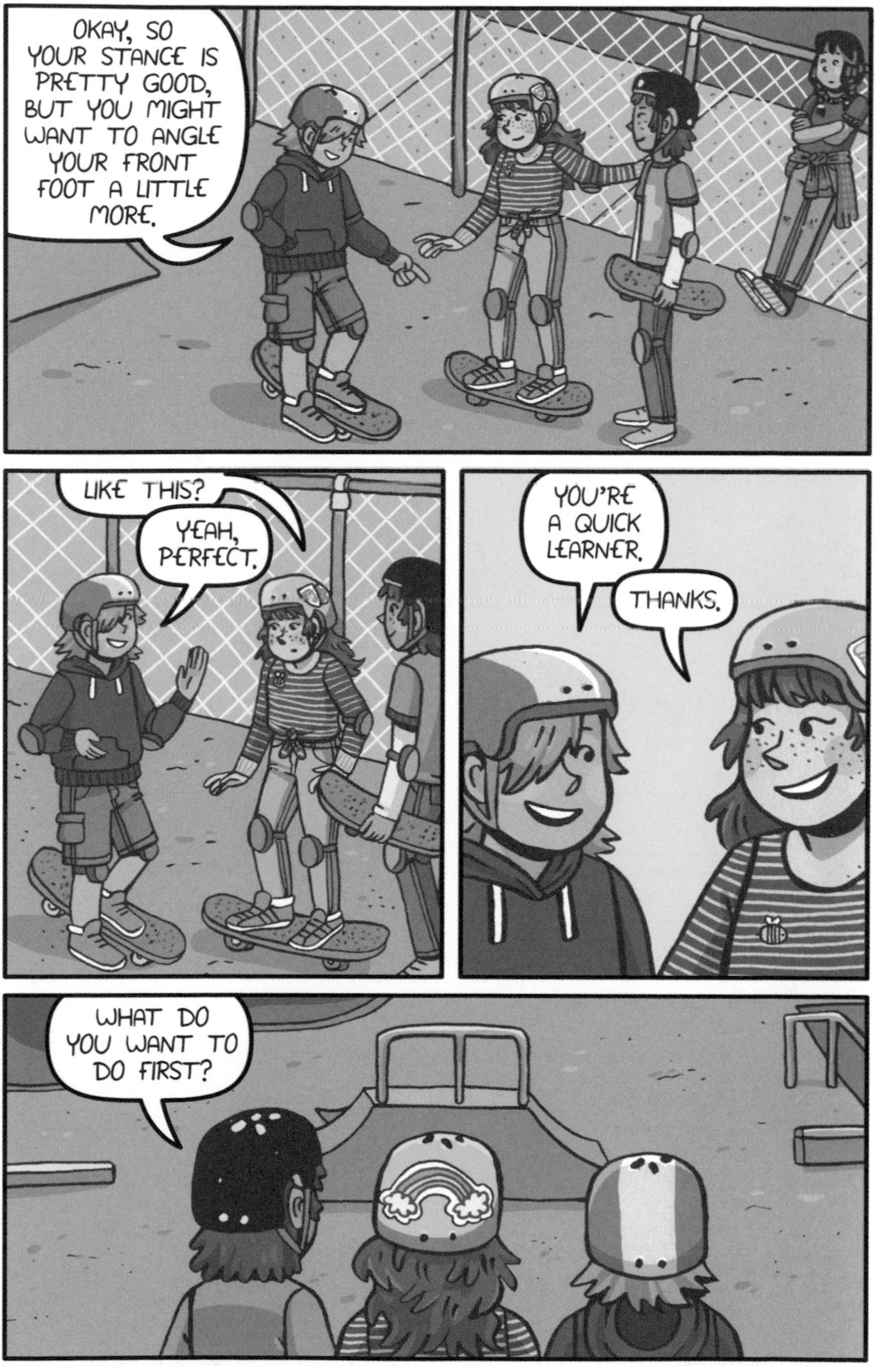
OKAY, SO YOUR STANCE IS PRETTY GOOD, BUT YOU MIGHT WANT TO ANGLE YOUR FRONT FOOT A LITTLE MORE.
LIKE THIS?
YEAH, PERFECT.
YOU'RE A QUICK LEARNER.
THANKS.
WHAT DO YOU WANT TO DO FIRST?

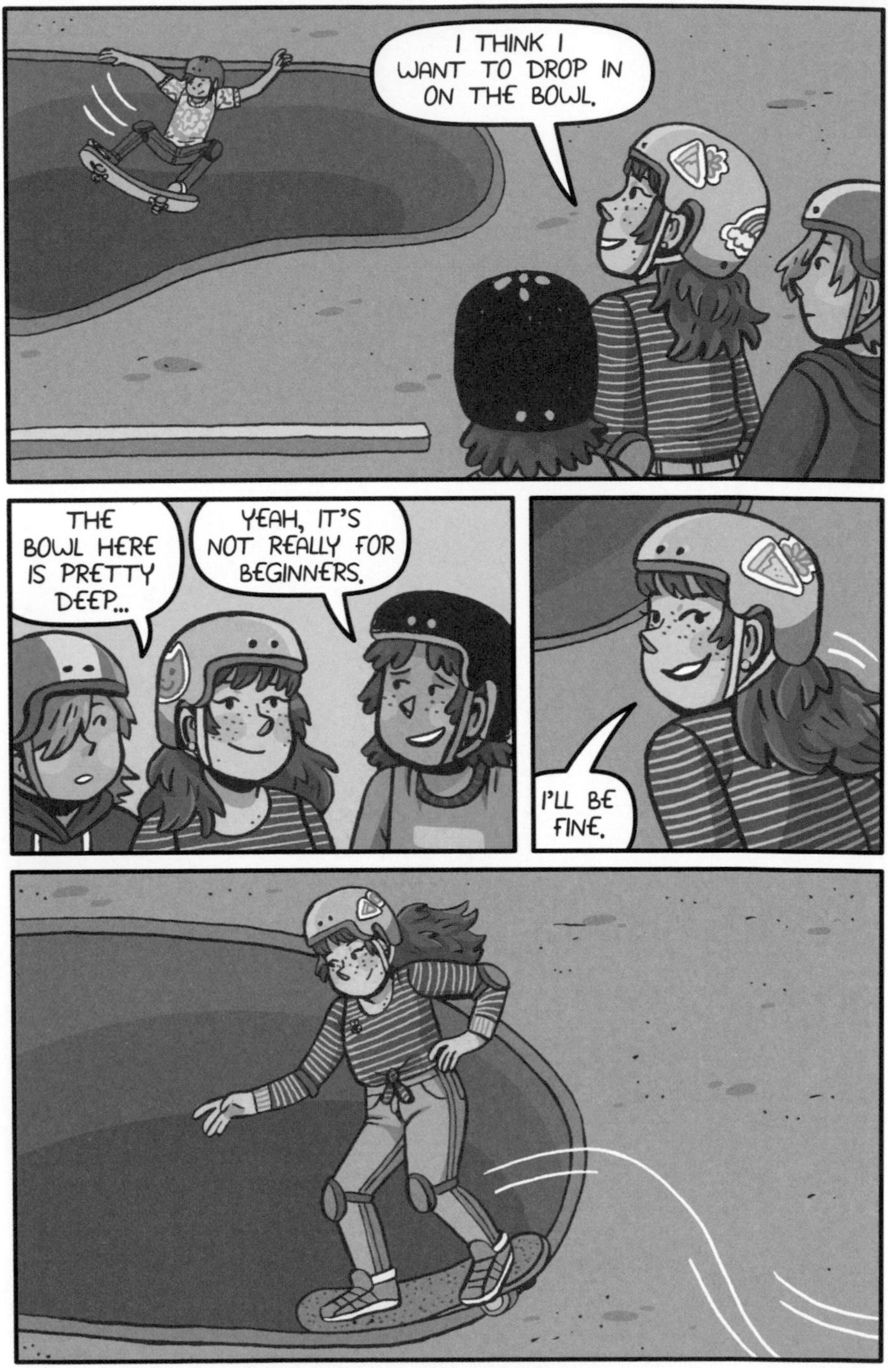
I THINK I WANT TO DROP IN ON THE BOWL.
THE BOWL HERE IS PRETTY DEEP...
YEAH, IT'S NOT REALLY FOR BEGINNERS.
I'LL BE FINE.

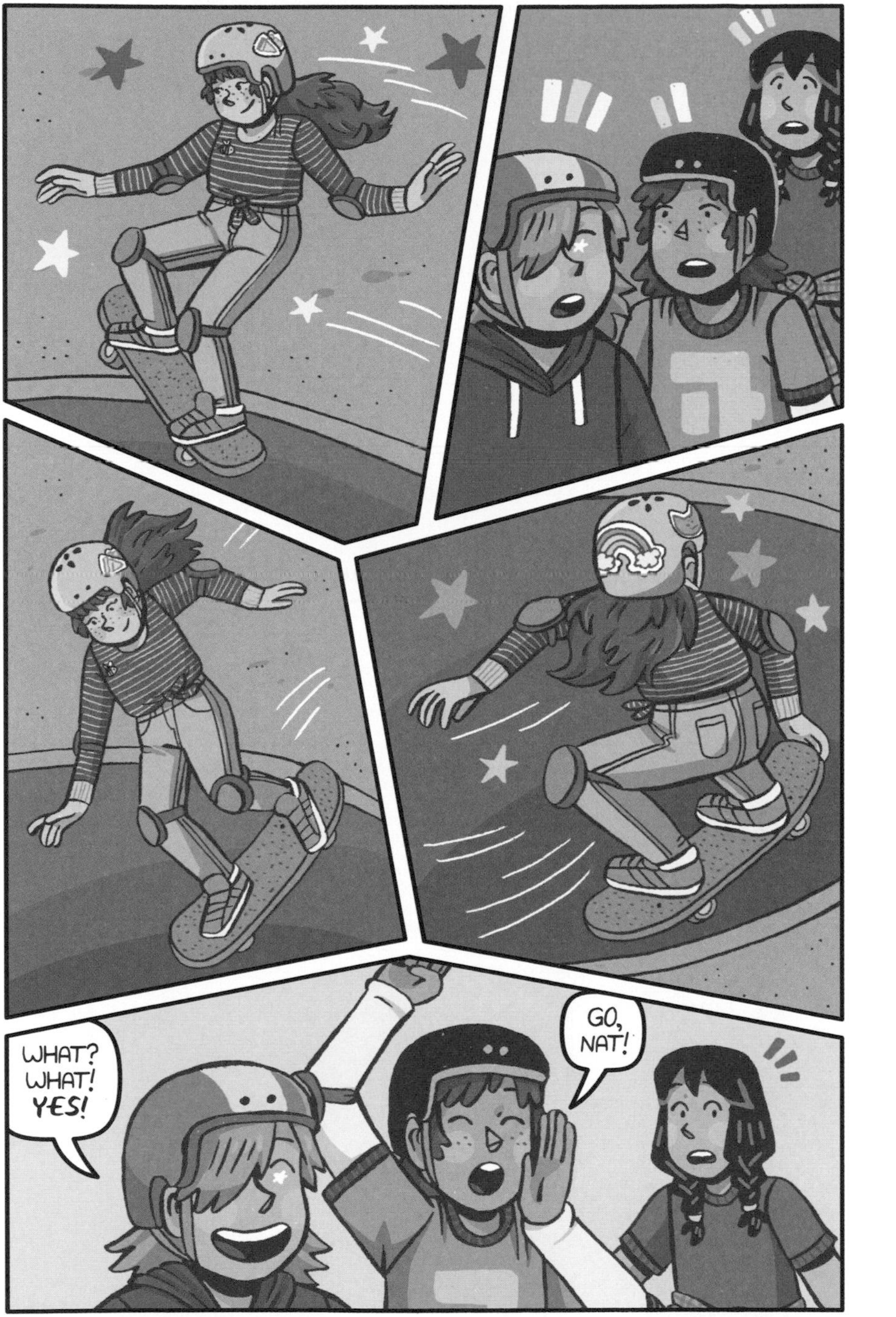
WHAT? WHAT! YES!
GO, NAT!

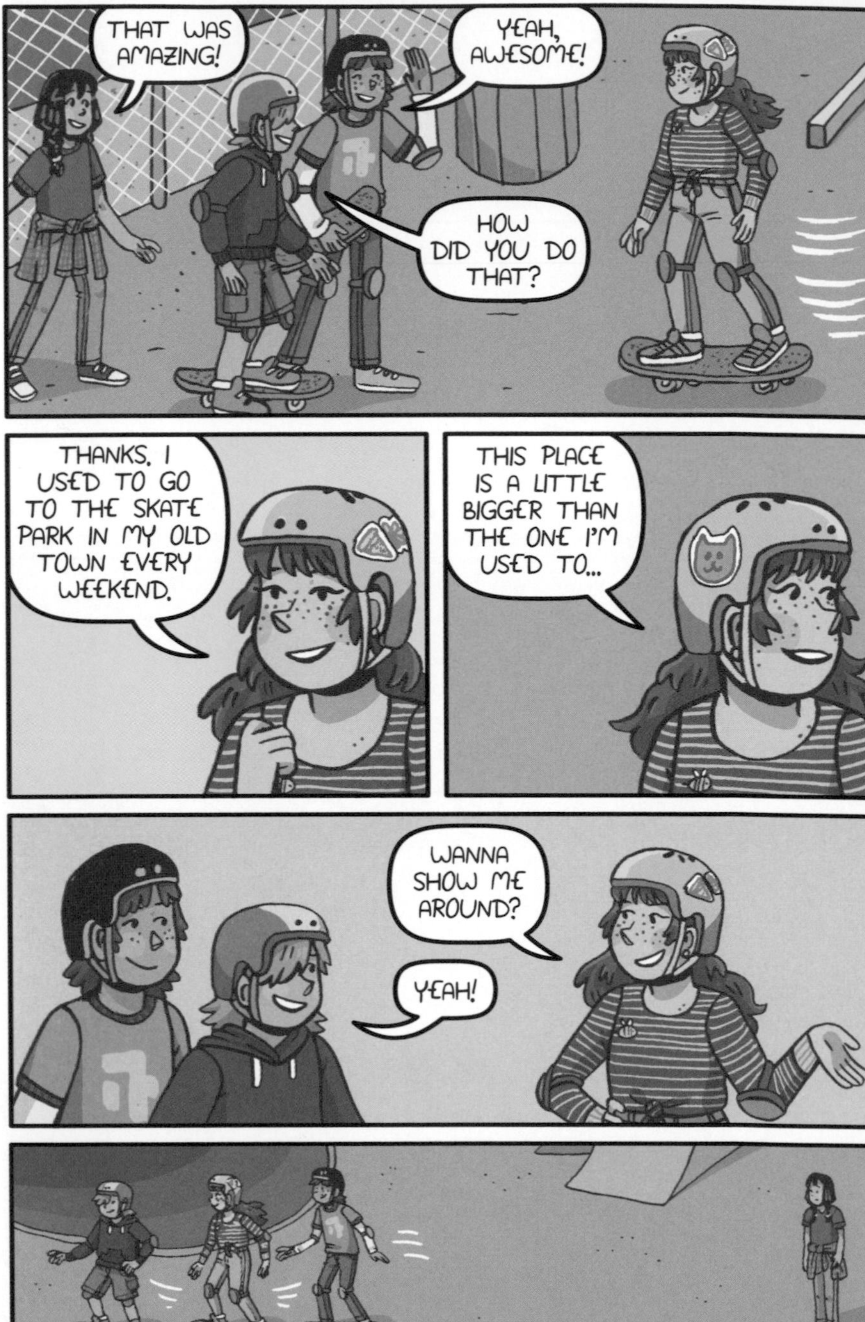
THAT WAS AMAZING!
YEAH, AWESOME!
HOW DID YOU DO THAT?
THANKS. I USED TO GO TO THE SKATE PARK IN MY OLD TOWN EVERY WEEKEND.
THIS PLACE IS A LITTLE BIGGER THAN THE ONE I'M USED TO...
WANNA SHOW ME AROUND?
YEAH!

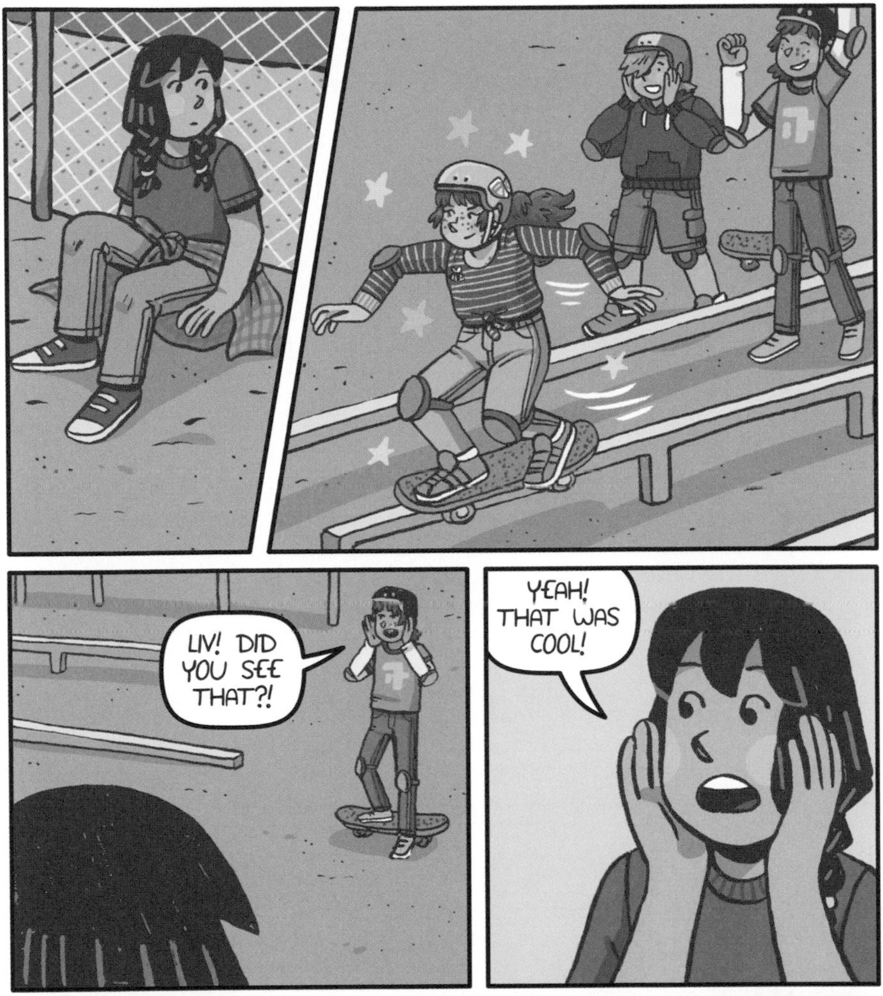
LIV! DID YOU SEE THAT?!
YEAH! THAT WAS COOL!

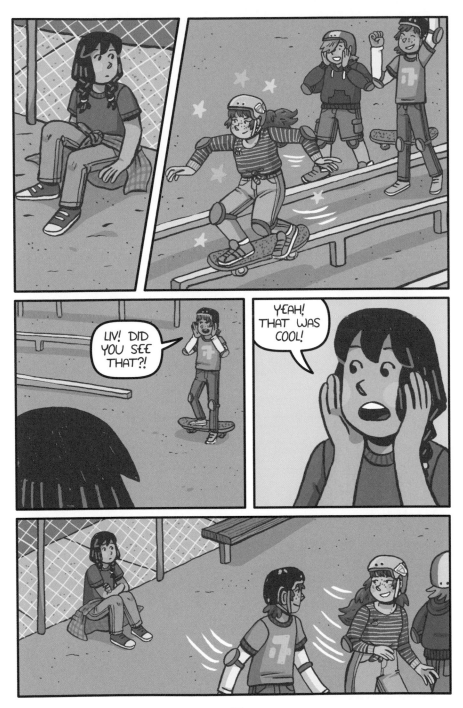

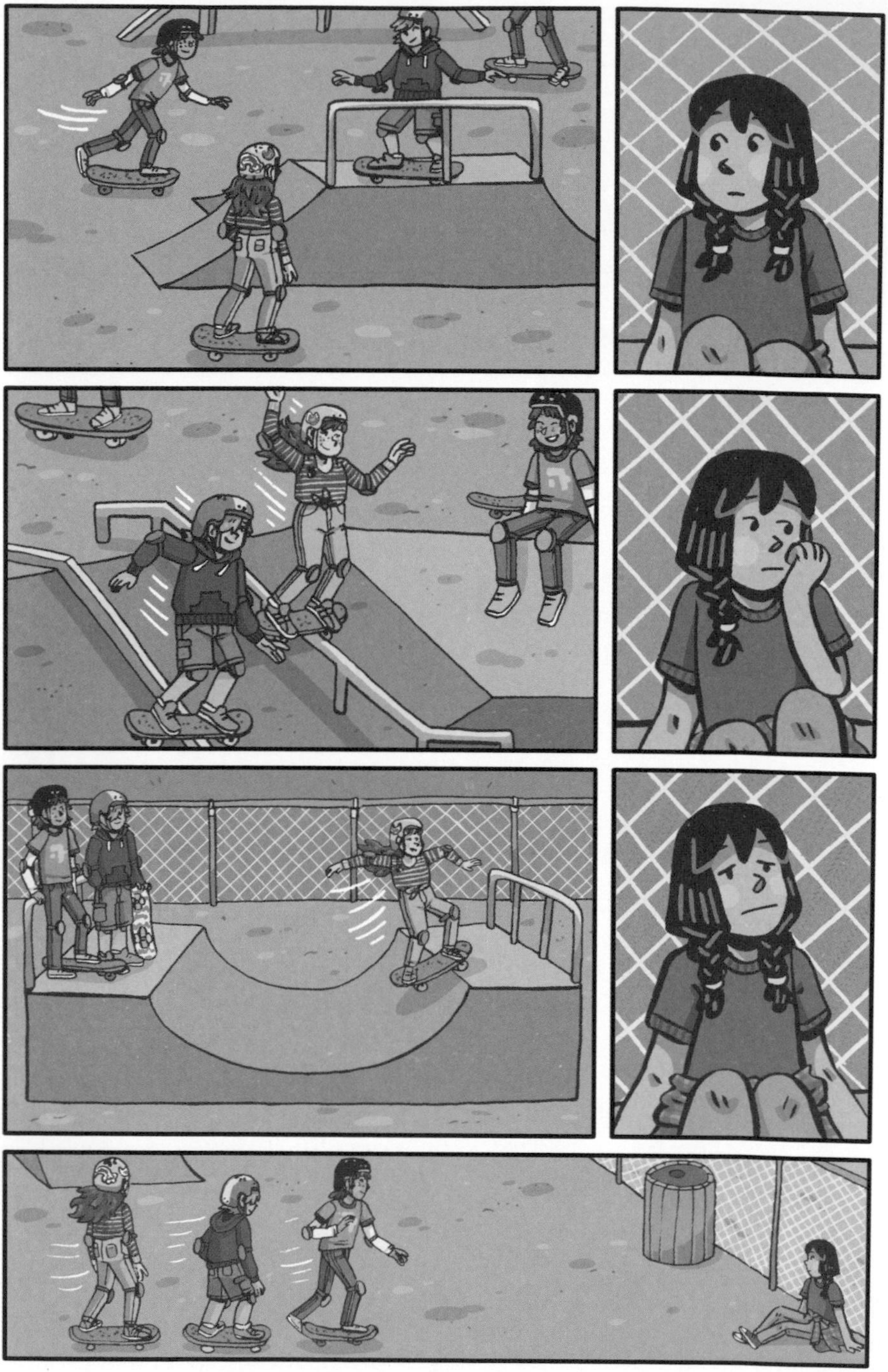

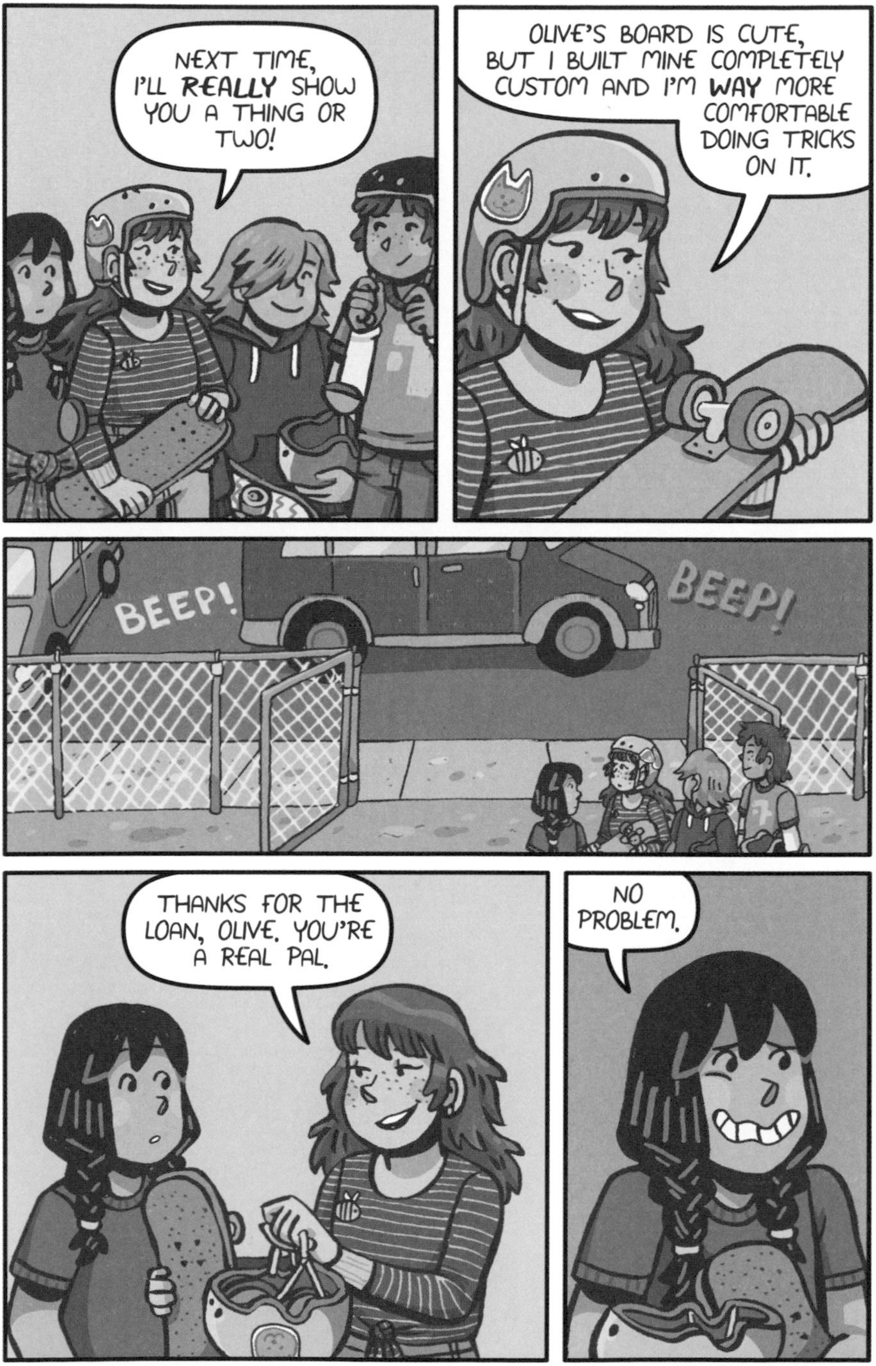
NEXT TIME, I'LL **REALLY** SHOW YOU A THING OR TWO!
OLIVE'S BOARD IS CUTE, BUT I BUILT MINE COMPLETELY CUSTOM AND I'M **WAY** MORE COMFORTABLE DOING TRICKS ON IT.
BEEP!
BEEP!
THANKS FOR THE LOAN, OLIVE. YOU'RE A REAL PAL.
NO PROBLEM.

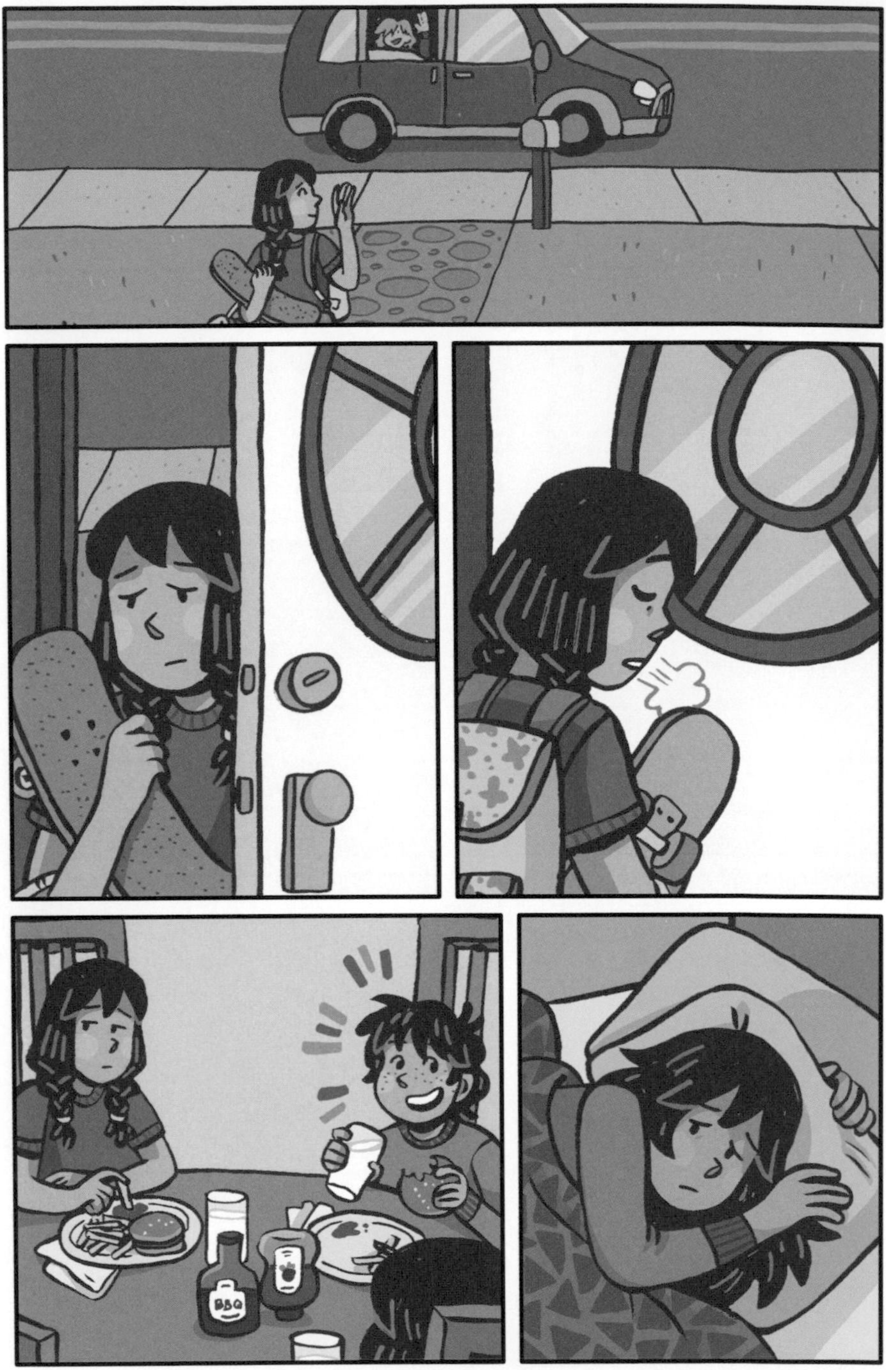

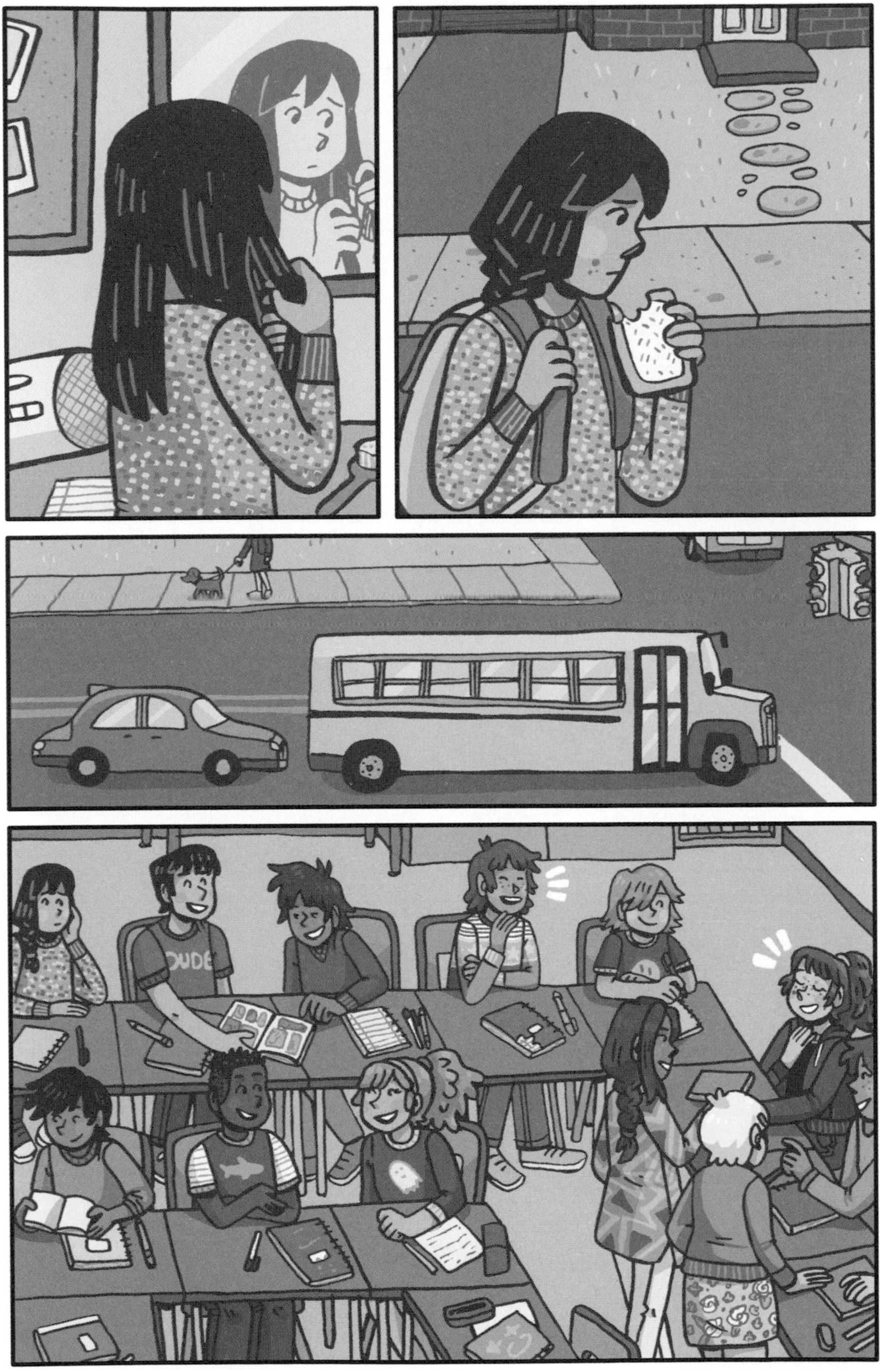
DUDE

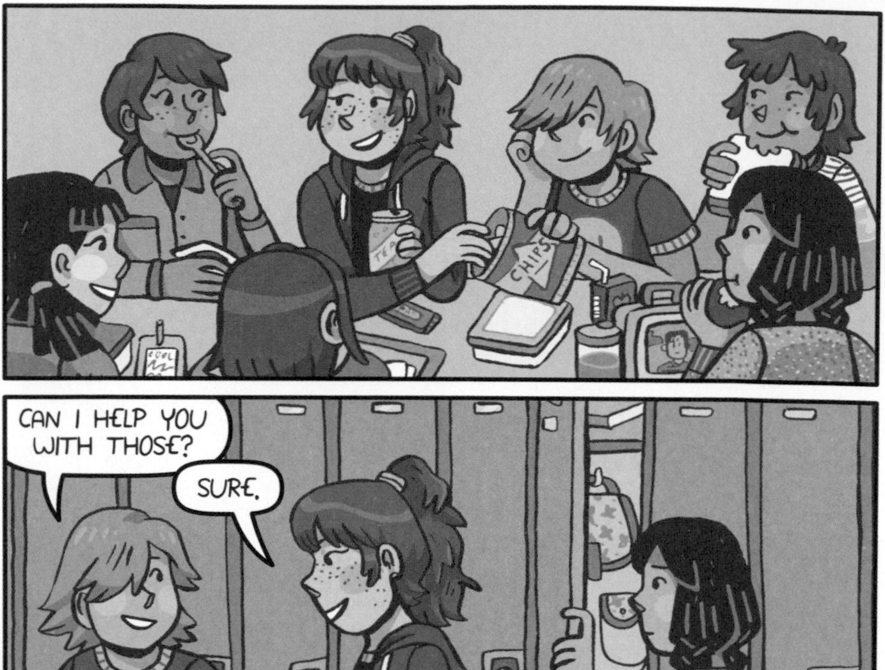
CHIPS
CAN I HELP YOU WITH THOSE?
SURE.

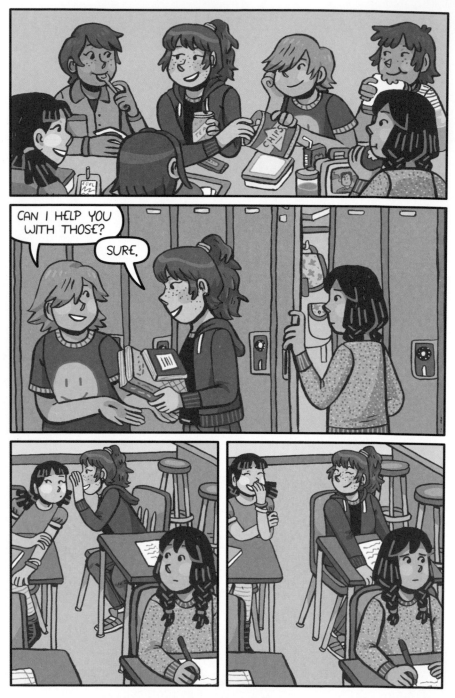

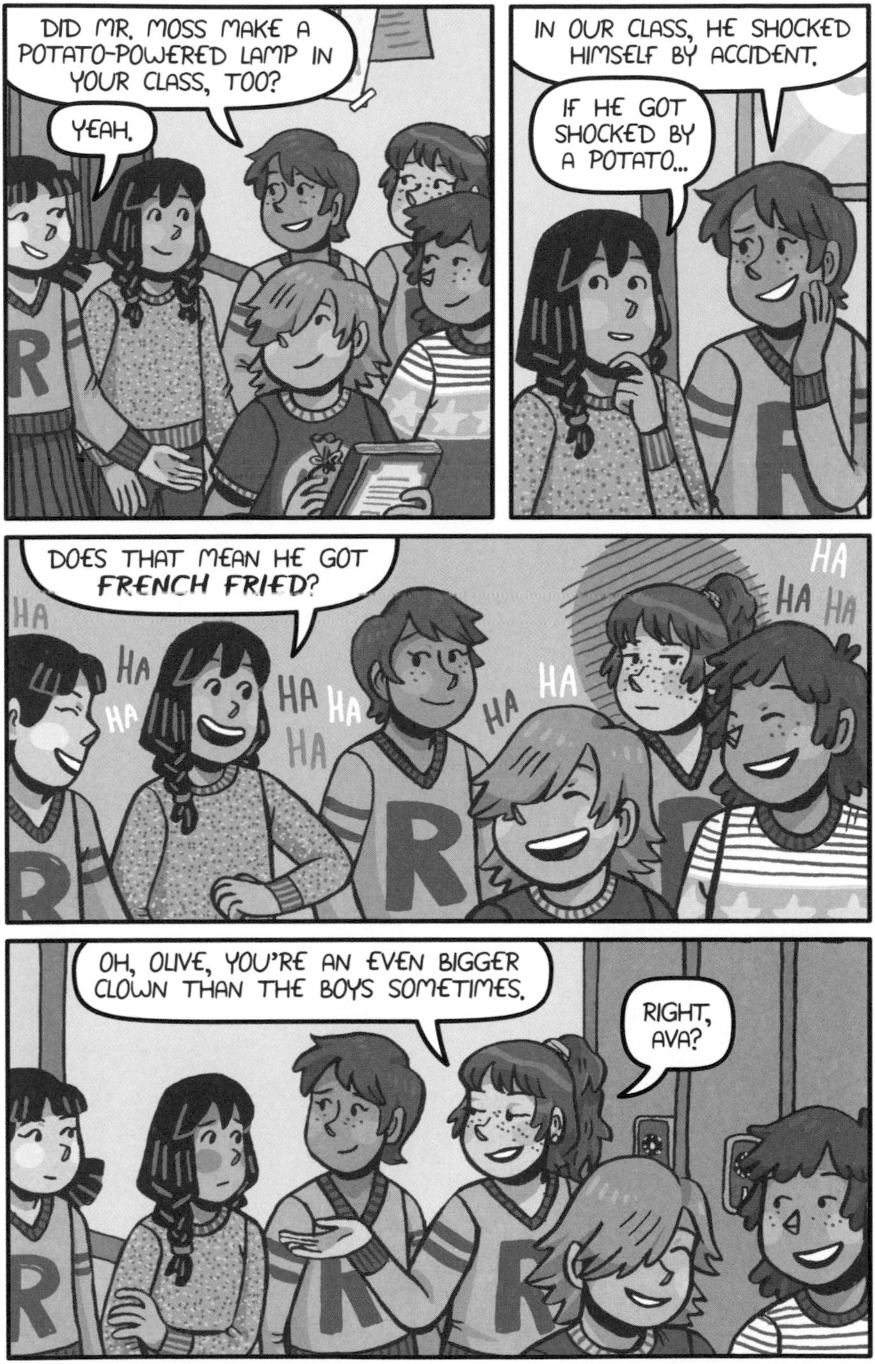
DID MR. MOSS MAKE A POTATO-POWERED LAMP IN YOUR CLASS, TOO?
YEAH.
IN OUR CLASS, HE SHOCKED HIMSELF BY ACCIDENT.
IF HE GOT SHOCKED BY A POTATO...
DOES THAT MEAN HE GOT **FRENCH FRIED**?
HA HA HA HA HA HA HA HA HA HA HA HA
OH, OLIVE, YOU'RE AN EVEN BIGGER CLOWN THAN THE BOYS SOMETIMES.
RIGHT, AVA?

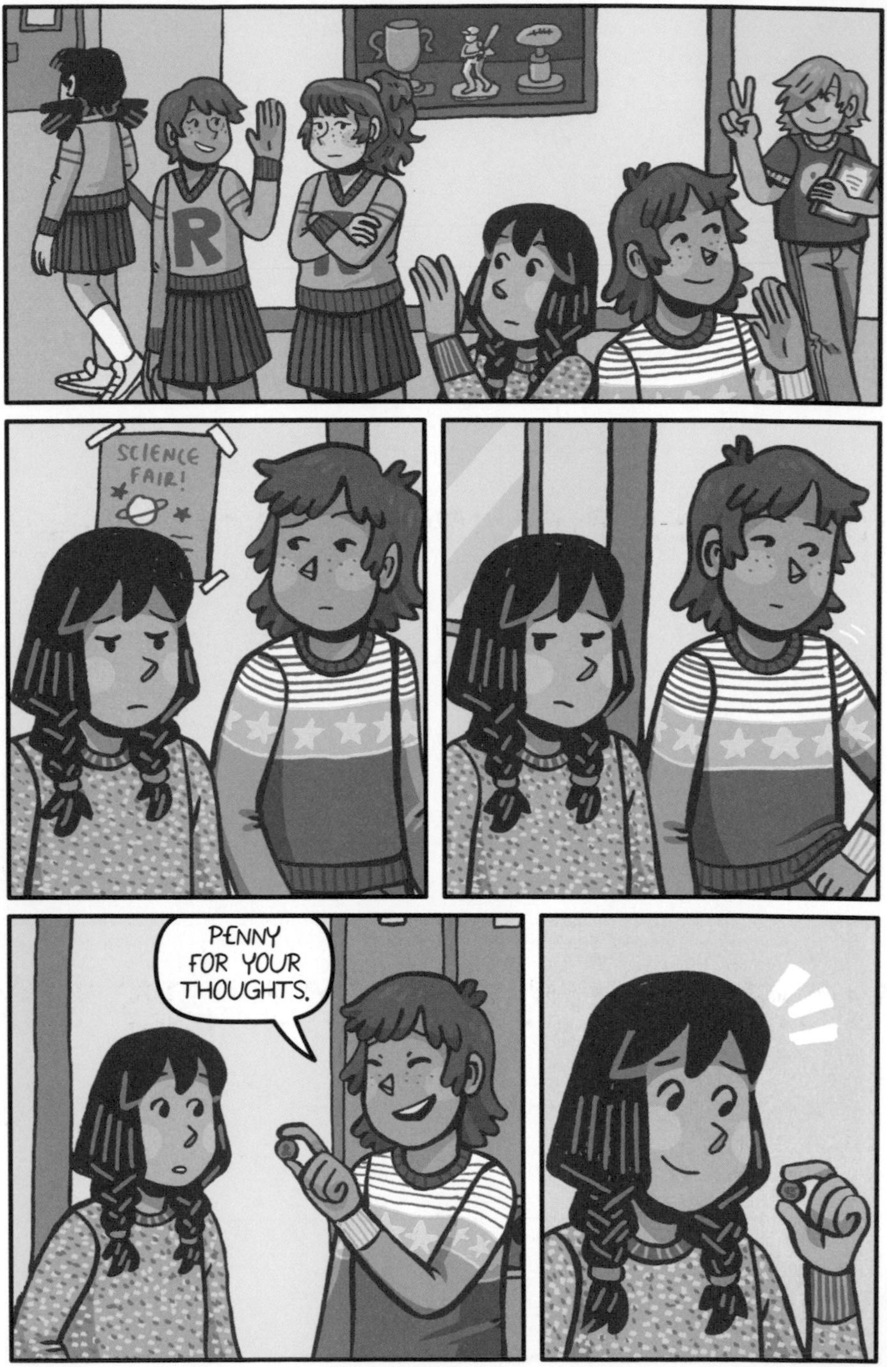
SCIENCE FAIR!
PENNY FOR YOUR THOUGHTS.

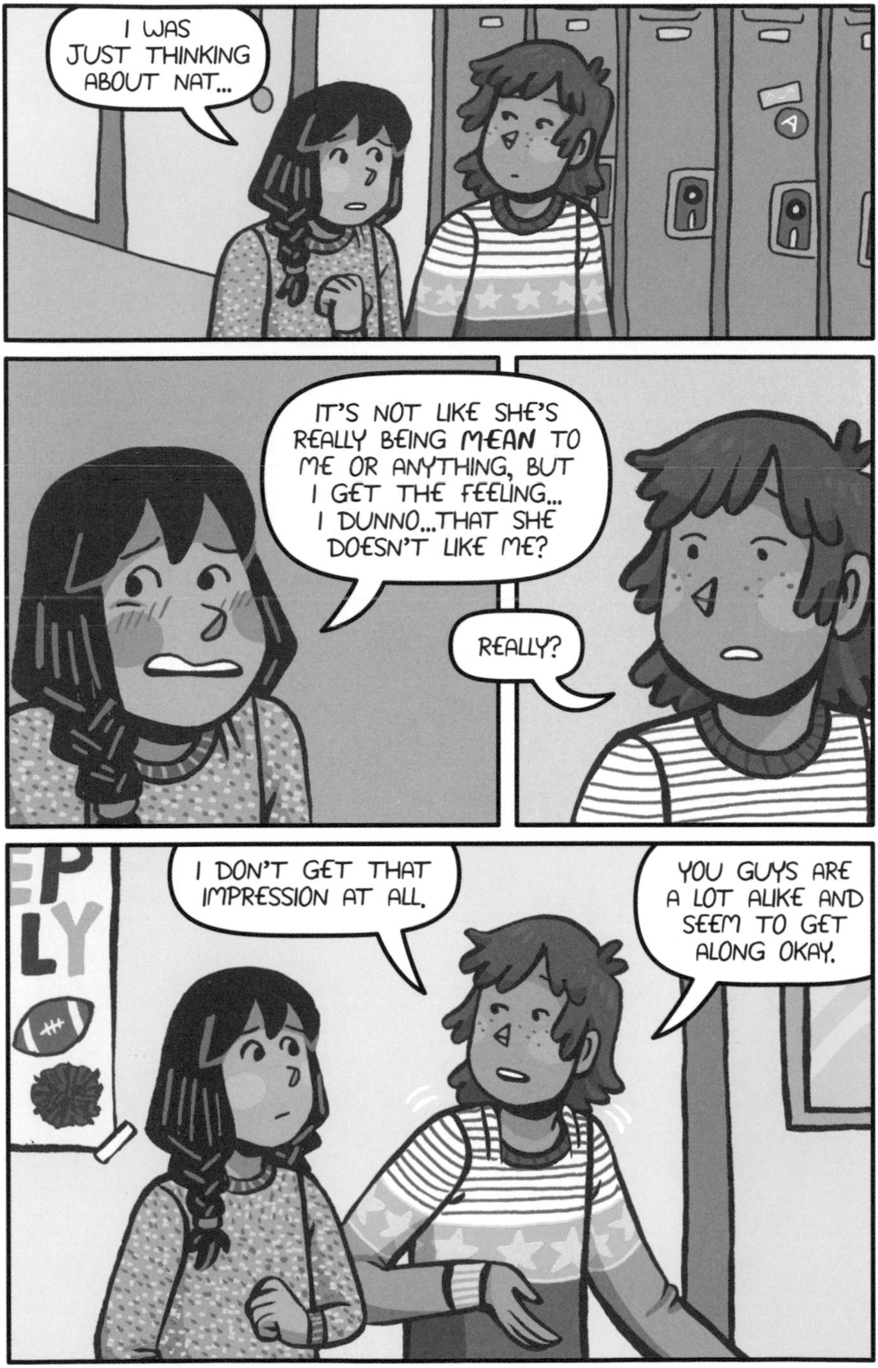
I WAS JUST THINKING ABOUT NAT...
IT'S NOT LIKE SHE'S REALLY BEING MEAN TO ME OR ANYTHING, BUT I GET THE FEELING... I DUNNO...THAT SHE DOESN'T LIKE ME?
REALLY?
I DON'T GET THAT IMPRESSION AT ALL.
YOU GUYS ARE A LOT ALIKE AND SEEM TO GET ALONG OKAY.

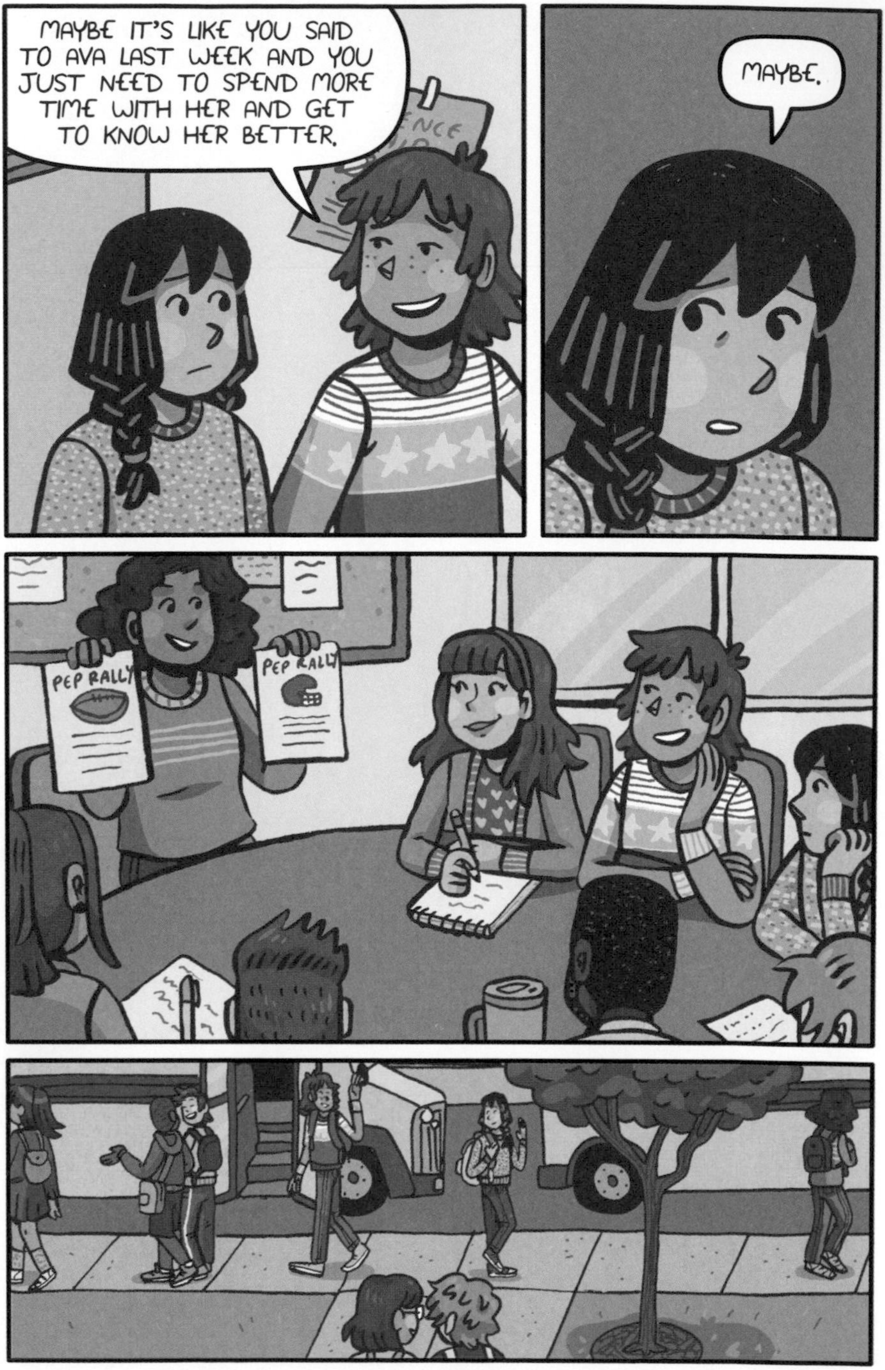
MAYBE IT'S LIKE YOU SAID TO AVA LAST WEEK AND YOU JUST NEED TO SPEND MORE TIME WITH HER AND GET TO KNOW HER BETTER.
MAYBE.
PEP RALLY
PEP RALLY

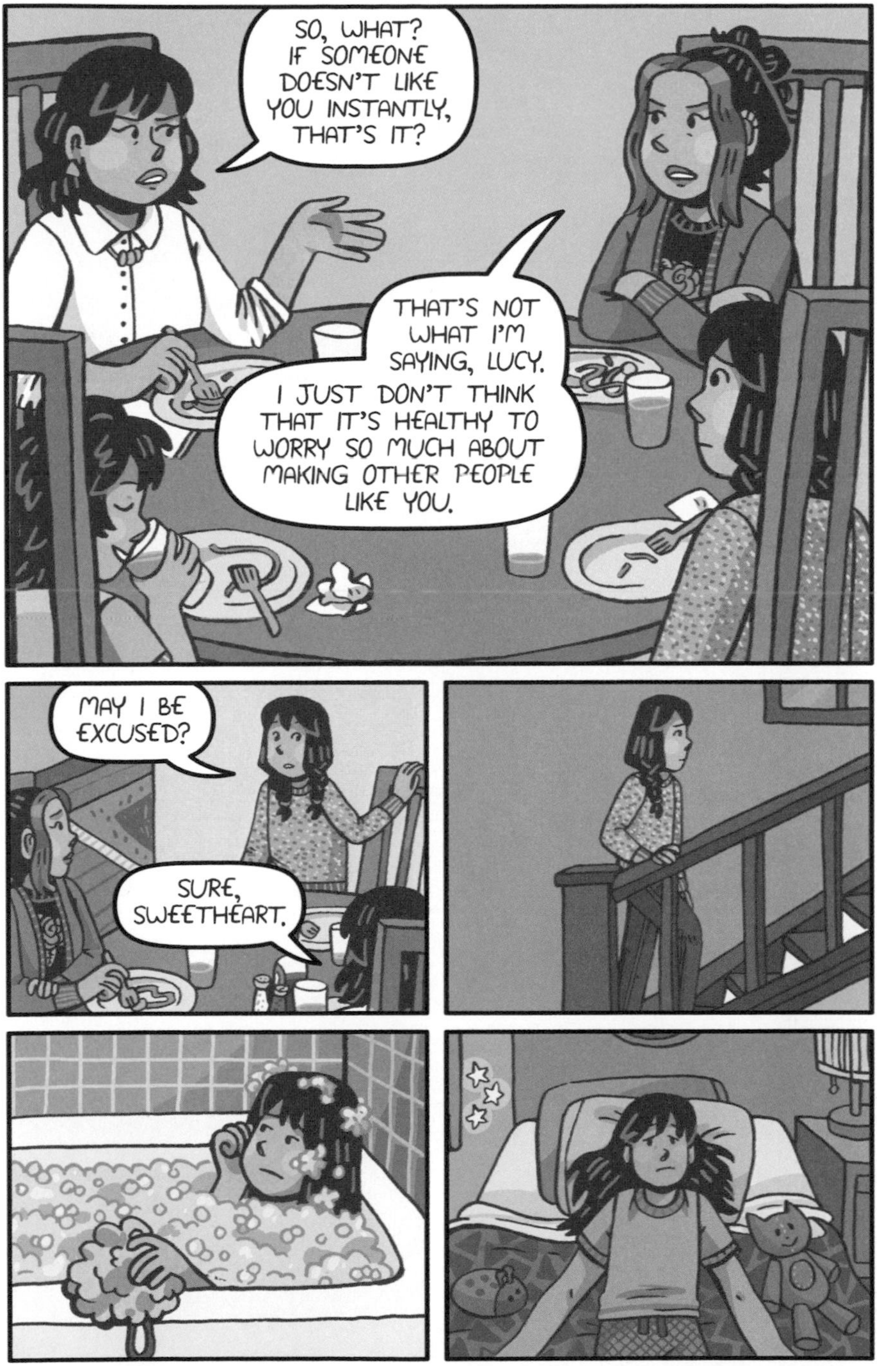
SO, WHAT? IF SOMEONE DOESN'T LIKE YOU INSTANTLY, THAT'S IT?
THAT'S NOT WHAT I'M SAYING, LUCY. I JUST DON'T THINK THAT IT'S HEALTHY TO WORRY SO MUCH ABOUT MAKING OTHER PEOPLE LIKE YOU.
MAY I BE EXCUSED?
SURE, SWEETHEART.

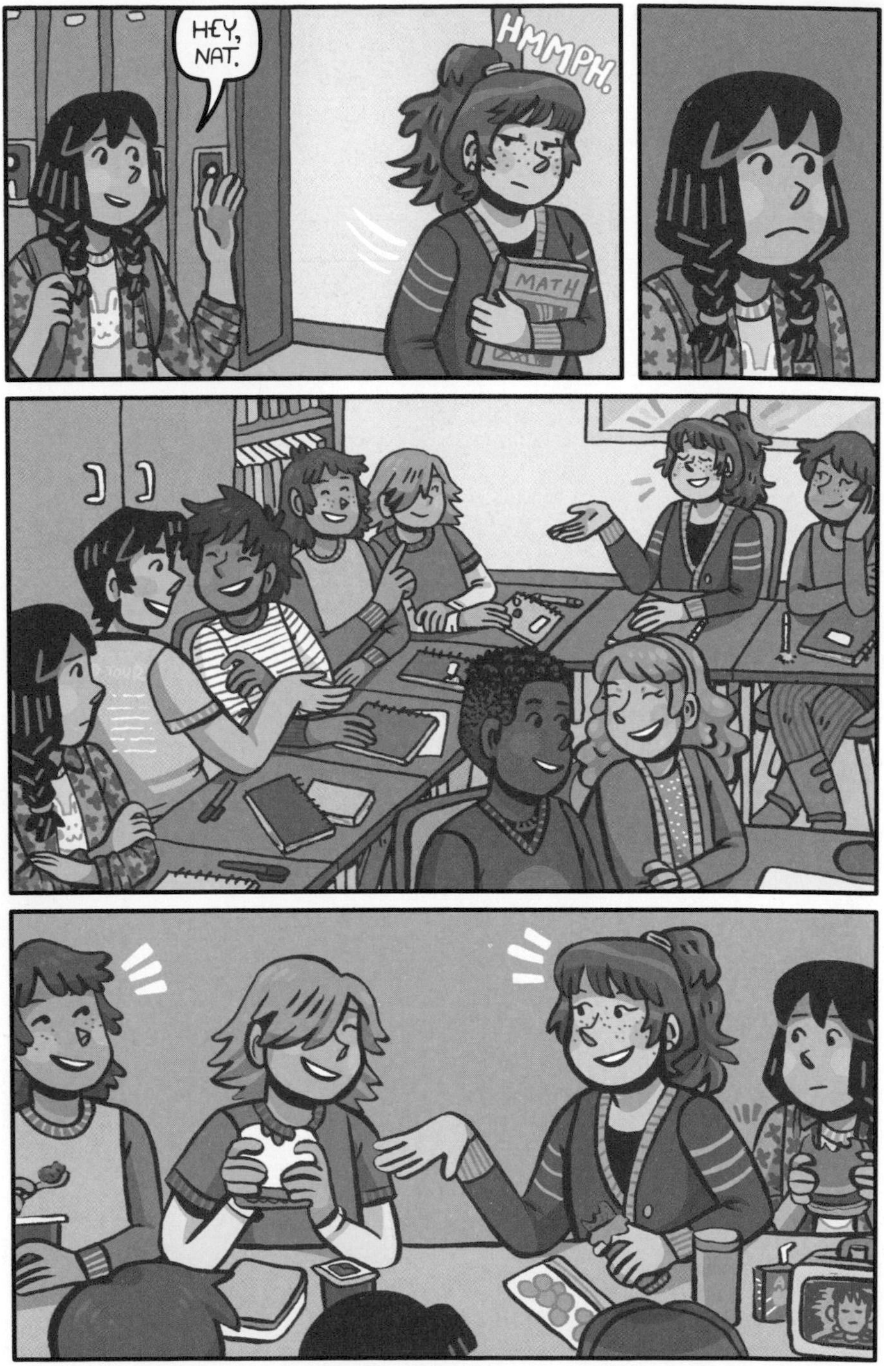
HEY, NAT.
HMMPH.
MATH

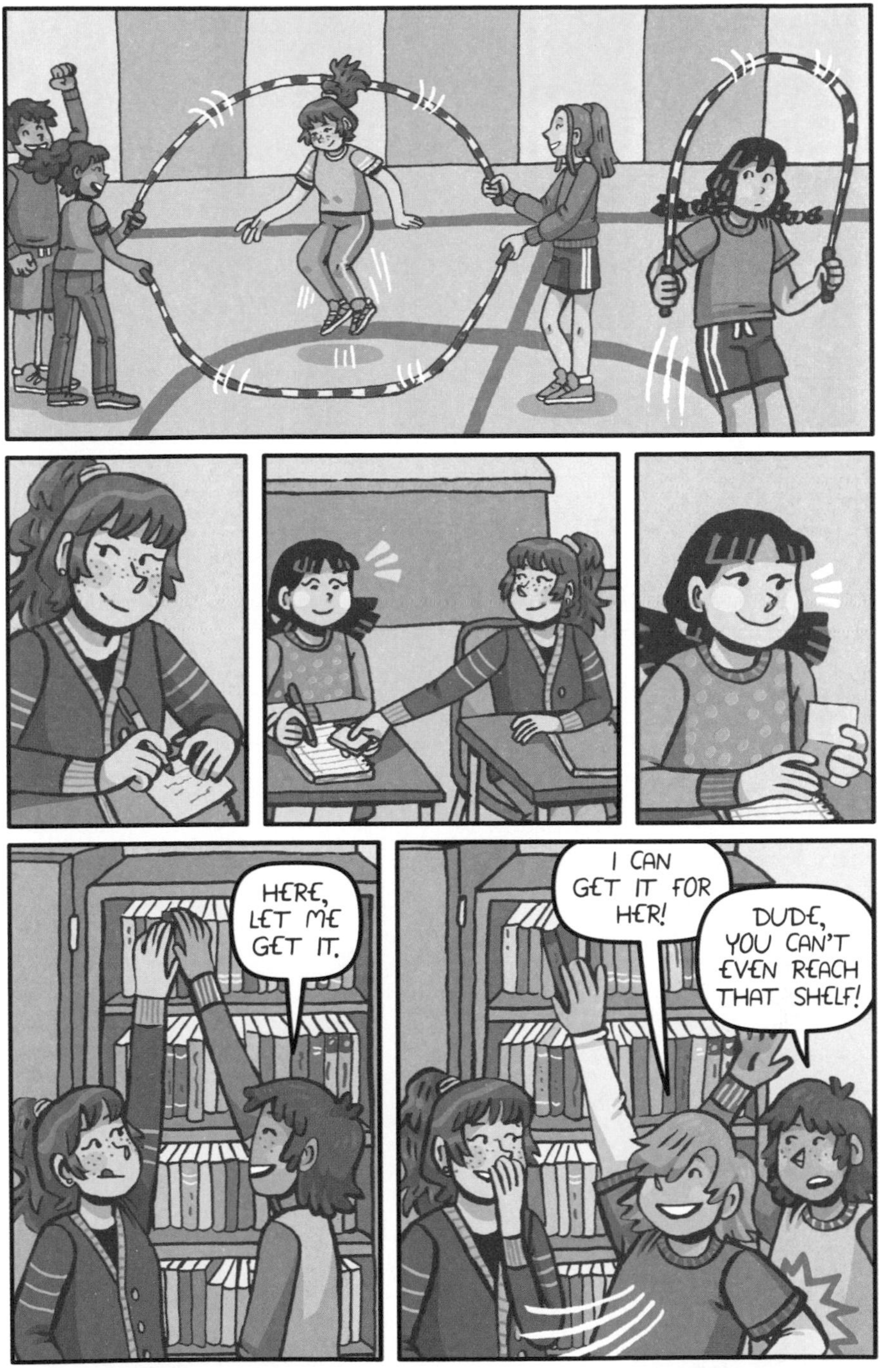
HERE, LET ME GET IT.
I CAN GET IT FOR HER!
DUDE, YOU CAN'T EVEN REACH THAT SHELF!

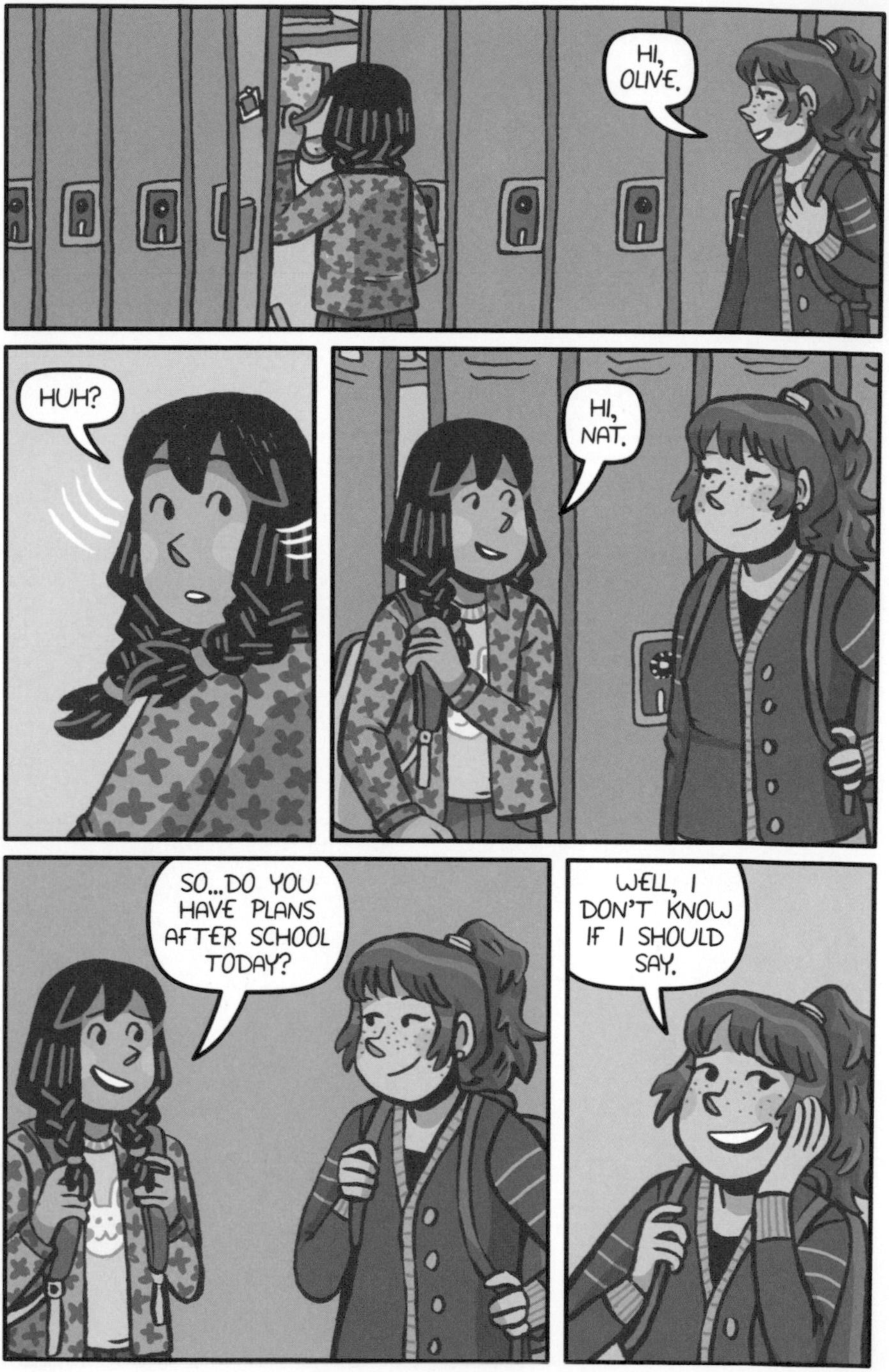
HI, OLIVE.
HUH?
HI, NAT.
SO...DO YOU HAVE PLANS AFTER SCHOOL TODAY?
WELL, I DON'T KNOW IF I SHOULD SAY.

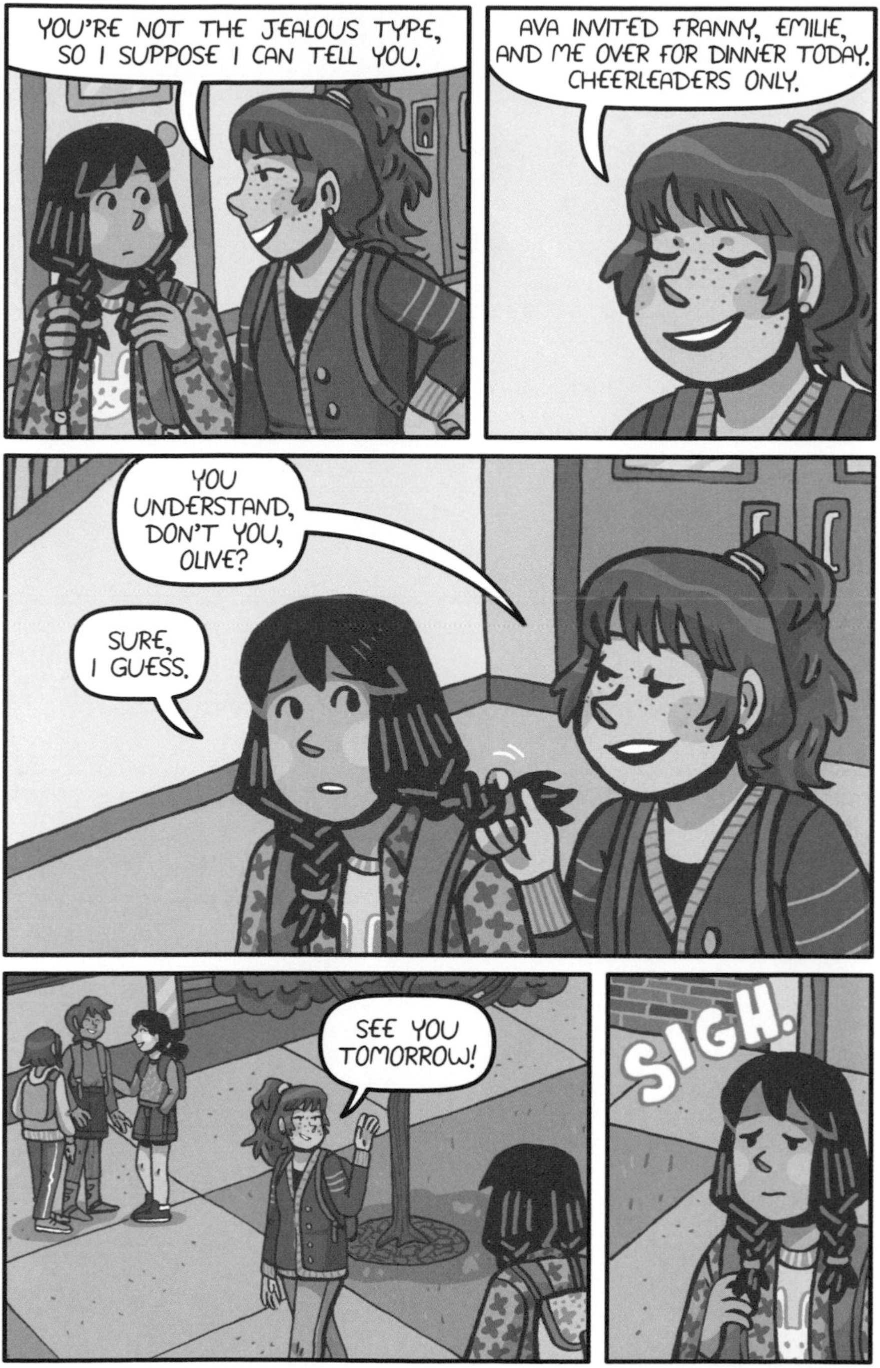
YOU'RE NOT THE JEALOUS TYPE, SO I SUPPOSE I CAN TELL YOU.
AVA INVITED FRANNY, EMILIE, AND ME OVER FOR DINNER TODAY. CHEERLEADERS ONLY.
YOU UNDERSTAND, DON'T YOU, OLIVE?
SURE, I GUESS.
SEE YOU TOMORROW!
SIGH.

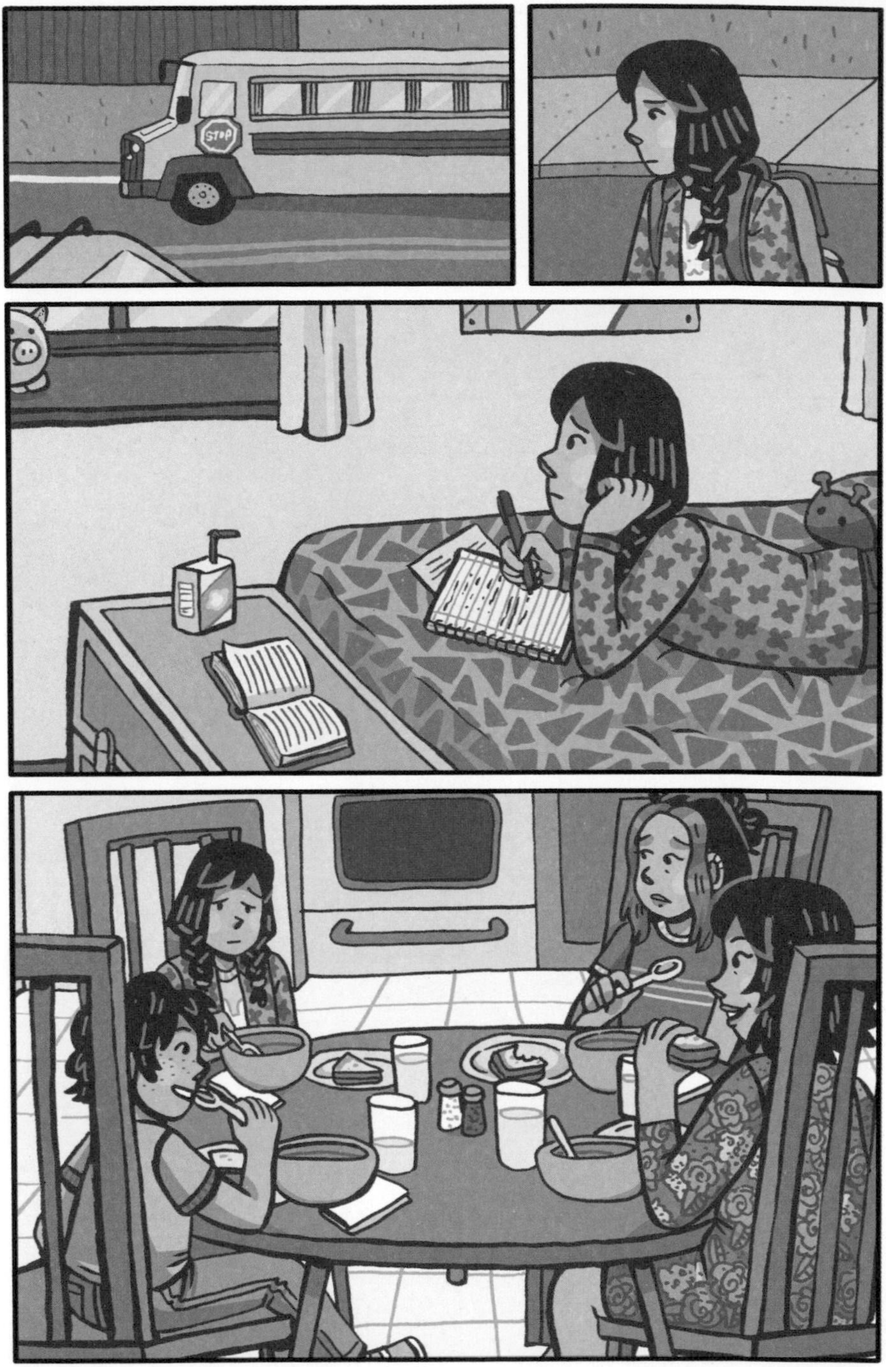
STOP

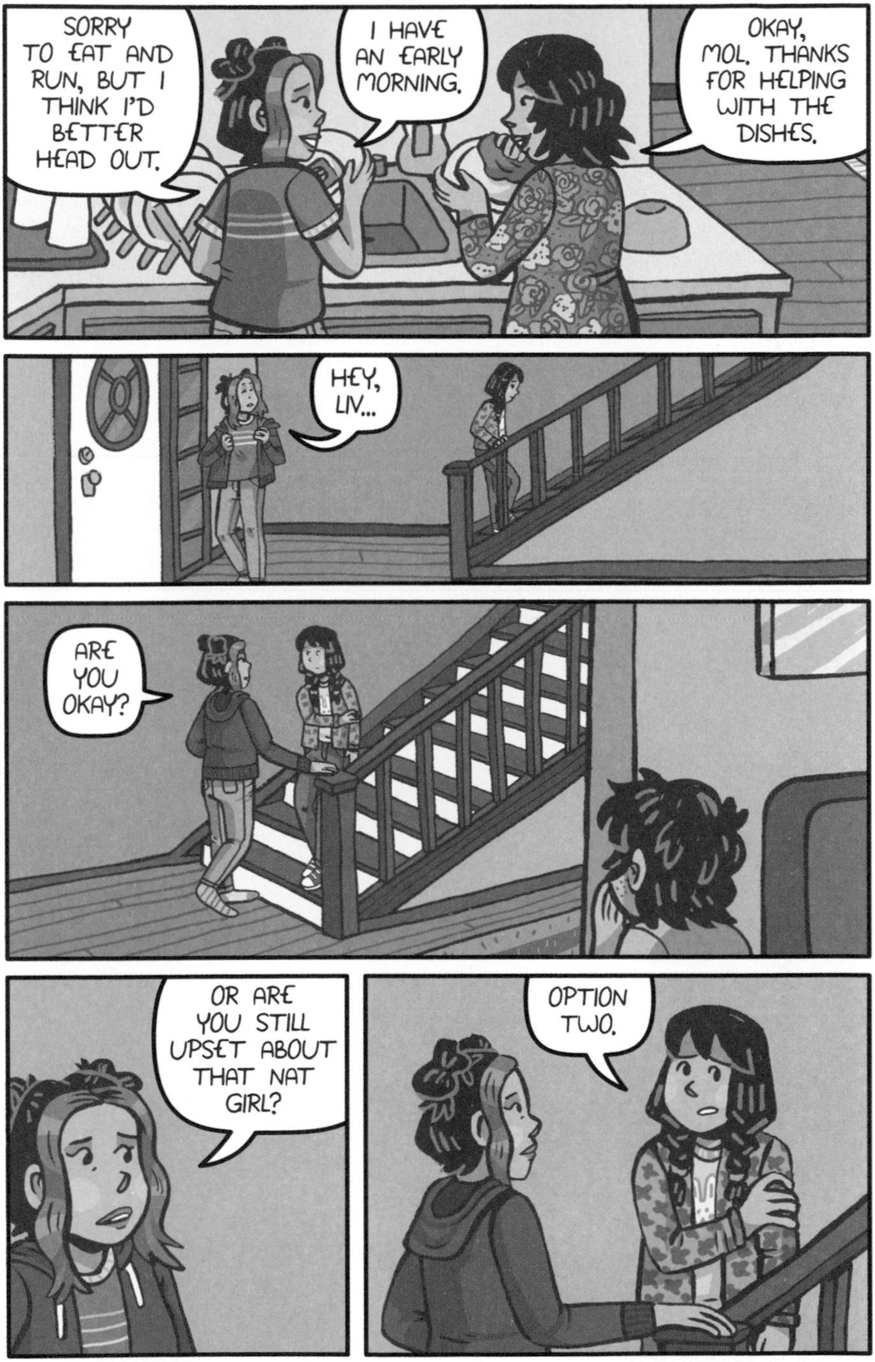
SORRY TO EAT AND RUN, BUT I THINK I'D BETTER HEAD OUT.
I HAVE AN EARLY MORNING.
OKAY, MOL. THANKS FOR HELPING WITH THE DISHES.
HEY, LIV...
ARE YOU OKAY?
OR ARE YOU STILL UPSET ABOUT THAT NAT GIRL?
OPTION TWO.

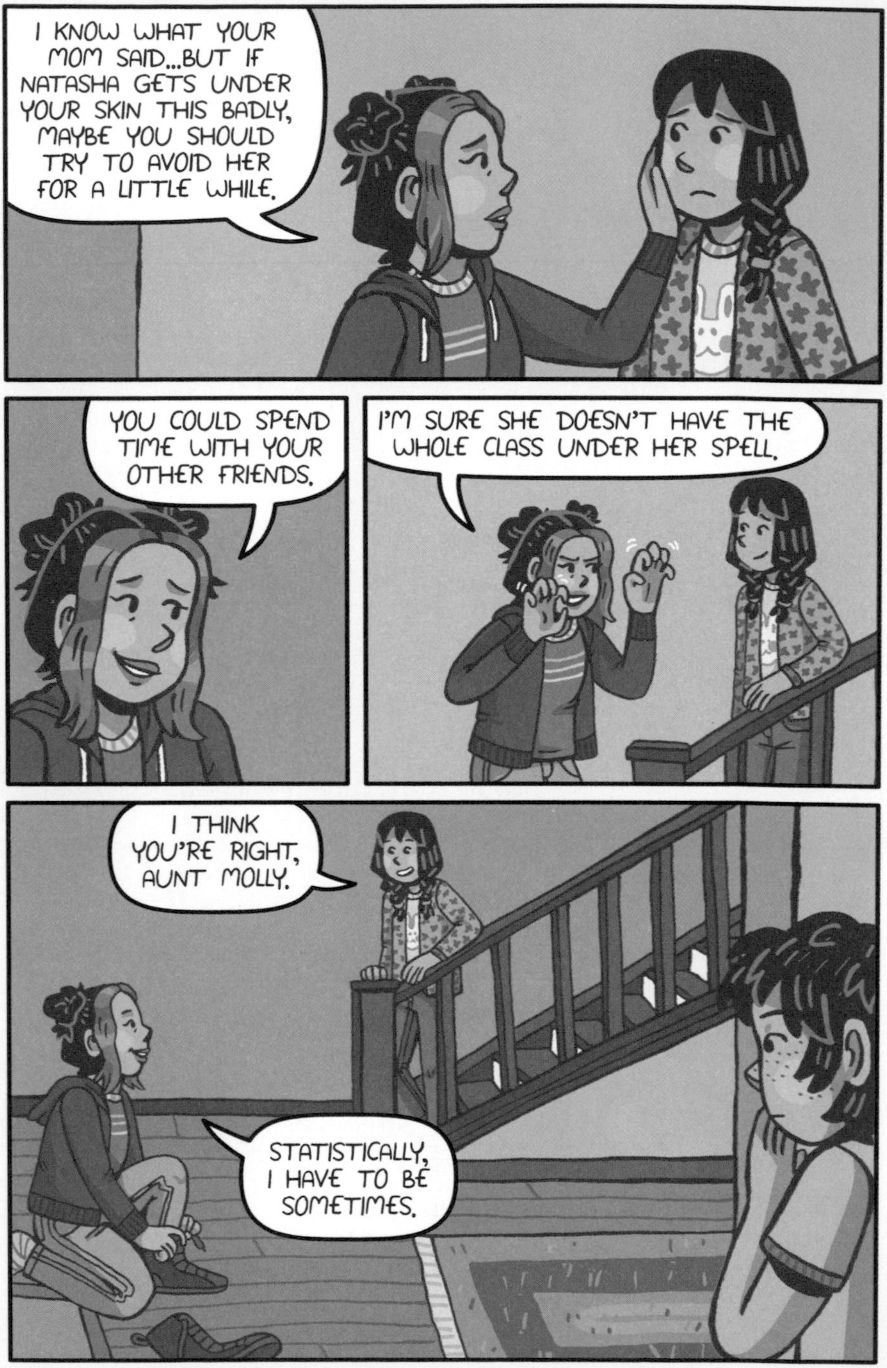
I KNOW WHAT YOUR MOM SAID...BUT IF NATASHA GETS UNDER YOUR SKIN THIS BADLY, MAYBE YOU SHOULD TRY TO AVOID HER FOR A LITTLE WHILE.
YOU COULD SPEND TIME WITH YOUR OTHER FRIENDS.
I'M SURE SHE DOESN'T HAVE THE WHOLE CLASS UNDER HER SPELL.
I THINK YOU'RE RIGHT, AUNT MOLLY.
STATISTICALLY, I HAVE TO BE SOMETIMES.

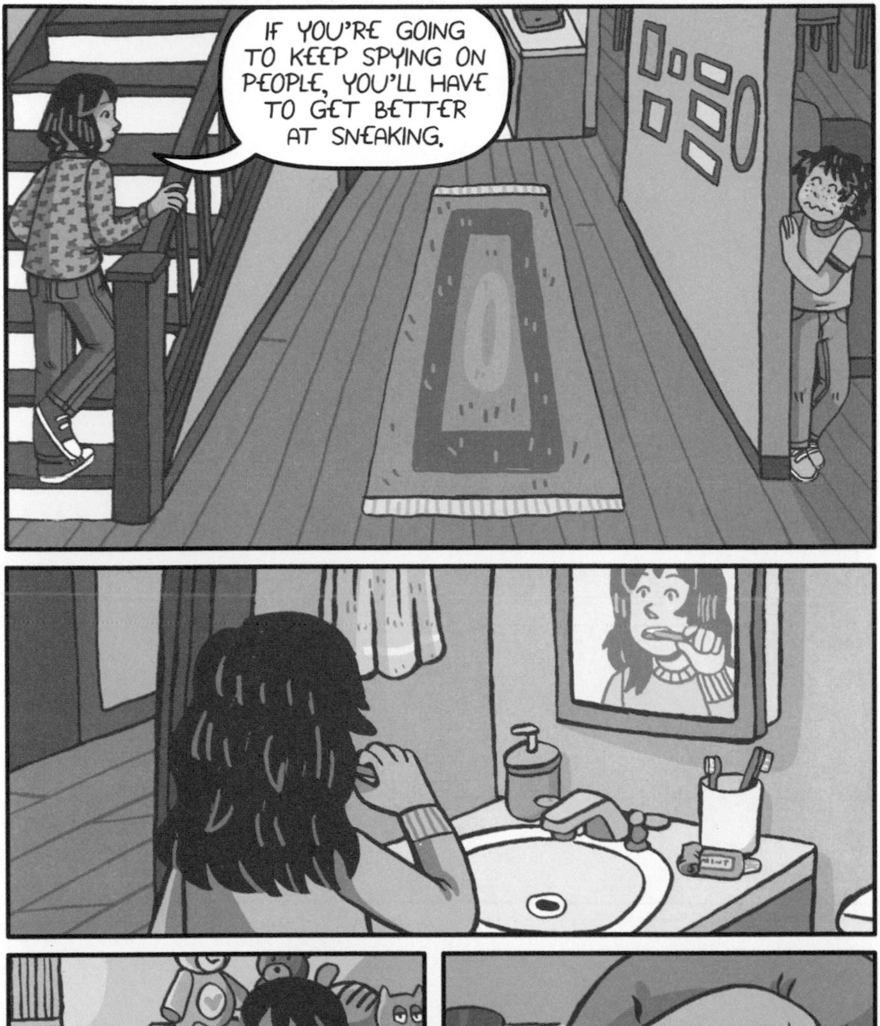
IF YOU'RE GOING TO KEEP SPYING ON PEOPLE, YOU'LL HAVE TO GET BETTER AT SNEAKING.

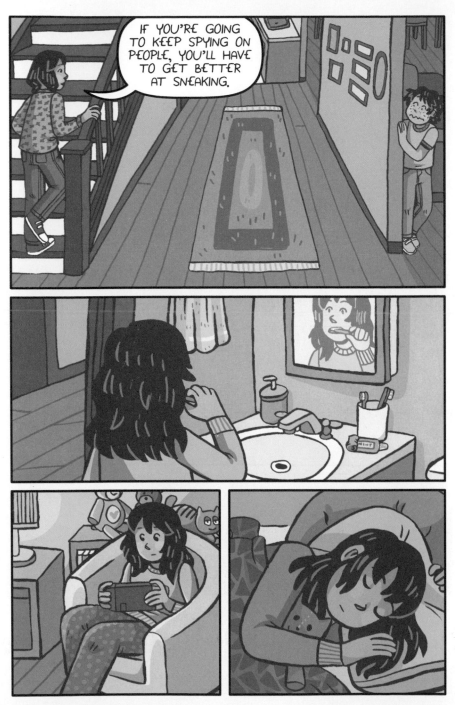

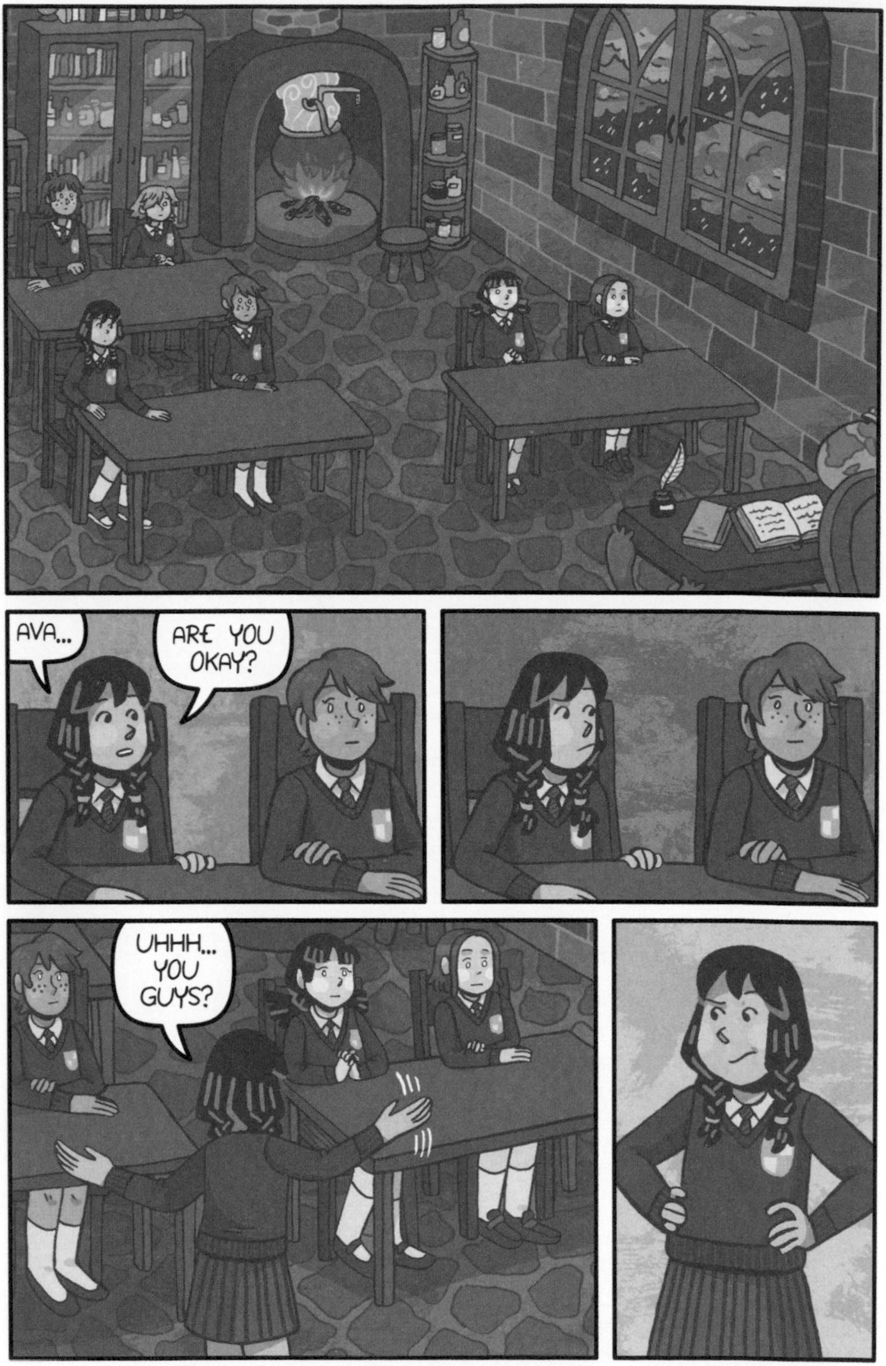
AVA...
ARE YOU OKAY?
UHHH... YOU GUYS?

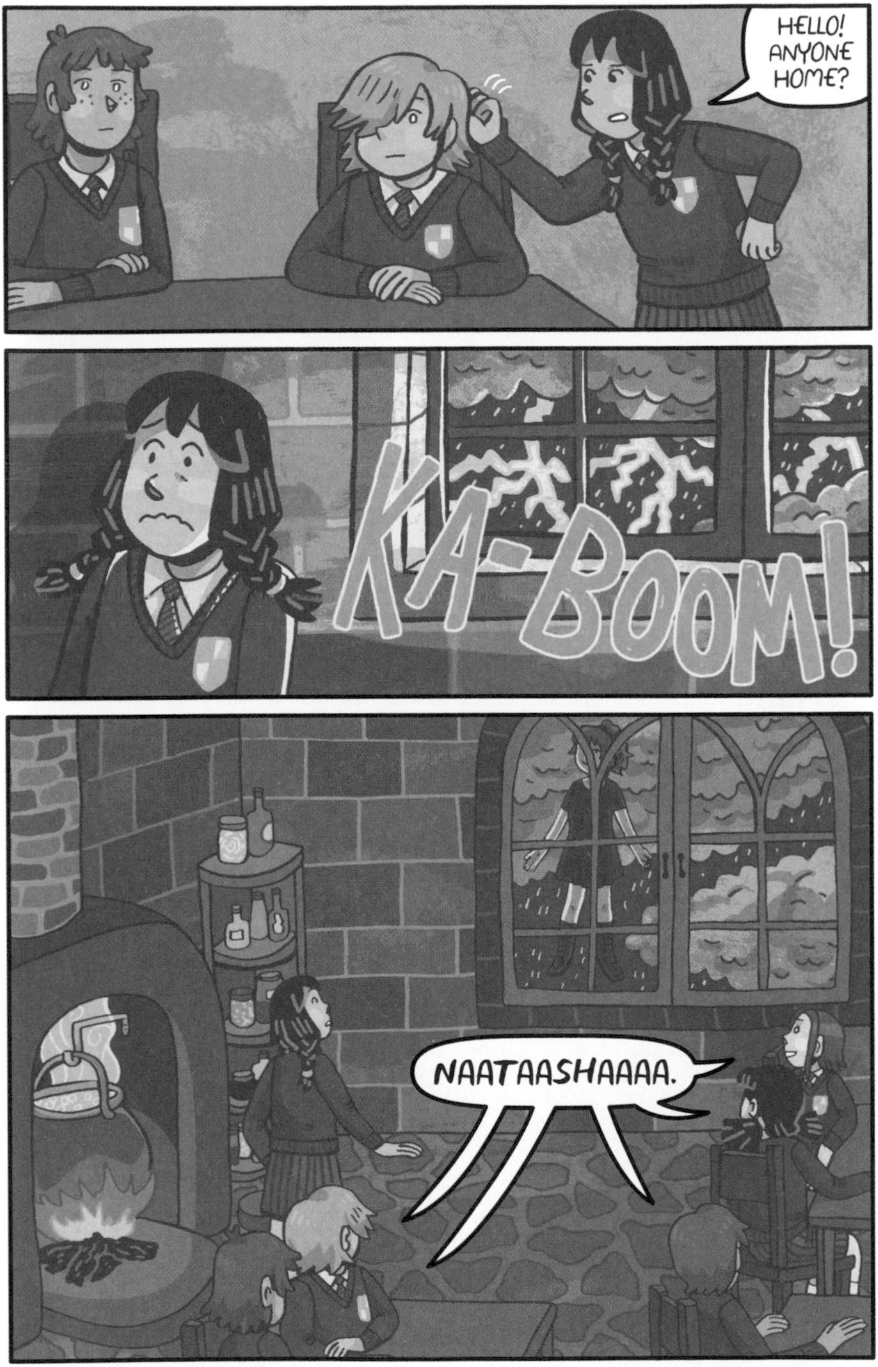
HELLO! ANYONE HOME?
KA-BOOM!
NAATAASHAAAA.

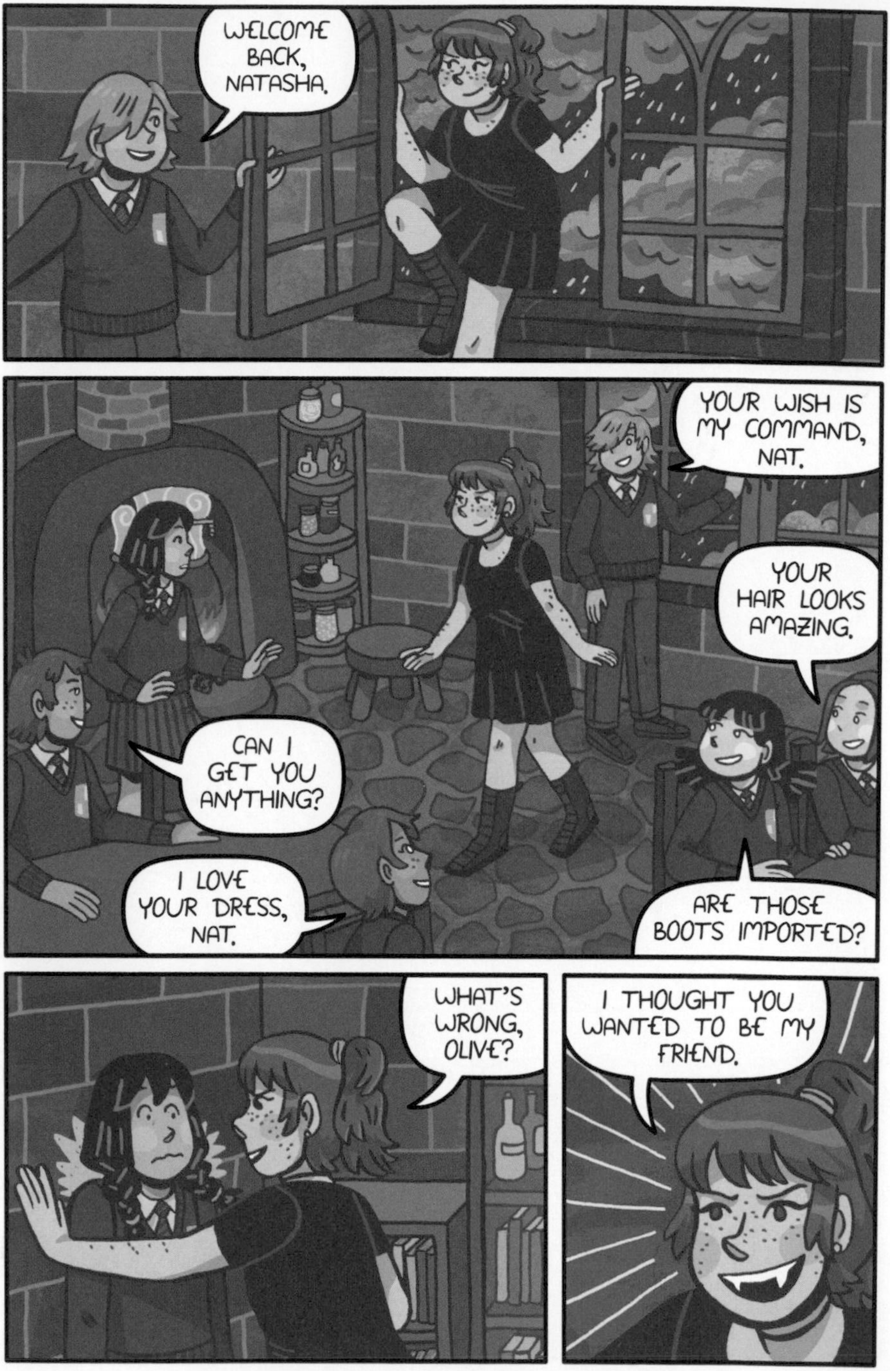

WELCOME BACK, NATASHA.
YOUR WISH IS MY COMMAND, NAT.
YOUR HAIR LOOKS AMAZING.
CAN I GET YOU ANYTHING?
I LOVE YOUR DRESS, NAT.
ARE THOSE BOOTS IMPORTED?
WHAT'S WRONG, OLIVE?
I THOUGHT YOU WANTED TO BE MY FRIEND.

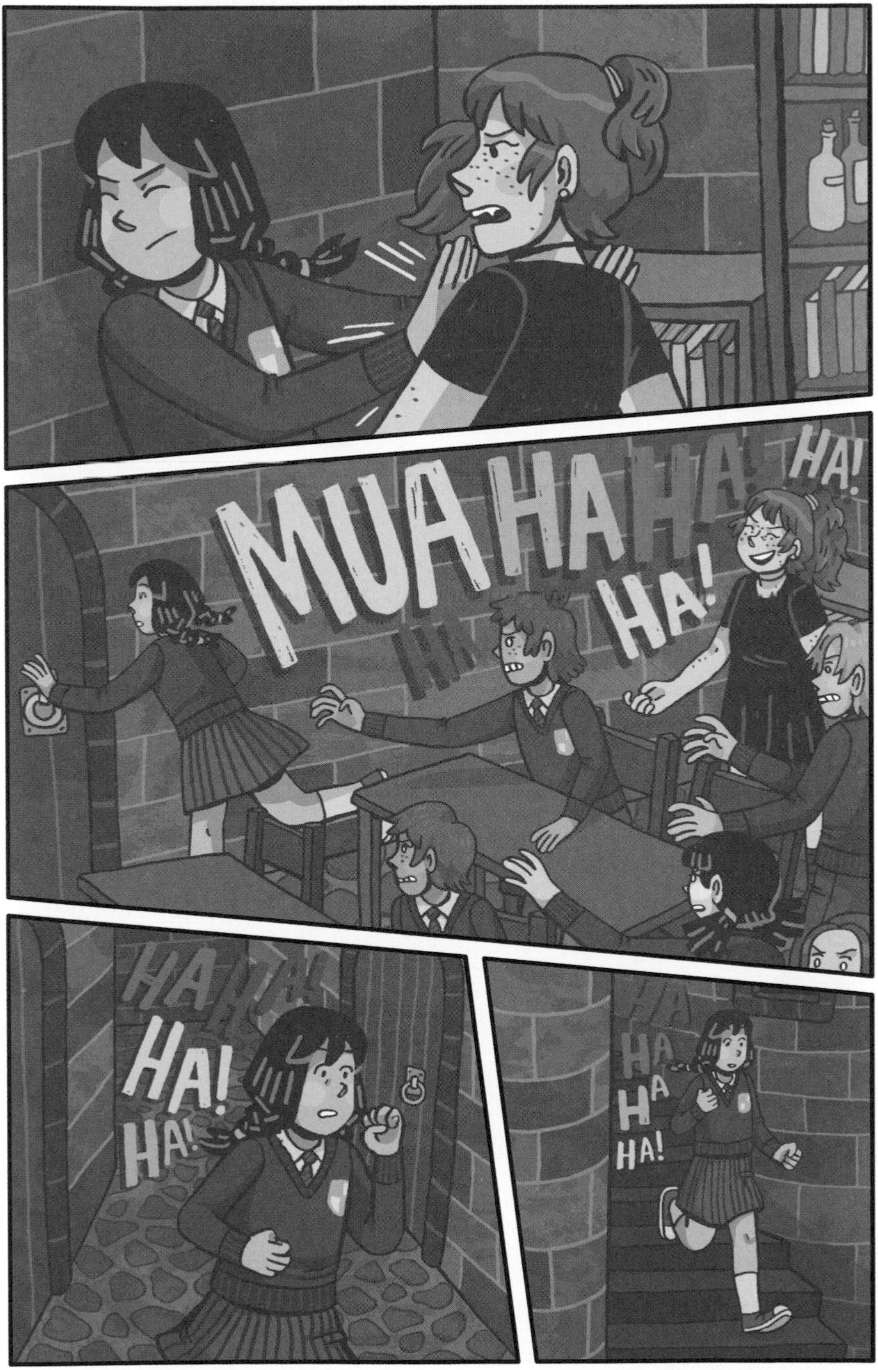
MUAHAHA! HA!
HA HA HA!
HA!
HAHA!
HA!
HA!
HA
HA
HA
HA
HA!

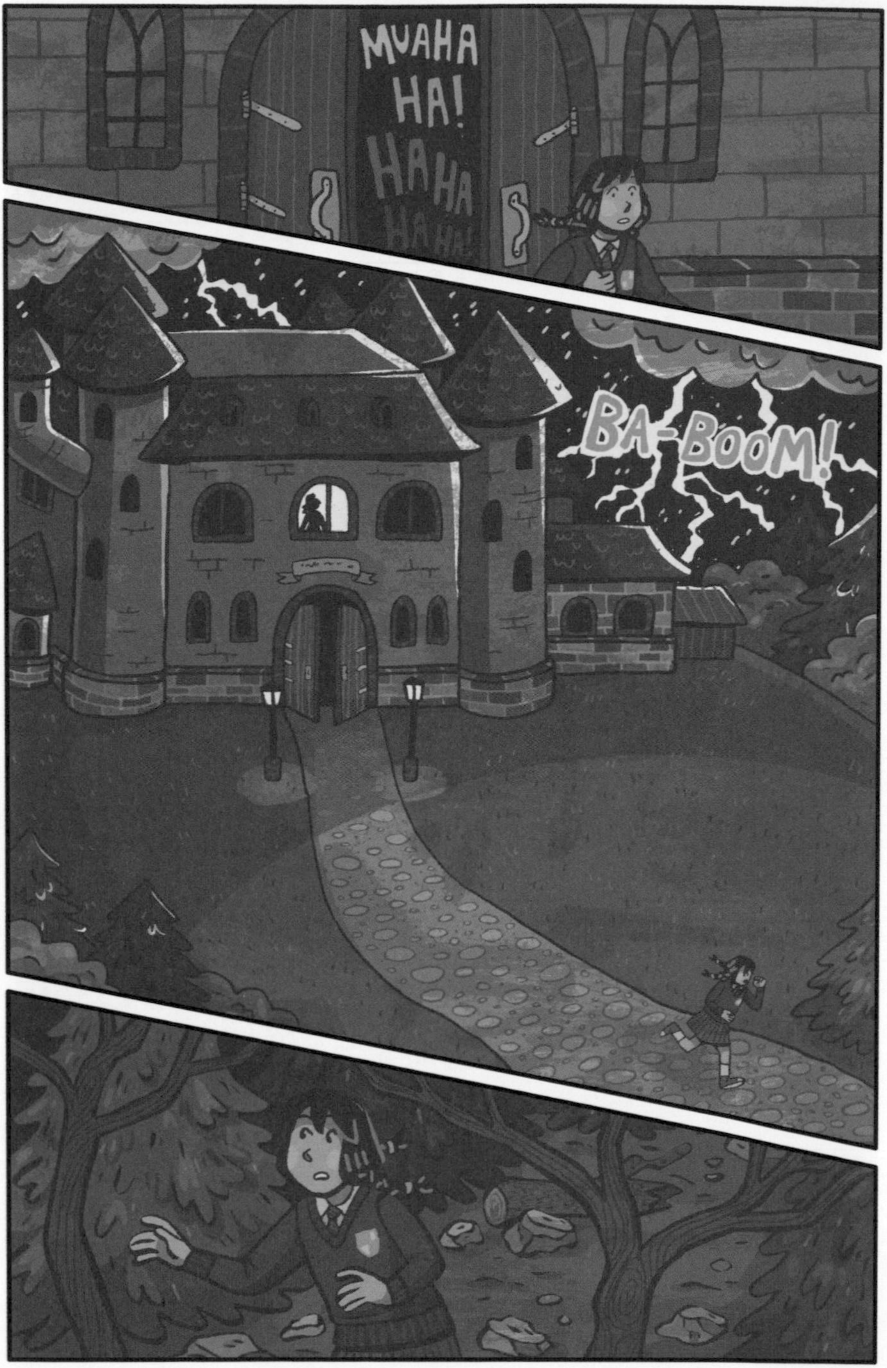
MUAHA HA! HAHA HAHA!
BA-BOOM!

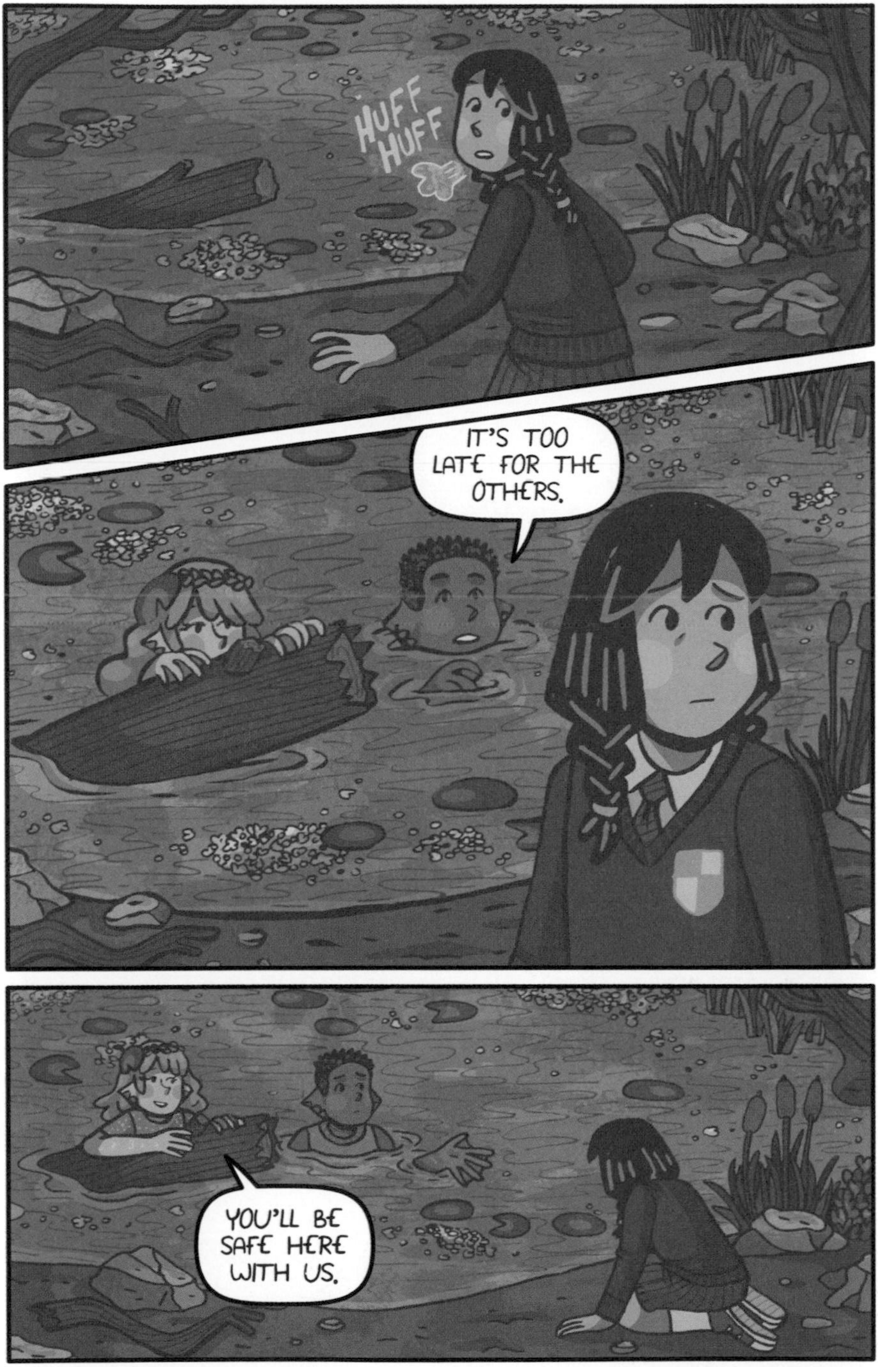
HUFF HUFF
IT'S TOO LATE FOR THE OTHERS.
YOU'LL BE SAFE HERE WITH US.

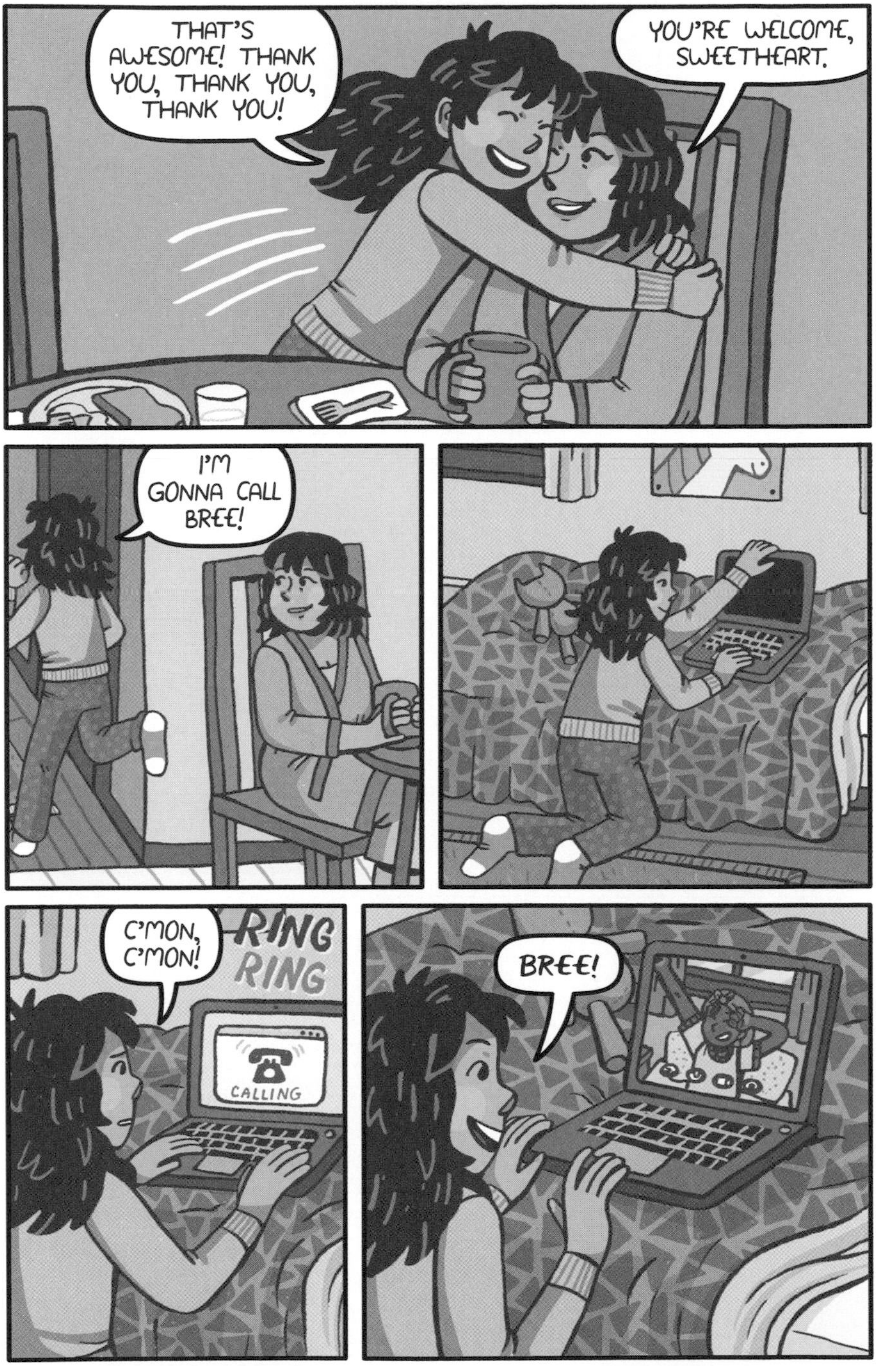
THAT'S AWESOME! THANK YOU, THANK YOU, THANK YOU!
YOU'RE WELCOME, SWEETHEART.
I'M GONNA CALL BREE!
C'MON, C'MON!
RING RING
CALLING
BREE!

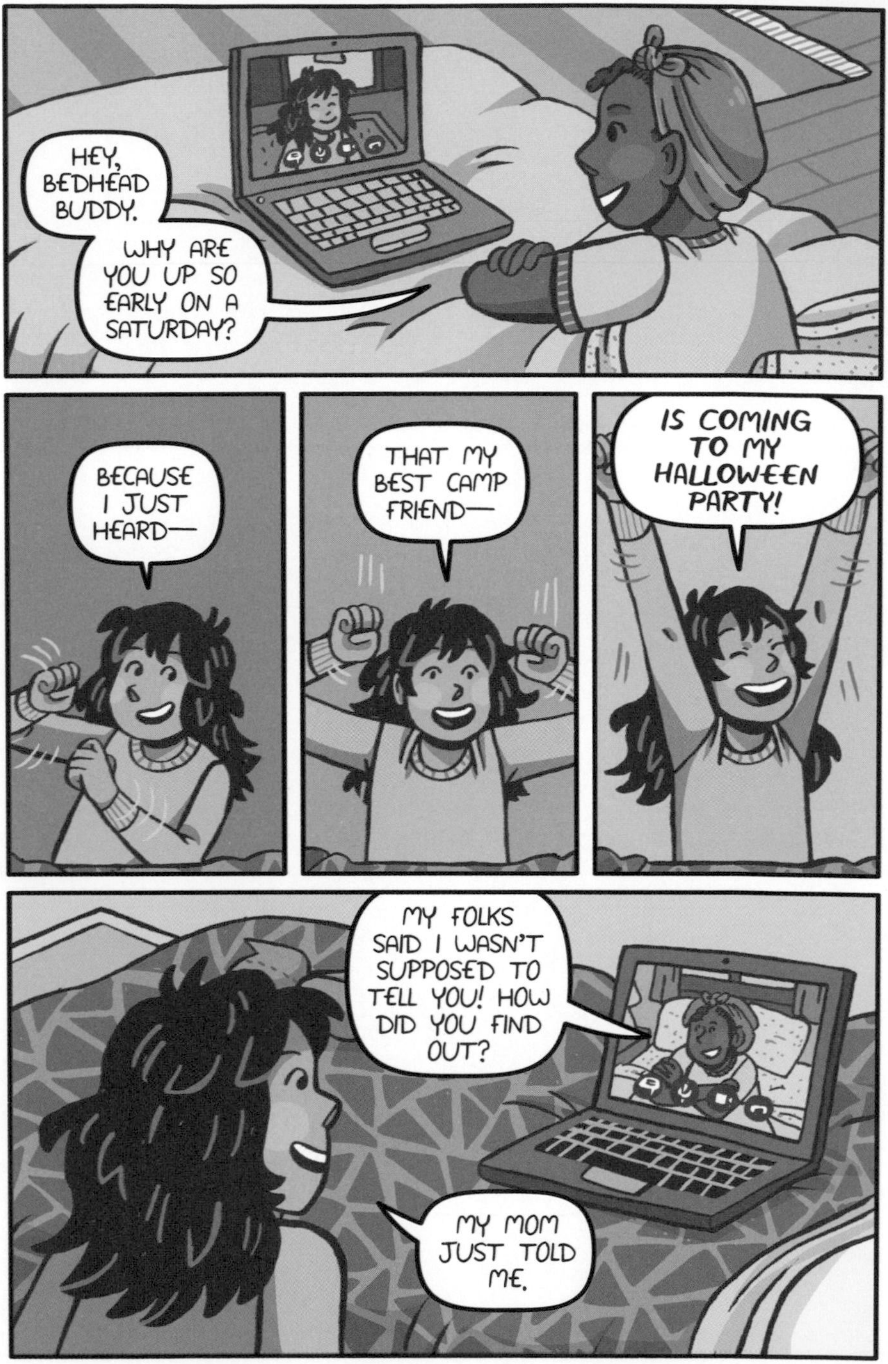
HEY, BEDHEAD BUDDY.
WHY ARE YOU UP SO EARLY ON A SATURDAY?
BECAUSE I JUST HEARD—
THAT MY BEST CAMP FRIEND—
IS COMING TO MY HALLOWEEN PARTY!
MY FOLKS SAID I WASN'T SUPPOSED TO TELL YOU! HOW DID YOU FIND OUT?
MY MOM JUST TOLD ME.

97

98

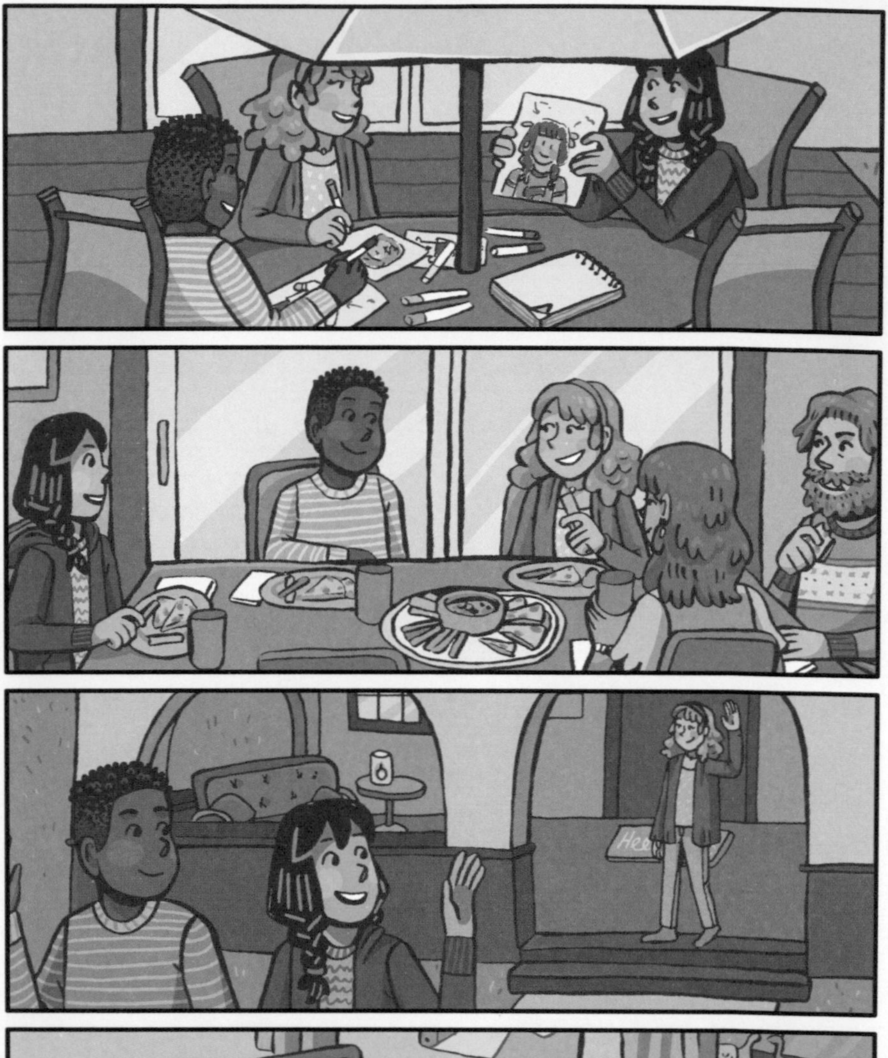

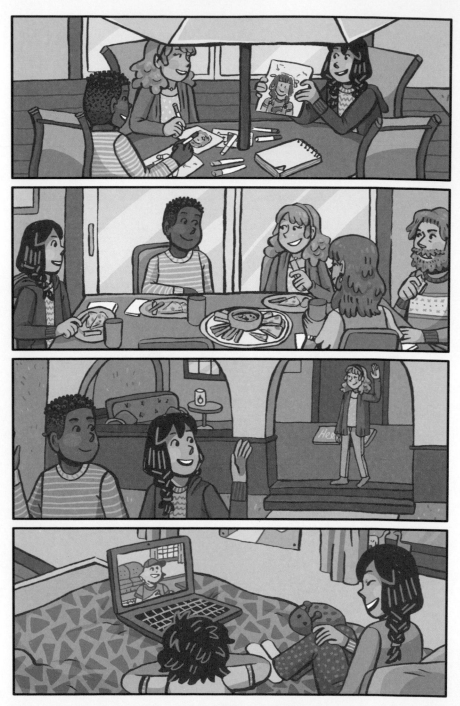

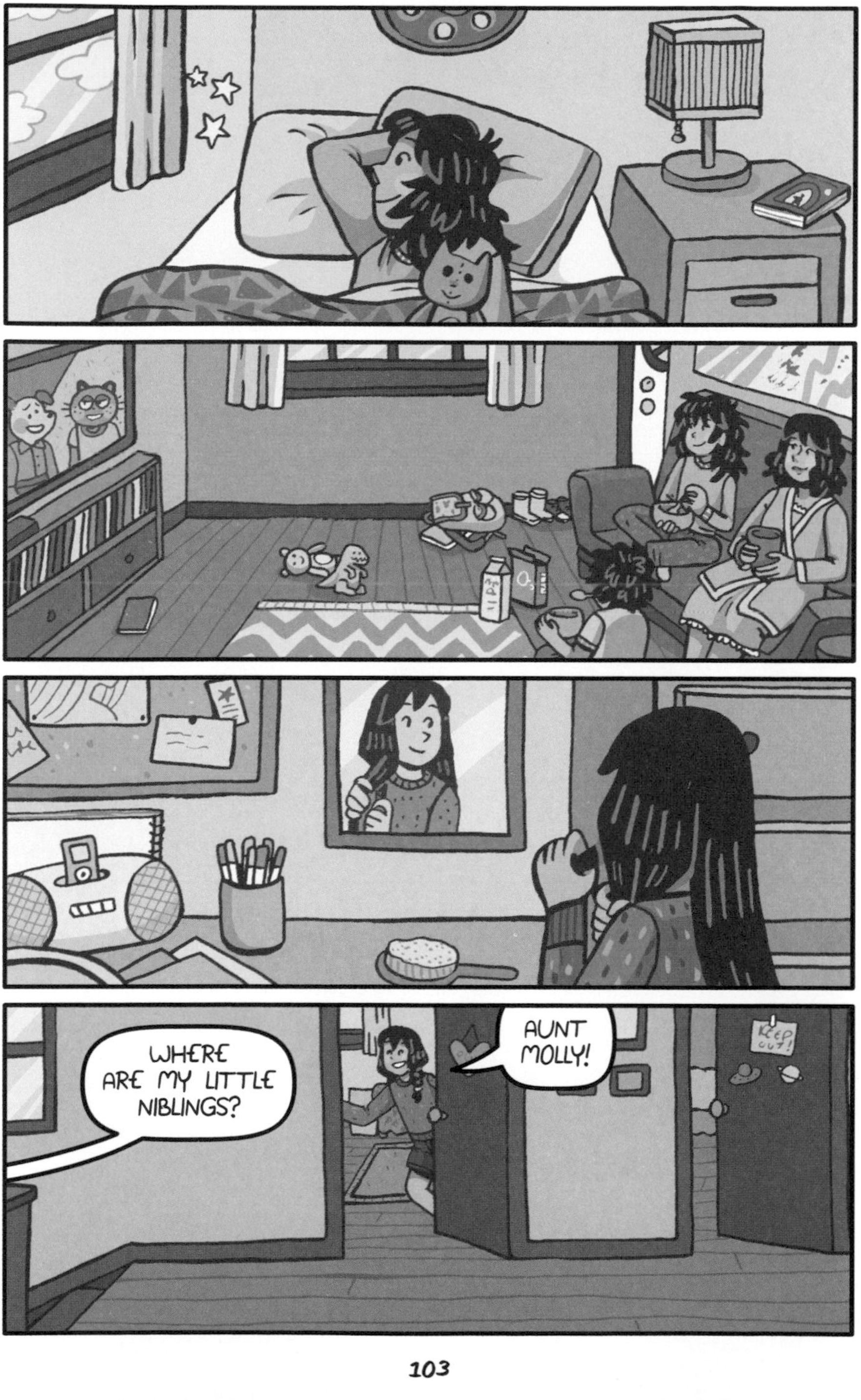
WHERE ARE MY LITTLE NIBLINGS?
AUNT MOLLY!
KEEP OUT!

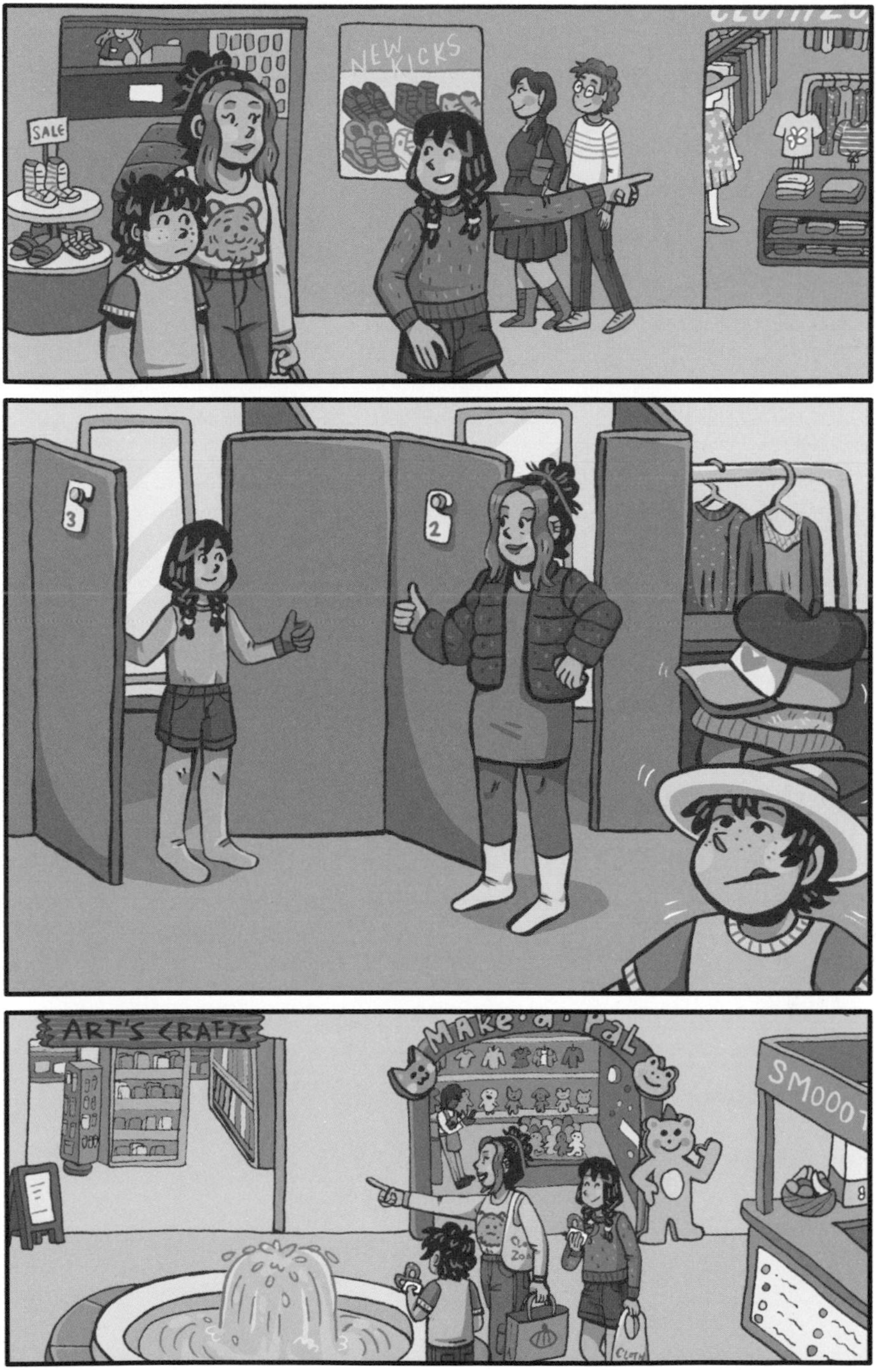
SALE
NEW KICKS
3
2
ART'S CRAFTS
Make·a·Pal

109

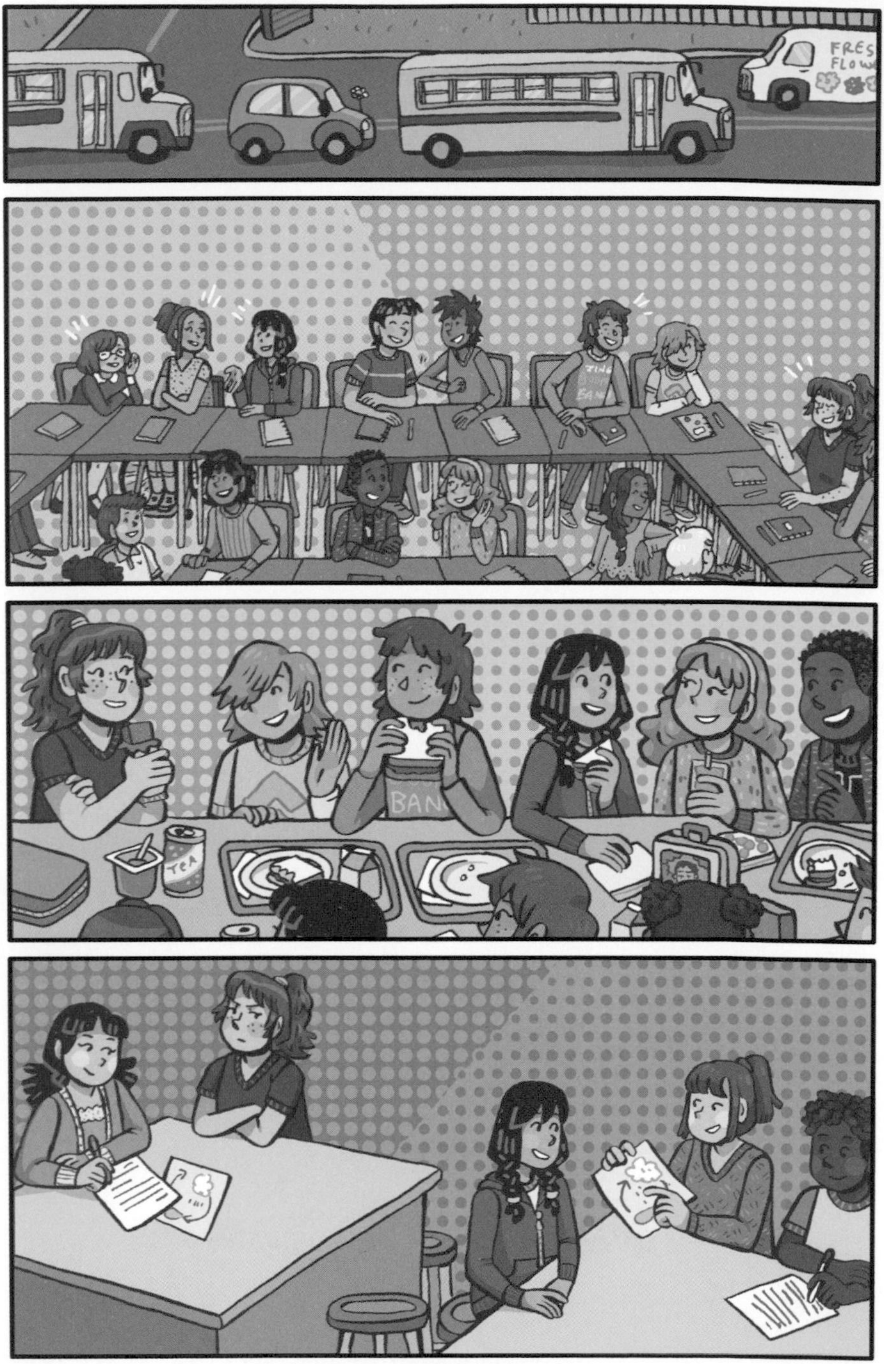
FRES
FLOW
TEA
BAN

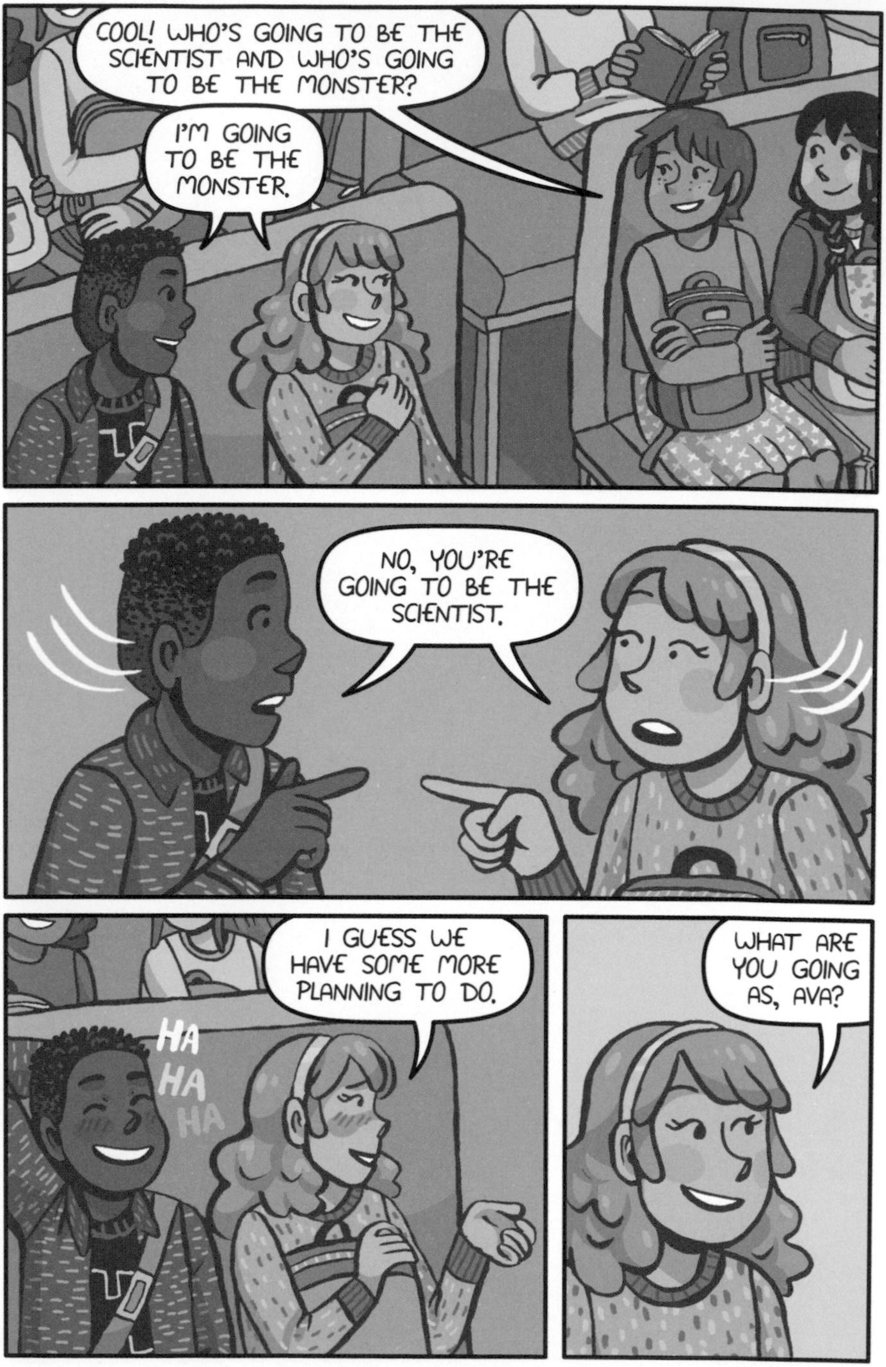
COOL! WHO'S GOING TO BE THE SCIENTIST AND WHO'S GOING TO BE THE MONSTER?
I'M GOING TO BE THE MONSTER.
NO, YOU'RE GOING TO BE THE SCIENTIST.
HA HA HA
I GUESS WE HAVE SOME MORE PLANNING TO DO.
WHAT ARE YOU GOING AS, AVA?

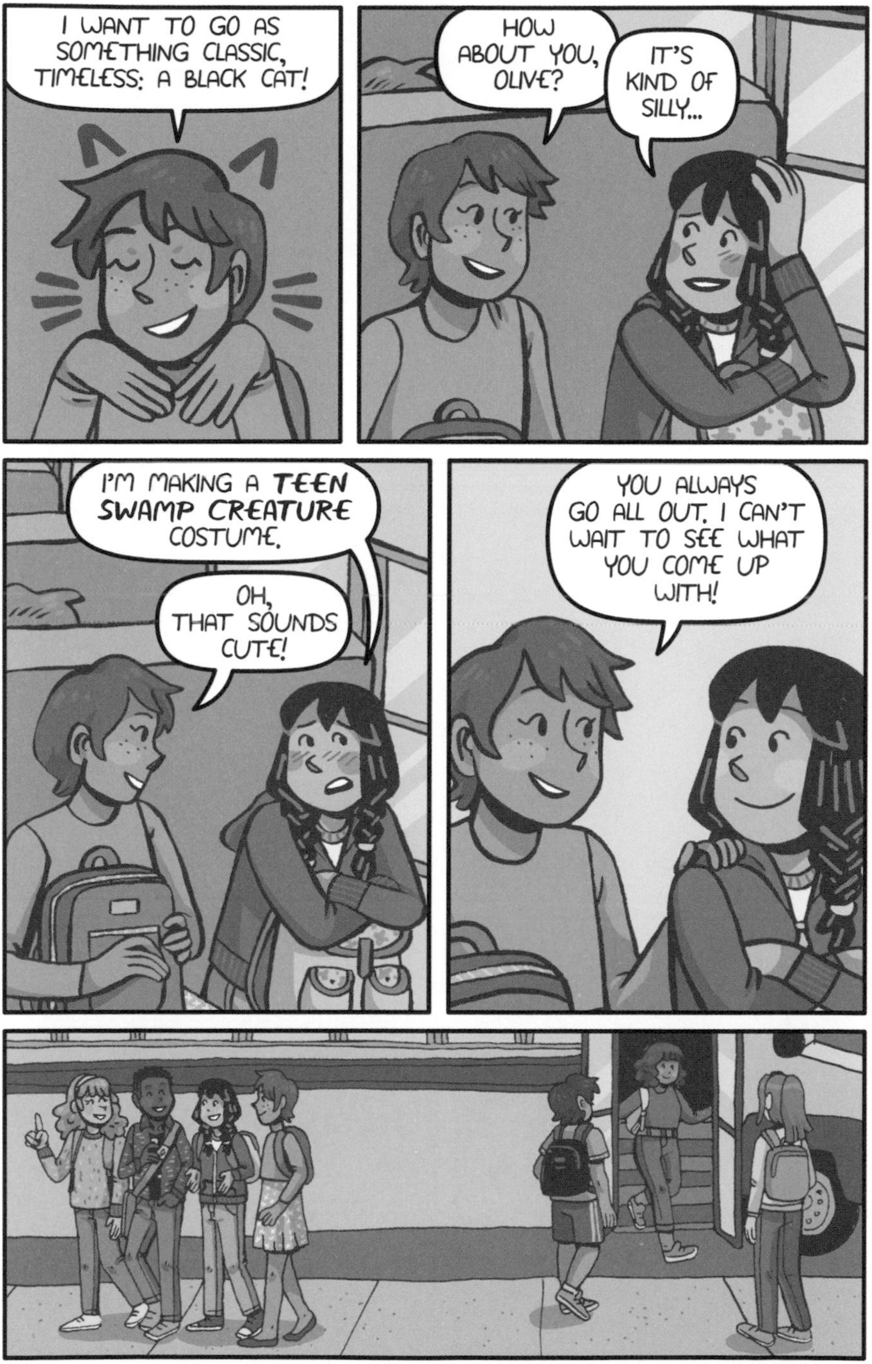
I WANT TO GO AS SOMETHING CLASSIC, TIMELESS: A BLACK CAT!
HOW ABOUT YOU, OLIVE?
IT'S KIND OF SILLY...
I'M MAKING A **TEEN SWAMP CREATURE** COSTUME.
OH, THAT SOUNDS CUTE!
YOU ALWAYS GO ALL OUT. I CAN'T WAIT TO SEE WHAT YOU COME UP WITH!

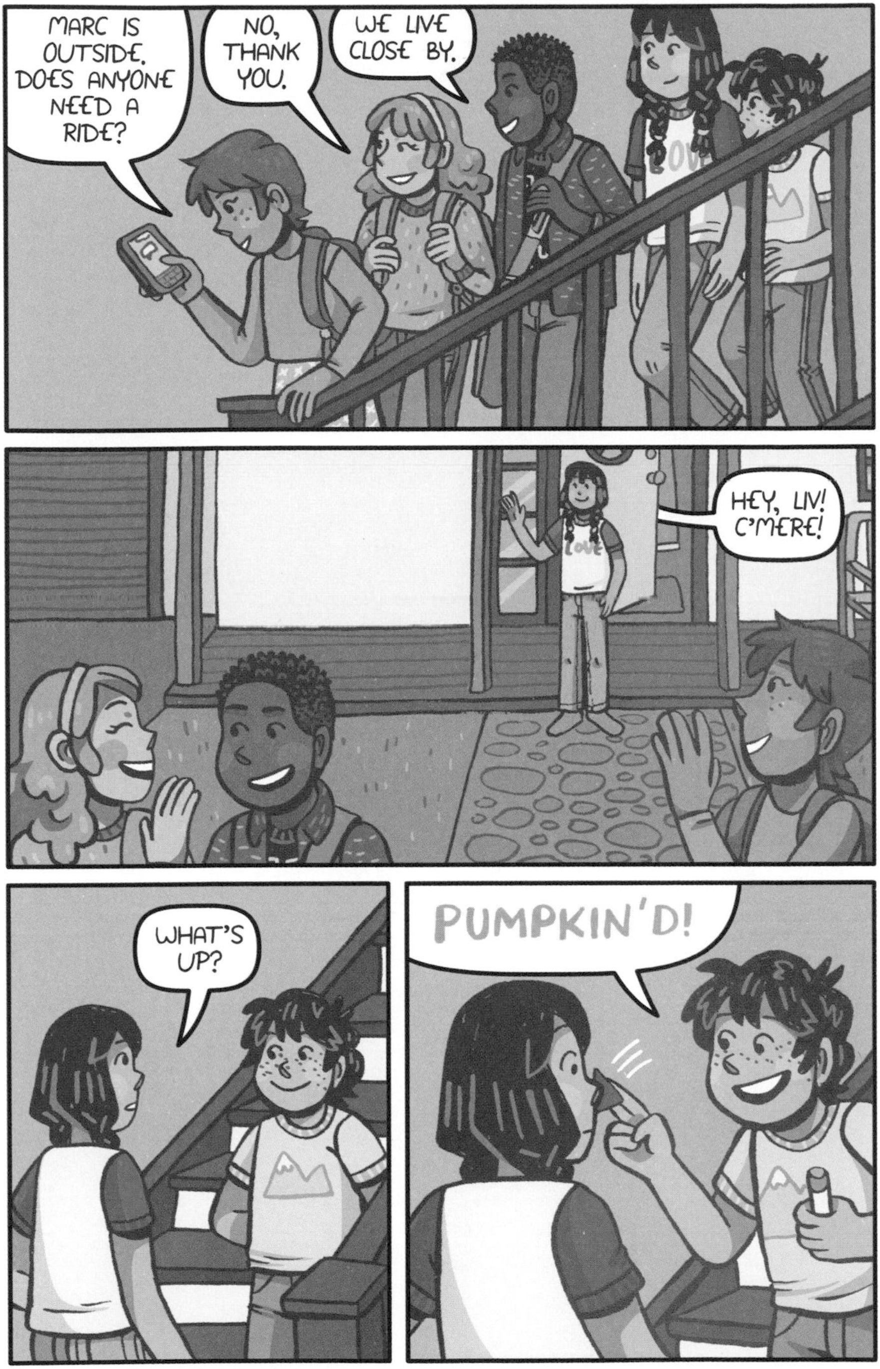
MARC IS OUTSIDE. DOES ANYONE NEED A RIDE?
NO, THANK YOU.
WE LIVE CLOSE BY.
HEY, LIV! C'MERE!
WHAT'S UP?
PUMPKIN'D!

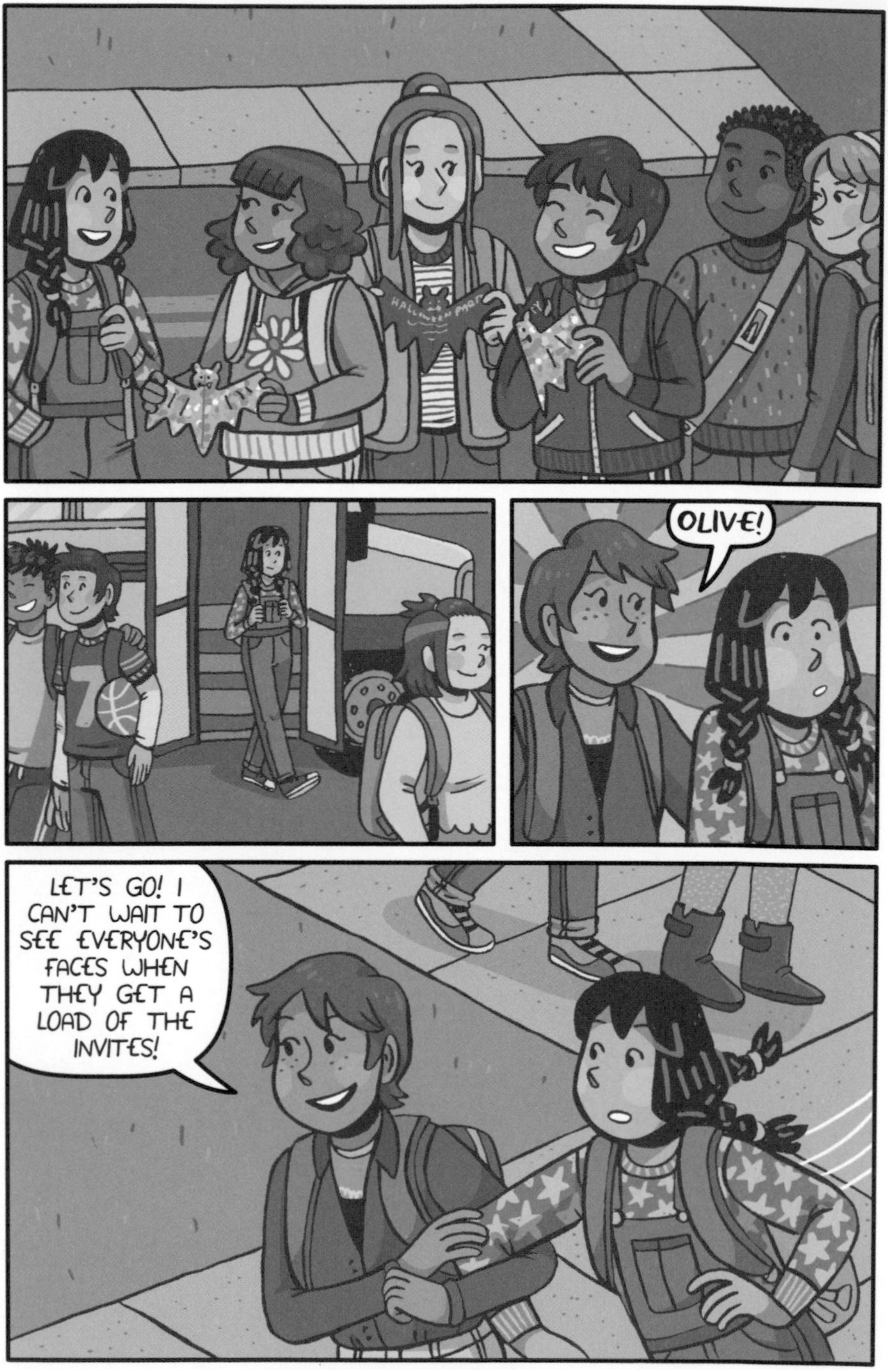
OLIVE!
LET'S GO! I CAN'T WAIT TO SEE EVERYONE'S FACES WHEN THEY GET A LOAD OF THE INVITES!

123

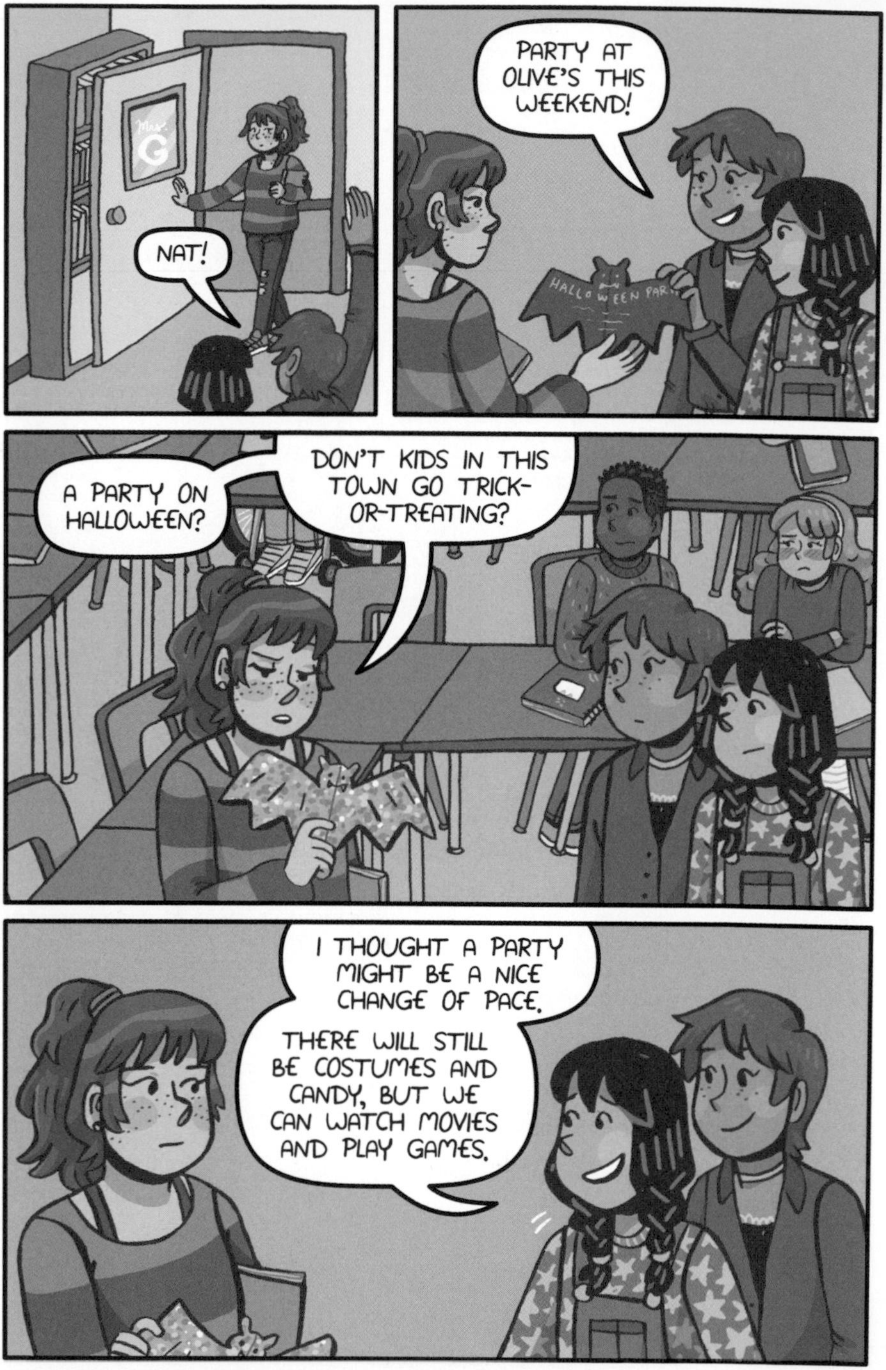
NAT!
PARTY AT OLIVE'S THIS WEEKEND!
A PARTY ON HALLOWEEN?
DON'T KIDS IN THIS TOWN GO TRICK-OR-TREATING?
I THOUGHT A PARTY MIGHT BE A NICE CHANGE OF PACE.
THERE WILL STILL BE COSTUMES AND CANDY, BUT WE CAN WATCH MOVIES AND PLAY GAMES.

125

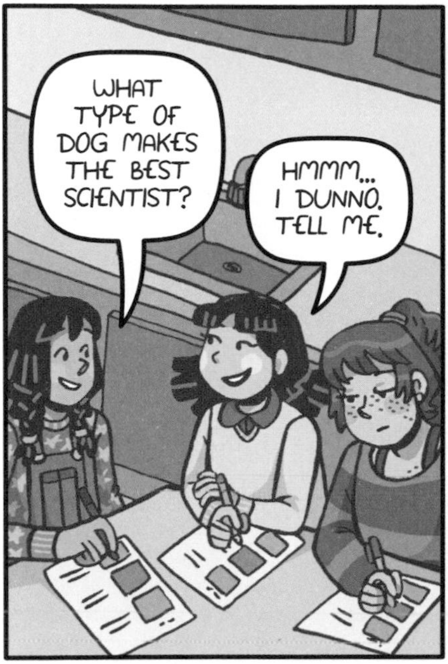
WHAT TYPE OF DOG MAKES THE BEST SCIENTIST?
HMMM... I DUNNO. TELL ME.

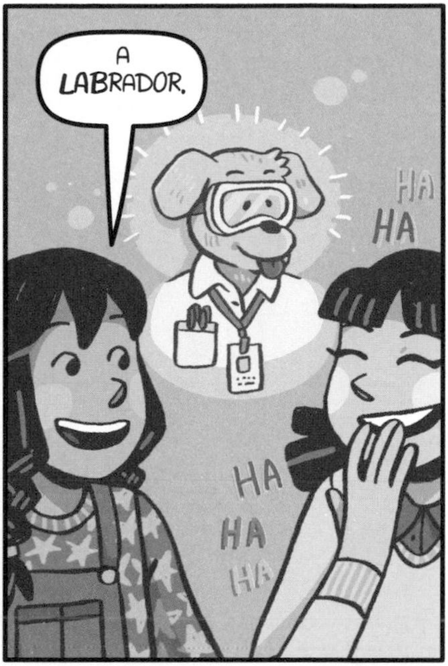
A LABRADOR.
HA HA
HA HA HA

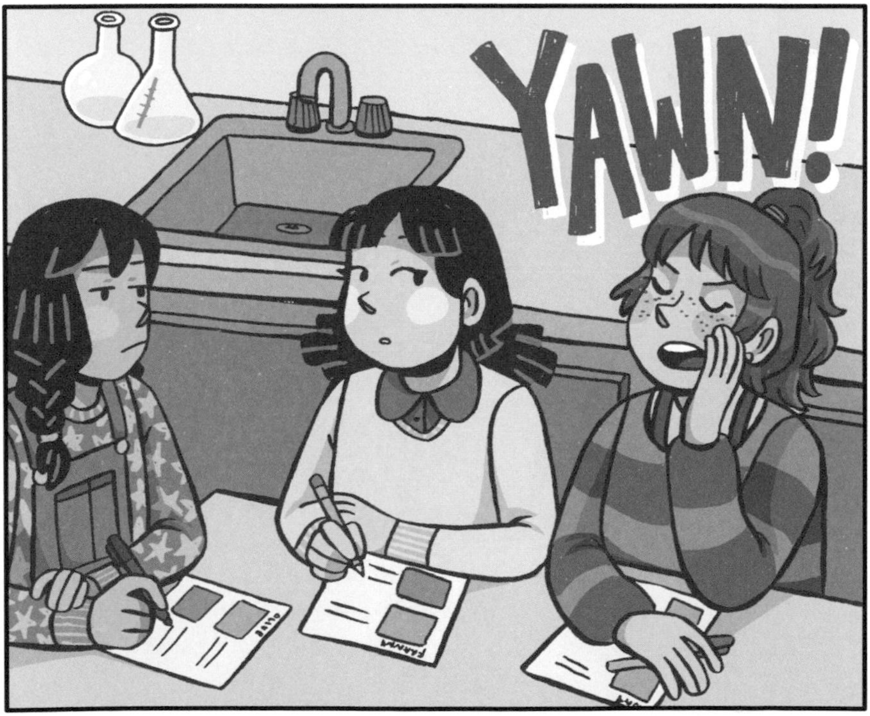
YAWN!

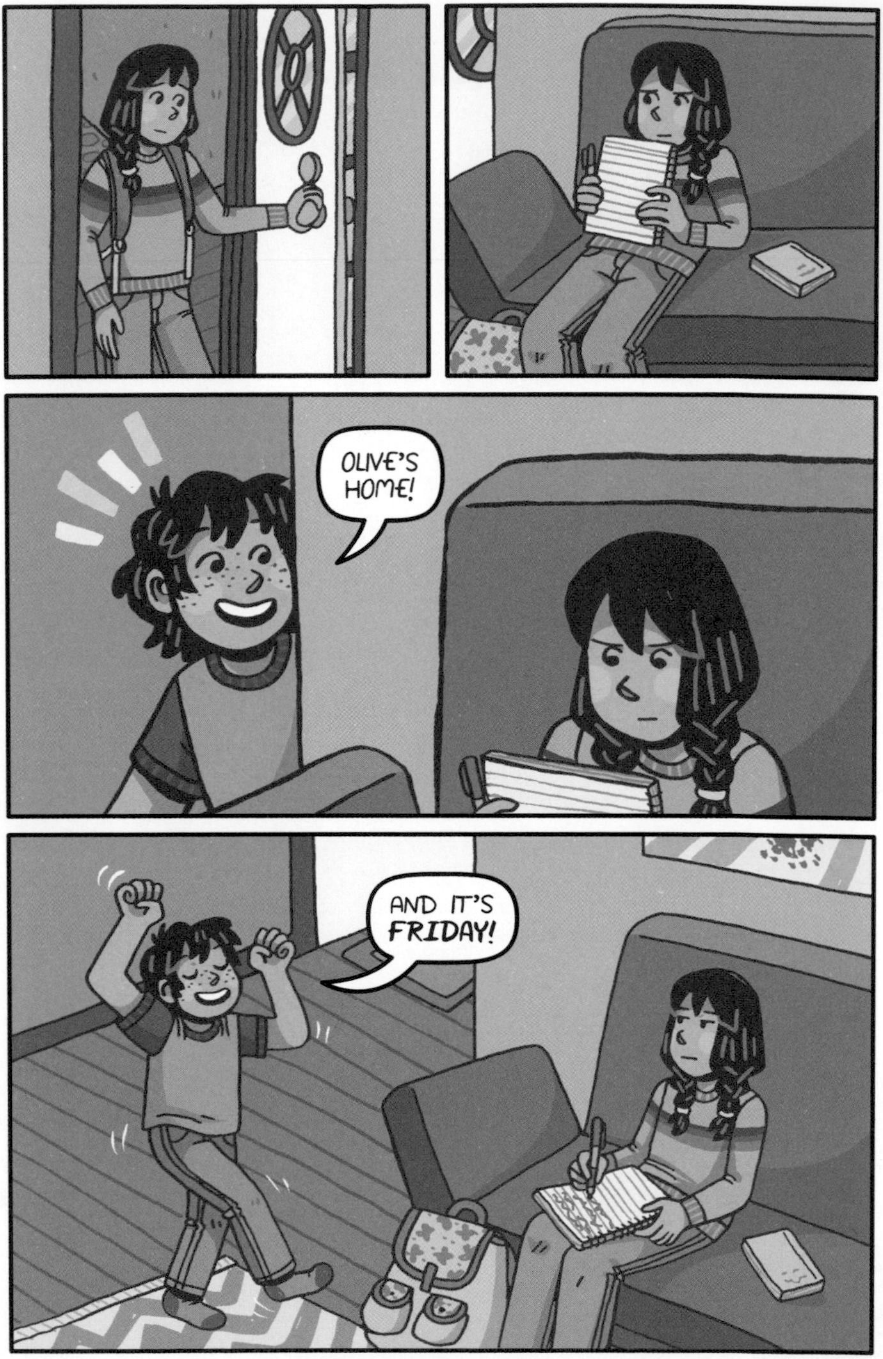
OLIVE'S HOME!
AND IT'S **FRIDAY**!

137

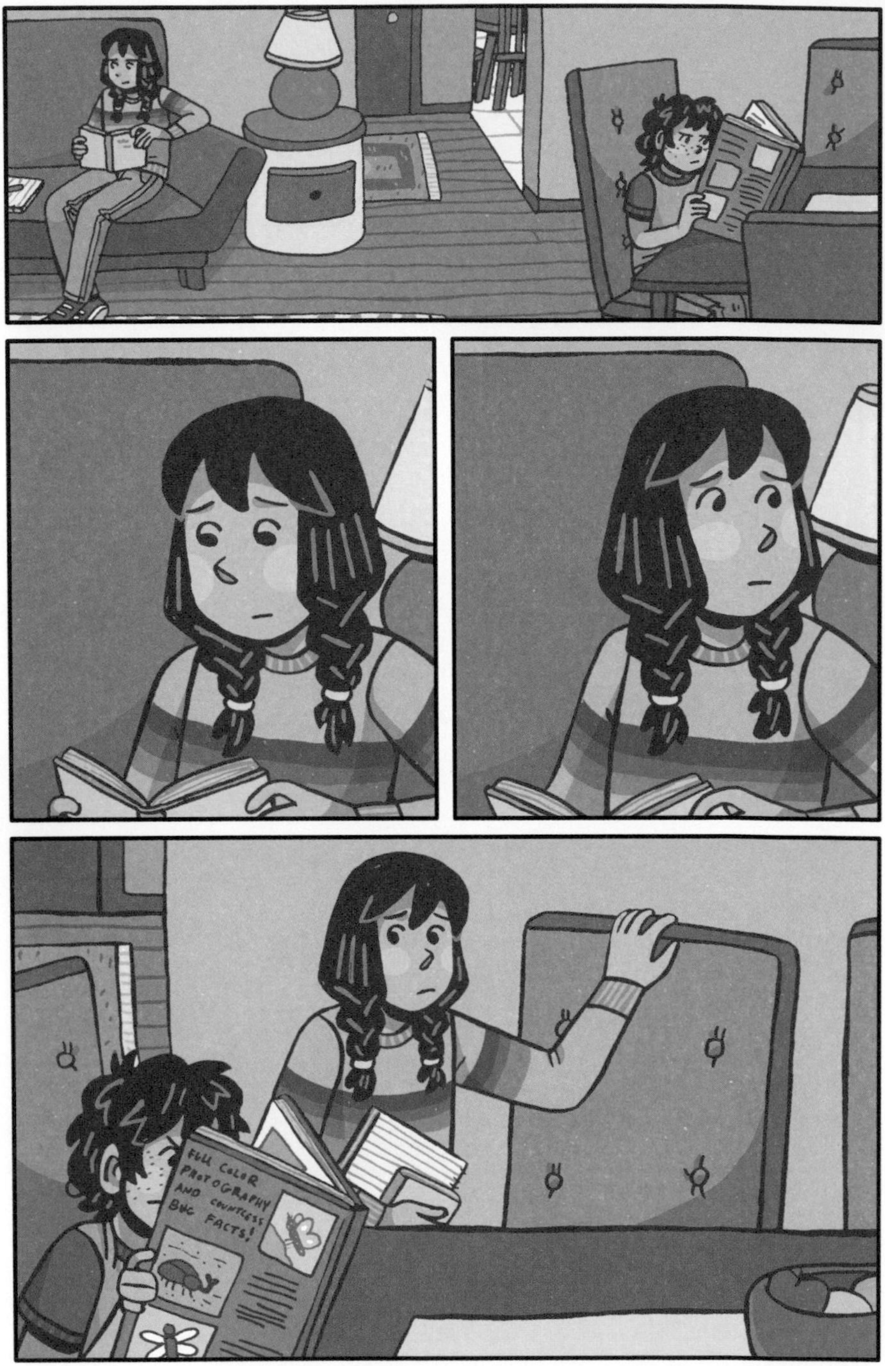
FULL COLOR PHOTOGRAPHY AND COUNTLESS BUG FACTS!

141

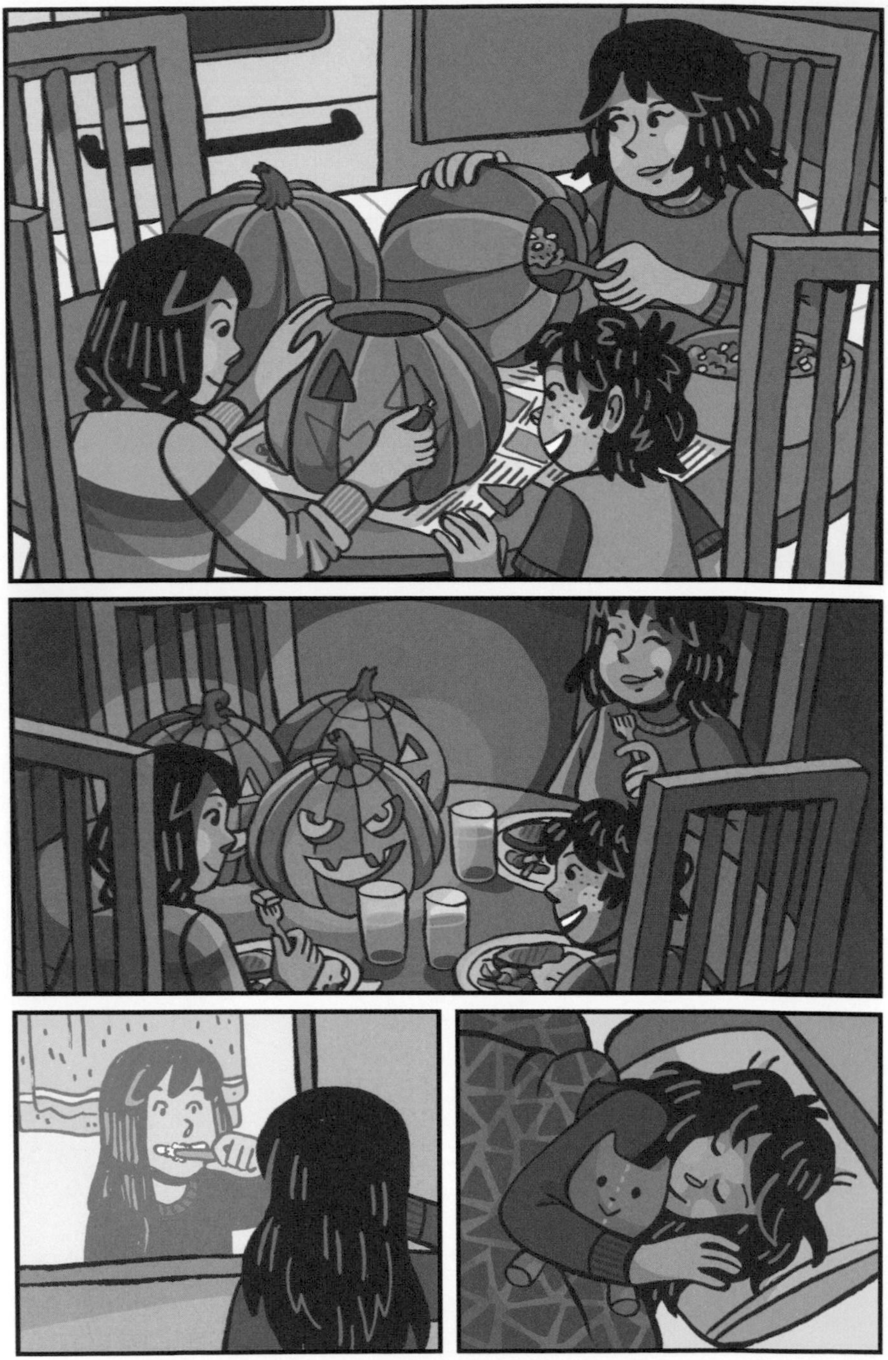

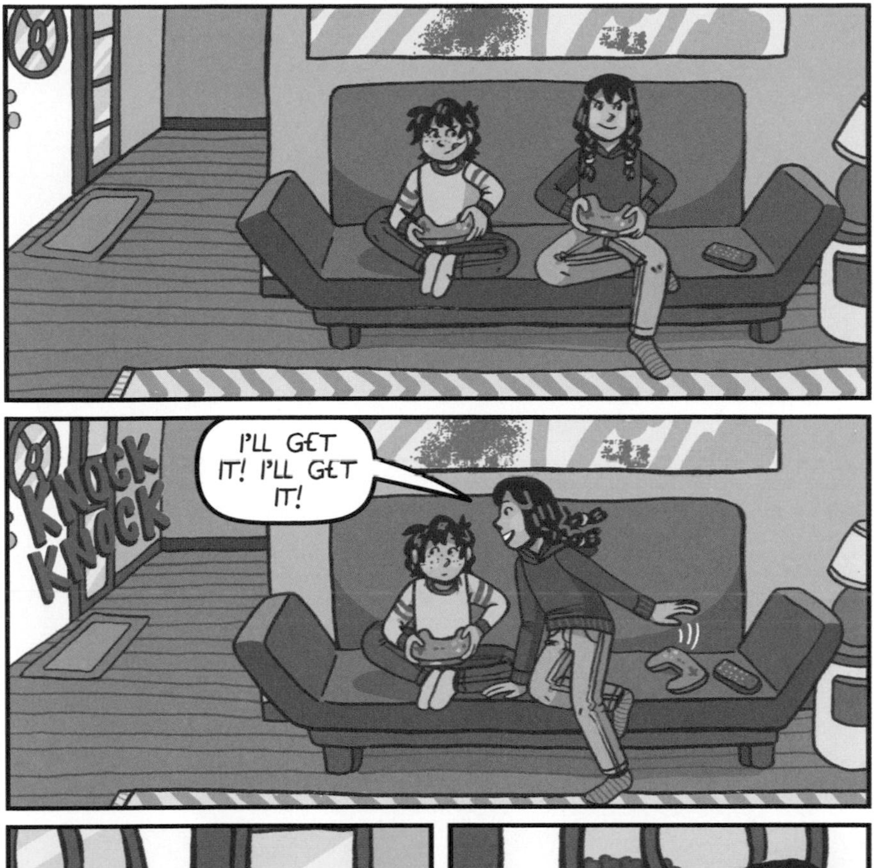
KNOCK KNOCK
I'LL GET IT! I'LL GET IT!

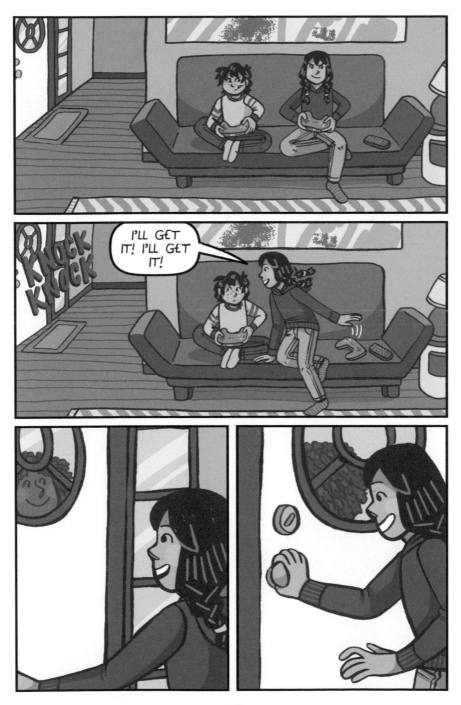

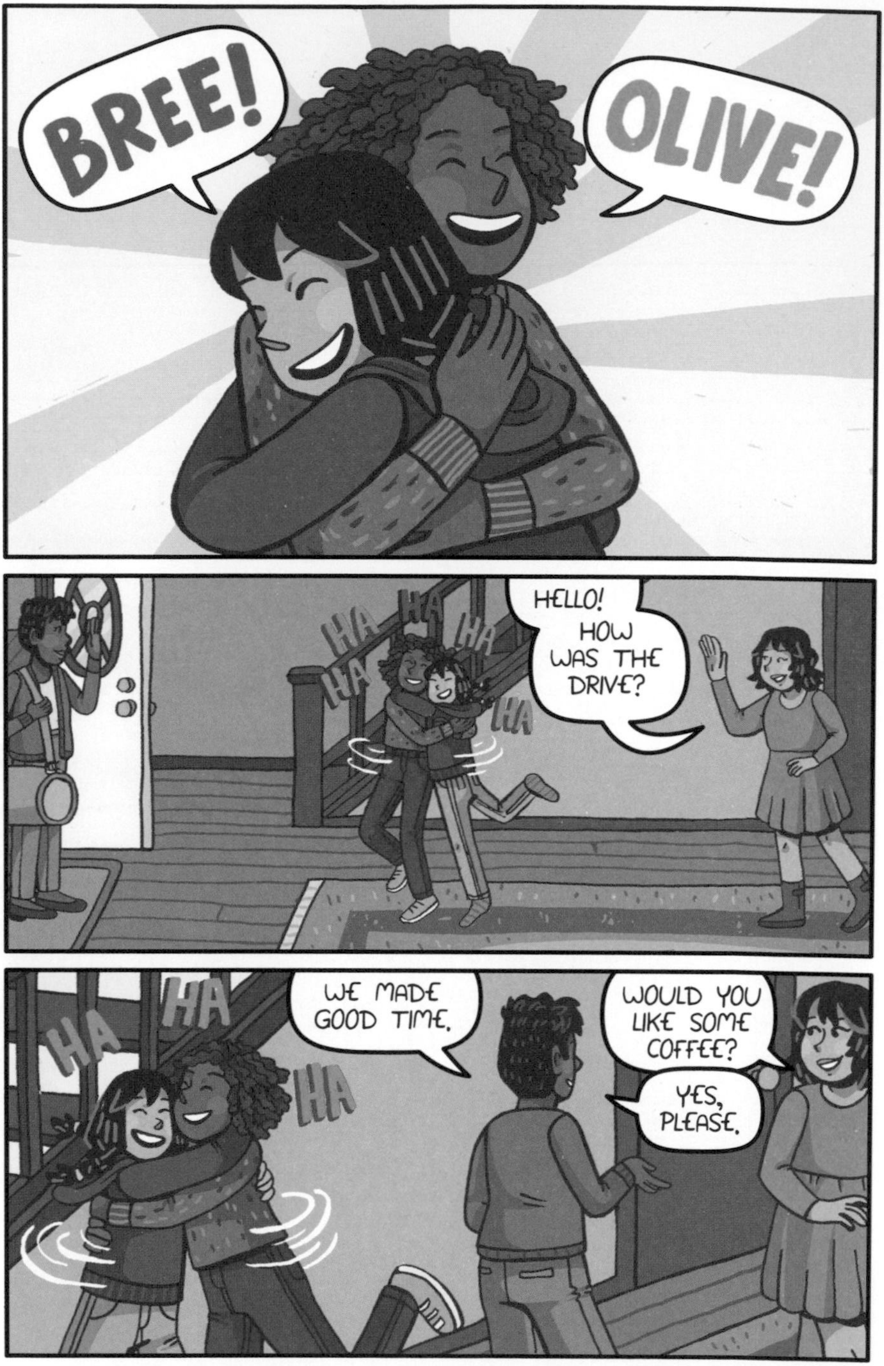
BREE!
OLIVE!
HA HA HA HA HA
HELLO! HOW WAS THE DRIVE?
HA HA HA
WE MADE GOOD TIME.
WOULD YOU LIKE SOME COFFEE?
YES, PLEASE.

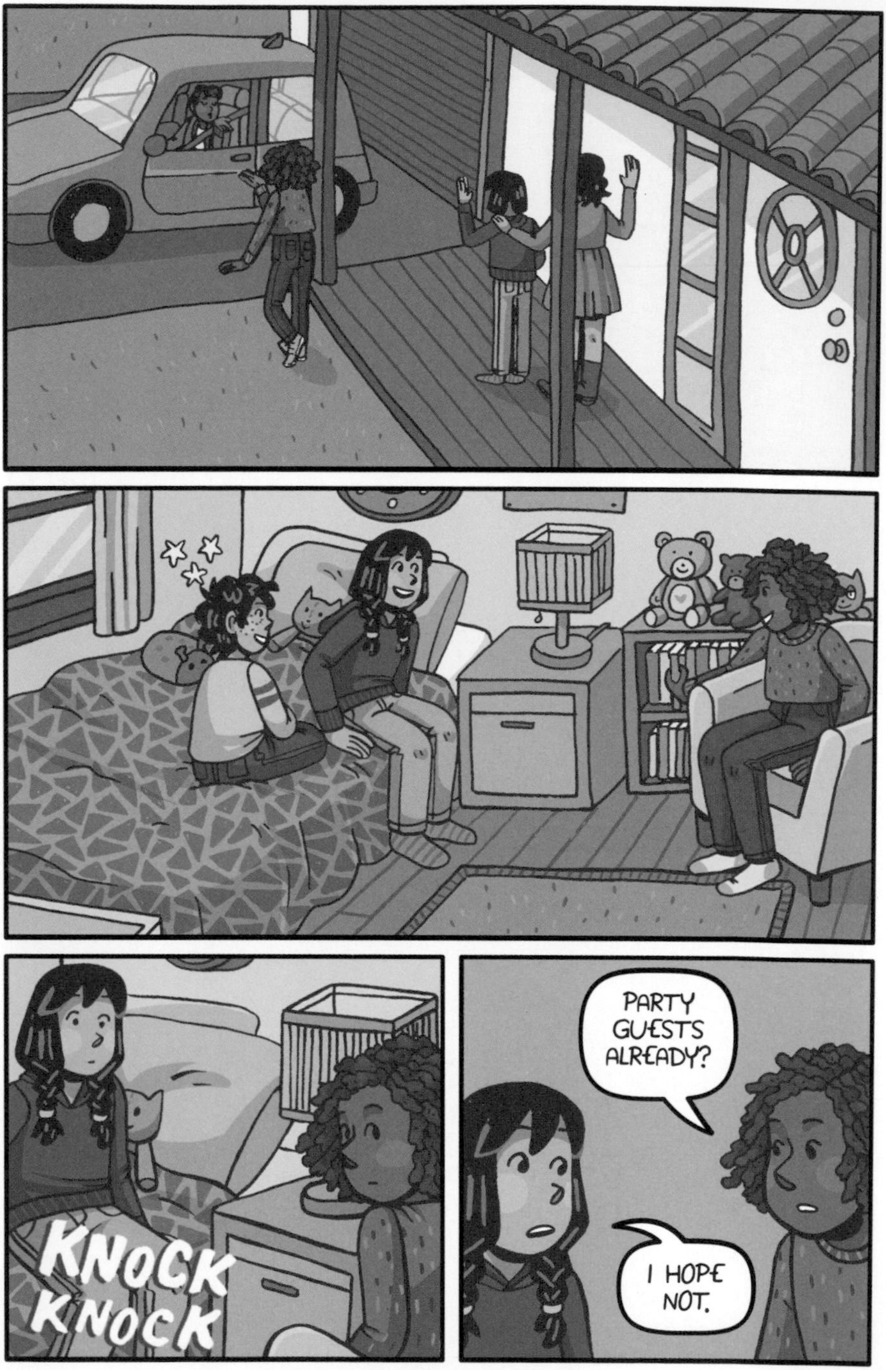
KNOCK KNOCK
PARTY GUESTS ALREADY?
I HOPE NOT.

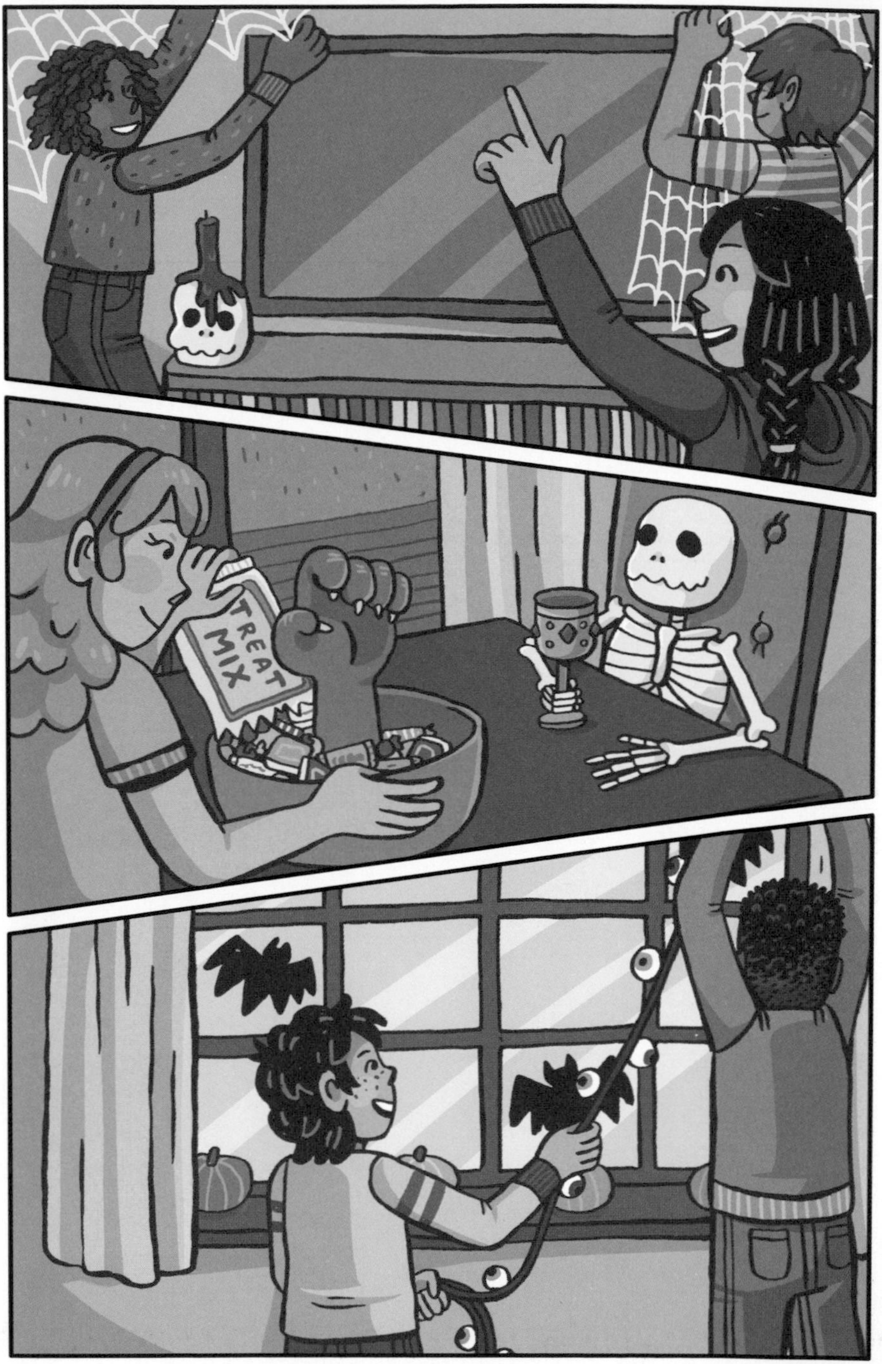
TREAT MIX

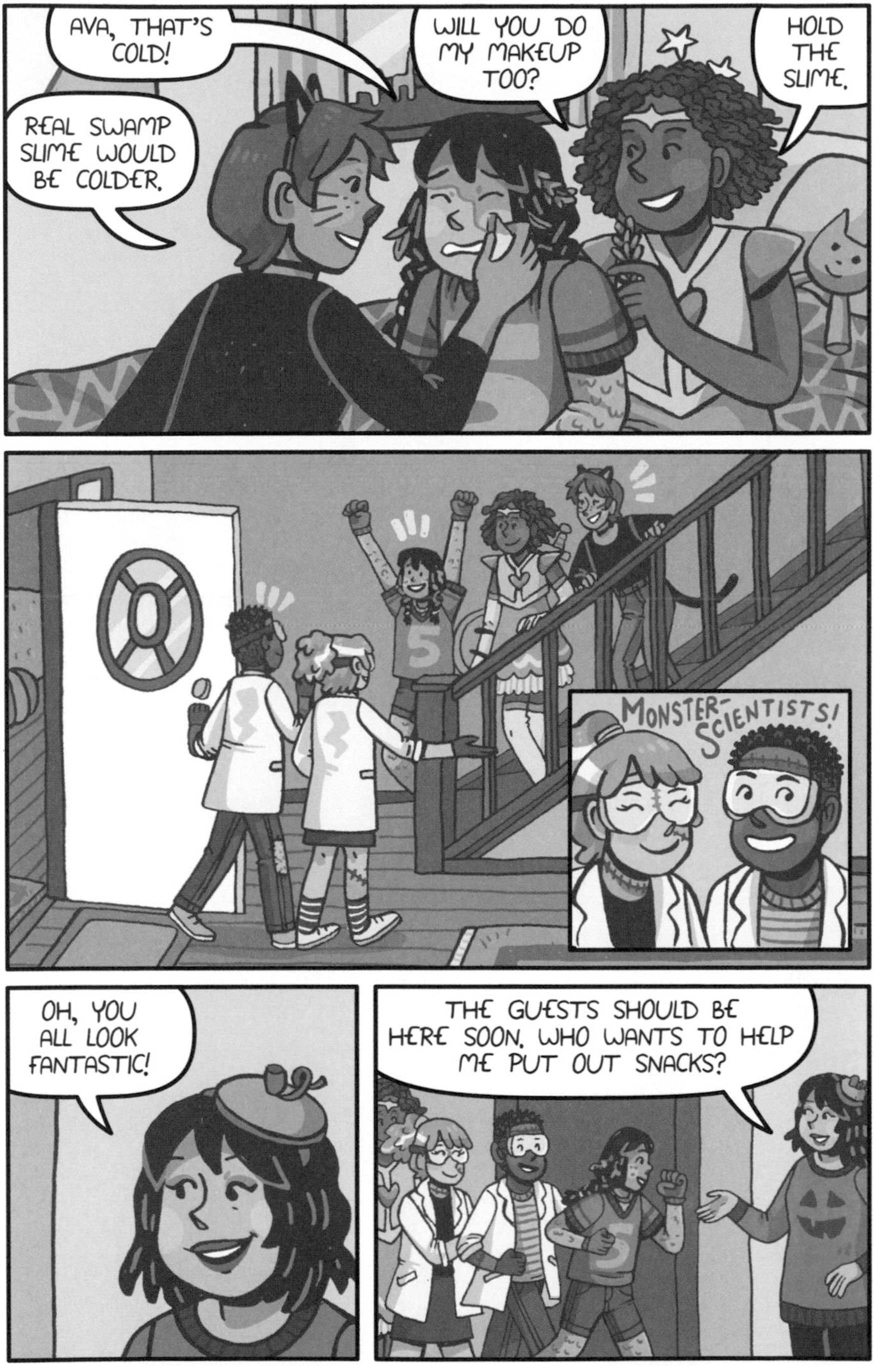
AVA, THAT'S COLD!
REAL SWAMP SLIME WOULD BE COLDER.
WILL YOU DO MY MAKEUP TOO?
HOLD THE SLIME.
MONSTER-SCIENTISTS!
OH, YOU ALL LOOK FANTASTIC!
THE GUESTS SHOULD BE HERE SOON. WHO WANTS TO HELP ME PUT OUT SNACKS?

157

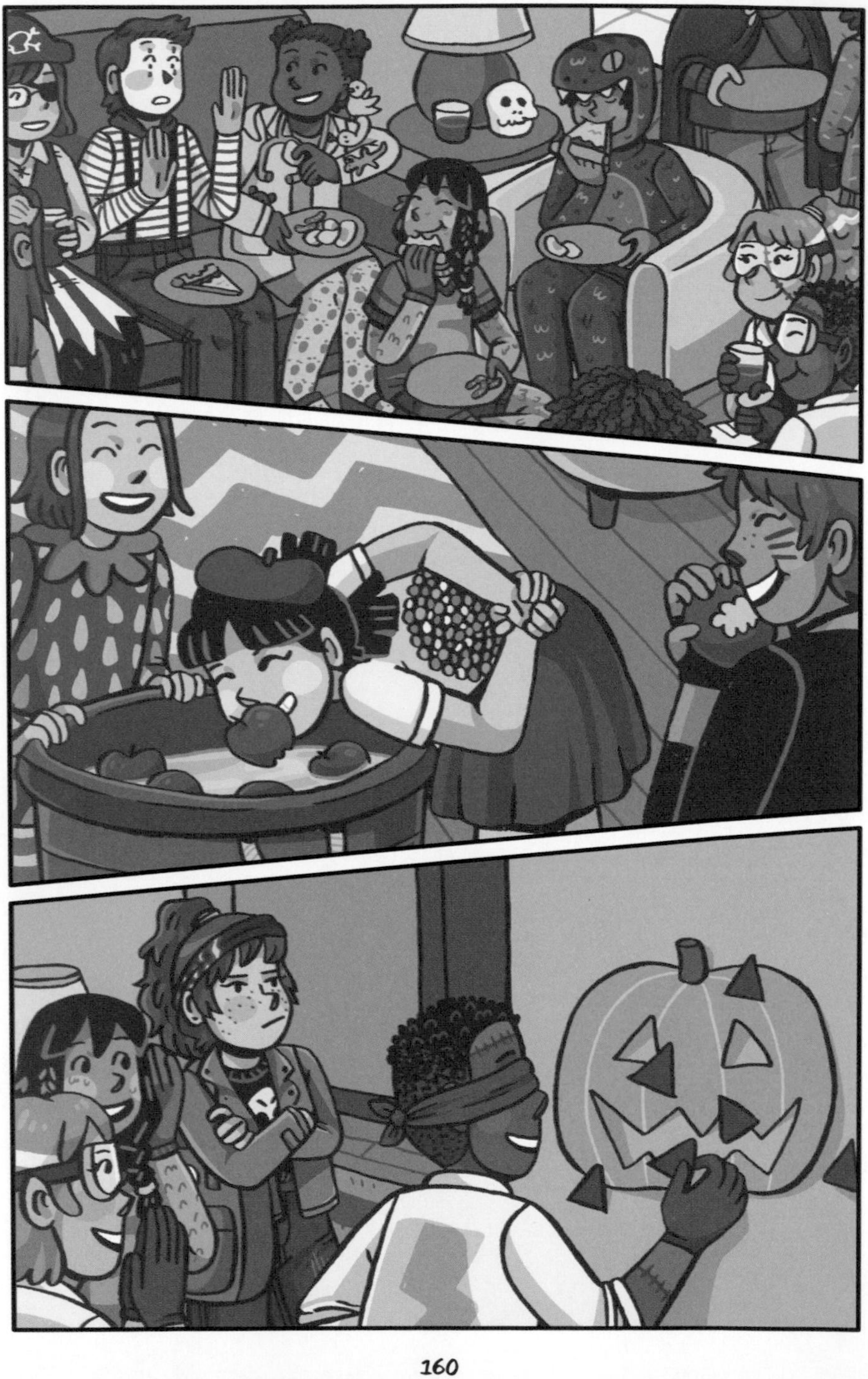

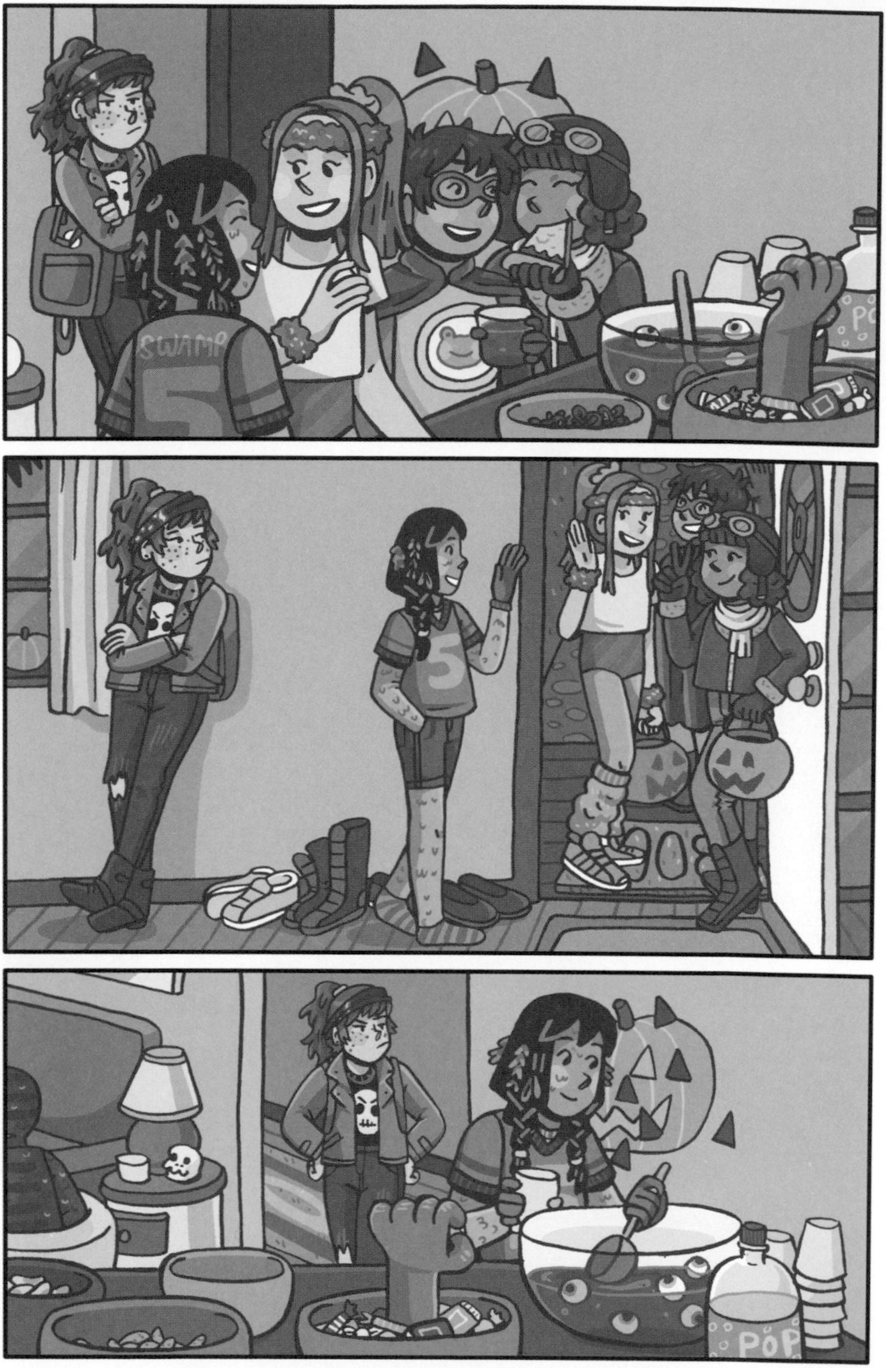
SWAMP
POP

163

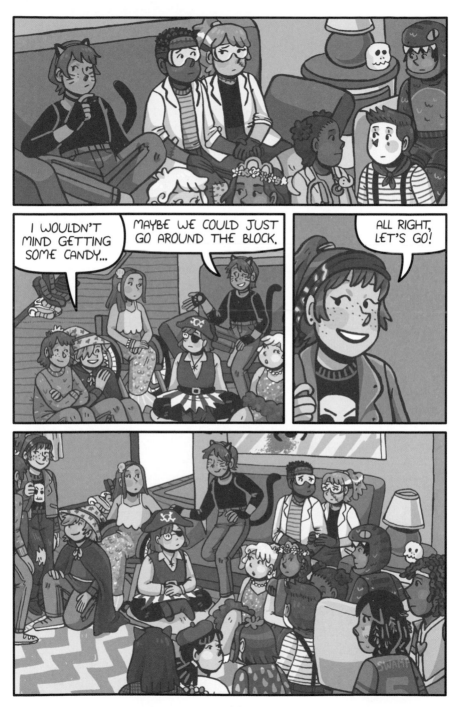

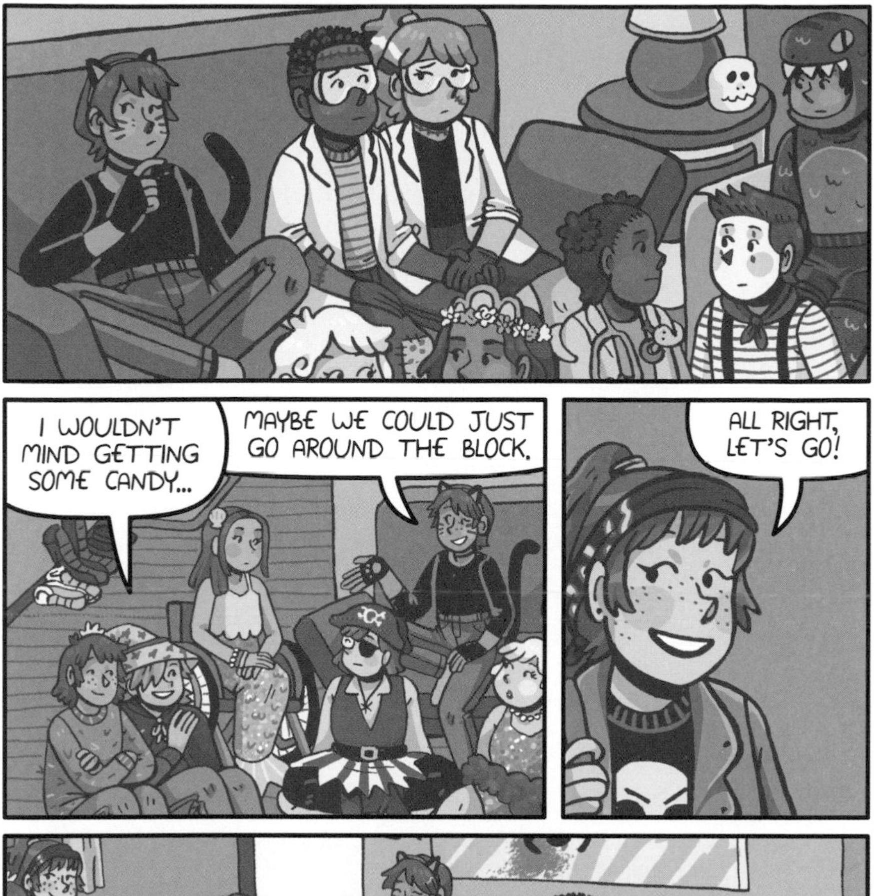
I WOULDN'T MIND GETTING SOME CANDY...
MAYBE WE COULD JUST GO AROUND THE BLOCK.
ALL RIGHT, LET'S GO!

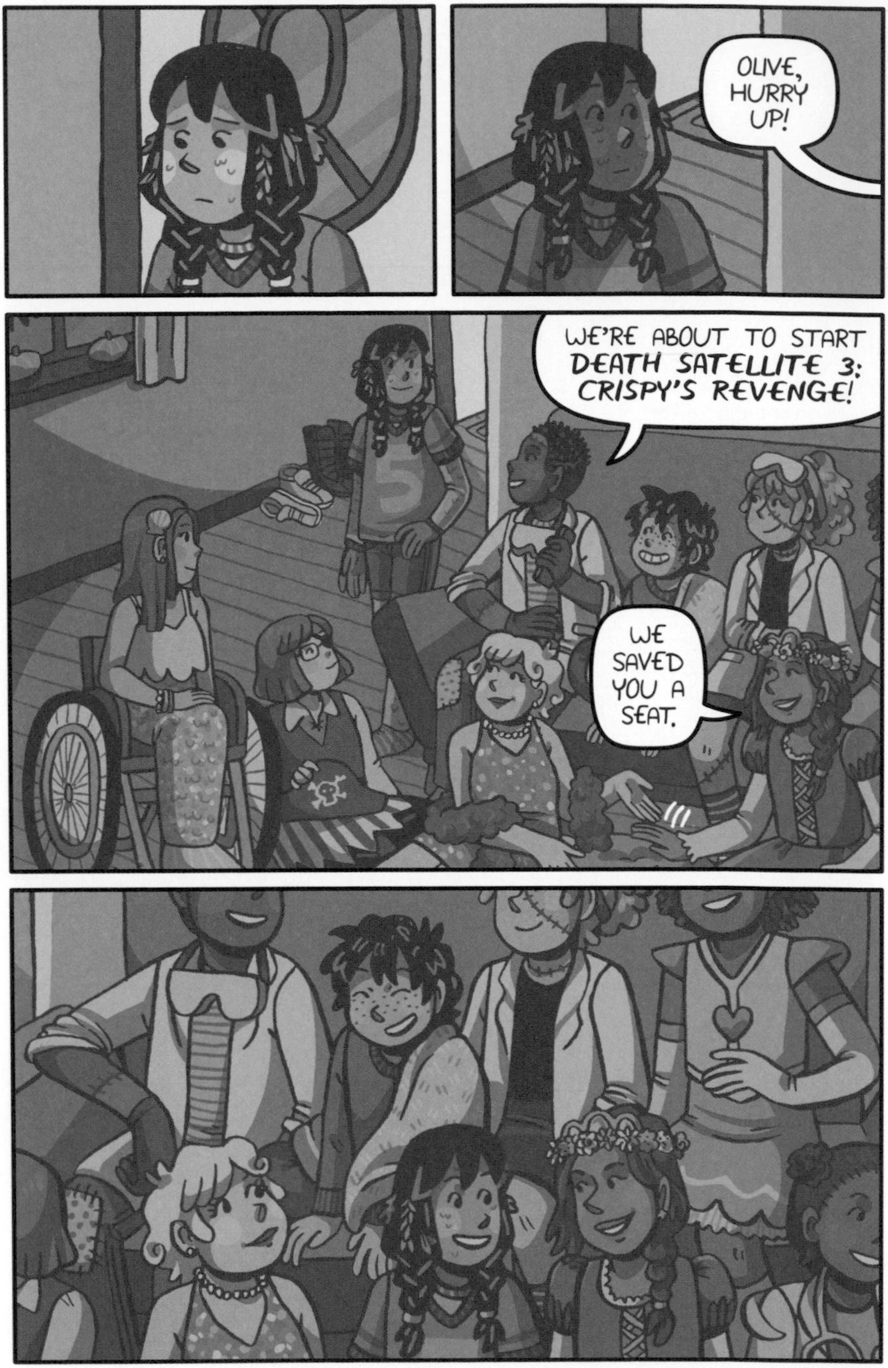
OLIVE, HURRY UP!
WE'RE ABOUT TO START DEATH SATELLITE 3: CRISPY'S REVENGE!
WE SAVED YOU A SEAT.

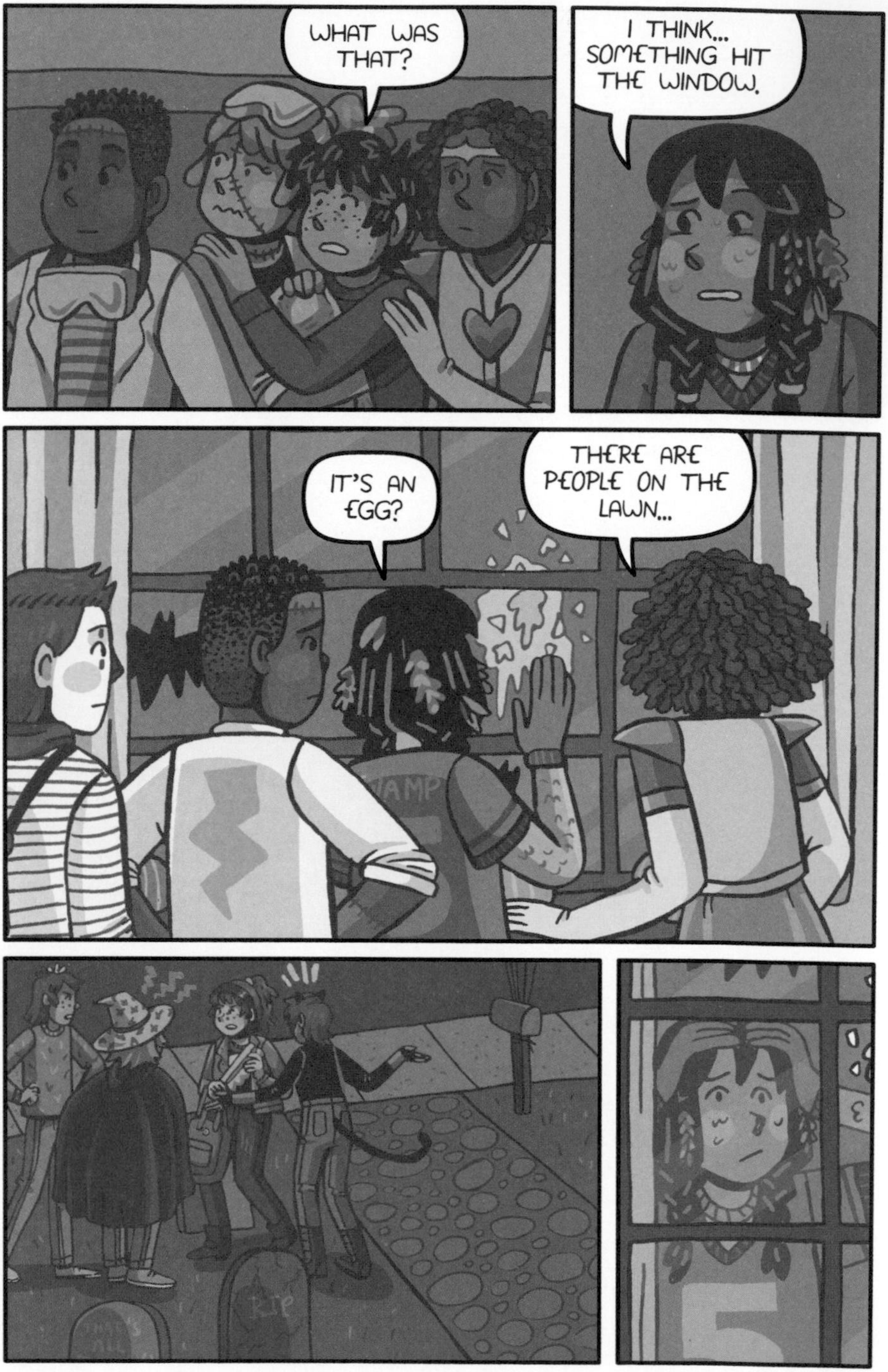
WHAT WAS THAT?
I THINK... SOMETHING HIT THE WINDOW.
IT'S AN EGG?
THERE ARE PEOPLE ON THE LAWN...
RIP

179

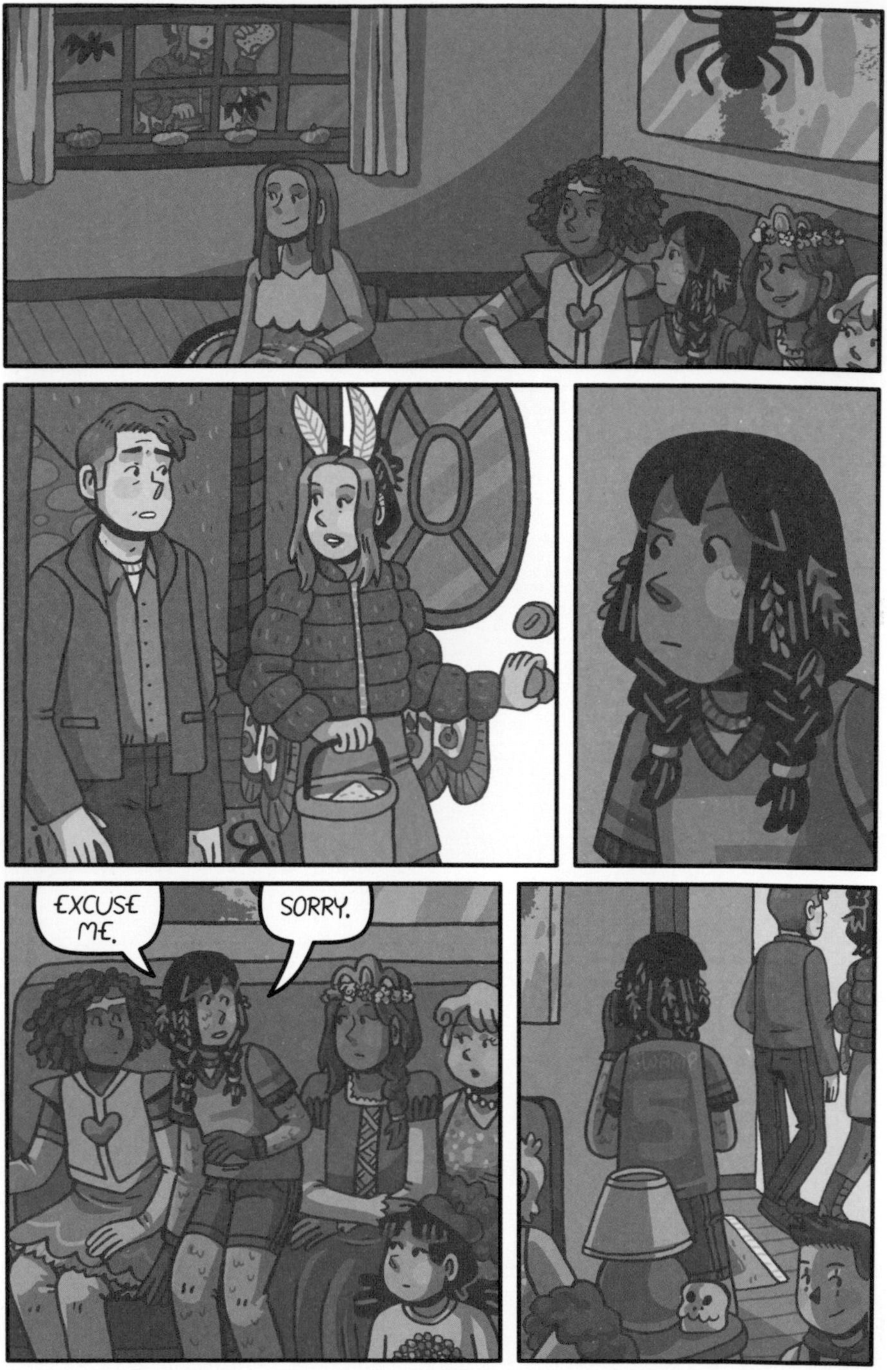
EXCUSE ME.
SORRY.

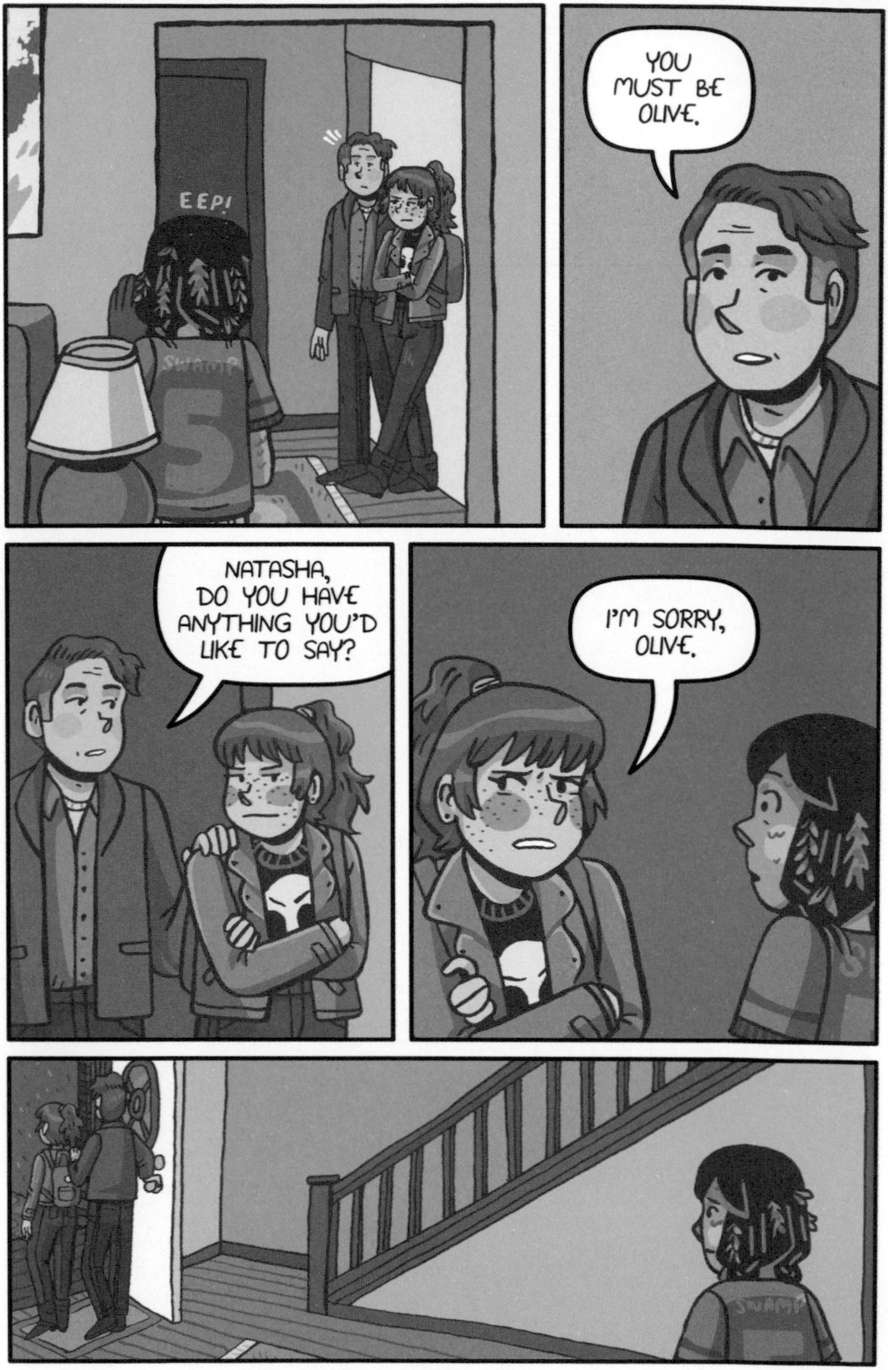
EEP!
SWAMP
5
YOU MUST BE OLIVE.
NATASHA, DO YOU HAVE ANYTHING YOU'D LIKE TO SAY?
I'M SORRY, OLIVE.
SWAMP

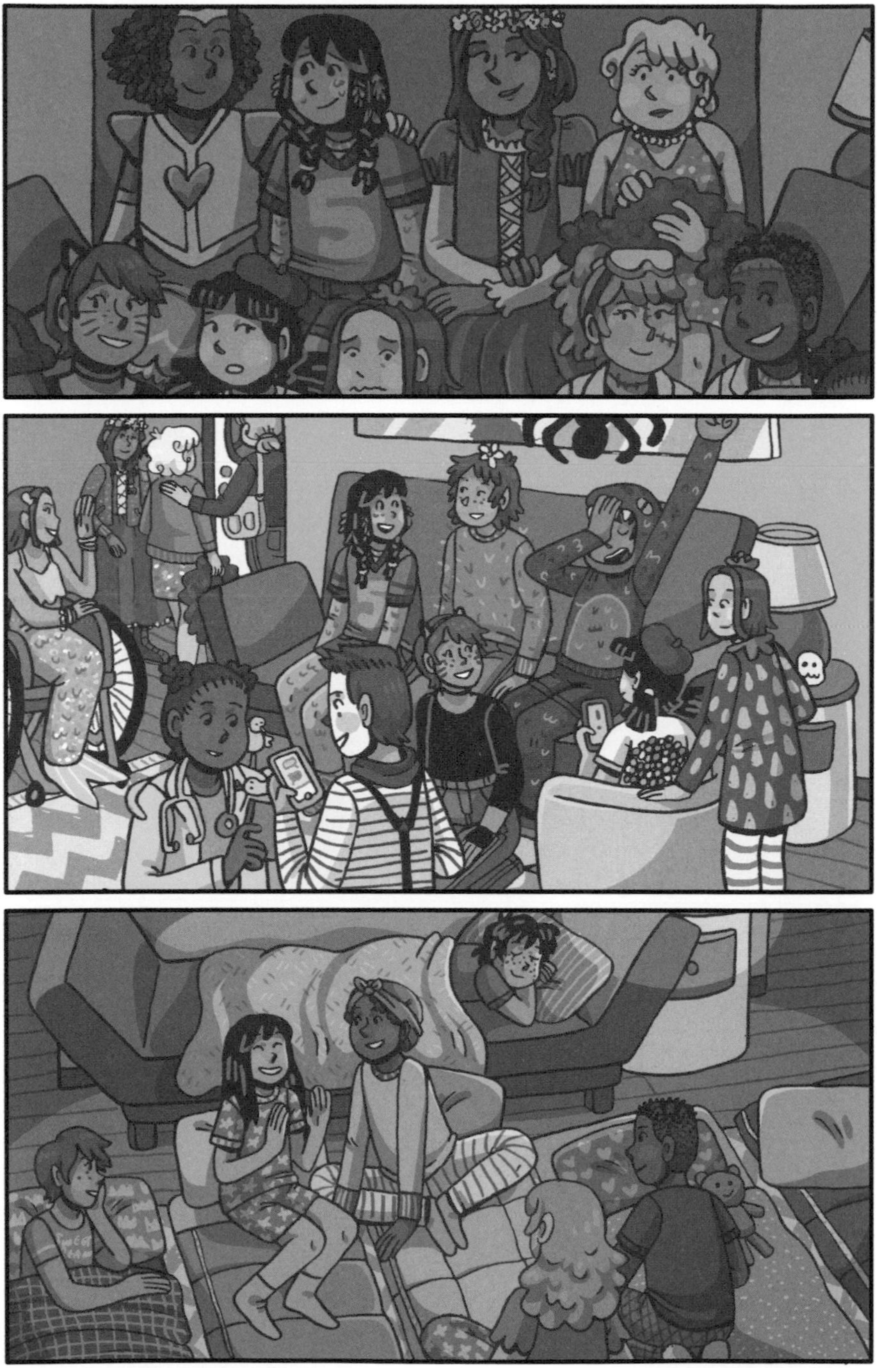

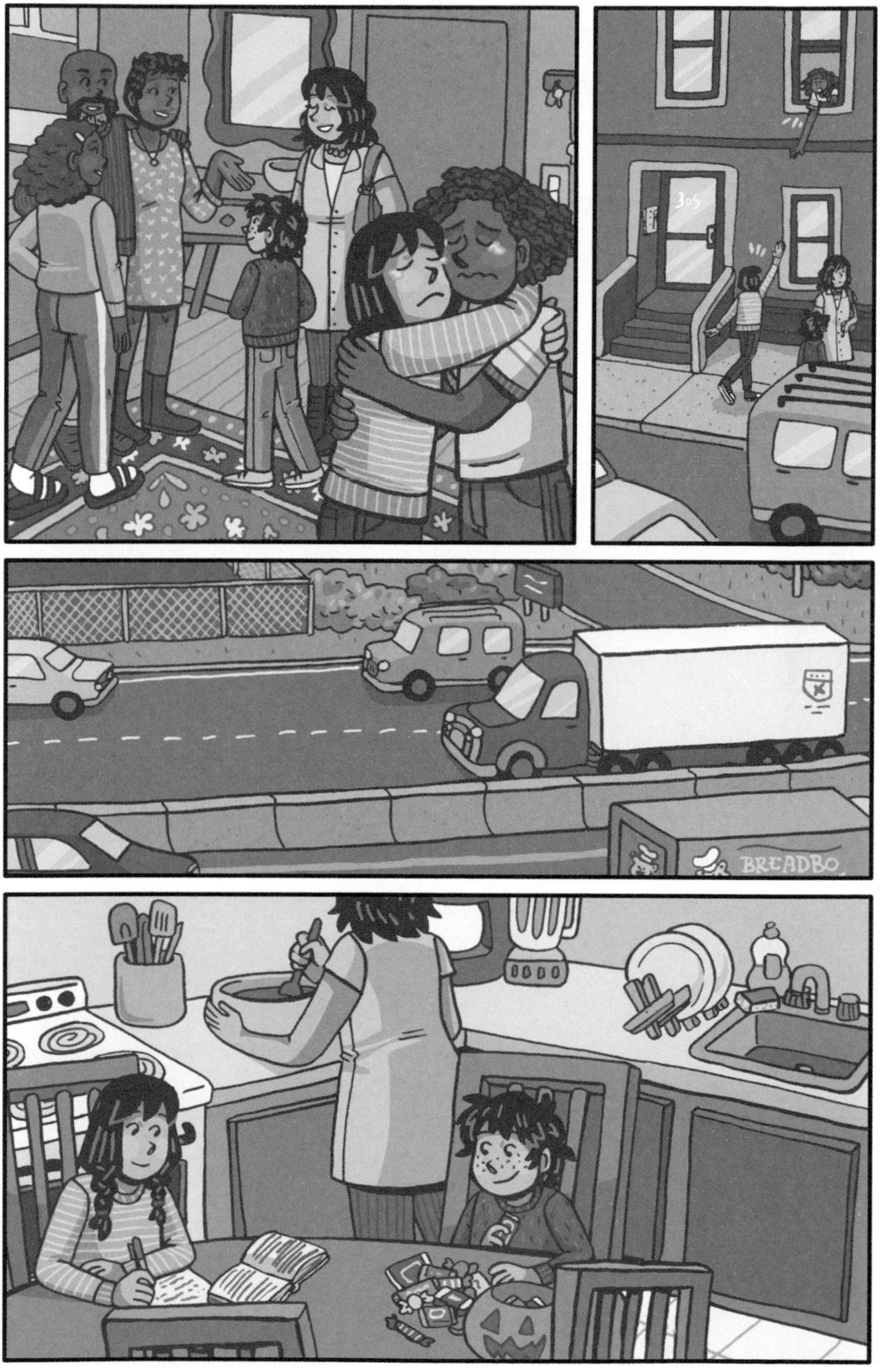
305
BREADBO

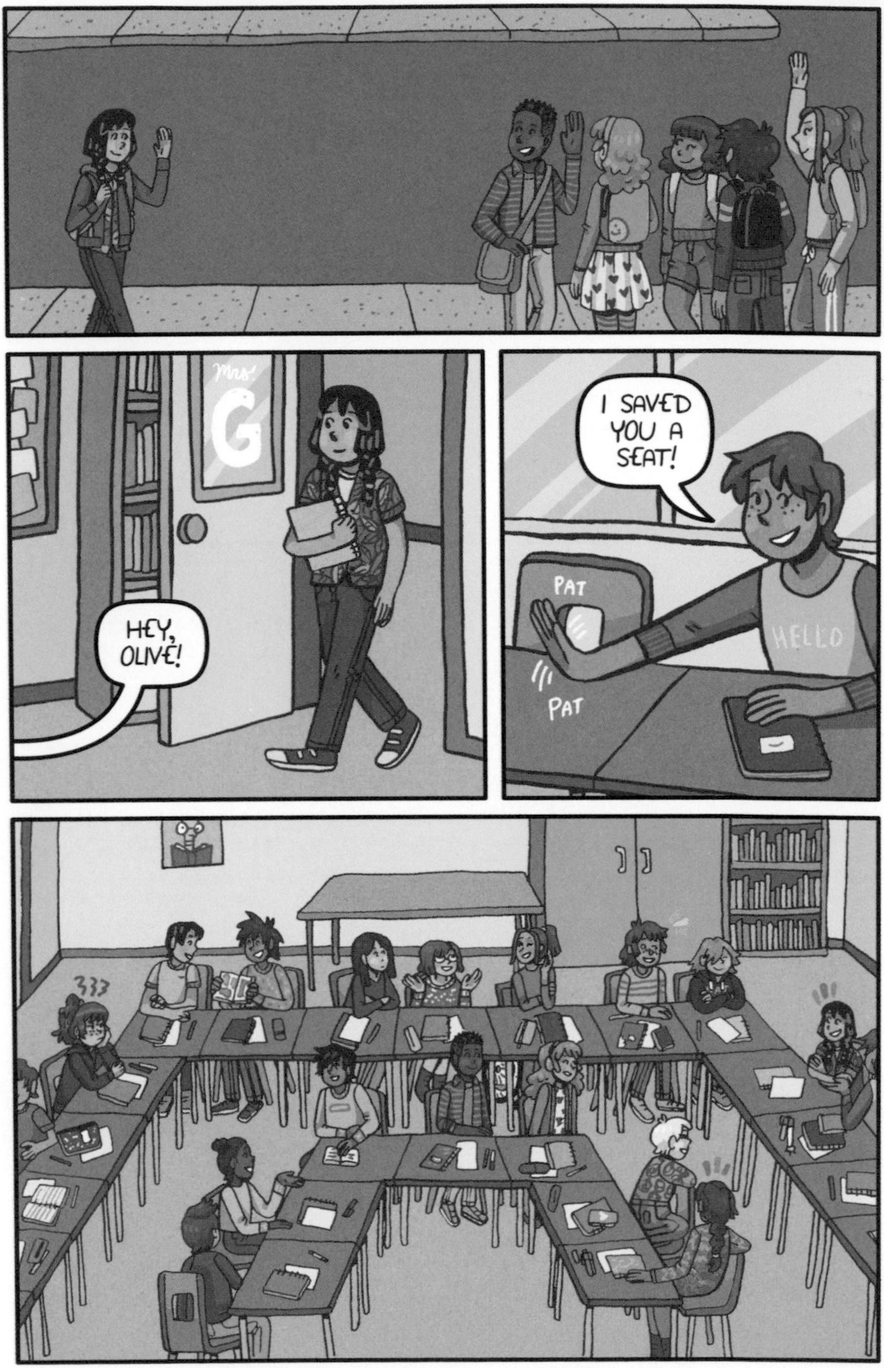
G
HEY, OLIVE!
I SAVED YOU A SEAT!
PAT
PAT
HELLO

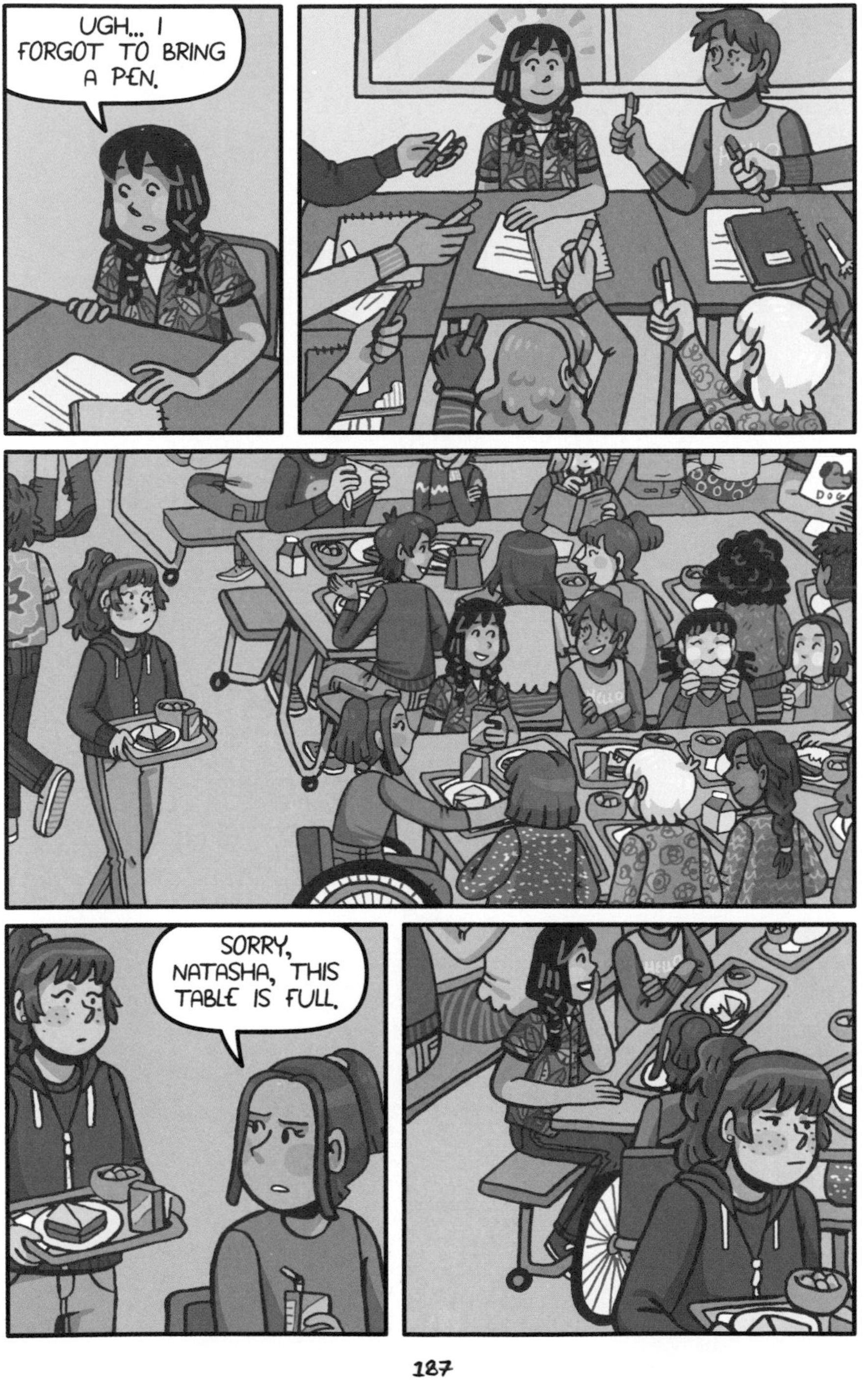
UGH... I FORGOT TO BRING A PEN.
DOG
SORRY, NATASHA, THIS TABLE IS FULL.

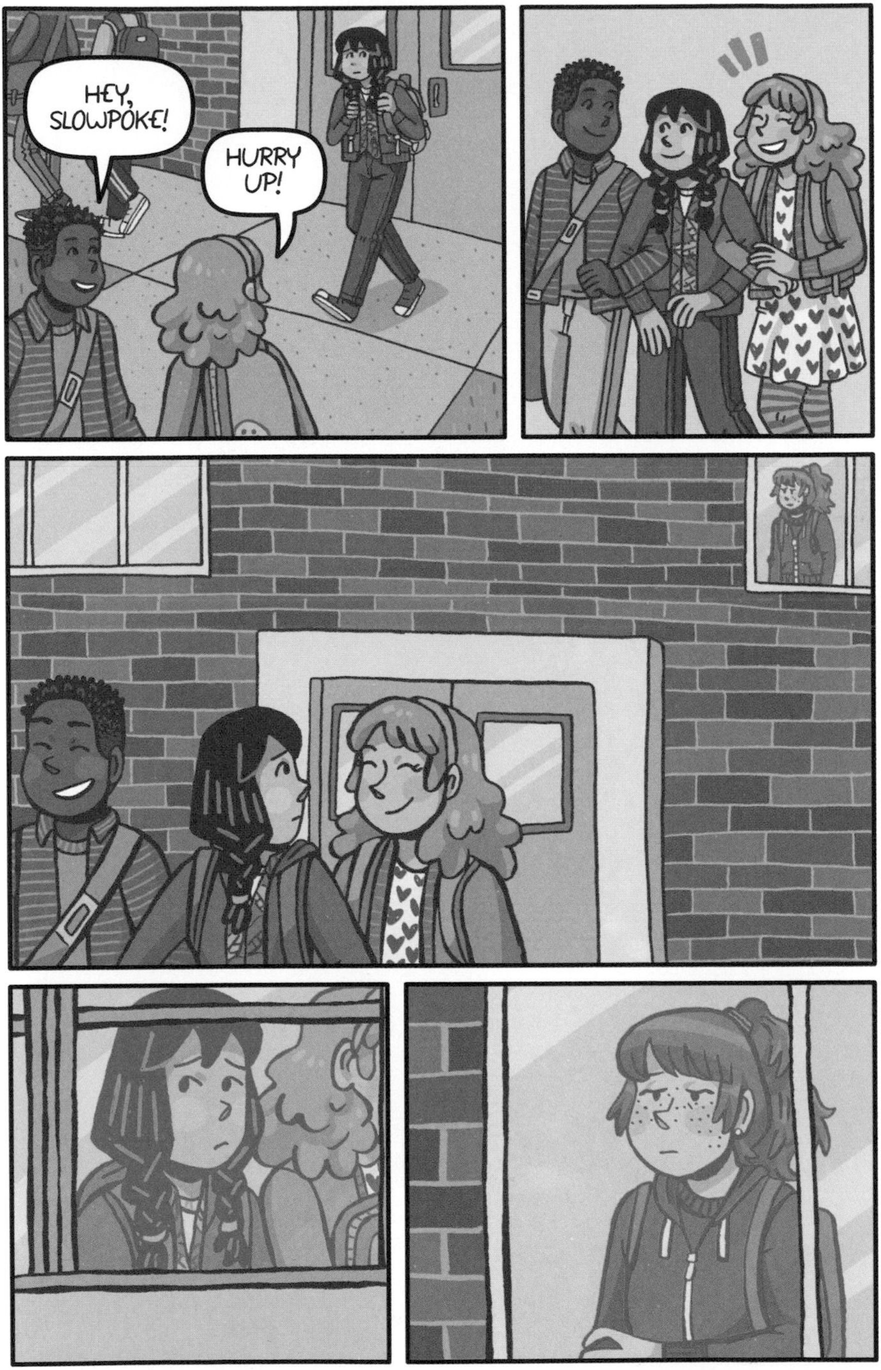
HEY, SLOWPOKE!
HURRY UP!

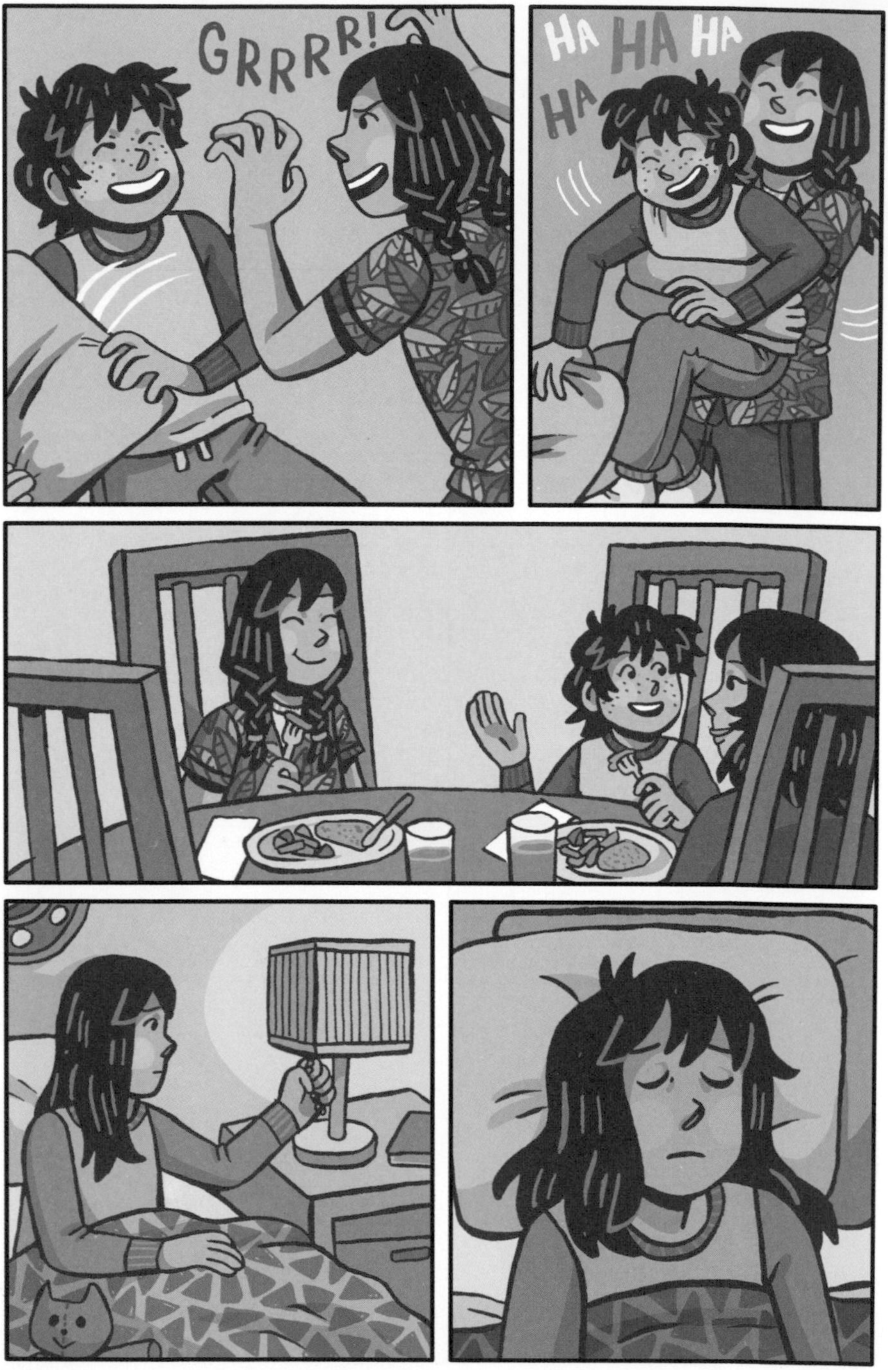
GRRRRR!
HA HA HA HA
HA

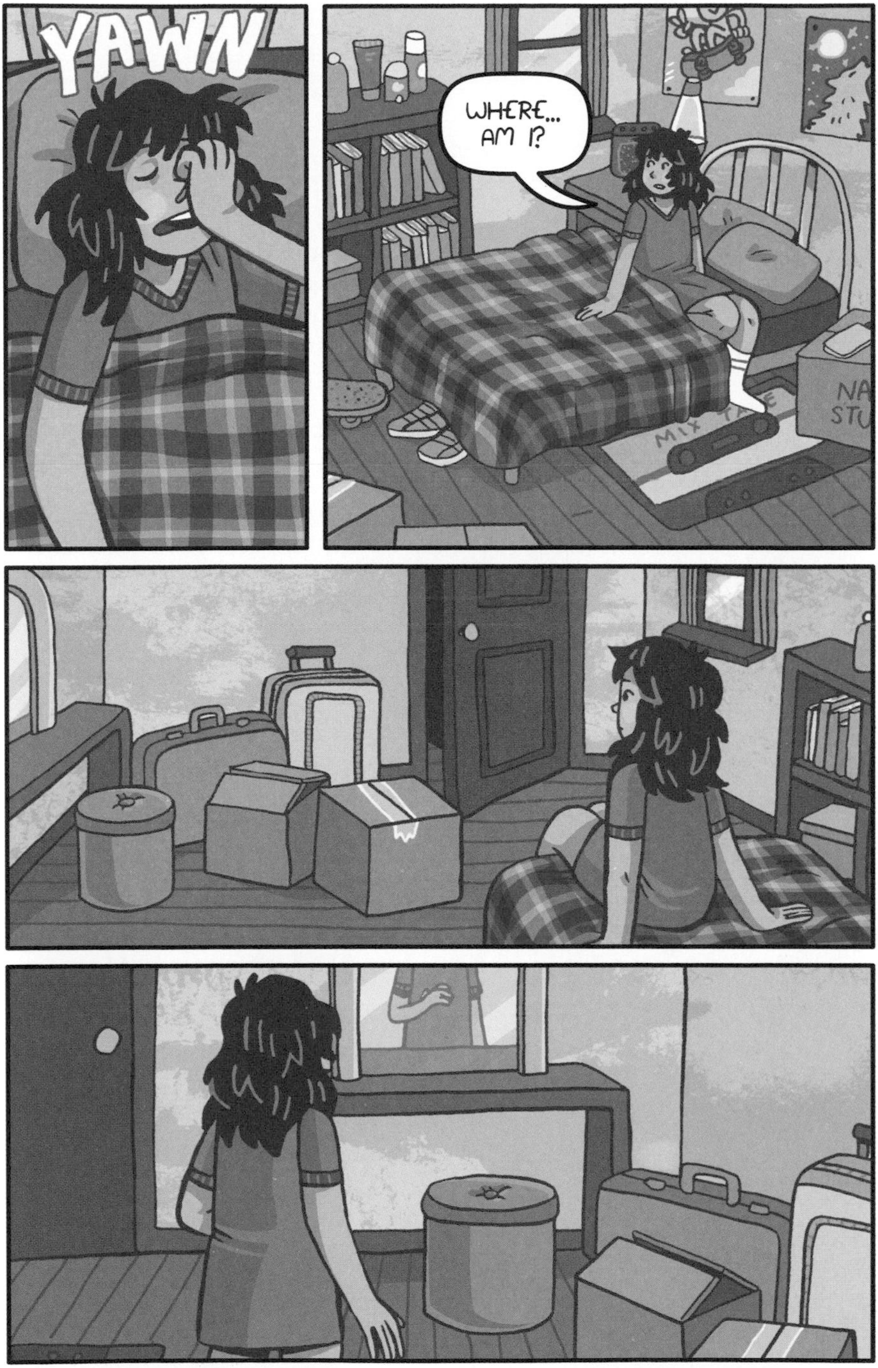
YAWN
WHERE... AM I?
MIX TAPE
NA
STU

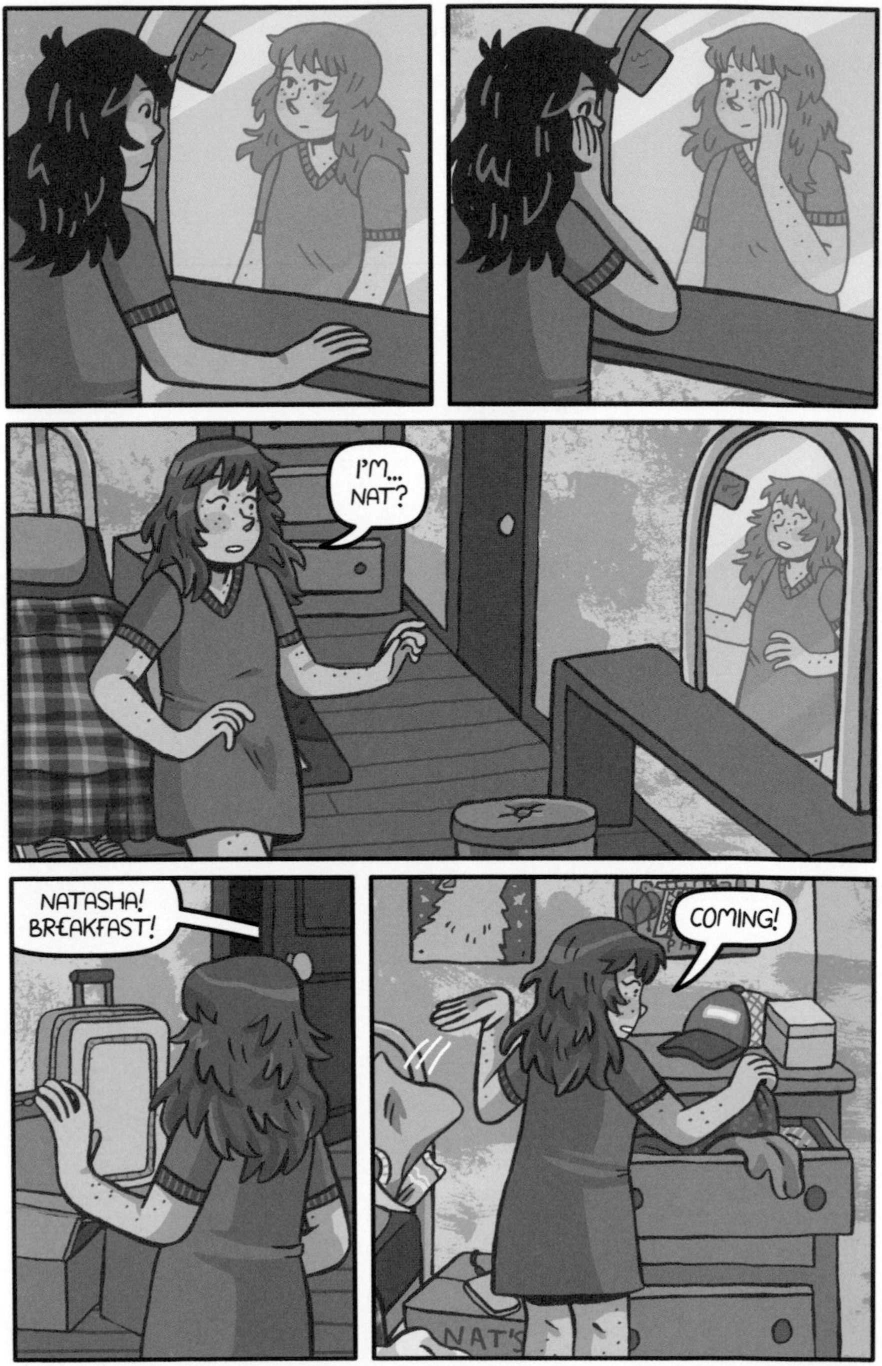
I'M... NAT?
NATASHA! BREAKFAST!
COMING!
NAT'S

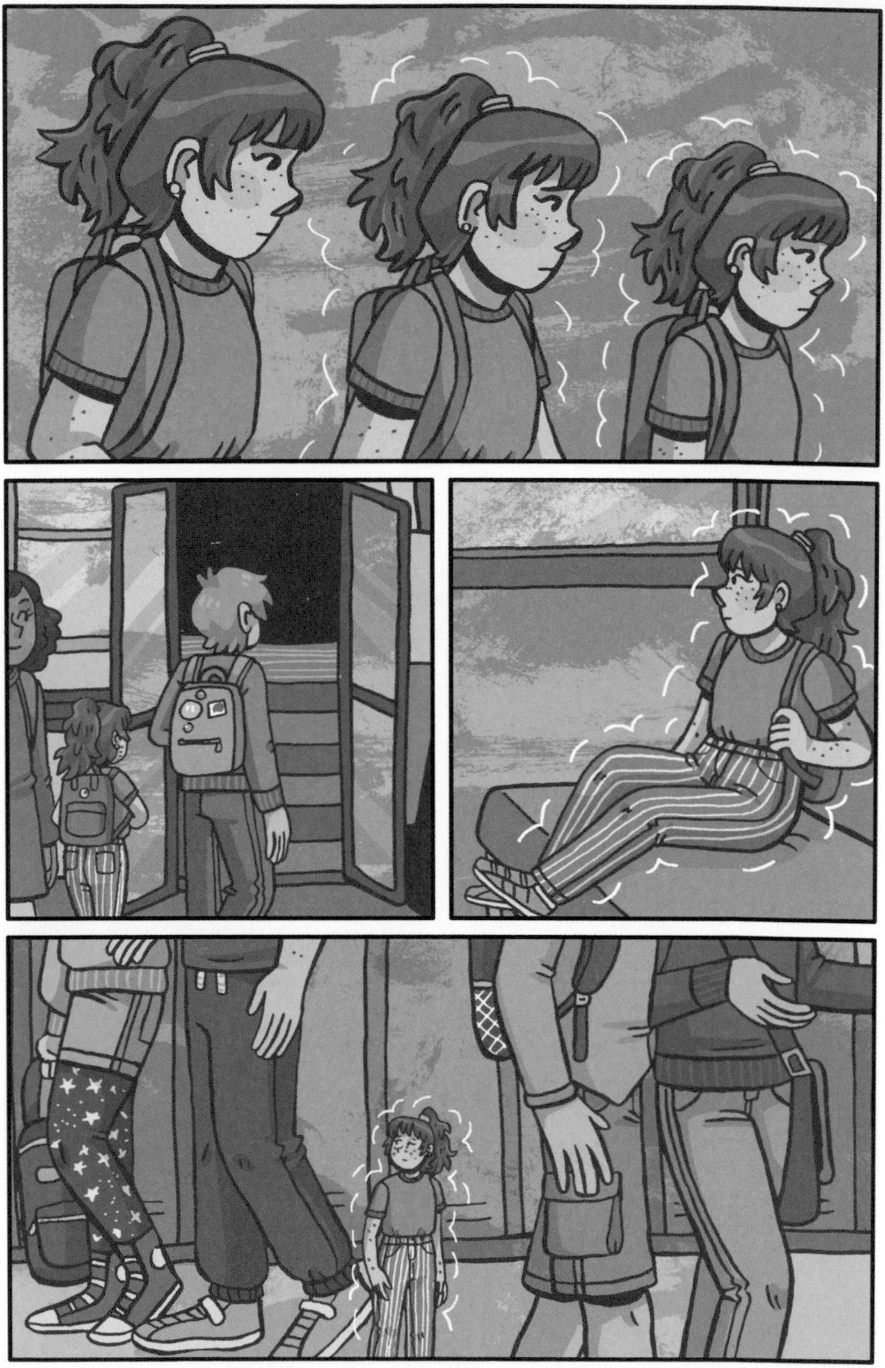

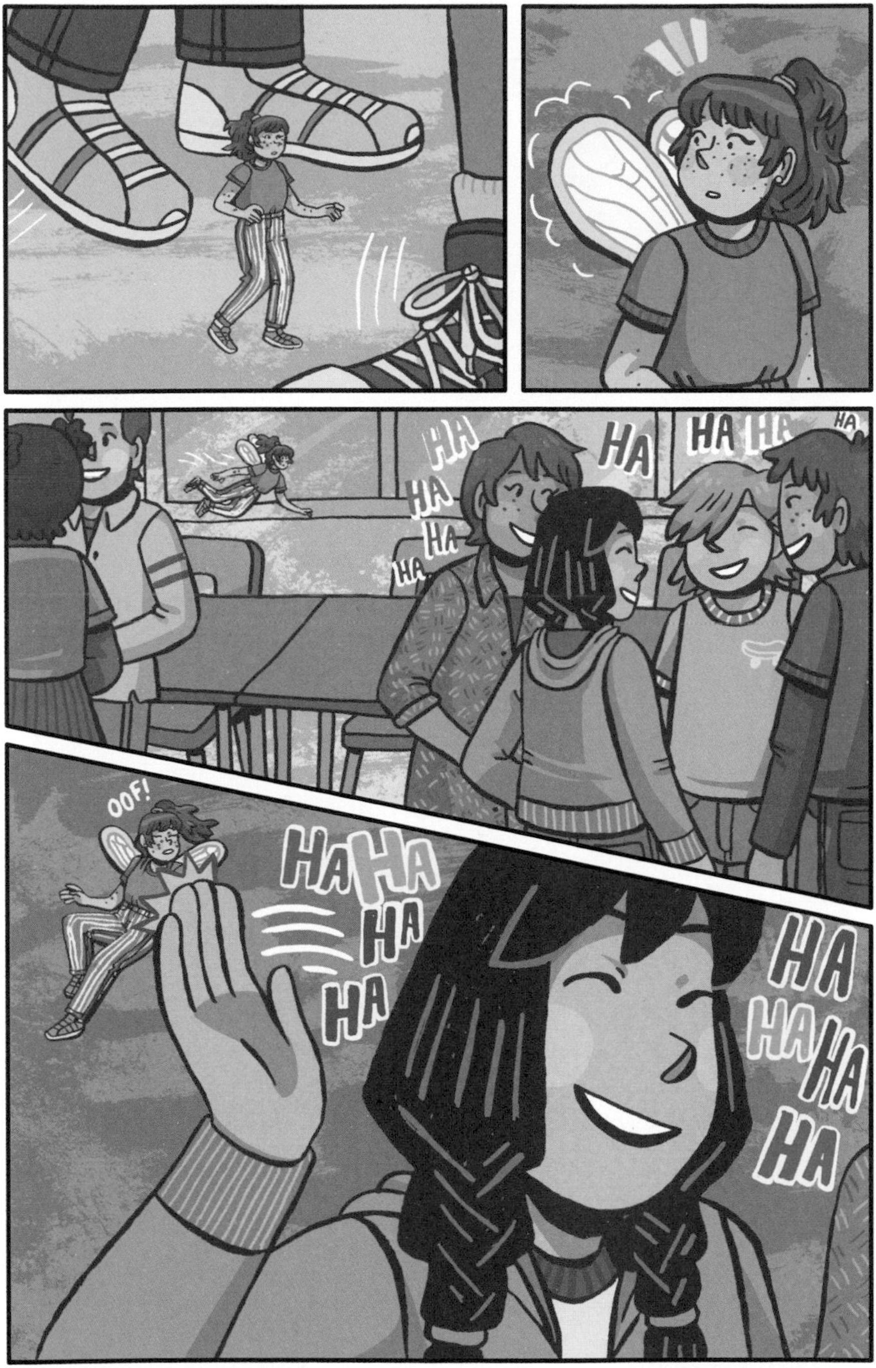
HA
HA
HA
HA
HA
HA
HA HA
HA
OOF!
HAHA
HA
HA
HA
HAHA
HA
HA
HA

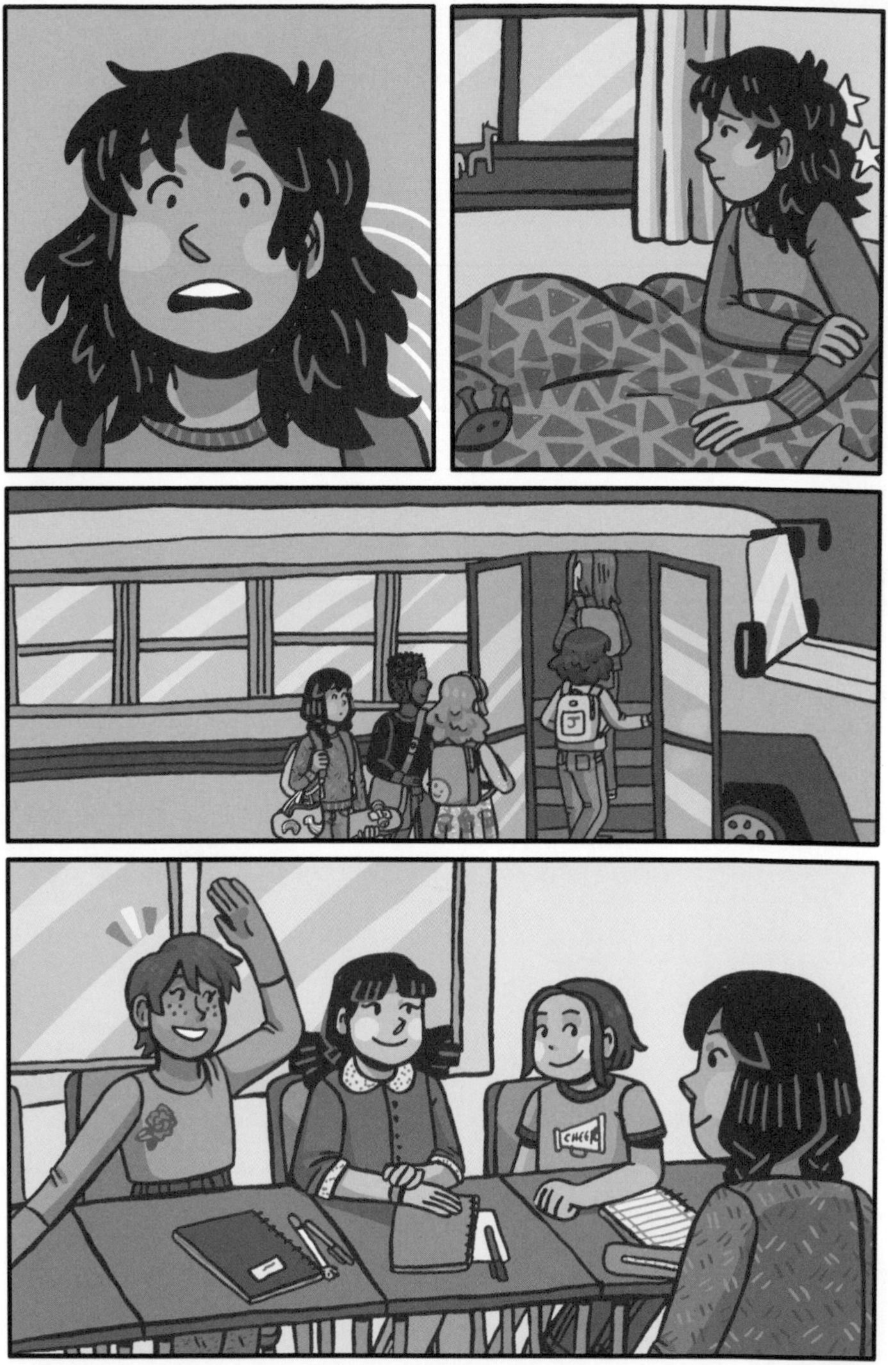

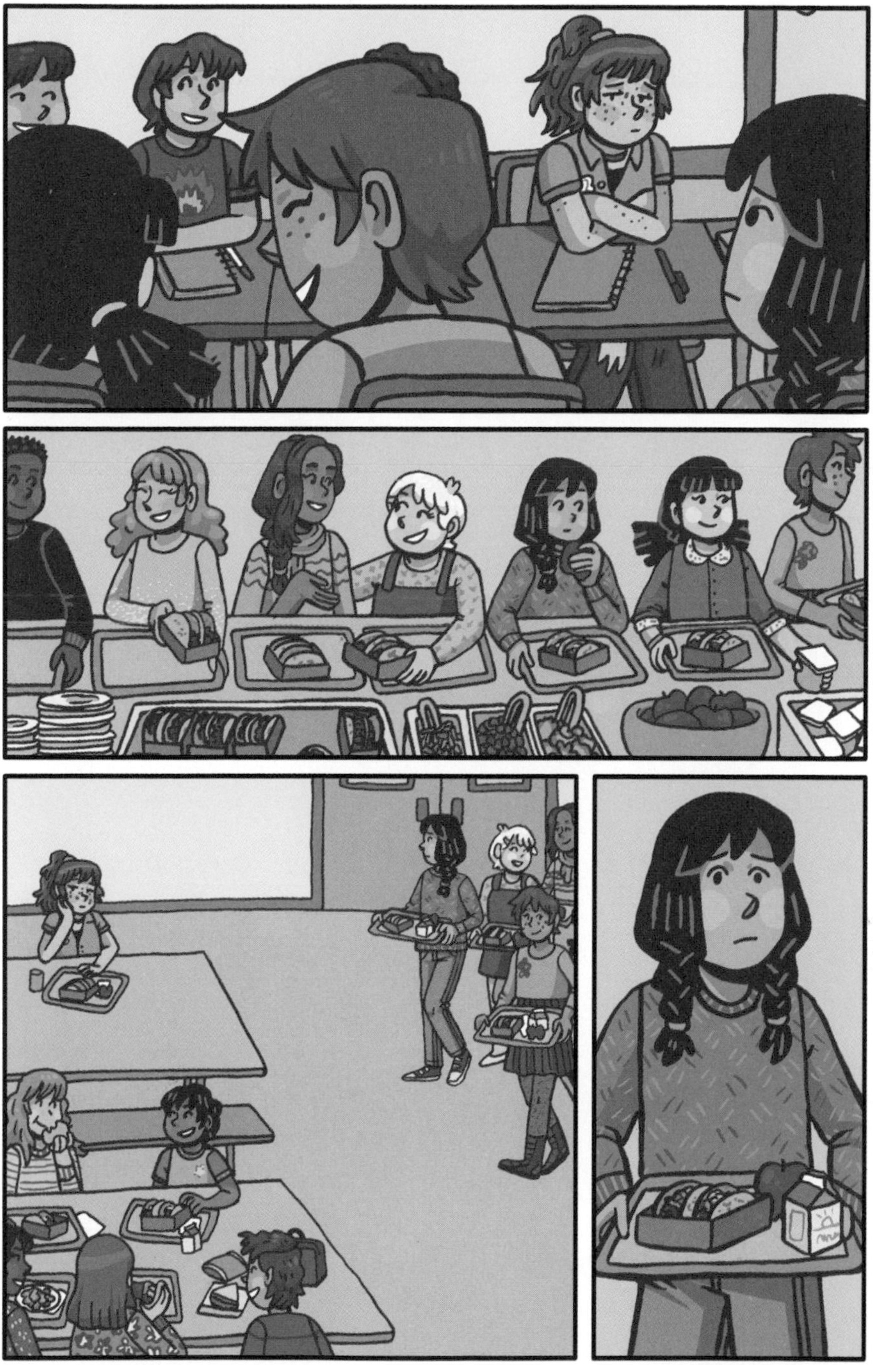

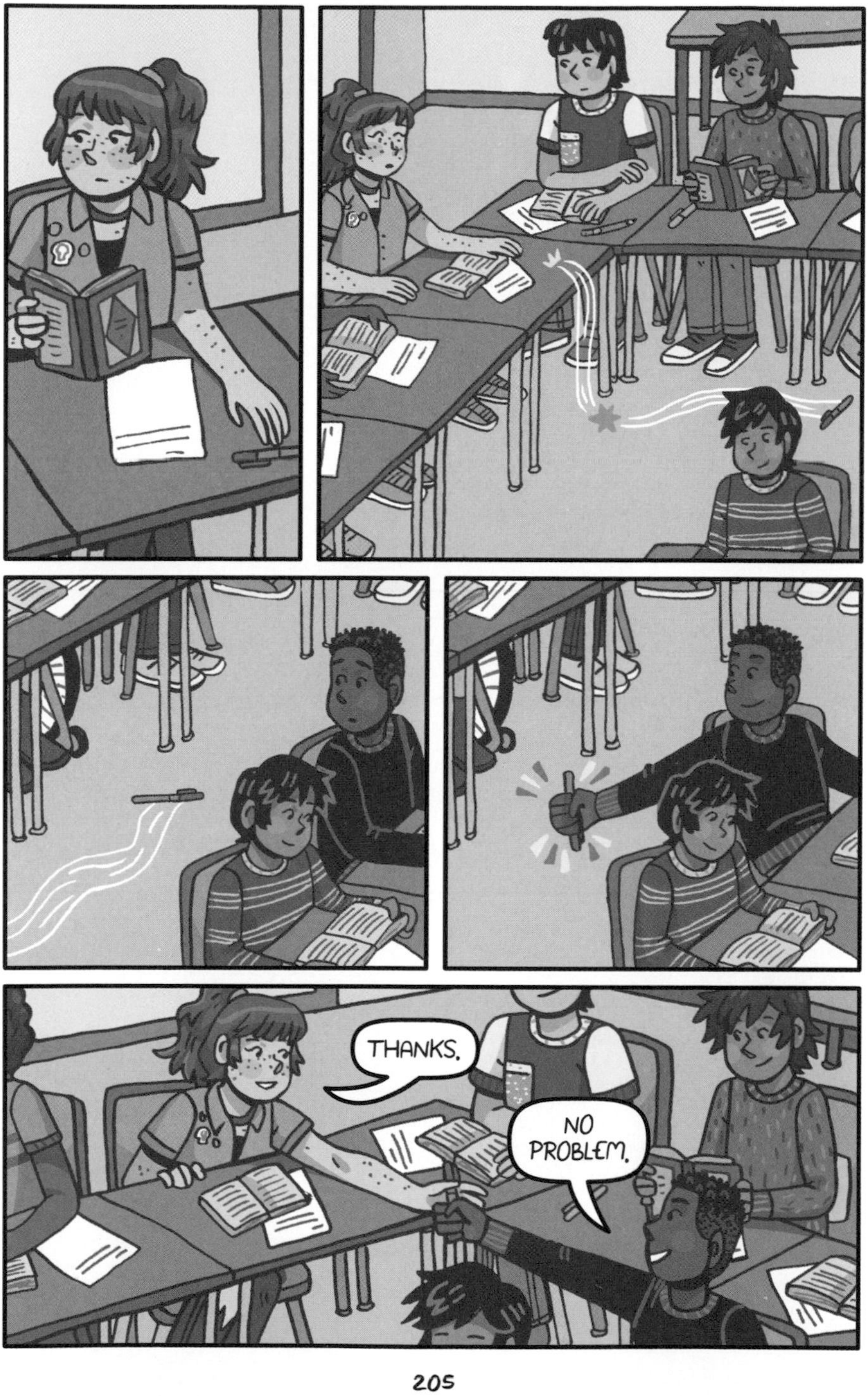
THANKS.
NO PROBLEM.

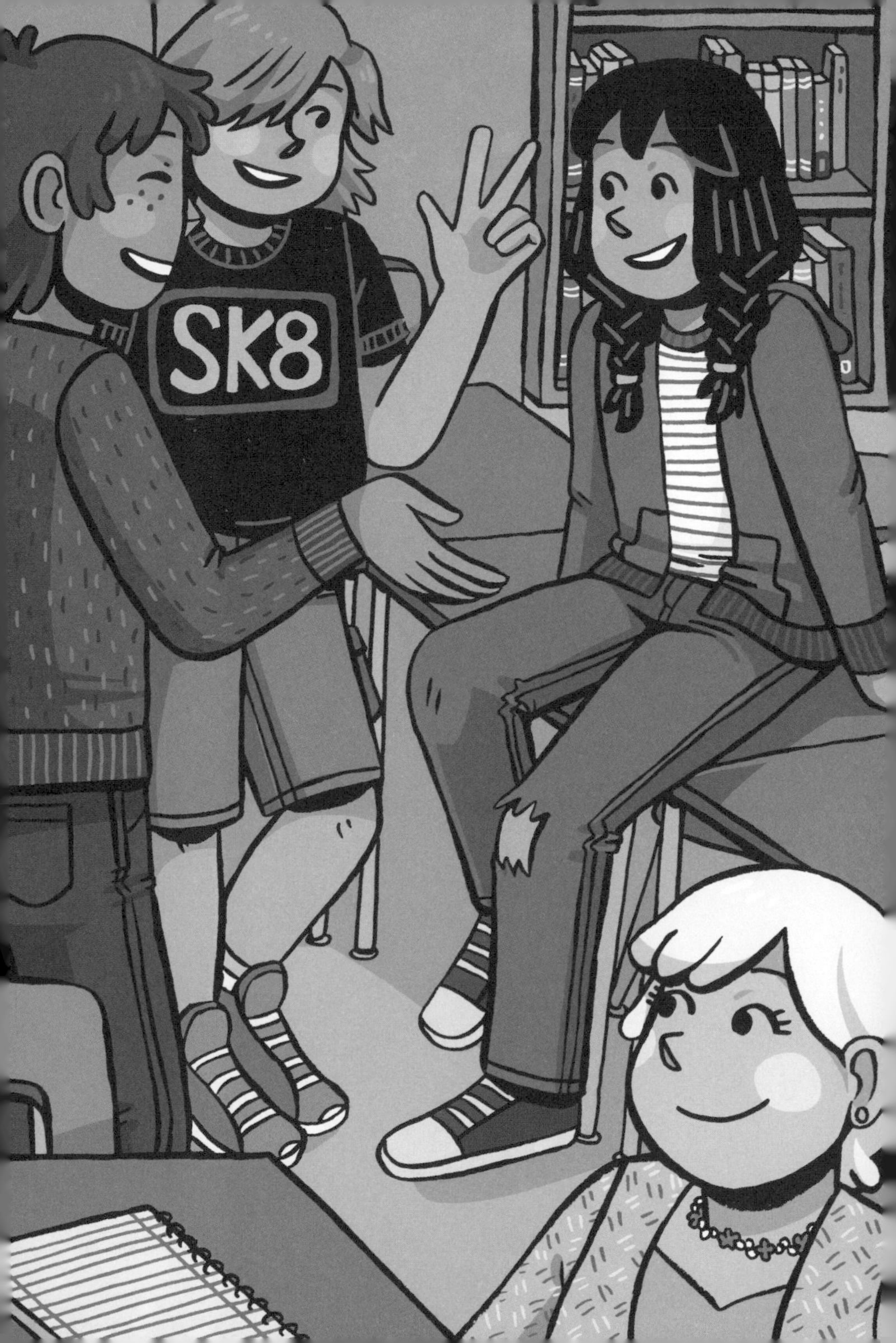
SK8

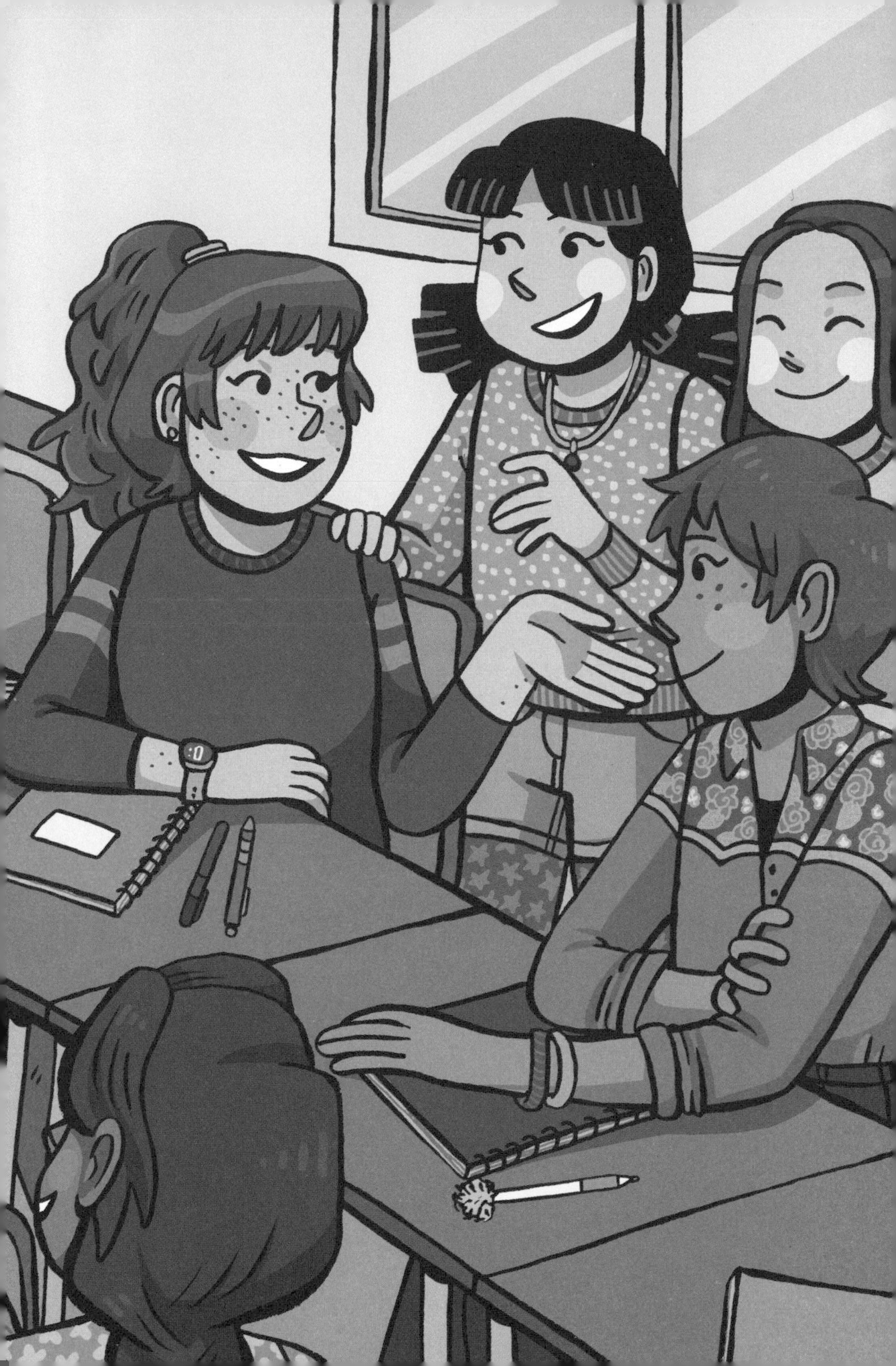

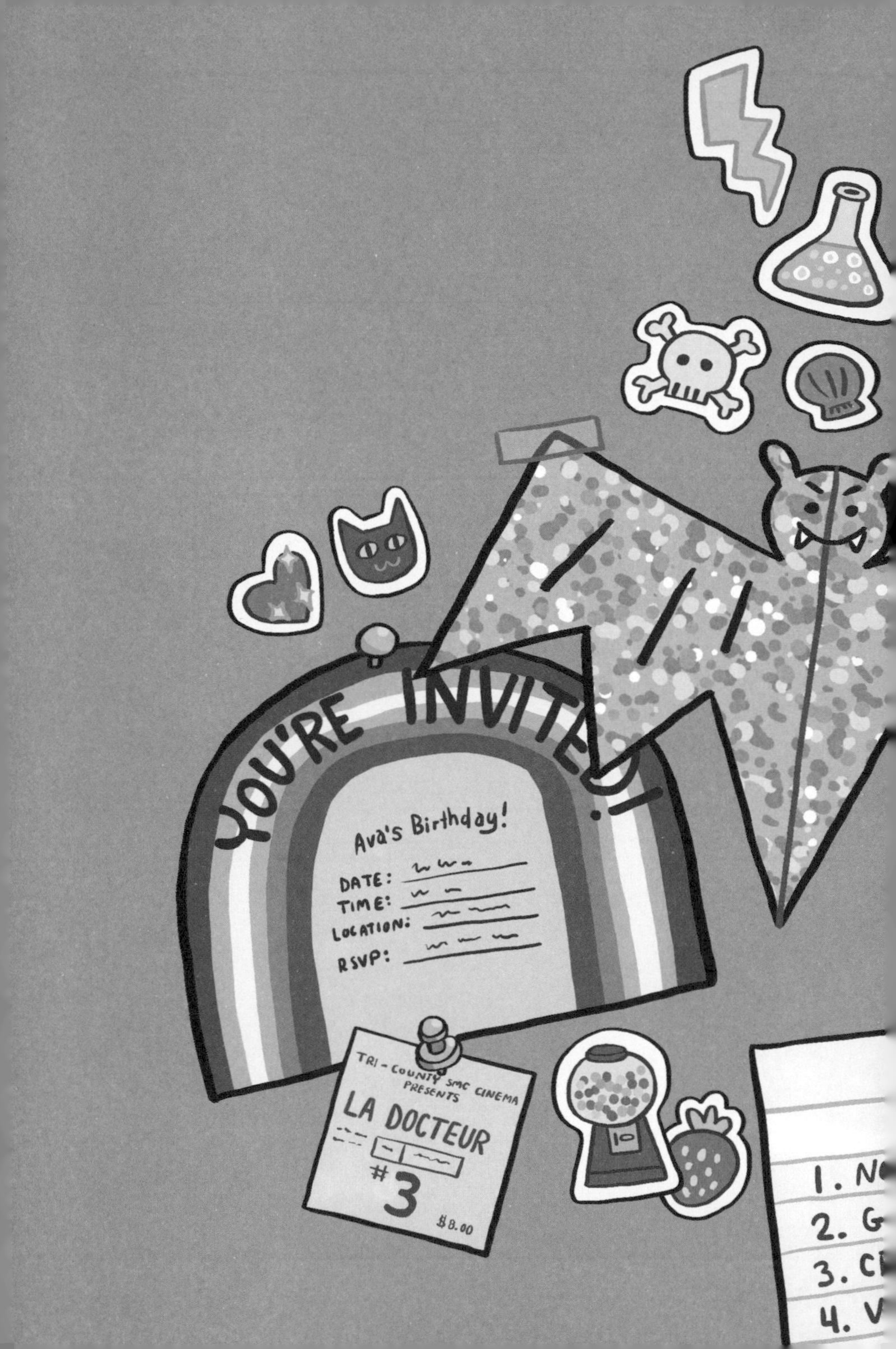
YOU'RE INVITED!
Ava's Birthday!
DATE:
TIME:
LOCATION:
RSVP:
TRI-COUNTY SMC CINEMA PRESENTS
LA DOCTEUR
#3
$8.00
1.
2.
3.
4.

CRAFTY COSTUMES

You don't have to spend a ton of money or know how to sew to make your own cool costumes! Here are some quick and easy costume ideas from Olive's friends that use some items you might already have.

What crafty costumes can you come up with?
Here are some ideas to spark your creativity.

PRETZEL: Brown clothes, cotton balls, and fabric glue
ROBOT: Cardboard boxes, tin foil, and duct tape
SCARECROW: flannel shirt, hay, and face paint
GRAPES: Purple balloons and green paper (for the leaf)

Q & A

Q: With *Clash*, we join Olive in her fourth book...and her friendly nature is challenged like never before! What drew you toward exploring this story?

An early sketch of Natasha!

KAYLA: Olive is a people person, and we see her make friends easily in the other books. I thought it would be interesting to write a story where she didn't get along with someone, since that would be a first for her. In our lives we all meet people whom we don't connect with or don't interact well with, and a lot of the time they're going to be people whom we have to spend time with, whether we like it or not. I wanted to show Olive finding peace with this sort of situation, even if it doesn't end with them becoming best friends.

Q: Have you ever dealt with a situation like the one in *Clash*?

KAYLA: Yes, sort of! When I was Olive's age, there was a kid who really got under my skin—and we saw each other constantly since we had all the same friends and participated in the same sports and activities. We tried to be friends, but our personalities were just too different and all we ever did was rile each other up over nothing. We were never mature enough to talk things out like Olive and Natasha do. I wanted to write a story where someone handles that difficult situation in a healthier manner.

Q: You get a lot of feedback from your readers either at the conferences you attend or on social media. What are some things that you hear most often from readers?

KAYLA: I get a lot of feedback about the characters that readers like (or don't like) and whom they'd like to see more of in future books. For a lot of readers, I think the characters are the element they connect with.

The feedback I get most often from parents is about how graphic novels have gotten their reluctant readers into reading—reading for fun and reading on their own! These kinds of comments are super important to me. I think everyone should enjoy reading and be able to read the kinds of books that make them happy.